NONE SO
DEADLY

NONE SO

A CULLEN AND COBB MYSTERY

DEADLY

DAVID A. POULSEN

DUNDURN

TORONTO

Cover image: istock.com/welcomia
Printer: Webcom, a division of Marquis Book Printing Inc.

Library and Archives Canada Cataloguing in Publication

Poulsen, David A., 1946-, author
    None so deadly / David A. Poulsen.

(A Cullen and Cobb mystery)
Issued in print and electronic formats.
ISBN 978-1-4597-4141-6 (softcover).--ISBN 978-1-4597-4142-3 (PDF).--
ISBN 978-1-4597-4143-0 (EPUB)

I. Title. II. Series: Poulsen, David A., 1946- . Cullen and Cobb mystery.

PS8581.O848N66 2019   C813'.54   C2018-904815-8
                                                C2018-904816-6

1   2   3   4   5   23   22   21   20   19

Conseil des Arts
du Canada

Canada Council
for the Arts

Canada

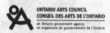
ONTARIO ARTS COUNCIL
CONSEIL DES ARTS DE L'ONTARIO
an Ontario government agency
un organisme du gouvernement de l'Ontario

We acknowledge the support of the Canada Council for the Arts, which last year invested $153 million to bring the arts to Canadians throughout the country, and the Ontario Arts Council for our publishing program. We also acknowledge the financial support of the Government of Ontario, through the Ontario Book Publishing Tax Credit and Ontario Creates, and the Government of Canada.

Nous remercions le Conseil des arts du Canada de son soutien. L'an dernier, le Conseil a investi 153 millions de dollars pour mettre de l'art dans la vie des Canadiennes et des Canadiens de tout le pays.

Care has been taken to trace the ownership of copyright material used in this book. The author and the publisher welcome any information enabling them to rectify any references or credits in subsequent editions.

The publisher is not responsible for websites or their content unless they are owned by the publisher.

Printed and bound in Canada.

VISIT US AT

 dundurn.com | @dundurnpress | dundurnpress | dundurnpress

Dundurn
3 Church Street, Suite 500
Toronto, Ontario, Canada
M5E 1M2

To Glenda and Mary

And to the teachers and librarians — with special mention to Mr. Reddick and Mr. Erickson — who inspired me to believe in the power of creating, whether on a stage, on a page, on canvas, or with music. All of you are the reason I am able to do this. All of you are the reason I love to do this.

PROLOGUE

My name is Adam Cullen. Some of you may have read my chronicles of cases I have worked previously with former Calgary homicide detective, now private investigator, Mike Cobb. You are then aware that I first met Cobb when I hired him to investigate the deliberately set fire that took the life of my wife, Donna, in May of 2005. Though he was unsuccessful in that effort, Cobb, in turn, recruited me almost a decade later to conduct research in connection with another case he was working. During that investigation we began to look again at Donna's murder, and this time the two of us were able to find and confront the arsonist/murderer. There was, I suppose, justice.

Cobb and I have worked other cases since — again, some of you may have seen my accounts of those investigations and their results. But since early in our work relationship, there has been one case, one terrible unsolved murder from 1991, that has hung over our heads like a guillotine blade and has become, at least for me, something of an obsession. For those of you who have never heard of or been interested in Cullen and Cobb, or for those of you who have forgotten the details of the Faith

Unruh murder, the following will, I hope, serve to update you as to where events stood as we began one of the most difficult times, certainly in my life, and, I suspect, in Cobb's, as well.

ONE

Marlon Kennedy had been dead for almost ten weeks.

Christmas had come and gone; cold, dark January had given way to the longer, more optimistic February days, and evenings that began after six o'clock. There had been more snow than the almanac had forecast, though its prediction of a milder, kinder February appeared, at least so far, to be accurate.

Cobb and I were sitting in the Sunterra Market at 12th Avenue and 1st Street East, just a few blocks from Cobb's office.

With Theory of a Deadman's "Santa Monica" rolling through the speakers, Cobb was working the prime rib lunch special while I had settled for soup and a sandwich, my appetite dampened somewhat by the topic of conversation. We were talking about Marlon Kennedy. Except, of course, that wasn't his real name.

Kendall Mark had been a Calgary Police Service detective at the time eleven-year-old Faith Unruh was murdered while walking home from school in 1991. Cobb had been on the force at that time, as well, but he was only two years into his career and not yet working homicide. It was in that department that he would spend much of his career before leaving the police service to become a private investigator. I had worked with Cobb on a few cases, including the search for the arsonist who set fire to my home and killed my wife, who was in the house at the time. Almost a decade later, we found that person.

Cobb told me the details of the Faith Unruh murder after my girlfriend's daughter and her best friend had stunned us with their knowledge of the horror that had taken place fifteen years before either of them had been born.

Faith Unruh had celebrated her eleventh birthday the day before she died. She was walking home from school with a friend on a pleasant June day. The two lived just a block from one another and had parted company at the friend's house, leaving Faith to travel the remaining block of her walk alone.

She never arrived home. Her killer somehow lured her into the backyard of a house two doors down and across the street from where she lived, strangled her in broad daylight and left her next to a garage with a piece of plywood over her. She was found several hours later, naked but not having been sexually assaulted.

Cobb told me that everyone in homicide had thought this would be a quick solve — that they'd have the guy within a day or two. The investigators figured it had to be someone who knew Faith, or at least knew her route home, and was also aware that she'd be alone for that final block. There was, of course, the possibility that it had happened by chance — that a predator had happened upon a near-perfect victim and had acted on impulse. Cobb said most investigators had ruled out that scenario, believing that the perfect storm of luck and opportunity was improbable. And that view was compounded by the belief that Faith would not have gone into the backyard of a neighbouring house with someone she didn't know.

There was a fair amount of blood near the body that wasn't Faith's, so the police figured they'd have physical evidence, as well. There were also indications that the girl had fought for her life, which meant she had likely screamed. But as the investigation continued, it became clear that if Faith had screamed, no one heard her. As unlikely as it seemed, apparently no one had seen or heard anything out of the ordinary. The investigating team talked to everyone in the neighbourhood, even appealed on radio and TV for anyone who might have been driving by to come forward — several people had responded, most of whom must have been very near when the murder took place. But there were simply no concrete leads — no actual witnesses, no fingerprints or DNA match, and no apparent motive for the killing — unless it had been a sex crime, and the killer got spooked and fled before completing what he had started.

The original investigating team was two veteran guys who Cobb said had worked their tails off. One was named Lennie Hansel. He was only three years from retirement at the time. The Faith Unruh case apparently haunted the man to the point that he was dead less than a year after receiving his gold watch.

His partner at the time was Tony Gaspari, although cop logic or humour dictated that all of Hansel's partners over the years were given the nickname Gretel.

Like his partner, this Gretel had become obsessed with the case, and the obsession eventually cost him his family and finally his mental health. Tony Gaspari ended up in a home, unable to look after himself or communicate beyond guttural sounds.

And there was a third cop. It wasn't his case but he had got caught up in it. Spent all of his non-work hours on it … for years. He became more and more immersed in the case and finally just disappeared.

That man was Kendall Mark. He resurfaced years later and it turned out he had changed both his name — to Marlon Kennedy — and his appearance — from Caucasian to black. He had spent the last several years living on the Unruhs' street, operating a sophisticated surveillance system that watched both the former Unruh family home and the one across the road, where Faith's body had been found. He was convinced that one day the killer would show up again at one of the locations associated with the murder, and when that happened, Mark, a.k.a. Kennedy, would spring his trap.

I'd met him under circumstances I hoped never to face again. Because I had become fascinated by the case myself, I had driven and walked the area around both houses, unaware that I was being watched … unaware, that is, until the night Kennedy jumped me in the alley behind my own apartment and came very close to administering his own justice on me before I was able, barely, to persuade him that I wasn't Faith Unruh's killer.

And now Kennedy was dead.

Theory of a Deadman had given way, first to Sinatra, then to Corb Lund — apparently whoever was in charge of music selection at Sunterra was nothing if not eclectic. Cobb pushed away the last of his prime rib at about the same time I finished half my sandwich and wrapped up the other half. We topped up our coffee and looked at each other across the table, neither of us eager to pick up the conversation thread that had brought us there.

Cobb started it. "Cops still haven't got much — it's another one of those *nobody saw anything, nobody heard anything* deals that drive cops crazy," Cobb said as he stirred Equal into his coffee.

"That shit'll kill you." I pointed.

"But not as fast as real sugar."

"Ever hear of no sweetener at all?"

"Boring." He grinned. "And boredom will kill you quickest of all."

There's no answer to that, so I decided to get back on task. "Hard to believe that a guy gets run over in a back alley of a populated neighbourhood in the early evening, and there isn't someone who knows something."

"Hard to believe, but it happens. Look at the Faith Unruh murder."

"So, what *do* we know?"

He pulled out his notebook, flipped it open.

"Not a lot more — he was run down in the alley behind the garage where Faith Unruh's body had been found. The vehicle went back and forth over him at least a couple of times."

"Making sure?"

Cobb shrugged. "Maybe. Although it could have been rage — like the killer who stabs his victim forty or fifty times, knowing that death has already occurred. The police determined it was a car, probably an SUV, not a pickup, and they know the make of the tires."

"Jesus," I said. "Tire-tread impressions on the body?"

Cobb nodded. "That, and I'm guessing in Kennedy's blood and the area right around the body."

I thought about what he'd said, shook my head. "Something's bothering me," I said. "Kennedy was a fit guy and pretty athletic. I know that from first-hand experience. I'm having trouble figuring how somebody managed to drive down that alley and nail him without his being able to jump out of the way."

"Probably didn't happen that way," Cobb answered. "More likely the killer drove in there, Kennedy came along and they talked at the driver's side window. Casual stuff — how ya doin', sure is cold. Kennedy let down his guard. Then as he stepped away, he made the mistake of moving either in front of or behind the car. The driver punched the accelerator and knocked him down. Even if Kennedy was still alive at that point, he was likely too injured to escape or even roll out of the way, at least not easily or quickly. The killer drove back and forth a few times and the job was done."

"The part I don't get is that Kennedy was the most suspicious guy I've ever known. Hard to believe he'd put himself in a position to be harmed. Especially like that."

"He made a mistake," Cobb said, no trace of doubt in his voice. "We don't know exactly what the killer did to lure him in there and let him feel secure right up until the moment when Kennedy realized — too late — what was happening."

I thought about that. "Lure him in there," I repeated. "To almost the same place Faith Unruh was lured the day she lost her life."

"Yeah," Cobb said. "I've thought about that. He died maybe twenty or twenty-five feet from where Faith's body was found."

"Damn." In the three years I'd been working with Cobb — my background as a former crime writer with the *Calgary Herald* had proved useful in researching various aspects of the cases he'd involved me in — I had come face to face with the depravity of the criminal mind and the violence that is often a trademark of that depravity. Here was further evidence.

"And we know that the tape that would have shown what happened in that alley was taken," I said.

"Meaning the driver of the car killed Kennedy, took his keys, then drove out of the alley, parked somewhere nearby and got into Kennedy's house, took the incriminating tape and left."

"Cool customer," I said.

"Very."

"And had to know about the surveillance set-up in Kennedy's house."

"Yeah."

I was also familiar with Kennedy's surveillance system, as he'd recruited me a few weeks before his death to babysit the operation while he was in Vancouver with his ex-wife, who was terminally ill. I was stationed in Kennedy's house for ten days, until she died and the funeral had taken place. There were two surveillance locations in the house; one was upstairs, and it was focused on the backyard and alley behind the house across the street, the one where Faith's body had been found. The second was on the main floor and was directed at the former Unruh house — Faith's home for eleven years and one day.

"The killer had to know about the cameras and the tapes." I knew I was stating the obvious but I needed to say it: not for Cobb, for me. "He *had* to know. You don't kill someone, then search their home for a camera *just in case*."

"No, but it's possible the killer was searching the house for something else altogether or maybe planning a robbery. He stumbled across the surveillance set-up, figured out what it was all about, and the tape that mattered disappeared."

"You think that's likely?"

"No." Cobb shook his head. "I think he was after the tapes. There were no signs of searching or the kind of disturbance associated with robbery in any other parts of the house. And that means Kennedy had to have told someone about what he had been doing all those years in that house."

I nodded. It was the only answer — however improbable.

Cobb sipped his coffee, set the cup down, and looked at me. "Did he ever indicate to you that he'd let anyone else besides you and me know about the surveillance?"

I thought back to that time and the conversations I'd had with Kennedy. They were seldom long conversations — never expansive.

"I can't remember if he said one way or the other. But my gut was that he was extremely secretive about what he was doing, that I was the only one who knew — well, me and you — who'd ever seen the set-up," I said. "I mean, this was a guy who changed his appearance, his name — Christ, his life — in his obsession with finding Faith's killer. It doesn't make sense that he told *a bunch of* people."

"Not a bunch of people. But he had to have told one."

"I guess you're right."

"Because if he didn't, that leaves only one other alternative," Cobb said. "And that is that either you or I killed him."

I looked at Cobb. He wasn't laughing or even smiling.

"I hope you're not serious."

He leaned forward. "I know you didn't kill Kennedy. But the police don't know that. And they are going to find out that you have a working knowledge of Kennedy's surveillance equipment and that you've been in that alley. I'm warning you that you are likely to be, if not a suspect, at least a person of interest."

"Which is a phrase used to point to someone they don't have enough evidence to call a suspect, but who is, in fact, a suspect."

"Something like that." Cobb's face formed a smile best described as sardonic. "By the way, I'm likely to be on their radar, too." He paused, straightened up. "And for the record, there is another possibility."

"I'm glad you feel that way." I was feeling a little taken aback by the direction of the conversation so far and it probably showed on my face. "And that possibility is?"

"That Faith's killer somehow learned, maybe even accidentally, of the surveillance and was playing Kennedy. Biding his time, waiting for the right moment."

I thought about that. "Which would mean the times Kennedy and I saw shadows — something — in that alley … maybe it wasn't an animal or … whatever. Maybe it was … the guy."

Cobb shrugged.

"And that makes the marks on the trash can platform significant," I went on. "Not some silly record of the times the person living in the house had taken out the trash or something equally banal and unbelievable."

Kennedy had discovered a series of marks — four perpendicular marks, then a diagonal line through them to make a group of five marks, then another set of five and one single perpendicular line on its own — eleven marks in all. In the hours before he went into that alley for the last time, he'd sent me an email telling me that a twelfth scratch had appeared. Whoever had been making those marks — Faith's killer? — had been back in the alley again. And though I'd never know for sure, my guess was that Kennedy had gone back there to check on it again, to see if there was anything that might tell him something … and that was when the person driving the SUV-cum-murder weapon had somehow surprised and killed him.

"Okay," I said. "So, what do we do? I know we have no client. But Kennedy was … what … an associate? Are we in on it or not?"

"I say we're in. At least we sniff around, see if we can learn anything useful. We owe the guy that much. But it'll have to wait a few days. I have to go out of town for a while on another case. Three, maybe four days at the most."

He was right. We didn't have a client for the Unruh-Kennedy murders, so whatever investigating we might do was pro bono. And the truth was I had a magazine piece I needed to move forward with, so the time I could devote to that would be welcome. And though it sounded callous to say it, the Kennedy murder and its connection — if there was one — to the Faith Unruh murder of a quarter of a century earlier would be there when Cobb got back.

"If the cops do decide to follow up on my surveillance connection to Kennedy, you think I need a lawyer?"

He shrugged. "Like I said, my guess is that at some point they'll want to talk to you. Even so, I can't see how they could possibly decide to charge you. Still, I'd have your lawyer ready in case you need him."

I nodded, not particularly reassured. "Where you off to?"

"Victoria. Forty-year-old woman runs off with twenty-year-old mechanic who worked on her car. Sixty-year-old husband wants her back."

"Sounds like fun."

"Fun like a case of malaria."

"What are you supposed to do — drag her back? I'm pretty sure that sort of thing is frowned upon in the justice community."

Cobb shook his head. "I just have to find them. Husband's pretty sure they're in Victoria or somewhere on the island. Somebody saw them on the ferry, gave him a call. Told him they'd seen his wife and their son but didn't get a chance to say hi."

"Their son. Ouch."

"Yeah, so I find them, report back, and I'm out of it. Tidy paycheque that will offset the pro bono aspect of the Kennedy investigation."

Cobb left that afternoon.

TWO

The kid looked to be fifteen, maybe sixteen.

He was good-looking, clean-cut, a tattoo on one bare arm but without metal in or on his face. He had clearly taken the time to dress in a way he felt appropriate for the meeting he had come for. Short-sleeved checked shirt (with collar), dress pants, and shoes — no ball cap, backwards or otherwise.

I'd met him at the door to Cobb's office, where he'd shaken my hand and asked if he could speak to me. I'd invited him in, told him to throw his coat and mitts on the window ledge.

Now I was sitting at Cobb's desk. The kid was across from me, nervous but seemingly unafraid. I reached back, turned down Sarah Slean on the CD player I'd brought into the office to background the piece I was writing for the *National Post* on Naheed Nenshi, the mayor who had been re-elected a few months earlier after a neck and neck campaign that it was predicted he would lose. The *Post* wanted me to examine whether Nenshi was, in fact, more popular outside Calgary than he was in the city. I doubted the premise but had to admit that I was a Nenshi fan, which might have tainted my ability to be unbiased. I was still in the research phase of the piece, and it was interesting, as it got me closer to the man than I had previously been. And while he had won a third term, there was little doubt that the lustre of the early years had been somewhat diminished.

The music reduced to a murmur, I pushed my notes to one side and studied the young man opposite me.

"Mr. Cobb, my name is Danny Luft," he said.

"Good to meet you, Danny," I answered him. "But I'm not Cobb. He's away on business and won't be back for a couple of days. I'm Adam Cullen. Is there anything I can help you with?"

"Do you do the same thing he does?"

I shook my head. "Not quite. Mr. Cobb is the private investigator. I'm a freelance writer. I used to cover crime for the *Calgary Herald*. Mr. Cobb and I have worked together on a number of cases. When required, I conduct research that assists him in the work he does. Can I help you with anything?"

I repeated that last bit, convinced that the kid had been caught by his parents with a little weed under the bed, or maybe he'd shoplifted a wallet or a CD from somewhere and was looking for advice, maybe even a little counselling. Stuff I could handle without Cobb.

The kid shifted in his chair. "You ever kill anybody?"

I swallowed once and moved some facial muscles around before I answered.

"No, I haven't, Danny."

"Me neither." A beat. "How about Mr. Cobb? He kill anybody?"

I thought about how to reply to that, decided to answer the question with one of my own — a tactic I'd seen

Cobb use more than once. "Why do you feel you need to know that?"

He looked at me for a long moment before answering. "I guess it's … it would probably help if he at least knew stuff about it."

"About killing people?"

"Yeah."

I opted for honesty, or at least something close to it. "I believe in carrying out his duties as a policeman and later as a private investigator, he may have had to do that, yes."

"He's probably the guy I should be talking to, then."

"Are you in some trouble, Danny?"

"I don't know. I don't think so. At least, not yet."

I leaned forward, my elbows on the desk. "Here's the thing," I said, "Mr. Cobb is out of town on a case. He phones in every morning. Maybe if you tell me what's going on that makes you think you need a private detective's help, I can relay that information to him, and he and I can discuss how best to help you. In the meantime, I'll certainly do all I can for you."

He considered this and finally nodded slowly. "Yeah, that should be okay," he said. "What's it going to cost me?"

"How about we talk about that after you've told me what brought you here?"

"Yeah, okay."

"Would you like a pop? I've got a couple of Cokes in the fridge."

He shook his head. "No thanks."

"What grade are you in, Danny?"

"Ten," he said. "I go to Beaverbrook."

Lord Beaverbrook High School. Southeast Calgary. A long way from Cobb's office.

"You drive here this morning?"

"Uh-uh. I'm only fifteen. Took the bus and the CTrain."

I nodded. "Okay. So, why don't you go ahead and tell me about it?"

He moved his head slowly up and down once, then a second time, fidgeted in the big, brown leather chair that could have held two of him, and finally spoke, slowly enunciating the words, his voice quieter now, as if he were guarding a secret.

"I have a girlfriend … Glenna."

He paused and I waited for more.

"Her dad is kind of a big deal in Calgary. He's got a lot of money; he's on quite a few of those boards, you know?"

"Boards of directors?"

"Yeah, for different companies and stuff, quite a few of them," he repeated. "Glenna told me that makes him pretty important and also pretty rich. He was the head of the Chamber of Commerce, and he was on city council for a few years."

I sat back and thought about that. "Are you talking about Wendell Claiborne, Danny?"

"Yeah, that's Glenna's dad."

The kid was bang on. Wendell Claiborne was a *very* big deal, one of Calgary's uber-rich, seriously powerful and a major player in Alberta's newly amalgamated United Conservative Party. I'd never met Claiborne, but had read enough about him and seen him being interviewed often enough that I didn't much like the man. From accounts I'd read, he and the mayor had butted heads repeatedly both in and out of council chambers when Claiborne was on council.

"He doesn't like you dating his daughter?" I said.

Danny shook his head. "No, that's not it."

"Okay, go on."

"Well, he … he wants me to kill his wife."

I reached over and picked up the cup of coffee I'd been working on for the half-hour or so before Danny Luft had knocked on the door of Cobb's office. It was cold now, but I needed a minute to think about what I'd just heard, and sipped the tepid brew as I considered my response.

After I set the cup back down, I said, "He told you that."

"Yeah, he did."

"Are you sure you heard him right? Understood correctly what he was saying?"

"I understood him all right."

"Okay, let's go back a bit. How did all this come about?"

"I started going out with Glenna about three months ago. She's great and her parents seemed okay … at first, anyway, but then one night I was over at Glenna's place and we heard them having this huge fight and —"

"When you say fight," I interrupted, "are you talking physical? Was anyone hitting anyone else?"

He shook his head. "I don't know. They were in a different part of the house, so we couldn't tell, but Glenna said she's heard them screaming at each other like that other times."

"Did she say if it happened a lot?"

Danny shrugged. "I don't think so. I mean, she didn't say how often her parents were like that, just that she'd heard it before."

"Okay, go on."

"So, last Saturday night, Glenna's parents were out, not together. I mean, they were both out, but they had gone to different places, you know?"

"I understand."

"Anyway, Mr. Claiborne came home early and caught us smoking some weed. I thought he'd freak but he didn't. He just told me to go home and to never bring dope into his house again. I thought he was, like, pretty cool to deal with it like that. Then yesterday morning he phoned me at home before I left for school and told me he wanted me to come to his office after school."

"And you went to his office."

He shook his head. "He texted me later and said he wanted me to meet him at this park not far from my school instead."

"And?"

"And that's what I did. I met him there."

"Was there anyone else at the park when you and Claiborne were there?"

"I didn't see anybody except for a couple of little kids on a set of swings. There was a woman with them, maybe one of their moms or a babysitter or something, I couldn't tell. We were at the other end of the park from them."

"Right. So, what happened?"

"That's when he told me that he wanted me to kill Mrs. Claiborne."

"Just like that? He said, 'I want you to kill my wife.'"

"Pretty much, yeah. And then he said I had to do it because if I didn't he was going to tell my dad I was a druggie."

"Did he tell you how he wanted you to do it?"

Danny nodded. "He told me he'd help me to make it look like somebody broke into their house to rob the place and then shot Mrs. Claiborne when she discovered the intruder in their home."

"And you were to shoot Mrs. Claiborne."

"Yeah, I was supposed to come over there and after I … did it, that's when he would make it look like someone broke in. He said he had somebody who would help him with that part."

"And what were you supposed to shoot Mrs. Claiborne with?"

"He said he'd take care of that."

"What did he mean by that?"

"He said he'd have the gun there for me."

"He'd provide the gun," I said.

"That's what he told me."

"You know anything about guns?"

"My dad's ex-military. He takes me to the range sometimes. I can shoot okay."

"Did Claiborne say what kind of gun?"

"Revolver. That's all he said. I didn't ask what kind."

"And when is this all supposed to happen, Danny?"

"He said Saturday night."

"This *coming* Saturday night?"

"Yeah."

"So, he threatened to tell your parents that you'd been smoking weed."

"My dad, yeah."

"Danny, that's not a big enough deal to make you kill somebody. So you get grounded for a while."

He shook his head. "Did you hear what I said? My dad's ex-military. He's as straight as they come. No drugs, not weed … nothing. And it would be a hell of a lot worse than grounding."

When I didn't respond, he elaborated. "I missed school for a week one time."

"Because of your dad."

"Yeah."

"He hit you?"

He nodded. I looked at him to see if he was lying. It didn't look like it. If anything, it looked like he was ashamed to have told me.

"Danny, that sounds like abuse."

He shook his head again. "It's not like he beats me up all the time or anything. And it's not like a couple of other kids I know where every time the old man gets drunk, somebody gets hurt. My dad's not like that. A lot of the time he's a pretty cool dad to have." He paused. "But if he loses it, like he would for this ..." He paused again. "And there's something else."

"What's that?"

"He told me he'd pay me ten thousand dollars if I did it."

"Claiborne said he'd pay you ten thousand dollars to shoot his wife," I repeated.

"Yeah."

"And rat you out to your dad if you didn't."

"Yeah."

"I can see where that would be a tough decision except for one thing."

"What's that?"

"We're talking about killing someone here — taking a person's life."

A pause, then a nod. "I know." His voice was soft and he spoke slowly. "That's why I'm here. What do you think I should do?"

"I'm guessing he told you not to tell anyone about his proposition."

"Yeah, but I figured maybe a private detective … you know, I couldn't really go to the cops."

I nodded. "Okay, Danny, what you do is you leave this with me. I'll talk to Cobb — Mr. Cobb — right away. How do I contact you?"

"Do you text?"

I smiled. "Yes, Danny, I text. I own a colour TV, too."

He missed the sarcasm or chose to ignore it, instead giving me his phone number.

"Okay, here's the deal," I said. "You don't do anything. You don't go to the Claiborne house; you don't take any calls from Claiborne; if he texts you, you don't reply. You do nothing, except maybe your homework, and you wait for me to contact you. You understand, Danny?"

"How do I see Glenna?"

"You see her at school; you see her at the mall, in the park, on a street corner. But you don't go near Claiborne — not at his house, not at his office, nowhere. You got that?"

"Yeah, yeah, I got it."

"By the way, have you told Glenna about her dad's … proposal?"

"Not yet." He was clenching and unclenching his fists one at a time. It wasn't anger, I didn't think. More frustration — a kid who'd been given a burden he was far from able to handle. I guessed that thought had occurred to Claiborne, too, and that was what made Danny Luft the ideal candidate for a psychological takeover. I was looking forward to a face to face with Claiborne, but decided that had better wait until after I talked to Cobb.

I'd been a little rougher than I needed to be on the kid and wanted to back things off a little. "Listen, Danny, we can help you. I'll talk to Mr. Cobb in the morning and, like I said, I'll text you, okay? The thing is you haven't done anything wrong, remember that. And you did the right thing asking for help. Everything's going to be okay."

He stood up. "Okay, Mr. ... what did you say your name was?"

"Cullen. Adam Cullen." I reached into a jacket pocket, pulled out a business card, and handed it to him. "My number's on there, Danny. You call me or text me if something happens that you think I should know about ... or if you're scared or you think Claiborne's up to something else ... anything ... you contact me, okay?"

"Right. Um, thanks a lot. I ..." He stopped talking and looked at the floor. "You haven't said how much this will cost."

"I'll discuss that as well with Mr. Cobb," I told him. "And I'll talk to you soon about ... all this," I said. "That's a promise."

When he'd gone I went to the big window that looked out over 1st Avenue and watched Danny come out of the building, turn north, and head for downtown and, I guessed, either a bus or the CTrain to take him home. I hoped the kid could be trusted to do two things — keep his mouth shut about Claiborne's offer and stay well away from the man who'd made that offer — until Cobb and I worked out a plan.

I called Cobb but didn't reach him. I left a message telling him to get back to me ASAP but wasn't sure if he'd be checking messages, especially if he was hot on the trail of the runaway lovers.

I reached back and cranked the volume on Sarah Slean. She had just begun a song called "The Devil & the Dove."

Cobb called at seven thirty the next morning. The call woke me up, but I was proud of how quickly I was able to be almost coherent.

"Sorry, Adam, I was tied up with the case out here and didn't get to my phone until now. What's up?"

I walked him through my conversation with Danny Luft. He stayed silent until I'd finished, and even then took a while before speaking.

"You think the kid is telling the truth?"

"I can't think why he wouldn't be," I said.

"I can." Cobb sounded like he was talking to me from the inside of a cave. Or the bottom of a well. "It happens from time to time. Kids with a real or imagined grievance accusing people in positions of authority of abuse, criminal actions, all kinds of stuff."

"I know that happens sometimes," I acknowledged. "But this doesn't feel like that. This feels like a kid telling the truth, and he's scared, and he doesn't know what to do."

"Okay, let's look at the positives. He hasn't shot Mrs. Claiborne and he came to us."

"I can't argue that. I'm just not sure, beyond counselling Danny not to kill anyone, what I should do."

"Well, you were right to tell him to stay away from Claiborne. I've got a couple of additional suggestions. We know Claiborne's a successful businessman, but that doesn't make him a good guy. Anyone who would try to hire-slash-blackmail a kid to kill his wife doesn't sound like a clean liver to me. Why don't you start working your magic and find out everything you can about him? We might just find something we can use to get the kid off Claiborne's radar. And you need to keep talking to Danny. Make sure he isn't having second thoughts or that Claiborne hasn't upped the ante and got him talked into a Saturday night shooting."

"Right, I'll get started on Claiborne right away."

"I'm in Ladysmith and I've found them. They're in a beach house by the ocean. I'm in the galley of a sailboat I rented. I have to confirm it's them, report to my client, and I'm wrapped up here. But I'm not sure I'll be back there by Saturday. So some of this is going to be on you. In the meantime you can call me anytime you need to."

"Wow, sailing on the ocean — tough case."

He laughed. "It would be better if I'd actually sailed the boat. I haven't left the mooring. I'm at a private little marina that's close to the beach house, perfect place to watch from. Anyway, I'll get there as fast as I can … call me when you need to."

"Good. That makes me feel a little better."

There was a pause on the line. "Adam."

"Yeah?"

"You can do this," Cobb, ever intuitive, hearing the hesitation in my voice, sensing the self-doubt, said. "Just make sure Claiborne doesn't get to Danny. I'll make a couple of calls and see if I can get you some help with that."

"Right."

I knew what help Cobb was referring to. He occasionally employed the services of a couple of people as operatives — I'd met them, and knew they were tough, fearless, and well-armed. He'd have them watching Danny to make sure the kid didn't succumb to some urgent message from Claiborne. That might help keep face-to-face contact from happening but there'd be nothing, save the desire to follow my advice, to keep the young man from phoning or texting Claiborne or responding to incoming calls or texts.

We ended the call. I got a pot of coffee going — old-school, *perked* coffee — and called Jill Sawley, the woman I'd met when I was working my first case with Cobb a couple of years previously and about whom I had been crazy ever since; actually, that applied to both Jill and her ten-year-old daughter, Kyla.

It was small talk for the moment — I'd bring Jill up to speed on Danny Luft's story over dinner later. The call completed, I texted Danny.

> Hey, Danny. I talked to Mike Cobb. He said to hang tough, stay away from Claiborne and we'll get him off your back … might take a couple of days. Stay strong and leave it to us, okay? Call or text anytime you need to or want to.

With that done, it was Google time. Coffee mug topped up and notebook at the ready, with Jann Arden's *Living Under June* providing the accompaniment, I began my examination of the life and times of Wendell Claiborne.

A couple of hours later, I had a fairly decent overview of the man's life. Claiborne had been born with the proverbial silver spoon firmly in place. His father, Orville

Claiborne, had been a major player in the oil industry. Orville's company, Flare and Derrick Oil, which later came to be known simply as FD Oil, made its mark — and its millions — on the exploration side of the industry.

Several of the largest companies in the oil patch, an Alberta-based bank, and even a wind-powered electricity producer all proudly pointed to Claiborne's name and influence on their boards of directors. And there were the continued rumblings that Alberta's United Conservative Party was hoping to woo him as a candidate for the next provincial election in the hope that he was a guy who could help oust the NDP government that currently presided over the province.

As I dug a little deeper, it appeared there might be some chinks in the sterling silver armour that surrounded the dapper businessman. I learned, for example, that the wife he was wanting Danny Luft to off was the third woman to fill that role, the first two having been eliminated in the more traditional, time-honoured fashion — divorce with a big settlement. Which raised the question: Why not employ a method that had worked before? Of course, there was a chance that Claiborne was tired of parting with large amounts of cash. Or maybe the current Mrs. Claiborne was less enthusiastic about taking the severance package.

There were a couple more red flags — one an incident four years earlier, when Claiborne was sued by a group of farmers and ranchers for alleged contamination of their wells, brought on by some drilling operations that Claiborne companies were part of. The matter had been settled out of court. The second was a break-in at the Claiborne house a week before Christmas. No one had been at home at the time, and while theft appeared to be at least part of the reason for the break-in, the newspaper account related that there had been considerable vandalism, resulting in thousands of dollars in damage to the home and contents. Claiborne had offered a ten-thousand-dollar reward for information leading to the arrest of those responsible, but a follow-up story indicated no arrests had been made. I found it interesting that the reward was the same amount he had offered Danny Luft to shoot his wife.

I was getting a sense that Claiborne might have a few enemies. I shut down my computer, changed, and headed for Jill's house, stopping to pick up a bottle of La Vieille Ferme, a French red wine I knew she liked. I made a second stop, this one at the Shawnessy Chapters, and picked up a couple of books for Kyla, who was the most voracious almost-eleven-year-old reader I'd ever seen. Just before I got to the house, I called Cobb and filled him in on what I'd learned about Claiborne. And I texted him my notes to date.

"Okay, that's good," he said. "Go enjoy dinner with your fair ladies and I'll call you later. I want to think about this and read what you've got — see if there's anything here that might help us."

My purchases netted me kisses from the older of the fair ladies and a high five from the younger. Dinner over, Kyla hunkered down in the bay window, earbuds and iPod dialed in to Marianas Trench, her current favourite band, as she plunged into one of the books I'd bought her — Susan Juby's *The Truth Commission*. Jill and I decided that an unusually warm night meant we should enjoy a glass of wine on the back deck.

For several minutes we sat in silence, enjoying the wine and the night sky.

"This one bothers me, Adam," Jill finally said.

I'd told her most of the Claiborne story while we were preparing salad before dinner. "Yeah, me too."

"I can't imagine first of all that someone can be that evil … to recruit a fifteen-year-old boy to kill his wife."

"Sadly, I *can* imagine it," I told her. "When I was at the *Herald*, the one thing I learned is that there's a lot of evil in the world, some of it unspeakable. This certainly falls into that category, but it's not unique in its malevolence."

"What are you going to do?"

"For the moment our strategy is to keep Danny away from Claiborne and vice versa. It's a temporary measure — we know that — but until we figure a way to lean on Claiborne and get him to back off from Danny, it's all we've got."

"Can't you just confront that … that … creep and tell him you know what he's up to?"

I shook my head. "We do that and Claiborne's the kind of guy who would enjoy phoning Danny's dad and telling him about the weed. And likely embellishing the story some to include other drugs. If Danny's being truthful, and I think he is, we would be putting our client in harm's way … and failing to respect his confidentiality. So, no, we can't do that. What we need to do is get something on Claiborne that we can use to make him abandon the thing with no repercussions for Danny. And in a way that ensures the safety of Mrs. Claiborne."

"How are you going to do that?"

I shrugged. "I have to admit I'd feel a lot more confident if Cobb were here. I know I'm not as good at this stuff as he is." I glanced at my watch. "Which reminds me, I need to get back to my computer to see if I can come up with something, anything, we can use."

Much as I looked forward to and enjoyed the nights I stayed over at Jill's place, or she at mine, I knew this wouldn't be one of those nights. Jill knew it, too, although that didn't stop her from giving me a good-night kiss that had a lot more hello than goodbye in it.

Once back at my apartment I drank a can of Rolling Rock, before switching to coffee as I sat at my computer, delving again into the mostly boring, occasionally sordid chronicling of Wendell Claiborne's life. Ben Heppner's *Airs Français* made the experience, if not pleasant, at least bearable. I fell asleep at my computer sometime after 4:00 a.m., having been singularly unsuccessful at finding anything even slightly useful.

Turns out it didn't matter, at least not in the way we thought it would. At 6:08 a.m., everything changed.

That's when the phone rang. I managed to pry one eye open and glared at the device, willing it to spontaneously combust so that my sleep-deprived brain wouldn't have to deal with whatever the news was — surely a call at that hour meant there *was* news of some kind. The bearer of that news was no longer my friend.

My phone-hate, and just about every other thought in my head at the time, was quickly pushed aside when the caller turned out to be Danny Luft. The kid's voice was shaking and his first words jerked me upright and instantly wide awake.

"This is Danny," he said. "I'm at the police station. Can you help me?"

"What's happened, Danny?"

"I don't know. They said I could phone my parents but I told them I wanted to call you first. Mr. Cullen, I'm scared."

"Danny, have you talked to Mr. Claiborne? I need the truth here."

"He called last night and left a message, and he texted me, too. Told me to get back to him right away."

"What did you do?" I could feel a shiver starting to work its way up my back.

"I called him back. I'm sorry but I didn't know what else to do … I was afraid he'd —"

"What did he say?" I interrupted.

"I didn't get him."

"What do you mean?"

"He didn't answer. I didn't get to talk to him and now he's —"

"What time was this, Danny?"

"He called me a little after nine. But I didn't call him back until about ten, I guess."

"But you *didn't* talk to him." I wanted to be totally clear on that point.

"No."

"Did you text him?"

"No, I left a message when I phoned, but I didn't text him and now —"

"What did you say in the message?"

"I just said I was sorry I missed his call. Then I ended it."

"Okay, that's good."

"I didn't kill him, Mr. Cullen."

"What?" All traces of leftover sleep leaped from my body.

"I didn't kill him."

"Danny, are you telling me Claiborne's dead? *Mister* Claiborne?"

"That's what the cops said … they came to the house this morning and told me I had to come with them. I asked them what happened and one of them told me that Mr. Claiborne had been shot. Then he read me that thing that says I can remain silent and all that stuff."

"Okay." It wasn't much of a response but I'd need time to come up with something better.

"What should I do?"

"Where are your parents?"

"They spent yesterday at the lake. They were coming home this morning — they might be home by now. Mr. Cullen, what should I do?"

I thought about that. "You do nothing, Danny. You won't have to talk to them until your parents and your lawyer are there. So just sit tight until they get there."

"But I didn't shoot him. Wouldn't it be better to tell them about —"

"No, Danny, that wouldn't be better." *Have you never watched a cop show on TV?* I thought. "What happened after they came to your house?"

"When I got here, they searched me and took my fingerprints. And they took my phone. All the texts and messages and stuff with Mr. Claiborne are on there and —"

"Danny."

"And what if —"

"Danny."

It was all I could do not to let my inner groan explode into the phone. "Now listen to me. I'll phone your parents; then I'll be there. Where are you?"

"At the main police … um … headquarters, I guess. I don't know the address or anything."

"I do. I'll be there. What's your home phone number?"

"Are you sure you have to —"

"Danny, you're a suspect or at least a person of interest in a murder investigation. I have to call your parents. Now give me the number."

"Sorry." He recited the number.

"No, Danny, *I'm* sorry. I didn't mean to be harsh. But I do need to speak to your mom *and* dad. And I'm sure your parents will be there very soon. Listen to me. The big thing you need to do now is just be calm and quiet and say nothing to anyone other than to tell them that you want me to be there. Otherwise it'll just be your parents and the lawyer. Tell the detectives that you are a client of Cobb and me. They'll probably know that already from your phone but you tell them that you want me there. You understand me …? And when I get there you need to be totally honest with me. You with me on those two things?"

"Uh-huh."

"Good, I'll see you shortly."

Next I called Cobb. "Yeah," his response an indication that he was busy and didn't have time right now. He'd have to make time.

I said, "Yeah, you know the shit and the fan? They've met."

"Okay, what's up?"

I told him. When I'd finished he said, "Goddamn it."

"Yeah."

"Okay, call the kid's dad; tell him to get a lawyer and get there fast. I can wrap things up here later today.

I'll see if I can change my flight and get an earlier one. Meantime I'll make a couple of calls."

I knew he meant he'd be calling some of his former police associates to find out what they had on Danny Luft. The police aren't eager to arrest kids and charge them with murder unless they've got pretty solid evidence. Of course, Danny hadn't been charged, at least I didn't think he had, but that old adage about smoke and fire felt pretty appropriate right now. Right up there with the fan and the caca. Next came the call I wasn't looking forward to making. I hoped Danny's parents were home from the cabin.

A male voice answered.

"Mr. Luft?"

"Yes, who's this?"

"My name's Adam Cullen. I'm a freelance journalist and I occasionally work with a private investigator named Mike Cobb."

"Yeah?" The voice was that of a man who expected some kind of extortion threat to be the next words he heard.

"I'll make this fast, Mr. Luft, because you need to move quickly."

"What is this shit?"

"I understand your suspicion, sir, but I need you to listen carefully for a couple of minutes. This is about Danny."

Silence for a beat. "What about Danny?"

I gave it to him quickly and unabridged — from Danny's visit to Cobb's office to the conversation I'd just had with him.

"You're telling me my kid's in jail."

"I'm telling you your son has been taken into custody. He hasn't, as far as I know, been charged yet, but that may happen soon or it may not happen at all. Depends on what evidence the police have."

"And he's been doing drugs, as well … Jesus Christ."

"Mr. Luft, I'm not going to tell you how to raise your son, but I think you might want to put yourself and how you feel on the back burner for the moment."

"Listen, bud, I don't need you to —"

"Danny needs his parents right now, and he needs you to be about more than discipline. Do you have a lawyer?"

Another beat. "Sure, for mortgages and stuff — nothing like this."

"I suggest you call your lawyer and ask him to recommend an attorney who handles criminal cases. Then you need to get to the police station and have that lawyer get there as quickly as possible, too."

"Criminal lawyer." He said the words slowly and softly — like a man who hadn't thought they were ones he'd ever have to use.

"Mr. Luft, I don't believe your son shot Wendell Claiborne. It would be really helpful if, when you get to where Danny is being held, you conducted yourself like a man who felt the same way."

"Yeah, yeah, I get that." Same dull, disembodied voice.

"Are you okay?" I asked him.

There was a long pause.

"Yeah, I'm okay. I better get moving on these calls."

"Right," I said. "I'm leaving now. I'll see you shortly."

They call it the campus because of its size — two enormous buildings in northeast Calgary surrounded by fast-food outlets, mini-malls, and middle-class residential neighbourhoods. Homicide is located in the smaller of the two — the Investigative Services Building. A detective met me at the front door and was polite, even friendly.

"Are you Cullen?"

"That's right."

"I'm Rivers," he said as we shook hands. "You and your partner are kind of a big deal."

I wasn't sure how to answer that. "We've been lucky a time or two." That seemed to be the right answer, as Rivers smiled and squired me through security and to the elevator.

As the door of the elevator closed he shook his head. "We hate these."

"What?"

"Arresting kids. Our worst nightmare. So many more regulations and protocols with young offenders."

"So, you haven't talked to Danny yet?"

He shrugged. "We can't … not without either a parent or a lawyer or both being in the room with him."

"Right," I said as the elevator door slid open. We stepped out and turned left down a hall and into a room that housed the holding and interview rooms. It was a busy night, with several witnesses and suspects standing around, some in handcuffs, waiting their turn. Rivers guided me through the crowd to one of the holding rooms.

"He's in there. You can have a few minutes with him. We've heard from the lawyer. He's on his way."

I thanked Rivers and stepped into the holding room. Rivers stayed at the door, I guessed to see the reaction from Danny and confirm that I was legitimate. Danny was slumped in a chair, his head down. He looked up and managed a half-smile when he saw me.

"A uniformed officer will be right outside the door if you …" Rivers looked at Danny. "If either of you need him." He stepped out and closed the door quietly behind him.

The room was small — one table, two chairs, nothing on the walls. I moved to the chair opposite Danny and sat. I could see he'd been crying but he sat up a little straighter and tried to look, if not brave, at least resolute.

"You okay, Danny?"

"Yeah." He gave a small shrug. "I guess so."

"You want anything, water or something?"

He shook his head.

"Since I spoke with you on the phone, have you talked any more to the police?"

A few seconds passed before he lifted his head and looked at me for the first time. "No," he said in a voice barely above a whisper. "I guess I'm sort of screwed, huh?" He tried for a smile. Failed.

"Nothing we can't handle," I said, trying to sound confident and reassuring. "Your parents and a lawyer are on their way."

His eyes opened wide at that and he sat up straight, then leaned on the table. "Yeah, I guess that had to happen."

"Pretty much. When they get here, you're going to have to go through all of it again."

"All of it?"

"All of it."

"The weed?"

He was still thinking that was the biggest problem he had. After talking to his old man, I wasn't sure the kid was wrong.

"All of it," I said.

He shook his head.

"First of all, Danny, your dad knows about the weed. And second —"

"You told him?"

"Yes, I told him. This isn't about smoking some dope. Your dad understands that and you need to, as well. You haven't been charged yet, but there's a chance that you will be charged with murder. We need to be ready when that happens. So, when your parents and the lawyer get here, you'll be questioned by the police. The lawyer will tell you if he doesn't want you to answer a question, but when you do answer questions, you need to be totally truthful. You can't tell people what you think they want to hear. There's no time for that, you understand that, right?"

"Yeah." He nodded, but I wasn't sure he got it.

There was a rap at the door. A bulky uniformed cop opened it and poked his head in. "There's a lawyer out here. Says he's been asked by the family's attorney to come down and talk to the kid."

"Sure," I said, "send him in, if that's okay. His parents should be here pretty soon, too." The cop nodded and let the door swing open a little more. He stepped back and a tall, thin, slightly greying man in a fifteen-hundred-dollar suit walked in.

I have a natural aversion to lawyers, but forced myself not to pass judgment — an admitted flaw of mine — until I heard what the man was all about. He stretched out a hand. "Brandon Kemper."

"Adam Cullen." We shook, then he reached across the table and shook Danny's hand. I stood up and offered the chair to the lawyer.

He nodded a thank you, pulled out a tape recorder and set it on the table. He got right to it. "Here's the thing, Danny, we don't have a lot of time. I've spoken to your parents. They will be here shortly and I'd like to hear as much of this as I can before they get here. Your dad is quite distraught and it might be a while before he's ... helpful."

"Okay," Danny said in a small voice; he leaned forward.

Kemper looked at me. "I imagine you've heard all this before, but I'd appreciate it if you wouldn't interrupt or add anything until Danny is finished."

I nodded. I was quickly impressed with the guy, especially his being able to accurately assess Danny's dad without having met the man.

Danny told his story again, and I didn't detect any deviations from what he'd told me. I was relieved about that. But my mood was about to change.

"Okay, Danny," Kemper said. "That's good. I appreciate all that you've told me. But there's one thing you didn't mention that I think is quite important. The police have indicated that your fingerprints are on the gun that killed Mr. Claiborne. We need to talk about that."

I was hoping Kemper wasn't looking at me, because if my face reflected what was going on inside my head, it wouldn't have been pretty. I looked across the table at Danny, determined not to allow my voice to scream the words that were crashing around in my brain.

Danny was looking down again, his eyes not meeting mine or Kemper's.

"Would you say the police are right in making that statement, Danny?" Kemper asked.

"Uh, yeah … I guess they are."

"Well, we need to talk about that."

We damn sure do.

But we didn't. As Danny looked up, glancing quickly at me before turning his gaze to Kemper, there was another knock at the door.

Burly-Cop opened the door wide this time and stepped into the room. "Mr. and Mrs. Luft are here."

THREE

Cobb was sitting across from me, sipping a Scotch while I nursed a rye and Diet Coke without enthusiasm. I'd related, twice, everything about the Danny Luft case.

We were in the lounge of the Earl's on 4th Street Southwest. Cobb, sharing my frustration, shook his head again when I got to the part about the kid's fingerprints on the murder weapon.

"Any chance there's some mistake?" I asked.

He shrugged. "Fingerprint evidence is not infallible. There have been mistakes over the years. But they're rare. And you said he didn't deny it or even register surprise when the lawyer brought it up. My guess is the cops got it right."

"Which means the kid's in trouble."

"Well, it's not good news, that's for sure. But it's not a slam dunk either. Fingerprints on a gun don't mean that that person necessarily pulled the trigger."

"So, what's our next move?"

"Well, first of all, we don't really have a client here." Cobb shrugged. "And from what you've said, it doesn't seem likely the kid's dad is about to hire us. Tell me that part one more time."

"I wasn't there that long," I recounted. "He wasn't in the holding room for much longer than a minute or two before he told the lawyer that he wanted, and I'm quoting here, my 'sorry ass out of here and right fucking now.'"

Cobb sipped his Scotch and it was a while before he answered. "See, that seems like overkill to me," he said. "All you did was try to help his son — at the kid's request. So, why the animosity?"

"Don't know," I admitted. "Maybe he's from the school of *all media are bad guys* — there's a fair amount of that going around the last couple of years."

Cobb smiled. "I hadn't noticed."

"Or maybe he didn't like the fact that Danny had confided in me and along the way revealed a few family secrets."

"And he'd know that how?"

"Well, when I told him to cool his jets and think about his kid as more than an object needing discipline, maybe he put two and two together."

"That's possible." Cobb nodded. "Anyway, that doesn't alter the fact that we don't have a client."

"Maybe. Maybe not. I mean, technically the kid sort of hired us to help him deal with Claiborne's proposition that he kill his wife."

"Proposition," Cobb repeated.

"Maybe not the right word. Doesn't matter. Danny did come to the office and wanted to hire you. In your absence I advised him. Not sure if that constitutes being a client or not."

Cobb sat back and looked at the ceiling. "If we do have a client or a case to work on, it's likely to be pro bono. Don't get me wrong, I'm all for being a good Samaritan, but I'm also not averse to being paid."

"Meaning?"

"I'm not sure. Let's think about this. Here's this teenage kid who has a story about his girlfriend's dad, one of the city's leading citizens, wanting the kid to off his wife. The cops hear a story like that and they're likely to say, 'How dumb do you think we are?' Then Mr. C ends up being shot with what was very likely the same gun the kid alleges he was being set up to use on Mrs. C. And think about this — if the police do actually give Danny's story any credence at all, then what we have is motive. Because now the scenario becomes this: Danny pops Claiborne to make sure he doesn't rat the kid out on the drug thing to his old man or to keep from having to shoot Mrs. Claiborne. Or both. And just to put the bow on the wrapping paper, there's the murder weapon with the kid's fingerprints conveniently in place. I don't like his chances."

I nodded. "I get that it sounds bad."

"And yet you, someone whose judgment I trust, feel that Danny was telling the truth when he came to you at my office."

I nodded again. "I would have bet the ranch that there wasn't a trace of larceny in that kid, at least not that I saw."

"But he didn't tell you he'd handled the gun?"

"No, but that might have happened after we talked."

Cobb regarded me thoughtfully. "Okay, you're a writer, how about you give me a storyline that explains some of the things we're dealing with here."

It was my turn to think. "Okay … I don't know, but maybe Claiborne had the gun with him when he saw Danny at the park and Danny was reluctant to admit he handled it."

"Which isn't the way the kid related it to you."

"No," I conceded, "it's not. But maybe he was embarrassed that he was dumb enough to actually handle the gun and didn't want to tell me that part."

"Okay, that's one possibility. I don't like it as credible, but it's a possibility. Got anything else?"

"Or when Claiborne was out of the house, Danny and Glenna snuck up to his bedroom and checked out the gun. Kids do some dumb shit."

Cobb let out a loud *hmmf*, and since I didn't know what that meant, I didn't answer. He went on. "Or how about Danny snuck out of his house the night of the murder and actually met with Claiborne even though you'd urged him not to. He handled the gun, and later that night somebody — Danny or someone else — got hold of the gun and popped Mr. C. The cops will like that one because they could argue that Claiborne gave Danny the gun, ostensibly to kill Mrs. Claiborne, and Danny decided to shoot Mr. C instead."

"But you said the cops wouldn't believe the hired assassin part of the story."

"They would in that scenario."

"Yeah, I guess."

"Bottom line," Cobb said, "is the kid is definitely the underdog in this thing, even with a good lawyer."

"And I still say he's … *sort of* your client."

Cobb took a sip of his drink, then stared at his glass for a long time. Finally, he said, "Okay, let's give this thing a try. I want you to dig deeper on Claiborne — get everything you can. Mrs. Claiborne, too. I'll see what I can learn from a few of my police friends. I'll try to find out where this thing's at from their perspective. We need to move fast if we're going to do any good at all. How's your time?"

"I'll make time."

"Okay, let's roll." He stood up, tossed a twenty-dollar bill on the table, and shook my hand, as he often did when we were about to embark on an investigative mission. "I'll call you tomorrow and we can exchange findings."

I dug deeper. That night after a dinner that featured a couple of dishes Jill had mastered in her gourmet cooking class — one a spectacular fish creation, the other a risotto-like compilation of rice and vegetables that was a definite ten out of ten — I hit the computer, this time at Jill's house.

During dinner we had talked about Danny Luft and the trouble he was in. I'd learned a long time ago that Jill and occasionally Kyla could offer useful suggestions about cases Mike and I were working.

Both of them were convinced that Mrs. Claiborne had shot her husband having found out about his plot to have her murdered. A pre-emptive strike. It made at least some sense and I tucked that potential solution in the back of my mind as I set my laptop up in a small quasi-bedroom Jill and I had rejigged into an office so that I wouldn't have to go home every time I had work to do. More and more of my writing files and paraphernalia had made their way to the room that Kyla had insisted on repainting a colour that could best be described as autumn off-pink with a hint of oh, I don't know, let's call it aged pumpkin.

She was sure I'd become the male equivalent of J.K. Rowling, working in a room as inspiring as this one. I dialed up some Barenaked Ladies and the Halifax band Hillsburn as a soundtrack and dug in. I had noticed that more and more of my all-Canadian music collection had also found its way into Jill's house.

I decided to focus my research on the personal as opposed to the corporate Wendell Claiborne. It didn't take long to come up with a few interesting bits to ponder, though I wasn't sure any of them would amount to anything resembling a breakthrough. Mrs. Claiborne was the former Rachel Coverdon; the Coverdons were in retail clothing in London, Ontario, and backed that up with a few multi-family dwellings they owned and rented out for fairly large sums.

Rachel had a brother, Elwood, who died suddenly at age fourteen (no details in the accounts I found), and another brother, Lance, who'd had some brushes with the law as a teen and young twenty-something. Borrowing cars without the express written consent of the owners seemed to be his crime of choice, but he had apparently righted the ship and was now a pipefitter by day and a successful DJ ("I'll Make Your Wedding Unforgettable!") by night. Married, with twin girls, eleven years old. I came across a five-year-old photo of a good-looking character home on Waterloo Street in London.

On the surface, everything sounded okay, but I made a note to check on the more recent whereabouts of Lance Coverdon.

Rachel Claiborne had a couple of skeletons of her own tucked away. Turns out the now respectable Mrs. C was once an exotic dancer who may have taken her relationship with certain members of her audience to a somewhat more personal and financially rewarding level.

She'd given up her career as an entertainer and moved in with a high school phys. ed teacher several years her junior, whom she later sued for a significant amount of money, alleging that he drove away potential employers for her dancing talents by behaving in a menacing manner when the club owners and managers came around to sign the lovely Rachel to a contract.

I circled back to Wendell Claiborne and it turned out that Claiborne, not to be outdone, had a younger brother of his own with somewhat nefarious leanings. Wilson Claiborne had run up against the regulatory authorities when he'd operated a limousine service in Edmonton. He finally closed up shop after three colourful years in the business and turned his attention to investment counselling. He had that licence revoked when several clients protested that the junior Claiborne had failed to invest the clients' money in the various platforms he had indicated he would.

I sat back and listened to Hillsburn perform "Sun Ought to Shine" while I thought about the Claiborne clan. Often in my work with Cobb, I struggled to find someone who might fit the role of perpetrator of the crime we were investigating. This time around it was damn tough to point to someone who didn't.

I wasn't sure I liked this better.

I was about to dive back into the morass that was the house of Claiborne when there was a tap at the door. Kyla poked her head in. "Sorry to interrupt," she said softly.

I beckoned her in. "You are most definitely not interrupting," I told her, and pulled a chair from against the wall a little closer for her to sit on. "What's up?"

"I wanted to ask you something."

"Ask away."

She sat, fidgeted for a minute, then folded her hands. Ready. "How soon do you think I should make a decision about what I'm going to be when I grow up?"

Several responses quickly came to mind, but I could see she was serious and I realized that none of my witticisms were going to be seen as either funny or appropriate.

"I'm not sure, sweetheart," I said. "I don't know that there's any rush. You have lots of time to consider the possibilities, and if you think there's something that sounds pretty good right now but you change your mind a time or two as you get older, that's okay, too."

"When did you decide you wanted to be a writer?"

I thought for a minute. "It's funny, but I can remember sitting at the kitchen table with my dad and reading the newspaper on Saturday mornings. He'd go down to the corner store and get the paper and we'd sit there and read it. He'd be drinking coffee and we'd trade sections of the paper — I was mostly about sports but my dad made sure I at least looked at the news and some of the other stuff. And sometimes we'd talk about what was going on in the world as we read about it. It was kind of cool actually."

It *was* cool and a memory I'd all but forgotten until right then.

"So, that's when you knew?"

"That I wanted to be a newspaper guy? No, I don't think so, not right then. I don't remember thinking seriously about journalism until I realized I was never going to be a ball player."

"Rotator cuff," she said. I'd told her before about my baseball dream dying during my third year at Oklahoma State, during a game against Texas Tech.

"Uh-huh. For a while I didn't know what I was going to do. But I'd always liked writing — even those essays in English classes — so I figured maybe I'd better switch gears and take a look at journalism. See, that's what I mean about how things can change along the way."

"Yeah, I guess."

"Are you thinking about anything in particular right now?"

"Yeah, I think so. Kind of."

"You want to tell me about it or is it still a secret?"

"No, I can tell you … but I don't want you to laugh."

I reached over and touched her on the arm. "Sweetheart, I can promise you, I won't laugh."

"I was thinking about the police."

I didn't laugh. In fact, for several seconds I wasn't sure how to react or what to say. It hadn't been one of the careers dancing around in my mind as we were chatting.

"Wow," I said.

"You think it's dumb?"

"No, Kyla, dumb is the last thing I think wanting to be in the police service is. In fact, I think it's amazing. And, for the record, I think you'd be a terrific police officer. But don't forget, it's okay if next week or next year you decide that being a doctor or a pilot or a writer is what you want to do."

"A writer?" She screwed up her face. "You guys make any money?"

"Not a lot, no."

"How about a baseball player?" She was grinning as she said it.

I laughed. "Well, it would be okay with me, but I'm not sure your mom's heart could stand it." Jill, sometimes fan, sometimes coach, was, let's say, *passionate* in her support of her daughter and her daughter's team.

Kyla's voice got quieter. "There's just one thing I was thinking about," she said.

"What's that?"

"I just wondered if they let people become police officers if they, you know, have Crohn's disease."

It was a good question. "I don't know, Kyla. My guess is they do, but I'll tell you what, how about I check it out?"

She looked at me. "Can you do that?"

"I think I can. How about I see what I can find out and report back to you?"

"Yeah … yeah, thanks." Her voice had regained its enthusiasm and she was smiling again.

"Anyway," she said, "I just wanted to tell you."

"I really appreciate that you did. It means a lot to me."

"Okay, well, good night."

"Good night."

She hugged me and was gone.

It had taken me a while to get used to how Kyla often ended conversations. Not rudely but abruptly. She finished saying what it was she wanted to say, and she was off to the next thing in her endlessly busy mind.

I refocused and reviewed my notes again, then decided to put in a call to a long-time colleague and friend, Lorne Cooney — brilliantly funny, proudly Jamaican, and one of the best diggers I knew among my journalist pals.

He picked up after three rings, and as it almost always did, hearing his voice instantly raised the level of my mood. I say *almost*, because there was one terrible time when it did not. It was the night he had urged me to go home as quickly as possible — he knew something was wrong, and though he wasn't certain what it was, he had suspected it was bad. And he was right. That was the night a hate-crazed arsonist had set fire to the home my wife and I had lived in and loved. The fire had taken Donna's life, and though years later Cobb and I finally caught up with the killer, Lorne and I had both hated that he had been the one to sound the alarm bell.

We were past that now, and I was glad that someone who laughed and made me laugh as much as he did was back in my life.

"I recognized the number," he boomed, his voice fully accented, a feature he turned on and off at will. "And I know you want something — money, romance, advice, or maybe a winning horse at Aqueduct. Which is it?"

"Shut up and listen ... mon," I said.

We both laughed, exchanged how are yous, and laughed some more.

Finally, I got around to the reason for my call. "You're right, I do want something," I said. "Wendell Claiborne. You know him?"

"That's *knew* him, brother. Past tense. Don't you read the newspapers?"

"Yeah, I know Claiborne's dead. *Did* you know him?"

"Everybody knew Wendell Claiborne. Now, if you'd asked me if I liked him, well, that's a whole different thing."

"You know much about him? Professional life? Vices? Things I might need to know?"

"You and Cobb on this one?"

"Seems a possibility."

"I heard the homicide boys have the daughter's boyfriend under lock and key. The kid shoot him?"

"Also possible," I said. "But I don't think so."

"Anything specific you want to know?"

"Like I said, we're kind of interested in the dark side of Claiborne."

"I can probably help you with a few things. Might cost you a beer or two."

"Tomorrow too soon?"

"Let me see what I can pull together. Give me the morning. Maybe we can meet in the afternoon."

"You have a preferred drinking establishment?"

"I prefer quite a few, as a matter of fact, but how about the Kensington Pub — say two?"

"Two it is. See you then."

FOUR

I spent the next morning checking out the younger siblings of first Mrs., then Mr. Claiborne. I struck them both off my list of people we should talk to. Lance Coverdon was still on the straight and narrow in London, working and raising his family, with nothing more serious than a parking ticket in his recent past. As for Wilson Claiborne, while it appeared that Wendell's little brother might have wished to continue to skate on the fringes of the legal pond, with occasional forays into the out-of-bounds areas, all of that ended when he'd been diagnosed with ALS a year and a half ago. Those few words instantly moved him from potential villain to sympathetic character in my mind's catalogue. I didn't pursue how he was doing now. I knew the diagnosis was a death sentence and I found myself feeling bad for someone I'd never met and probably never would.

Lorne's head was down and he was a tapping on his cellphone as I walked into the pub. It gave me a chance to study the guy who had probably been my longest-serving best bud.

I noticed he had more facial hair this time, some of it black but a lot of it grey. His ensemble was part grunge, part seniors' home. Lorne was the only person I knew who could make that combination work. The face that most often reflected the hilarity with which Lorne viewed the world was not smiling now. Instead, there were furrows — deep lines that cut across cheeks and forehead. Lorne Cooney looked worried.

"Penny for your thoughts," I said as I moved alongside him.

"You've got to be kidding." He looked up and simultaneously moved the phone from hand to breast pocket. "It'll take more than that to get into my treasure trove of information. Shit you need, mon."

"Okay then, *mon*," I said. "What are you drinking?"

He gestured at the empty table. "I've been saving myself for you." He stood up; we embraced and he laughed, becoming the Cooney I knew best.

A young server arrived and Lorne greeted her by name — not a surprise, given his affinity for pubs in general and the KP in particular.

I raised an eyebrow in his direction and he said, "Stella, please, Corey."

"Two of those," I said.

"Okay, small talk until she gets back," Lorne said as he sat back down. I slid in on the other side and the exchange of *how ya doin's* and *keeping busys* lasted maybe three minutes.

The arrival of the Stella Artois triggered, as Lorne had said it would, the business part of the discussion.

"Where do you want me to start?" he asked.

I leaned forward, took a pull on my bottle of beer and shook my head. "Your call."

"Well. A good place to launch a discussion of Wendell Claiborne might be with a list of his ex-wives and assorted mistresses, some of the latter graduating to be among the former."

"Bit of a rake," I said.

"Shit, Adam, rake doesn't even warm up this guy's escapades."

"Libertine," I said.

"Try asshole."

"Ah."

He pulled out a battered notebook, flipped it open to a page near the back, and set the notebook down, adjusting glasses that looked as if they had last been cleaned when the first Trudeau was prime minister. "Cindy Marsh, the first Mrs. C, was probably the best of the lot. He said as much in a *Maclean's* interview a few months ago. As you might guess, that did not go down well with the incumbent."

"What do you mean by *best*?"

"Normal … not nuts … not obsessed with Claiborne's money, that sort of thing. And she was a few years older than him, as was her successor. After that he apparently gravitated toward younger women."

I nodded, took a sip of my drink, and waited. It was best to let Lorne find his own pace for relaying information. He'd get there eventually.

"She came from a good family, not mega-rich, but not hurting either. She earned a master's degree from McGill in child psychology, did a lot of volunteer work with kids, but didn't really get into the field professionally until after she and Claiborne said their goodbyes. She lasted four years, no kids. Stumbled across some incriminating texts and confronted her husband, who apparently was only too happy to confess his transgressions and move to his next amour. Rumour has it she wasn't the only love interest he had on the go at the time. Cindy got a nice settlement and moved on to different though not likely greener pastures. She's apparently writing a book now, but I don't know if

61

her ex is a character. I met her once at a fundraiser for the Calgary Zoo and I can't say she struck me as the type to off somebody, even somebody who was as big a dickhead as charming Wendell."

"Should I be taking notes?" I asked.

"I made a copy for you." He grinned at me. "Which is why this will be a two-beer meeting."

"Check."

He tossed back about half of his Stella and glanced down at his notes. Two fingers waggled in the air. "*Numero deux.* Susannah Hainsey, eight years older than 'da man.' She'd just buried her last younger man after he had an unfortunate encounter with a forklift at the warehouse full of the power tools his company manufactured."

"Sounds like it was an okay gig for Susannah … I mean, until the forklift incident."

Lorne nodded. "On the surface I think it was, but Dennis Hainsey was flawed in his own way. Apparently liked to zip down to Vegas, ostensibly on business, but was known to drop some serious cash at the tables."

"How serious?"

"Word is there were a couple of occasions that topped out at over a hundred large."

"Ouch!"

"Yeah, and a lot of smaller but still significant losses along the way, some of which were still outstanding at the time of his untimely demise. The result was that Susannah came out of that one with not much in the way of assets."

"Any hint that the forklift thing was anything less than adventitious?"

"Adventitious. You a writer by any chance?"

"Was it?"

"Deliberate? I never heard anything to suggest that. But I wasn't there."

"Fair enough."

"Anyway, Ms. Hainsey never became one of the Mrs. Claibornes. She moved in, stayed a while, a couple of years, I think, and left in a lot better situation than when she'd first taken up with him."

"Boring," I said.

"Wrong." Lorne shook his head. "Because the successor to Susannah, whose maiden name, by the way, was Pettimore, was a woman named Janine. Janine *did* become the next Mrs. Claiborne. Interesting thing about Janine is that her last name was … wait for it … Pettimore."

"Sisters?"

"Bingo, bro. Bing-go."

"Seems like that could have led to a little family tension."

"Does seem possible."

"So, Susannah, who has already lost a husband to unfortunate circumstances, sees her boyfriend take up with her sister; then *that* guy gets snuffed. Suze seem the type to carry a grudge?"

Lorne shrugged. "Can't answer that. Pretty much the same story as with Cindy. I may have met her at a cocktail thing or something, but if I did, it didn't register. I certainly didn't interview her."

"Too bad."

"Janine, who, by the way, was several years younger than her sibling, was also short-lived — couple of years, maybe less. Wasn't able to learn much about her. She's still around, but I'm told lives a quiet life. She's a church secretary at Central United downtown. Don't know much more." Lorne looked down at his notes, then back up. "Which leads us to the current Mrs. C. And I *have* met her. I interviewed her for a piece my editor called 'The Power Women Behind Calgary's Power Men.'"

"Catchy … and maybe a bit sexist?"

"Hey, baby, I just write 'em."

"Mrs. Claiborne the third, the former Rachel Coverdon — she a power woman?"

"Oh, yeah." That got an emphatic nod. "I remember thinking when I talked to her that Claiborne had met his match this time. In a lot of ways."

"Meaning?"

"Meaning she is maybe the sexiest over-forty lady I've ever met. Power and … well, you know."

"They have a daughter?"

"Yeah, had her in the first year they were married. I remember her telling me that."

"So, in addition to power and sex, the lady has staying power — like fifteen or sixteen years' worth. Must be some kind of record."

"Uh-huh." Lorne nodded. "He kind of smoothed the stormy seas with money for the others. I'm not sure that would work with the current. She'd leave when she was damn good and ready to go."

I thought about that. "Interesting."

Lorne didn't reply.

"Okay," I told him, "now I've got a story for you."

He touched an ear. "Listening."

"Off the record."

"The good ones always are."

I told Lorne about my visit with Danny Luft and what had happened since, while we worked on our second round of Stellas. When I got to the part about the kid's prints on the gun, he whistled: "Holy shit."

"Yeah," I said.

"Now I get your interest in the women in Claiborne's life."

"And anybody else who might be intriguing."

"Tell you what. I'll keep the ol' antennae on high def. If I hear something, I'll call you."

"I'd appreciate that."

He leaned forward. "And if something comes of this that might earn a poor hard-working scribe a CJF, well, that scribe would appreciate a little quid pro quo."

"I think the Canadian Journalism Federation insists on at least some ability to write before it hands over awards."

"Shut up. We got a deal or not?" He stuck out a hand.

"Deal," I said.

We shook on it.

I stayed the night at Jill's, and though we had a wonderful dinner — seafood lasagna and a Tuscan salad Jill had discovered in a travel magazine — followed by a quiet night of wine, soft talk, and softer music, then easy, comfortable love-making, I slept poorly.

That was a rarity when I stayed there, but on this night my sleep was intermittent when it happened at all and was punctuated by dreams that seemed to be a non-stop pulsing of images on a brick wall — first of Wendell Claiborne, then Marlon Kennedy, and finally Faith Unruh. All of them dead, all of them victims of violent crimes.

Every time I woke up, I felt worse than I had the time before. When the sun's first rays pushed their way into the room, I was relieved that the night was coming to an end, again a feeling I had seldom — no, never — experienced with Jill lying beside me.

I was first to the kitchen and had cantaloupe sliced, croissants warming in the oven, and the coffee perked and ready when the two ladies I loved entered the kitchen.

Kyla said, "I think he's a keeper, Mom."

"Hey," I protested. "This isn't a one-off. I'm not one of those guys who never sets foot in the kitchen or can't handle a vacuum cleaner." Even I sensed the unnecessary edge in my voice that ended what should have an exchange of humorous jibes.

I started to say something, decided that whatever I came up with would probably make things worse, and instead poured coffee for two and juice for Kyla. It was a quieter breakfast than usual until Jill asked Kyla what was on her schedule for the day and we got the rundown of sports, lunch activities (library club was the highlight), and a request for help that evening with her science project — the creation of a balloon solar system with special emphasis on the planets.

"I feel bad for Pluto," I said, trying for levity. "It must be tough being punted as a planet when you've been one for a few billion years."

Polite chuckles from my audience.

Kyla headed off to brush her teeth and gather her books while Jill and I cleared the table and loaded the dishwasher. Kyla stopped for hugs and paused for a moment to look at me. Then she said, "I hope you have a good day, Adam."

I knew it could well be the only time that day when I would hear that phrase and the speaker would actually mean it. "I'm pretty sure it's going to be just fine now," I told her.

She'd been out the door for maybe three minutes when Jill topped up our coffee, took my hand, guided me to a kitchen chair, and sat down across the table from me.

"I know," I said. "I was a jerk. I'm sorry."

"Not a jerk." Jill shook her head. "Troubled."

I didn't answer.

"So, what's the trouble?"

I thought about how to answer her.

"It's not us, is it? Because if it is, I must have missed something? And if you say *it's not you, it's me*, I will punch you in the face."

I laughed. "There are some things bothering me. But you and Kyla aren't on the list. In fact, when I do feel down, and I admit I'm a bit that way right now, you two really are my port in the storm. I know it's a cliché, but it's true. It's just one of the things I love about you. Both of you."

"Good, that's out of the way. Your face is safe. Do you want to talk about the things that *are* bothering you?"

I picked up my coffee cup but set it back down without drinking any. "You know, I wonder sometimes how cops do it. How are they able, day after day, to look into the face of the evil around us and still maintain an outlook that isn't as dark as the part of the world they inhabit? I know I did something similar when I was at the *Herald*, but writing about crime isn't the same as what I'm doing now with Cobb. That was more distant somehow. Now I feel like I'm up to my neck in it, and I don't like it."

"I've talked to Lindsay Cobb about that," Jill said. "And she says there are days when Mike really struggles with it. Even after all this time and all he's seen, there are times ..." She didn't need to finish the sentence.

"That surprises me," I said. "He always seems so … together, so in charge of what's happening around him. I guess I should have known that he had to have those down moments, too."

"And you've seen the face of evil … again. And you're troubled."

I looked at her. "Yes," I said.

"Is it the boy you told me about? Danny?"

"Yeah, him. This is a tough one. I believe … no, I guess I want to believe the kid didn't shoot Claiborne."

"Then that's what you *should* believe."

"Although I hasten to add that *someone* needed to shoot the guy."

"Not a solid citizen?"

"Outwardly a model guy — successful, rich, gave to charities. Everybody loved Wendell. But there was another side, the dark side. Pretty creepy. And he's not alone. There's enough sleaze in that family to service an entire neighbourhood. The trouble with a case like this is that I want so badly to help the kid, but I'm not sure I can."

"You'll help him."

"Just like that?"

"Just like that."

"And in those rare moments when I'm not thinking about the plight of Danny Luft, there's Kennedy. And Faith Unruh. Some days there's just too damn much." I didn't tell her there was something else. Something that was killing me and that I wanted more than anything to tell her … and couldn't.

A few months before, Jill had told me that the combination food bank/homeless shelter she volunteered at, Let the Sunshine Inn, was in financial trouble. The government grant the Inn relied on had gone away and the place was going to have to close if alternate funding wasn't found.

And, of course, given the financial turndown in Alberta after the oil price collapse of 2015, that funding wasn't coming from a struggling private sector.

That's when I made one of the biggest mistakes of my life. I approached the MFs, a criminal motorcycle gang Cobb and I had encountered before. I had this idea that maybe they'd provide the money — twenty-five thousand dollars — to keep the doors of the Inn open. Stupid. Naive. Ridiculous. Check, check, and check.

Except that they *did* agree to come up with the money. But not without a few conditions that I should have foreseen. That *anyone* would have foreseen. Anyone, that is, who didn't desperately want to help someone they loved. Desperately being the operative word.

The MFs made it clear that I was theirs, that there would be payback and there wouldn't be negotiations when the time came for me to do something or a series of somethings to repay them — simply returning the twenty-five thousand dollars wasn't an option, even if I had a way to come up with the money.

The leader of the MFs was a ruthless and evil bastard named Rock Scubberd. But surprisingly and disturbingly, it was his beautiful and clearly influential wife who had been instrumental first in brokering the deal, then in explaining what it meant for me. *The Power Woman Behind the Power Man.* I doubted that Lorne Cooney had included the Scubberds in his feature.

But somehow, hearing it from a woman, this woman, in her measured, calm, almost mesmerizing voice, made the promised (though unstated) outcome, if I didn't deliver when the time came, all the more threatening.

I had known almost immediately the seriousness of my mistake. I also knew there was no turning back. I had literally made a deal with the devil, and the price I would one day pay was going to be very, very high.

And when the day came when they made their demand, I knew it wouldn't be the beautiful, enigmatic Mrs. Scubberd who would invite me for coffee at Starbucks and gently, almost apologetically, lay out the details of my ... assignment. No, it wouldn't be like that. Nor would it be Scubberd himself; he'd see the whole thing as beneath him. No, it would be one or more of his lieutenants, thoroughly dangerous and not giving a damn whether I lived another day or not. And one of those lieutenants would be Minnis — I knew only the one name — the most vicious, the most frightening, and the one most without feeling. He would kill me, if given the order, like the rest of us stomp out the lives of insects on the sidewalk.

Yes, it would be Minnis.

I hadn't intended to tell Cobb, but eventually I did. He was angrier than I'd ever seen him and was stunned at my stupidity. He essentially reiterated what the lovely Mrs. Scubberd had said — that the payback, when the time came, would be something I almost assuredly would not want to have any part of, and he added that there would be other, just as unpleasant demands to follow and the consequences, if I decided not to comply, were unthinkable.

One of the worst things about what I'd done, and something else I hadn't considered as I planned my approach to the MFs, was that I had put Jill and Kyla in harm's way. When the MFs made their initial, and subsequent, demands of me — were I to refuse, no matter how impossibly awful those demands — these were people to whom family was simply human currency to be used in whatever way was needed to make others do what they wanted. And Cobb had made it horribly clear that there were no limits to what Scubberd and his people would do. I could not, of course, tell Jill. I had long ago promised her and myself that I would never lie to her about anything and while I technically hadn't, at least not yet, I was a long way from being forthcoming about the money that she believed had come from a good and unnamed Samaritan.

This Samaritan was anything but good.

"More coffee?"

I shook my head. "I should probably get moving. I've got some calls to make and a couple of people I need to see." I stood up. "I'll call you later."

"Don't go just yet," she said. "There's something I want to talk about, too. Or at least something I want to ask you."

For a second, panic grabbed me as I thought she had somehow heard about the MFs and my arrangement with them ... or rather their arrangement with me.

"You might want a little more coffee for this one."

She was smiling and I didn't think she'd be doing that if this was about the MFs. I sat and watched her pour the coffee.

Jill returned the pot to the counter, sat back down, and looked at me. "Adam, what do you think about us?"

"Listen, if this is about this morning, I'm sorry I was a pain in the ass, I really am. But I love you guys to death, you know that, and —"

She leaned across the table and put her fingers on my lips. "Shut up and listen a minute." Her voice the soft, throaty sound I loved.

"Okay," I said through her fingers.

"Kyla and I have been talking … about us. About the three of us."

I started to say something, but thought better of it and settled for a nod.

"We think of us as a family and wondered if you feel that way, too."

I couldn't tell her that moments before, I had been thinking about the possible looming danger to her and Kyla.

"I do, yes," I said. "Consciously. Unconsciously. All the time. You *are* my family."

"I can't tell you how happy that makes me. How happy that makes both of us."

"What are we talking about here? Are you proposing to me?"

Her face lit up. "Let's just say I'm proposing a proposal."

"I love you, Jill. I love you guys more than I can even express — and I'm a wordsmith, for God's sake."

"If there's a *but* coming …"

"I know, you'll punch me in the face." I held up my hands. "It won't be necessary. But I am a bit of a traditionalist. I'd like to ask you, and then I'd like us to be engaged for a while … I don't know if that's weird for people who have been married before, but I'd really like that."

I didn't tell her that being engaged would allow some time for me to figure out a way to extricate myself from the clutches of the MFs. Of course, I knew that extrication was not possible, but I needed to at least have some idea as to what I was facing and whether, in fact, Jill and Kyla were in danger. Because if they were, there could be no wedding; there could be no family.

"How traditional are we talking here?"

"Down-on-one-knee-ring-in-hand traditional. I know that's chauvinist and hopelessly old-fashioned but I'd really like to do that, you know?"

She nodded, smiling widely. "Okay, but there's something I want, too — that you might think is just as strange."

"And that is …?"

"The first time around, I was married by a justice of the peace. Lovely man, and he made everything as nice as he could. There were six people at the ceremony, including the JP, Keith, and me. I'd like you and me to be married in a church. It can be a little church, and I don't care if there are more than six people there. But I always felt bad that I'd missed out on that and I was hoping you'd be okay with it."

"Of course, I'm okay with it. I'd marry you in a bathroom if it came to that, but a church might be better."

"I can almost guarantee it."

"When do we tell Kyla?"

"I think, for now, I'll tell her that you and I have talked about it — which isn't a lie — I just won't tell her what we've decided until some of that tradition kicks in."

I leaned in toward her. "It seems to me that two people who have just decided to get married should maybe kiss and hug and stuff."

She put a hand to my cheek and said, "I couldn't agree more, but I thought you had calls to make and people to see."

"Calls? People? I don't remember saying that."

She laughed, then punched me playfully in the chest.

Cobb was working on a Reuben while I was in full attack mode on a little something called the Portobello

Perkalator Burger. We were in the Purple Perk and conversation had ground to a halt while we ate. Both of us liked the place. Good food, interesting clientele, great coffee, all just a few blocks from Cobb's office.

Once the food was gone, we both sat back and sighed. "They have to start supplying cots in this place," Cobb said.

"No argument over here." But the truth was I wasn't in the mood to kibitz. "You ready for the rundown?"

"Ready," he said, and sat up a little straighter, presumably the better to take in what I had on Claiborne and family. Between what I had gathered and what Lorne Cooney had passed along, there was a fair amount of information. I hoped there was more fact than fiction, but you could never be sure when taking data from a source other than the subject. Nevertheless, based on volume alone, it made for an impressive report.

"There's a lot there," he acknowledged. "Plenty of skeletons in plenty of closets. All we need now is a client who shaves more than once a month and has money."

"In the meantime?"

"In the meantime, we keep working it. I don't like what's happening with the kid any more than you do."

"So, what's next?"

"We shut off the computers and put away the press clippings and do some real detecting. Face to face."

"Gumshoe."

"The very word I was looking for."

FIVE

It was pretty much a coin flip as to where the gumshoe-ing would begin, but we agreed we were both intrigued with the sister thing. Susannah Hainsey hadn't married after she and Claiborne parted company. She lived alone in what looked from the outside like a very nice condo in Lower Mount Royal. I was wondering whether her parting settlement had left her enough to purchase the place or whether she had settled into a lucrative career. Cobb's ability to get us an appointment with her at two in the afternoon on a workday was telling. He'd called her and explained that while he knew she had spoken with the police, we were representing Danny Luft, who had been detained and was likely to be charged in the case. She'd heard about Danny and was appropriately sympathetic.

Ms. Hainsey greeted us wearing a top and long skirt that I guessed came from Africa. Both garments were predominantly black but were far from widow's weeds. The top sported a frenzied pattern of bright colours, flamboyant colours, cheerful colours, while the skirt featured stripes, mostly white, but some yellow and light blue. It wasn't an outfit I'd expect to see at an office party or oil company board meeting — maybe a CD launch for the

Barenaked Ladies. Thing is, it looked good on her, as I suspected most clothes did.

Susannah Hainsey was a beautiful woman; in fact, she possessed a mesmerizing beauty, combined with an elegant, almost perfect way of carrying herself that made it difficult not to stare. Seconds after she had ushered us into her living room, I glanced over at Cobb. He appeared to be as intrigued as I was.

"Mike Cobb," he said, recovering and extending a hand, "and this is Adam Cullen."

I followed suit on the handshake and was surprised, I'm not sure why, at the firmness of her grip. She gestured in the direction of a coffee-brown leather couch and Cobb and I sat. She settled on a loveseat opposite us, her legs tucked up beneath her. I remembered Lorne Cooney saying she was older than Claiborne by eight years, putting her in her midfifties, but she had the fluid movement and the litheness of a much younger person.

I was a little surprised that she didn't offer anything in the way of refreshments. She hadn't appeared upset or annoyed at our being there, yet there was no mention of coffee, cookies … not even water. Maybe she was worried we would stay longer than she was comfortable with.

But while I was still pondering the point, from another room, a man wearing dress slacks and a light-blue sport jacket appeared. "Gentlemen, this is Trenton. What can he get you? We have alcoholic and non-alcoholic drinks of almost every kind, so please don't hesitate to ask for whatever it is you'd like."

"Just a Diet Coke for me," Cobb said, and though I was thinking how pleasant it might be to have a Caesar or maybe a Manhattan, I told Trenton water would be fine.

Ms. Hainsey looked disappointed in us, and I hoped my facial expression told her it was Cobb's fault.

"How can I help you gentlemen?"

"As I mentioned on the phone, Ms. Hains—"

She held up a hand. "Susannah, please."

"As I mentioned to you, Susannah, we're investigating the murder of your former … friend —"

Her hand went up again. "Please, Mr. Cobb, Wendell and I were lovers; then we lived together; then we split up and eventually ended up hating each other. But we were definitely never friends."

Cobb nodded. "I stand corrected. And before I go further, I should say that we are sorry for your —" Here he hesitated, certain that *loss* was not the correct word for how Susannah Hainsey viewed Claiborne's demise.

She was smiling, apparently enjoying his discomfort, and waved off the comment just as Trenton returned with the refreshments. I restrained myself from glaring at Cobb as Trenton deposited the Coke and bottled water in front of us and what looked very much like a well-constructed dry martini on an end table to Susannah's left. Trenton exited the room and Susannah sipped once, then settled back and looked at Cobb, clearly ready. I pulled my notebook and pen out of my pocket. She glanced at it but didn't comment.

Cobb said, "How did you and Claiborne meet?"

"I was a volunteer with the United Way and I met with Wendell to discuss a possible donation. He'd been a donor previously, but the amount wasn't particularly significant. We met at his office, then again a couple of days later over lunch, and he signed a cheque for fifty thousand dollars, more than five times the amount of his previous donations."

"And from there?"

"From there we saw more of each other — it was platonic at first, but not, I confess, for long."

"And he was married at the time?"

"Yes, but that didn't last a great deal longer."

"You and he never married."

"No. I'd been married and lost my husband in an accident. I just didn't feel that I wanted to marry again. And if I had wanted to marry someone, it wouldn't have been Wendell Claiborne, I can assure you."

"Why is that, Ms. … Susannah?"

"Why didn't I want to marry Wendell?" She considered before answering. "It's just … there wasn't real depth in what we felt for each other. I liked dating him, I liked sleeping with him, but I didn't want to marry him and I certainly didn't want to have children with him."

Cobb nodded, drank some Diet Coke. I looked at Susannah's martini. "Can we go back for a minute?" Cobb said. "I wanted to ask you about your first husband."

"Dennis? Yes?"

"You mentioned that he was killed in an accident. Can you tell us what happened?"

Again she didn't answer right away. A small smile toyed with the corners of her lovely mouth. "Because if it wasn't accidental, you just might be looking at a serial husband-killer, is that the thought here? Even if Wendell wasn't technically my husband?"

"Is that the thought you'd have if you were us?"

She smiled at that and I decided that if I were casting a *Helen of Troy* remake, Susannah Hainsey would be a frontrunner to play Helen. This was a face that could launch a thousand ships. With the smile, maybe two thousand.

"I don't think I look like a killer," she said. "And I know I don't have the physical strength to murder someone."

"So, that rules out beating someone to death, and maybe stabbing. Neither of the gentlemen died of those causes. And, of course, there's always the time-honoured practice of hiring someone to do the heavy lifting."

"True," she said. "Then I guess you'll just have to take my word for it. I didn't kill my husband and I didn't shoot Wendell Claiborne. And I didn't arrange for a hit man. That's a very sexist term, don't you think? I'm sure there are women who kill for money. Hit *person* perhaps?"

"When did you find out about Claiborne's death?"

She took a moment before answering. "My sister called. It was early, six thirty or so. Trenton took the call, and woke me."

"Trenton lives here?"

"Not all the time. He has his own room, and if I'm going to need him early or if he has had to work late, he will often stay. He lives a forty-five-minute drive away, over an hour in rush-hour traffic."

"Trenton's role in your life?"

"He works for me ... in several capacities, some of them domestic. Neither of us likes the term servant, so let's leave it at that. Anyway, he woke me, I took the call. Janine told me the news and I went back to bed."

Cobb didn't have a response for that.

"Sounds callous, doesn't it? Please don't think I wasn't affected by hearing a man I had lived with was dead. It was sad, but it wasn't a tragedy. Not to me. A tragedy is when a good person dies young. Wendell wasn't a particularly good person. What was most impactful, I suppose, was the way he died."

"Why was that impactful?"

She sipped her martini before answering and prefaced her answer with a gentle shake of her lovely head.

"Perhaps *impactful* is the wrong word. Maybe *dramatic* is better. Surely you'd agree that being shot by someone is a dramatic way to have one's life end."

Cobb waited a beat before saying, "Ms. Hainsey, do you have any idea who might have shot Wendell Claiborne?"

He'd gone back to calling her Ms. Hainsey. I wasn't surprised. Cobb didn't put interrogating witnesses in a murder investigation in the same category as a casual chat over an Americano at Starbucks. And there was something else. I didn't think Cobb liked Susannah Hainsey a whole lot. It was nothing he was doing or even the way he was phrasing his questions, but I'd known him long enough to get a sense that she was not someone he would care to spend a whole lot of time with. What surprised me was that although she was striking, I didn't much like her either. And I wasn't sure why.

"You mentioned the police have made an arrest."

"They have, yes," Cobb said.

Susannah Hainsey raised her hands, palms up as if to say, *Then it's settled; why are you asking me that question.*

"The person in police custody, who, by the way, has not yet been charged, is, as I mentioned on the phone, our client. He is fifteen years old and he did not kill your former partner. We'd like to make sure he is not imprisoned for something he didn't do. So I repeat my question: Do you have any thoughts as to who might have shot Wendell Claiborne?"

"Surely any conjecture on my part would be a waste of time. I'm sure the police have much more complete information to work from and it seems to me that they are doing that work."

"Humour me," Cobb pressed. "Let's pretend the police haven't made an arrest or maybe they have but they've got the wrong person. Any thoughts as to who might have wanted to kill your ex—?" He almost said husband, but caught himself.

"I can think of lots of people who might have liked the idea of killing Wendell." A slight smile, mouth only this time. "But as to someone who could actually have pulled the trigger, well, I'm sure you can appreciate, it's difficult to be definitive."

"Would you include your sister Janine in the group that might have liked to see Claiborne dead?"

"No, I wouldn't." Maybe the quickest response she had given so far.

"You seem quite certain on that point."

"I am, yes."

Cobb looked over at me as he often did at about this time in the questioning, the silent invitation to ask any questions of my own.

"Susannah," I began — first name was okay with me; I was, after all, just the researcher, not the investigator. And in this scenario, the good cop. "How well do you know the current Mrs. Claiborne?"

"Rachel? Well, I know her, of course. We were on a committee together at the Calgary Public Library. We were looking at the history of the library, how best to preserve and present that history. But I can't say I know her well. Not well enough to know if she'd — what's the word on all those shows? — *snuff* her husband." She smiled.

"What do you do for a living?"

"I'm a life coach. I work from here and stay pretty busy. I have a philosophy degree and it's difficult to put it to work in any sort of lucrative way."

I looked around the apartment. "Life coach work seems lucrative enough."

All vestiges of her smile disappeared. So much for good cop. And so much for working my way onto Susannah Hainsey's Christmas card list.

"It does," she said in a voice that was icicle-cold. "That and my investments keep me comfortable."

Having destroyed all prospects of my becoming Paris to this particular Helen, I plunged ahead. "Did the settlement from parting company with Claiborne provide the seed money for those investments?"

"I'm not sure that has anything to do with what we're talking about or that it is any of your business." Colder still.

"Actually, it might," I said. "I'm wondering if the settlement was one large transaction or if the money has been paid out in smaller amounts over a longer period of time."

"We weren't married."

"So you mentioned. But there *was* a settlement of sorts. You didn't leave the relationship with nothing." I thought if I spoke assertively enough, I might convince her that I knew things that, in fact, I was guessing at, although Lorne Cooney had seemed fairly certain she was in pretty fair financial shape after her breakup with Claiborne.

"And why would you think that might be important?"

"A few reasons," I said. "For example, if he was continuing to pay you, then it would seem less likely that you would want him dead, as that might put an end to the … uh … income. Kind of like a motive in reverse." I smiled, but the gesture was not returned.

"Then I guess I'm off your suspects list."

"Or conversely, if he had threatened to cut off the cash flow, why then … you see where I'm going with that." I wasn't sure why I had suddenly gone rogue. But I found this stunning woman very easy to dislike. And her indifference to the possibility that a fifteen-year-old kid was charged with a crime he may not have committed was, I think, the tipping point.

She didn't answer.

"Care to tell us how much the payments are?"

"No." She stood up to let us know our conversation was over.

Cobb said, "I want to thank you for your time, Ms. Hainsey. One last thing …"

"Yes?" Her tone was less than inviting.

"I'm sure you've answered this question for the police, but it would help us a lot."

"Yes," she repeated.

"Can you tell us where you were at around midnight three nights ago?"

"Ah," she said. "Of course you'd ask that. The answer is I was right here. Trenton can corroborate that. That's the right word, isn't it? *Corroborate?*"

"That's the right word. And if we want to talk to Trenton, is it best to call here?"

"I think you've inconvenienced us enough. You aren't the police, so we probably won't be chatting further. *Either* of us."

Cobb nodded. "Thank you again for your time."

Once we were outside the building, Cobb looked at me. "What'd you think?"

"I don't think she liked us."

"No." Cobb shook his head. "I don't think she liked *you*."

"Probably saw me eyeing her martini."

"Yeah, that must have been it."

We climbed into his Cherokee. "What's next?" I asked.

"The other half of the sisters. Tomorrow morning. Ten. Coffee first?"

"I always want coffee first."

"Purple Perk at nine then."

SIX

A tragedy is when a good person dies young. Susannah Hainsey's words were particularly appropriate on a morning when I was writing a piece about one of the people in Canadian music I had most admired. Gord Downie had left us the previous October 17, coincidentally the day of the Calgary civic election, about which I had also written. *Maclean's* had contracted me to write an in-depth follow-up article to the dozens of tribute pieces that had come out immediately after his passing.

I'd been in the Purple Perk for almost an hour but had barely touched my coffee. I stared at my computer screen, trying to come up with something fresh, something that hadn't already been said.

In the years that followed Donna's death, I had struggled to find something to give meaning to my life. And while it would never mend the heartbreak that losing Donna had caused, I found solace in music, Canadian music specifically. I'd never been able to *make* music in any form, not really. Like a lot of thirteen- or fourteen-year-old kids, I'd dreamed of being part of the garage band that made it. Bought the guitar, learned a few chords, wrote a handful of terrible songs, played like crazy for a couple of months. When no one discovered me and the three friends who'd formed Nude Reality, we put the instruments away and went back to baseball and hockey.

But after the arsonist took Donna from me, I returned to music, not as a music-*maker* but as an observer and fan of Canadian music, and perhaps even something of an authority on the subject. My collection of records and CDs still took up close to a third of the space in my living room. Not to mention the files on my computer and my iPod.

And more than any other, with the possible exceptions of Blue Rodeo and Arcade Fire, the Hip had become my band of choice. The music and the musicianship were amazing but driving the experience was the poetry, Downie's words.

I'd met him only once, briefly, but through his lyrics — which conveyed the thoughts of this immensely decent, enormously talented man — I felt I knew him. Knew him well.

I continued to stare at my coffee as Cobb arrived and sat down across from me. Cobb, who was one of the most perceptive people I had ever met, after a couple of minutes said, "Tough day?"

"Yeah, working on the Gord Downie story. It's not going well."

Cobb picked up my coffee cup and disappeared for a minute. He returned with a fresh cup for me and one for himself.

"I met him once," I said, "after a concert in 2013. Outdoors at Shaw Millennium Park. It was raining and nobody cared, nobody left. It was amazing. The Hip played like it was thirty degrees and sunny. I hung around after, thinking wouldn't it be cool to meet the guy and knowing there was no chance. So, there I was, leaning against this fence and I looked up and there was Gord. He leaned against the fence with me and we talked for maybe ten minutes. In the rain. But the most incredible thing was he mostly wanted to talk about me. I told him that Donna was crazy about the Hip and he wanted to know what happened to her. I told him, and the guy was genuinely sad. You can tell when it's not just words — when someone means it. He meant it. Finally, we shook hands and said so long. It was one of those really great moments in your life that comes along totally unexpectedly."

"Cool story," Cobb said.

"I've just been rereading the obits and the features — a lot of good stuff. I'd like to say something that hasn't been said."

"Why don't you write what you just told me? Talking to Gord Downie in the rain."

"You think so?"

"Why not? I just learned something about the guy I didn't know. And I'm glad I know that now. Why not share that story with a bunch of people?"

"You know something, that's not bad."

Cobb smiled and nodded. "I'm actually a very smart guy. You want something to eat?"

I started to shake my head, then realized I was starving. "Yeah, that might be good."

"What'll you have? I'm buying."

"They make a pretty good breakfast sandwich," I said.

"On it."

Cobb left again, eventually returning with the sandwiches in hand. I closed up my laptop and we ate, for the most part in silence. When we'd finished, a server cleared the plates and we got refills of coffee.

"Looks like we're going to have to pick up the pace on Claiborne. Danny's been charged and the prosecutor is already making noise about trying him in adult court."

"What are the chances of that happening?"

Cobb shrugged. "I'd like to believe they aren't very good, but there are no guarantees."

I nodded. "Okay, let's get going. Thanks for breakfast. And the help with the Downie piece."

"Anytime." Cobb pulled out his notebook. "Before we head out, I ran a check of the lady. Seems Janine has a slightly checkered past."

Lorne Cooney didn't have that, or if he did he hadn't mentioned it.

"As in a criminal record?"

Cobb nodded. "Exactly. Care to guess what her sin was?"

"So far this crowd seems fairly keen on money and acquiring it. Not always by means that endear them to the authorities. I'll go down that road."

"Good call. She defrauded not one but two banks — some kind of phony mortgage scheme. Borrowed money against properties she didn't actually own. When she failed to make the payments, the financial institutions moved to foreclose, only to find out that the person they loaned the money to was fictional. She pulled it off twice, got caught the third time. Did three years at the Fraser Valley Institution for Women. Got out in '94, married Claiborne two years later. Spent less time married than she did in the Big House. But the inter-esting thing is that Claiborne and company have been pretty successful at sweeping this one under the ol' rug. It's a well-guarded secret."

That helped to explain why Lorne didn't have that one in his packet of info.

"I suspect there are a few of those. And it seems fair to say that money is a bit of an ongoing theme."

"Yeah, except for one thing. She's found religion in the years since Claiborne."

"Really found it or *bullshit* found it?"

"What does that mean?"

"I go to church and I pray lots but I'm actually a racist and I'm okay with white supremacy and the person I love most in the world is me. That's bullshit religion."

"I can't imagine there are people like that in the world."

"Maybe one or two," I said.

Cobb shrugged. "Can't say what kind of Christian Janine Claiborne is."

"Lorne said something about her being a church secretary."

"Correct. Of course, that doesn't guarantee that a person is sincere in their beliefs, or even that they have any. Maybe it's something we should inquire about."

"Wonder what happened to the money she acquired during the more sordid part of her past."

"Something else we might want to ask her."

"She never remarried?"

Cobb shook his head. "Don't know if there's a boy-friend or not. Let's add that to the list." He stood up, slipped his notebook into his pocket. "You have your car here?"

"Yeah, I didn't feel like walking this morning."

"How about you drive? I want to make some calls."

Janine Claiborne lived in Crescent Heights, a venerable Calgary neighbourhood perched at the top of the North Hill. One of my favourite parts of the city, in part because I went to high school there.

The house was small and older, but immaculate. The yard was the same. Unfortunately, the place was surrounded by infills and would probably itself be bulldozed or moved off the property in the next few years.

We sat in the car in front of Janine Claiborne's home as Cobb talked first to Danny's lawyer — not a lot of new information there — then Danny's dad. While I could only hear Cobb's side of the conversation, it seemed that Matthew Luft had mellowed some in the time since he'd tossed me out of the interview room at the police station. Cobb ended the call and turned to me. "He wants to meet with us later today."

"Us? As in you and me?"

Cobb grinned. "I guess you grow on people. I expect a call any time now from Susannah inviting us to dinner."

"We might both starve to death before that happens."

"You might be right." Cobb climbed out of the Accord and led the way to the house.

Janine Claiborne was clearly ready for us. She met us at the front door before Cobb even had a chance to ring the bell. After what felt like a warm greeting, she directed us inside, where coffee and tea were waiting.

The first couple of minutes were spent getting Cobb and me seated in matching blue recliners, coffee poured, shortbread biscuits distributed, and the mandatory small talk of introductions made.

She sat opposite us in an older easy chair that looked utilitarian but comfortable.

If Janine had money, it wasn't reflected in the furnishings of her home. Like the exterior, the living space inside was clean, pleasant, and comfortable but not the stuff of wealth. Our coffee was in mugs, not cups.

I liked her right off. Her smile seemed genuine and she appeared to be totally at ease with talking to a couple of guys who might be about to ask difficult questions.

"I understand you're representing the young man who is Glenna's boyfriend."

"That's right," Cobb said, after swallowing a bite of shortbread. "The police charged him this morning."

"Oh dear."

"It was expected," Cobb told her. "His fingerprints were on the murder weapon."

"I see," she murmured. "But you feel he didn't shoot Wendell, or if he did, you want to get him off." She was forthright but spoke without attitude, and she definitely lacked the venom her sister had displayed, although I reminded myself that Bad Susannah had only surfaced when the questioning got unpleasant.

"The former," Cobb replied. "We don't think Danny killed Claiborne. No, let me rephrase that. I haven't met Danny, but my partner" — he tilted his head in my direction — "has talked to him and feels strongly that Danny is a victim in all this."

Janine turned her gaze to me and I gave her an abridged version of my conversation with Danny in Cobb's office.

When I finished she looked thoughtful but remained silent.

"Based on what I've said, are you surprised that your former husband made the proposal he did to Danny?"

"That's difficult to answer, Mr. Cullen." She spoke slowly. "Wendell was not a good man in many ways. And I don't doubt that he might have wanted his wife dead. But conspiring with a teenage boy to kill her — that seems rather extreme even for him."

"Why do you think he might have wanted Mrs. Claiborne dead?"

"Well, Wendell made a habit of discarding women — I was one of them. It didn't seem that Rachel was as inclined to accept being thrown out of his home and his life as the rest of us were."

Cobb looked at me. I knew what he wanted. If there was to be *unpleasantness*, he wanted me to be the instigator. That way he could jump back as Mr. Nice Guy and pick up the pieces.

"Do you mind my asking, Mrs. Claiborne, was there a financial settlement that went with being exited from your ex's life?"

"First of all, I don't mind your asking that, and secondly, I really prefer Janine. Mrs. Claiborne carries with it some … unpleasantness. To answer your question, I received one hundred and fifty thousand dollars, which I know doesn't sound like much now, but I wanted out and probably would have taken less to be free of him. I used the money to buy this house, which was doable twenty years ago. I even had a little left over. I got a job, the one I have now, and the rest, as they say …"

I nodded. "On the subject of history, Janine, and again I apologize in advance for the question — we understand that you had previously acquired some fairly large sums of money."

"Mr. Cullen, in the first place, that's not a question, and secondly, again I'm happy to share that information with you. Once I was arrested, a lot of what money I still had went to my legal people. When I got out of jail, I had very little left, and what I had I frankly squandered. I was 'down on my luck,' I think the expression is, when I met Wendell."

Cobb jumped back in at that point. "Your meeting Claiborne, did that come about because of your sister's relationship with him?"

"It did, yes." She nodded. "And I'm happy to tell you about that, as well, but can I offer you more coffee first?"

Cobb declined but I thought back to the missed martini opportunity and decided that since I actually *wanted* more coffee, maybe I should say that. I did and Janine Claiborne refreshed mine then hers. As she came closer I was reminded that she was younger than Susannah. And though she was not the beauty her sister was, she was not unattractive.

When she had returned to her chair, she smiled and said, "I thought Wendell was charming — most women did — but I absolutely would not have entered into a relationship with him while he was with Susannah. My sister would probably see this differently, but sometime after that first meeting, Wendell told me he was attracted to me and assured me it was over between him and Susannah. I believed him, and I was wrong to do that. I know that now. It may have been over in his mind, but

Susannah was unaware that she was about to be … set aside. I think it's fair to say that she has hated me ever since. I don't blame her."

"She mentioned that you called her with the news of Claiborne's death."

"Yes, that's right."

"And how did you learn he'd been killed?"

"Glenna called me. It was very early — I guess about six."

"Were you and Glenna close?" Cobb asked.

"I always got along very well with Glenna. I'm not sure why. We met when she was maybe five or six and I've always felt more like an aunt where she's involved. Rachel, Glenna's mom and the current Mrs. Claiborne —" She stopped suddenly and shook her head. "That was stupid. You already know that, of course."

"That's all right," Cobb said lightly. "Please go on."

"Anyway, Rachel doesn't mind. I've taken Glenna to the movies the odd time and a Red Hot Chili Peppers concert a couple of years ago. I guess she thought I'd want to know and I got the feeling she wanted to talk to someone."

"Did she say who she thought might have shot her dad?"

"No. As I said, she was upset and emotional and though she seemed to want to talk, a lot of what she was saying sounded like nonsense, bordering on the hysterical, even though it had been hours since … but I guess that isn't really very long, is it, especially to one so young? But was it the kind of upset that would be the result of worrying about her boyfriend having something to do with it? If that *was* it, I couldn't say."

"Do you have any thoughts as to people who might have wanted to harm Wendell?"

She thought about it for quite a while before answering. "I assume you're considering all of the exes, including me. But I honestly have doubts about that. Wendell was a philanderer, no question, but he didn't mistreat his women, at least not that I'm aware of. Although I suppose it can be argued that cheating on them *is* mistreating them. But he was never abusive to me, not even verbally. Wendell loved falling in love, and when that had worn off, it was time to get rid of the old, find someone new, and fall in love again. Although I admit it didn't always happen in that order."

Both Cobb and I waited, thinking there might be more. There was.

"There were a number of women in Wendell's life over the years, beyond the ones he married or lived with. Not all of them were unmarried. I should think that might have created enemies for him. And I'm not sure Wendell displayed much more integrity in his business life than he did in his personal life. I suppose, if it were me, I might look into some of his business dealings and the people he had those dealings with. If you're sure, that is, that your young man … Danny was it? … if you're sure it wasn't him."

"We're quite certain about Danny," I said. "But it may not be easy to prove he's innocent unless we're able to find the real killer."

She nodded. "I wish you luck, I really do. I can't imagine how difficult it must be for that young man and his family. I'm very glad he has you working on his behalf."

"Thank you," I said.

Cobb scribbled something in his notebook, then looked up. "So ... angry husbands, business associates ... anybody else?"

"Well, there's Trenton, but of course, you know about him."

Cobb and I exchanged looks.

"Ah, I see you don't."

"We know he's your sister's employee. That's all we know. Would you mind enlightening us?"

"Trenton worked for Wendell in several capacities — chauffeur, personal secretary, valet. I don't know that he had an official title, but he'd been with Wendell quite a long time. When Susannah moved in with Wendell, Trenton fell for her. Hard. Head over heels. It was obvious to everyone, and eventually it became obvious to Wendell, as well. It grew awkward and Wendell had to let him go."

"And Trenton winds up working for your sister," Cobb noted. "Any thought that there might be something more to that relationship than employer-employee?"

"I couldn't say. Susannah has never said, and I haven't asked. We're no longer close enough that I would feel comfortable asking her something like that."

Cobb looked at me to see if there was anything else I wanted to ask. I gave a small head shake and he closed his notebook.

"We want to thank you, ma'am. Your candour has been much appreciated."

She smiled at him. "Ma'am," she repeated. "I must say, I like that almost as much as Mrs. Claiborne."

"Sorry." Cobb shook his head ruefully. "I didn't mean to be —"

She stopped him with an outstretched hand. "You haven't been anything but a gentleman." She looked at me as she got to her feet. "Both of you. And I sincerely hope you're successful in your quest."

I noted she didn't use the phrase *get him off* this time.

She walked us to the door; we shook hands, and I followed Cobb out into an unseasonably hot February day. Neither of us spoke until we were back in the car.

As I pulled away from the curb, Cobb said, "Trenton."

"Didn't see that one coming."

"What do you think?"

"Well, it's interesting," I said. "But it's a long way from having a crush on the boss's girlfriend to offing the boss, especially twenty years after the fact."

"True, but love and all its ramifications have been responsible for a hell of a lot of murders and mayhem throughout history. It's worth checking out."

"I agree."

"How about you work your investigative magic on him later today? Next up, Matthew Luft."

"Before or after lunch?"

Cobb consulted his watch. "After."

"Phew," I said. "You scared me there for a minute. That shortbread was amazing, but the trouble with shortbread is it's, well, short."

Cobb pushed back his chair, took a deep breath, then let it out slowly. "That, my friend, was mighty fine."

"No argument here."

We had chosen the Burger Inn on 4th Street. It was handy and the name was the only unimaginative thing about the place. Cobb, ever the old-school guy when it came to food choices, had gone with the prime rib burger, while I had been only slightly more daring with the elk burger. Both plates had been all but licked clean.

Cobb's phone beeped and he looked down for a minute, reading, then looked up at me. "While you were in the washroom I texted a former colleague. The bad news is he's retiring next year, which will leave me with one less contact on the force. The good news is that he ran Trenton through records and got a couple of hits."

"Enlighten me."

"I'll leave out the part where he cusses me for not giving him a full name. Hard to work with just *Trenton*. I knew that, told him that was all we had."

"And?"

"Full name Marcus Trenton. Anglicized version of a Croatian name I can't pronounce. Hmm … like damn near everybody involved with Claiborne, Trenton is less than squeaky clean. Did a little pimping, some bookmaking, and there were a couple of other charges, mostly assaults. Nasty stuff."

"He didn't look that tough."

"Which is why they invented baseball bats."

"He connected to organized crime?"

"Doesn't say. Could have been. Or maybe an independent who did a little work for them on the side."

"Like Janine, saw the error of his ways and decided to reform his life?"

"Doesn't say that either. That's part of your job." He glanced again at his watch. "Time to go. I don't want to keep Luft waiting."

"Right." I reached for the bill. "I've got this. It's my turn."

As I picked it up, Spirit of the West's "Home for a Rest" announced that I had a call. I looked at the screen. It was Jill. "I better take this."

Cobb nodded and made his way toward the washroom as I lifted the phone to my ear.

"I love you," I said.

"You need to come to my place, Adam, right away."

The chill that wormed its way around my spinal column was a combination of fear and dread.

"Are you okay?" I said, the urgency in my voice turning the heads of a couple of nearby diners.

"I'm okay. Kyla's fine. You need to come now."

"I'm on my way." I ended the call as Cobb came back from the washroom.

"I gotta go," I told him. "That was Jill. Something's wrong. I don't know what. She and Kyla are okay but I need to be there right away."

Cobb nodded and instantly was the ex-cop I'd seen in action before. "I'll come with you."

I shook my head. "I'm okay. I'll let you know what's going on as soon as I know."

"You sure?"

"I'm sure."

"Right, go. I'll walk back to the office."

"I can —"

He held up a hand. "It's six blocks; I can handle it. Call as soon as you know what's up. If there's anything I can do ..."

I nodded once and was out the door. I drove faster than meets with the approval of the authorities, but luckily I didn't encounter any of those authorities between the Burger Inn and Jill's house.

I slid the car in behind an Audi, jumped out, and started toward the house. I didn't make it.

"Hey, Cullen."

I turned to watch a human giant heave himself out of the Audi.

Audi. I should have known. I'd seen the car before. And as I turned I realized I'd seen the giant before, too.

Minnis.

I looked at the house, then back at Minnis. He shook his head.

"Your girlfriend's fine. No need for her not to be, right?"

I knew instantly what this was about. The day of reckoning had arrived. And I knew, too, why the MFs had chosen the meeting to be at Jill's house. The threat — unspoken — was palpable. Like the fear that gripped me as I looked at the imposing, deadly figure of one of the people I feared most in the world.

I realized that in none of my previous encounters with Minnis had I ever heard him speak. The voice didn't fit. Or maybe it fit perfectly. It was low and soft, forcing the listener to pay close attention to every syllable. Which I realized, as he came around the car toward me, heightened the menace of the man even more.

But there was more than menace to this man. There was *evil*.

"What did you tell her?"

He held his hands out, palms up. "Hey, you're way too suspicious, Scribe. You need to relax."

Scribe. His boss's term for me. "What did you tell her?" I repeated, hoping my voice conveyed more of the rage and less of the dread I was feeling in equal parts.

"I mentioned we'd met before and I had a message for you from the MFs, something you'd want to know. Don't worry, I didn't tell her about your ... arrangement with us. That could come later, of course."

There was no way of knowing if he was telling the truth. I'd know that as soon as I went inside and talked to Jill.

"What do you want?"

He stepped closer. I willed myself not to step back. "You'll be receiving a package in the next few days. There will be instructions with the package. Your job will be to get that package to a destination in the United States. How you do that is up to you."

"You want me to smuggle something across the border."

"You'll be receiving a package that you will deliver to someone in the U.S." The second time he said it was in the same disembodied voice as the first time.

"And if I tell you to shove it up your ass?"

Minnis glanced toward the house. "You probably don't want to do that."

That's when I stepped back, wanting to get into the house. I took a couple of steps, then turned back to him. "How do I get the package?"

"We'll get it to you. You don't need to worry about that part."

"Are you done?"

"For now, Scribe, I'm done. Now it's up to you. My advice? Don't fuck up."

I badly wanted to come back with something that would convey my loathing for this noxious mound of vile malevolence. I failed. This time when I turned away from him, I kept on going. I stepped in the front door and Jill was there.

"I was watching," she said.

I nodded. "I thought you might be. Thank you."

I knew that if things had gotten physical with Minnis, she'd have been out the door, doing what she could. It wouldn't have been nearly enough, of course, but that wouldn't have stopped her from trying.

"What did that …? What did he want?"

I knew I'd have to lie to her again. But I wanted to come as close to the truth as I could.

"He didn't say. Just told me that the MFs wanted to talk to Cobb and me about something. Down the road sometime. He was, I guess, setting the stage for that."

"Why here?"

I knew she'd ask that. And I knew, too, that this was the tough part.

"They're devious bastards, Jill. I think they want us to know that they know where you live. Which is ridiculous, of course. It's not like we're a secret. It's just part of the games they play."

"I need to know, Adam. Is Kyla in danger?"

Not *are we* in danger. Only *is Kyla* in danger.

"Kyla is not in any danger, Jill. Neither of you are."

And that wasn't a lie. Because I knew that whatever the package was — I was certain it was something illegal, probably drugs — I would do what they asked. I would soon be a lawbreaker, a smuggler. But Jill and Kyla would be safe.

That thought was accompanied by another. That, exactly as Cobb had predicted, there would be more demands. And I would comply. For as long as the horror lasted.

Jill's voice interrupted my brooding. "Do you feel like a coffee?"

"I feel like a whiskey," I said. "But a coffee would be good."

We didn't talk further until we were sitting at the kitchen table, mugs of coffee in front of us. Jill was holding hers in both her hands, like they were cold. Maybe they were.

"I wish you'd never had anything to do with those people."

"Yeah, me too," I said. "But it'll be okay, I promise."

Which, of course, was anything but a sure thing. It was, nevertheless, what I had to say right then. Probably more for me than for Jill.

John Mann and Spirit of the West announced an incoming call. I pulled my phone from my jacket pocket. "Hello."

"You doing okay?" Cobb's voice sounded worried.

"Yeah, let's talk about it later. How did you make out?"

"Okay. We have a client."

"Luft?"

"The same. Totally different guy this time. Maybe he figured out that his kid's in trouble and he's going to need some help."

"That's a big turnaround. As in one hundred and eighty degrees."

"Roger that. He came dangerously close to being a human being today. He is one scared dad."

"He have any thoughts that might help us?"

"I don't think so. I took some notes. I'll show them to you when I see you next, but I'm not sure there's anything there."

When I see you next. Leaving it to me to make that call.

"I want to get at this. When do you want to meet? I'm ready anytime."

Jill was watching me, neither approving nor disapproving.

"Let's confab at the office tomorrow morning, if that works."

"I can do that. I'll bring the Timbits," I said.

"Goody."

We ended the call and I stood up. Jill got up from her chair and came to me. We stood for a long time, holding each other, not hugging really, just together. It felt good to know that for now, at least, we were one for whatever came our way. I wondered if we'd still be together if Jill actually knew what it was that might come our way.

SEVEN

"It was the MFs, wasn't it?"

I was reminded that Cobb had been a homicide detective and, according to people who'd know, a good one. We were halfway through our first cup of coffee and had popped a couple of Timbits each. Neither of us had said much beyond good morning until Cobb's statement — because it *was* more of a statement than a question.

I knew it was better not to lie. The only question was how much of the truth I was prepared to share. There was still a small part of me — and getting smaller all the time — that believed that if I did what I'd been ordered to and didn't fuck up — which was, after all, part of the assignment — that maybe, just maybe, it would happen only once.

"Yeah, it was. Minnis."

"And?"

"Setting the stage. No assignment. Not yet." Again I'd stayed in the rough vicinity of the truth. "Told me I'd hear from them. I think the whole point was to intimidate me. Meeting me in front of Jill's house, that was part of it, but for now, nothing's really changed. I think they just wanted to remind me that the day is coming."

Cobb thought about that. "Doesn't make a lot of sense. You already knew that. It's not like those people to waste time. They don't have to. They know they hold the cards."

I shrugged. "Yeah, I was thinking that same thing as Minnis was talking to me. So, I don't know what to tell you. Guess I'll find out one of these days. For now, though, not much has changed."

I didn't know if Cobb believed me. But he seemed prepared to let it go for the moment.

"Your turn," I said. "Tell me about your meeting with Luft, then I'll tell you what I was able to learn last night about him."

"Well, I told you that he's hired us, so I don't need to go over that again." He reached into the inside pocket of the jacket he was wearing, pulled out first his reading glasses then a small notebook. "He told me he'd never met Claiborne but did know Rachel Claiborne from a couple of parent-teacher evenings at school. Just chit-chat. He was aware that Danny was seeing Glenna Claiborne and had met her a couple of times. He thought it was just kid stuff — his words — nothing serious. He never suspected his kid had ever done drugs — again his words — and pretty much confirmed what Danny said about how there would have been a lot of shit flying if he'd known the kid was smoking weed."

"Let me guess. A lot of shit flying — his words, as well?"

"A direct quote. But now he's the worried dad."

"Yeah, maybe the lawyer explained just how deep the kid is in this, or maybe his wife told him to drop the tough-guy stuff and start being a father. Not sure. Danny did say that his dad was a good guy most of the time."

"I guess this is one of those times. Okay, what've you got?" Cobb asked.

I pulled out my own notebook, though I had most of what I wanted to share with Cobb committed to memory. "Military record exemplary. Two overseas tours — Croatia and Afghanistan. In 1993 he and the rest of the second battalion Princess Patricia's Canadian Light Infantry were involved in the Battle of the Medak Pocket in Croatia. It's called the forgotten battle, but it was pretty big and pretty intense. Luft got a couple of commendations coming out of that and was promoted to sergeant not long after. He also saw action in Afghanistan in 2002, this time with the third battalion of the PPCLI, again some pretty heavy stuff. Sounds like the guy was a good soldier." I glanced down at my notes. "Married in '99. Elaine Darmody, Ontario girl, born, raised, and educated in Kitchener. Danny's their only child, born in 2001, not long before Luft went to Afghanistan. Mrs. Luft works part-time as a library assistant at a school."

"You find any criminal past in Luft?"

I shook my head. "Straight shooter, near as I can tell."

"Nice word choice." Cobb smiled.

I laughed. "Guess it was."

"Oh, and while we're on the topic of shooters, I got a look at the ballistics report. Only definable prints on the murder weapon were Danny's, Claiborne's, and Mrs. Claiborne's. And one other thing: Claiborne was shot once, upper chest, left side. I don't know all the medical jargon, but the bullet apparently destroyed the aortic valve and passed through the left ventricle. Catastrophic internal bleeding."

"Sounds like someone was a good shot."

"Maybe. Not a pro though. A pro wants to make sure; there's at least one head shot. And, by the way, nothing was missing. Claiborne's wallet with a fair amount of cash, an expensive ring — all of that was still in place. And the room wasn't tossed, so the killer didn't apparently search for anything."

"So, if Danny didn't shoot Claiborne, who did? You said it didn't look like a robbery."

"No evidence of anything taken, but we can't rule out that there actually was an intruder who just didn't have time to complete the robbery, or got hold of the gun, shot Claiborne, then panicked and ran off."

"I'm thinking that's awfully unlikely."

"I'd say you're right."

I flipped a page in my notebook. "The other thing I did was compile a list of possible shooters."

"Okay, what've you got? Let's see if your group matches mine."

"Well, first there's all the exes — wives, girlfriends, and the like. I don't have all those listed, but I've jotted down the main players."

"Shoot."

"Cindy Marsh Claiborne. First wife. We haven't talked to her yet."

"I'm planning to call her today."

"Susannah Hainsey and her sister, Janine Claiborne."

"Uh-huh. Anything new there or anything we missed?"

"Not sure off the top of my head. Be interesting to ask Susannah about Trenton, who, by the way, is the next name on my list. I've got the address he uses when he's not staying over at Susannah's. Bragg Creek, just west of the city."

"Good."

I surveyed my notes. "Then, of course, there's the incumbent Mrs. Claiborne, Rachel, who one suspects might come out of all this in pretty good shape financially."

"I'm guessing you're right. And there's Danny Luft, our client, and his dad and mom. Dad seems like the kind of guy with both the skills and the temperament to take someone down if he saw them as a threat to his family. Anything on Danny's mom?"

I shook my head. "Beyond the name, not really. Anybody I'm missing?"

"Yeah, I'd put the younger Claiborne on that list."

"Glenna?"

"Sure. Consider if Danny told her about her dad's effort to recruit him to kill Glenna's mom. Seems like a pretty strong motive to me. She saves both her mom and her boyfriend."

"Yeah … maybe. Takes a certain kind of kid to take out her old man, even if the guy's a grade-A slimeball."

"Can't argue that. Anyway, I like your work on this. I think we should get started talking to as many of the people on there as we can."

"Anybody in particular you want to start with?"

"I don't think it matters. I'd like to talk to all of them. And the sooner the better."

"On it," I said. "I can also call Cindy Claiborne, the first wife. Why don't you leave that with me?"

Cobb nodded. "That'll help a lot. I've got a meeting with Danny's lawyer. He's apparently willing to talk to me now that we're part of the outfit. You want to come along?"

"I think I'd rather get started making calls to the people we want to chat with. See how I make out."

"Sure, why don't you stay here, use the office while I'm downtown. I'll call or text when I'm out of my meeting."

Trenton was my first call; I'm not sure why, since he was the one guy I figured would be the hardest to catch up with. I wasn't sure how badly I wanted to call Susannah Hainsey's apartment, so I called his home first, fairly certain that at that time of day he wouldn't be there. When a male voice picked up on the third ring, I had to organize my thoughts quickly.

I introduced myself, told him I was one of the people who'd been at Ms. Hainsey's apartment two days before, and explained that Cobb and I would like to meet him at his convenience to ask him a few questions.

"What's it about?" he asked.

The question surprised me, but I didn't want to say, *You know exactly what it's about*, so I took a breath instead. "We're looking into the murder of Wendell Claiborne. We're acting on behalf of Danny Luft, the young man who has been charged with the murder. We understand you were employed by Claiborne before you went to work for Ms. Hainsey, and we'd like to chat with you."

"When would you like to meet?"

Again I was caught off guard. Maybe I was guilty of being a glass-half-empty guy, but I knew that there were times when getting to talk to someone connected to a case was a whole lot tougher than this. Trenton had responded, without hesitation, in the affirmative. A very different reaction from that of his employer by the end of our conversation with her.

"Are you working today, Mr. Trenton?"

"Just Trenton," he said. I thought I detected a chuckle or at least a smile in his voice. "I only have one name."

"Right … Trenton."

"And I am working today, but just noon to six. If tonight at seven or so works ...?"

"It absolutely works."

"I live in Bragg Creek and I prefer not to drive after dark. So if we could meet there, it would be helpful for me, though I realize less convenient for you."

"No problem at all," I said. "Is there a place you could suggest? I've been to Bragg Creek but I'm not all that familiar with the area."

"You'd be most welcome at my home, if that's all right."

"Appreciate the hospitality."

He gave me the address.

"We'll find it. See you tonight."

I rang off and my winning streak continued when I reached Cindy Claiborne on the first try. If I had to characterize the voice on the phone, I would have said tired, almost frail-sounding. My guess was that she would now be only in her fifties, but she sounded older than that. I wondered about the state of her health. However, after a couple of clarifications as to who I was and why I was calling, she agreed to meet us that afternoon.

"Two o'clock work for you, Ms. Claiborne?"

"I don't go out of the house too much," she said. "Would you be able to come here?"

I assured her we'd be happy to do that and took down the address. She lived just off 14th Street on the North Hill.

I was pretty full of myself after going two for two, but my luck ran out after that. No answer when I called Rachel Claiborne. I made an executive decision and included in my message that we'd like to speak to Glenna, as well, and that she was welcome to be present for the conversation with her daughter.

I decided to make some notes prior to our meetings and that, too, turned out to be an exercise in futility. Cindy Claiborne, formerly Cindy Marsh, had clearly been a low-key, low-profile figure when she was married to Claiborne and had remained that way after their breakup. I found a couple of early photos of the happy couple at charity events and one with Ralph Klein when he was mayor of Calgary. Virtually nothing since Cindy had ceased being the live-in Mrs. Claiborne. She was not on social media and I searched online for everything from "Cindy Claiborne, wife of Wendell Claiborne" to "Cindy Marsh, debutante," but came up empty.

Finally, I found a small piece about Cindy Marsh, graduate of William Aberhart High School, which talked about her winning a national photography competition for teens. It was from the *Herald* dated July 25, 1979. Then I logged into Classmates.com and was able to find a photo of Cindy as a student. Half-smile, almost shy look on a face surrounded by light-brown hair. A very average-looking kid. The bio below her picture indicated that she was an only child and was interested in music and photography. She'd had a part in the school's operetta that year, *The Pirates of Penzance*.

My notes about her were sketchy, to say the least, although they were *War and Peace* next to what I found out about Trenton, which was exactly nothing. Interesting, considering he'd had a criminal past.

I texted Cobb the times of our appointments and suggested he might want to ask the lawyer about Claiborne's will. Then I took a break and walked across the street to

PARM for a pizza. It was one of my favourite spots, but still felt a little weird. A few months before, Cobb and I had investigated the disappearance of a young folksinger in 1965 from a place called The Depression. The coffee house was Calgary's first, and had been located in the basement of the building now occupied by PARM.

The *Il Classico* pizza was excellent, but I ate one slice and wrapped up the rest to go. My appetite had been off for some time, and I knew why. The realization that the day of reckoning with the MFs would soon arrive had thrown me off my game in a number of ways. I hoped I was able to appear normal, whatever that means, when I was with Jill and Kyla. I knew that if Jill sensed there was something seriously amiss, she'd confront me, wanting to know what was wrong. And I knew, or at least I was pretty sure, that I couldn't lie to her. Not anymore.

Cobb arrived back at the office just before one thirty. I pointed at the pizza and he nodded, took a slice, and sat down.

"What did Kemper have to say?"

Cobb rubbed the back of his hand over his mouth and said, "He's a doom and gloomer. Already talking about working a deal with the prosecution — see if we can get the thing handled in juvenile court, get Danny some time in the YOC. Not a lot of enthusiasm for the idea that maybe somebody else offed Claiborne. But, and this is pretty much a quote, 'Even if the kid is innocent as spring rain, we'll have a hell of a time getting him off, so our best bet is to take what we can get and try to keep him out of big boy prison.'"

"And you said?"

"Not much. Fact is he might be right. Think about all the people who have done serious time for murders they didn't commit. In fact, didn't the Tragically Hip have a song about that?"

"Yeah, 'Wheat Kings,' about David Milgaard."

"Kemper's got a pretty good reputation, so if he says we're in trouble on the court front, then we're probably in trouble."

"How about a good old-fashioned alibi?"

Cobb ate more pizza, took his time before answering. "That whole alibi thing is one of the reasons we're in some hot water here. Danny doesn't have one. Kemper says the kid admitted that at about the time Claiborne was shot, he was back at home after a late-night bike ride to try to see Glenna."

"So he rode over to Claiborne's house."

"Yeah."

"Kid's not a good listener."

"He's a kid. Lots of them aren't."

"Okay, so after my explicit instruction that he stay away from Claiborne, he rides over to the house. Did he see Claiborne?"

"Says not. And he didn't see Glenna either. Said he just wanted to see her, not talk to her, make sure she was okay. He didn't actually go up to the house, and when he didn't see Glenna, he got back on his bike and headed home."

"Shit," I said.

Cobb waved that off. "You're premature, my friend; it gets worse. On the way either to or from trying to catch a glimpse of his girlfriend, Danny stopped off at a 7-Eleven to buy a bag of Cheezies. Store employee recognized him and has told the police the time, corroborated by cash machine tape, Danny was there. It was within a half-hour one way or the other of when the ME has stated was the time of Claiborne's death. And that is further corroborated by my guys who followed Danny that night. Saw him at the house, at the store, and saw him arrive back home. They lost him for a few minutes on the way back home but picked him up again about a block from his house. Saw him go inside. He didn't come out again that night."

"I thought they were supposed to keep him away from Claiborne's place."

Cobb shook his head. "They were supposed to keep him away from Claiborne. They were across the street and ready to move if the kid had actually started up to the house. I'd told them I didn't want them scaring the crap out of the kid for no reason, so they stayed back, which is exactly what they were supposed to do."

"So, our client's fingerprints are on the weapon, he's got motive, they've got him and Claiborne in conversation about killing Mrs. Claiborne, *and* he was near the scene of the crime at the approximate time of the murder."

"Pretty much, yeah."

"I'd say Kemper's right, then. Our client is in a very bad spot."

"Now you got it."

I slid my fairly pathetic notes across the table. It didn't take Cobb long to read them. He folded the paper, stuck it in a jacket pocket, and stood up. "I'm going to wash my hands," he said. "Then let's go see Cindy. We need something to go right, and we need it soon."

We thought we were at the wrong house. The address I had for Cindy Claiborne took us to a small bungalow on 21st Avenue NW, but the place was all wrong. I have nothing against small bungalows, but this place needed paint, the lawn hadn't seen a mower in a long time, and the garage door looked like it had taken a significant hit and was incapable of movement up or down. Infills flanked the house, and you got the feeling that this Mrs. Claiborne's place, if this was, in fact, the right house, would, like Janine Claiborne's, soon be replaced by something bigger and nicer. Which it seemed to me wouldn't be hard to accomplish. Almost any house would fit both those categories.

Cobb looked at me. He didn't say it, but I knew he was thinking the same thing. And there was a part of me that hoped I *was* wrong. Because the person who lived in this house could not have been doing well.

Cobb pressed the doorbell and we heard a healthy *ding-dong*. I was hoping the inside of the house would be quaint and clean and that Cindy was just waiting for the exterior renovation company to arrive for a makeover. Hoping but not believing.

My fear that things would not get better when the door opened was quickly realized. A woman stood looking at us through the screen. She was tiny, maybe five feet tall, and to call her thin would have been a kindness. In fact, the body matched almost exactly the voice I had heard on the phone. Frail.

"Mrs. Cindy Claiborne?" I stepped forward when I saw her, thinking it would be best if she realized she was dealing with the guy she'd talked to on the telephone.

"I'm Cindy Claiborne."

"I'm Adam Cullen, Mrs. Claiborne. This is my partner, Mike Cobb. I spoke to you on the telephone earlier today."

"Of course. Please come inside." She stood back and I stepped in ahead of Cobb, then waited for her to direct us where she wanted.

There weren't a lot of options. She moved across in front of me and we proceeded to the right, into the living room. It was hard to describe and harder to take. It didn't make sense that a woman who had once been married to one of Calgary's wealthiest men and was rumoured to have been well taken care of when the marriage ended was living like this as she got older.

"Would you like to sit over there?" she pointed to a worn sofa that wouldn't have been out of place in a re-mounting of *Annie*. There was a coffee table, same vintage, in front of the sofa, and on it were two glasses of water, one ice cube in each, and a plate of cookies.

"I read once that detectives are reluctant to accept beverages and things from people they are interviewing," she said, a small smile brightening her pale features. "Maybe it has to do with being compromised in their investigation. I hope water is all right. And I made peanut butter cookies this afternoon. I hope you like them."

"Peanut butter cookies are my favourite, ma'am," said Cobb, "and the water is perfect, thank you."

I smiled my thanks and we sipped our waters in unison. As we sat back on the sofa, Cobb nodded in my direction, handing me the lead, at least for the moment.

"As you know, Ms. Claiborne … is it all right to call you that, or do you prefer something else?"

"My first name is Cynthia, although I was most often called Cindy. I didn't like that much. If you were to call me Cynthia, I think that would be fine."

I nodded. "As you know, Cynthia, we're looking at the murder of your ex-husband. We're representing the young man, Danny Luft, who has been charged in connection with Wendell Claiborne's death. I wanted you to know that in case you're uncomfortable talking to us under those circumstances."

"Not at all," she said. "Please continue."

"Our client indicated to us that Mr. Claiborne had approached him with a proposal that Danny shoot Mrs. Claiborne. Then together they would set things up to look like Mrs. Claiborne had disturbed a prowler and was killed. Do you find that shocking or unbelievable, Cynthia?"

She sat for a long moment before responding. While she thought, she seemed to be staring at a spot just over Cobb's head. Finally, she refocused her gaze on me, shifted for a moment to Cobb, then back to me. Taking the time she needed. "Wendell was a man who was capable of a great many unpleasant things, as are most people who are completely lacking in empathy. I wouldn't have predicted something like this, but having heard of it now, I cannot say I'm shocked or surprised."

I thought about her answer. "Cynthia, I hope you won't mind this question. But our understanding is that you received a generous settlement when you and Claiborne divorced. And …" I hesitated, not knowing exactly how I wanted to phrase the rest of the question. I didn't have to.

"And as you look at me and my home and belongings, you're wondering what happened to all that wealth."

"Yes, ma'am, something like that, I guess."

"I grew up in this house. My parents were middle-class people: my father worked for the CPR as a machinist; my mother worked part-time at a postal outlet just a few blocks from here. I was an only child. When I married Wendell, it was quite honestly a step up financially for the family, though that had nothing to do with my wanting to marry him. He was handsome and charming. In fact, and I know it sounds silly now, but I thought of him as my Prince Charming. I was twenty-nine, had not a lot of experience with men, and I found Wendell perfect.

"I was, of course, very foolish, but as I said, he was a charmer. One night we were hosting a small cocktail party, and partway through the evening Wendell sang 'Some Enchanted Evening.' He sang it to me. It was one of the most romantic moments I could imagine and it was *my* moment. You can see how a woman who had few previous boyfriends, and none that were serious, might have been quite taken with a man like Wendell."

"Yes, I can," Cobb said. I nodded my agreement.

Cynthia took a breath, exhaled and continued. "And he was, at first, generous, even offered to buy my parents a new house, but they were unpretentious people and loved their modest little home.

"When the marriage ended, there was a settlement, but it wasn't nearly as bountiful as one might have expected. And he quite simply fooled me — some might say swindled. I'm not sure if that was the case — I'm not very knowledgeable about things financial. He set me up as a partner in a company he was starting. He swore it was a way for me to secure my financial future. The company was some kind of marketing/sales thing. And for a few months it really did look like Wendell had actually wanted to set me up to be, if not wealthy, at least comfortable. Then the company suffered some terrible reverses — now, there's a phrase I'll never forget. It was the one Wendell used over and over. By the end of the year, I was looking for a job that my psychology degree might have prepared me for. As you might guess, there aren't a lot of those. I have been in retail, selling ladies' wear, for the past twenty-one years. Three years ago my father passed away and Mom decided she wanted to move into a home. She offered to sell me the house, virtually gave it to me. And other than a leaky roof, especially when the wind is blowing from the north during a hard rain, it really isn't too bad. There are lovely memories of my parents in all the nooks and crannies."

I looked at Cobb and saw intensity in his eyes that I'd seen before, usually just before someone was about to be the victim of his wrath. If Claiborne wasn't already dead, I wouldn't have been surprised if Cobb had gone straight to the man's office and beat the crap out of him. And to be honest, I'd have been there cheering him on.

"Cynthia," I said. "Did you shoot your husband?"

The smile that had begun to form when she spoke of her parents' memories in the house grew broader now.

"A thousand times," she said. "Oh, it wasn't always shooting; I was a regular Agatha Christie. Sometimes I poisoned him, the odd time I suffocated him with a pillow, and one of my favourites was my idea to somehow smuggle a cougar into his bedroom and he'd wake up, startle the cougar, and … oh my, that would have been unpleasant." She chuckled at that one.

"Remind me never to make you angry!" I laughed with her and picked up one of the cookies.

Then she turned serious. "But despite all that nastiness in my mind and even in my dreams, I'm saddened that he's gone. I feel bad for his family and I even feel bad for Wendell. For all his cruelty, I didn't want him dead, not really. And there *was* a cruelty to him — it's barbarous and brutish to be married and carry on like he did; I actually first suspected him of cheating during our honeymoon. That, gentlemen, is cruelty. And yet I wish he wasn't dead. And no, I didn't kill him or even hire someone to do it for me — which, by the way, was another of my rather childish fantasies."

"Do you have any idea who might have killed Wendell?" Cobb asked.

"I haven't been part of his life for a very long time."

"So, no thoughts at all?"

"Thoughts? Lots of them. I haven't thought of much else since I heard. But ideas as to who might have done this — I would think there might be a number of people who had reasons. Wendell was, as I said, a nasty man."

"Was there ever physical abuse?"

She shook her head emphatically. "Never. I will say that for him. He never laid a hand on me. Other abuse? I don't know if that's the term one uses for the knowledge that when he wasn't home he was very likely in someone else's bed. I can't tell you how hard that is on one's self-esteem. That's the cruelty I referred to. But there was no physical abuse."

"Have you seen Claiborne in recent years?"

"A couple of times. Briefly. He called me about a year ago and wanted to have coffee. I'm not sure why."

"And did you meet him?"

"I did. It was very short. We had coffee and chatted about … not much. It was like he was checking up on me, to see if I was still alive and what I was doing. He lost interest rather quickly and left. A couple of days later, I received a cheque in the mail for two hundred and fifty dollars."

"Two hundred and fifty dollars," Cobb repeated.

One of the articles I had read on Claiborne stated that his salary as CEO of his firm was nine and a half million dollars. That was in 2015. And he had offered Cynthia Claiborne two hundred and fifty dollars.

"Asshole," I said under my breath.

"Yes." Cynthia Claiborne smiled, then added, "I didn't cash it."

Cobb looked at me and raised his eyebrows, wondering if I had anything else.

"Cynthia, we understand you're writing a book about your life with Claiborne."

"A memoir, yes. I'm quite close to the end of the first draft."

"Put me down for a signed copy," I told her, and a happy smile spread over features that didn't look as if they'd had much to smile about in recent times.

Cobb said, "We really appreciate your time, Cynthia."

She got to her feet. "I wish you gentlemen well in your undertaking. I truly hope that young man did not shoot Wendell."

"Thank you, ma'am," Cobb said as we shook hands with her.

"And thank you for the cookie," I said. "It reminded me of my mom's peanut butter cookies."

"I bet you say that to all the girls." She chuckled softly and patted the hand she'd been shaking.

"No, ma'am," I told her. "I can honestly say you are the first person I have ever said that to."

When Cobb and I were a few blocks away from Cynthia Claiborne's house, he pulled the Jeep to the curb and fumbled for his phone. He dialed without talking to me, looking straight ahead, concentrating. "Cliffy? Cliffy St. Jerome? Mike Cobb here ... Yeah, I'm good. Listen, Cliffy, you still in the roofing business? ... Yeah, when you're not in prison. You're a funny guy. Anyway, I need a favour. There's a house needs re-shingling. The bill comes to me and the lady who owns the house doesn't need to know who's paying for the job. You tell her you're an instructor at SAIT — yeah, I know that's a bit of a stretch, Cliffy, but I'm sure you can pull it off. You're an instructor and you need a class project and noticed her roof needs re-shingling ... Yeah, Cliffy, I'm serious. And I need this to happen as soon as possible. You get a crew together and call me. I'll give you the address ... Yeah ... And about that crew, Cliffy, if anything goes missing from her house or if anything happens that I'm not happy with, like inferior materials, I think you know what will happen ... Good, that's what I like to hear. Call me, and like I said, I'd like this to happen soon ... Yeah, Cliffy. We'll talk. See ya." He hung up the phone.

"You're kidding, right? You're going to get some felon that you probably know because you put the guy behind bars and you're going to turn him and his pals loose on that sweet lady's house?"

"Uh-huh. Cliffy's been off the felon wagon for a couple of years. Does a few things — one of them's roofing. He's pretty good. And he also knows that if he or one of his crew should happen to screw up, I will pay him a visit. And he doesn't want that."

I looked at Cobb for a long minute. "It's a damn decent thing you're doing, it really is. But, you know, I read once that in the Old West the lawmen and the guys on the other side of the law were almost interchangeable. Rob a bank this week. Grab a badge and chase down some rustlers the next week. I'm wondering if anything's changed."

Cobb shrugged and started the Cherokee. "Let's go chase down some rustlers."

During the pleasant, one-coffee drive to Bragg Creek, Cobb and I, without coordinating a plan, decided to talk about anything that wasn't related to crime and bad guys. We chatted mostly sports and kids, and forty-five min-utes after leaving Cynthia Claiborne's place, we were parking in front of Trenton's house, a high-ceilinged log structure that would have been right at home on the front of a Christmas card. For the second time in a matter of a few hours, the house didn't fit the occupant, or at least my clearly incorrect vision of that occupant.

Trenton was standing at the front door before we were out of the Cherokee.

"Gentlemen," he said as we approached.

He stepped aside to let us enter. I looked around, tak-ing in an open-beamed interior with a west-facing wall that was almost all window, offering a virtually unobstructed view of the Rockies. Nice pad. *Expensive* pad.

He pointed to a spacious leather sofa. Next to it was a table where he had laid out some snacks: crackers, a cheese ball, some small cocktail sausages. Very nice, but I was thinking I preferred Cynthia's peanut butter cookies.

"Please make yourselves comfortable and please help yourselves to the crackers and cheese," he said. "If you let me, I can promise you a world-class Caesar. I pride myself on my bartending skills and hope you might allow me to show off just a little."

"You can show off for me," I told him. "Unsalted, please."

"And yourself?" Trenton turned to Cobb.

"A short one."

Trenton busied himself at the bar mixing the drinks. It wasn't often, in fact, next to never, that people we were about to question viewed the occasion as a social event and rolled out the hospitality for us. And it had just happened twice in the last couple of hours.

I sat, but Cobb was on the move, checking out the room, examining the paintings — a lot of them — that populated the walls. I thought the room would have been perfect for western lifestyle decor — art, memorabilia, tack, lanterns, animal heads, and the like. But there was none of that. Instead it felt like an upscale art salon. I'm not an authority, but I did recognize a couple of pieces by a Saskatchewan artist I had long admired — Allen Sapp. I stood up and crossed the room for a closer look. I was right. Trenton owned what look like two original Sapp paintings. I wondered how much money he was being paid by Susannah Hainsey.

Trenton delivered the Caesars. He hadn't lied. Mine was perfect. And it looked like Cobb felt the same way about his. We sat. I chose one of the leather chairs and Cobb opted for the sofa. We were far enough apart that while Trenton was responding to a question from one of us, the other could study his facial expressions and body language from another angle. I knew this was Cobb's preference when it was possible to arrange it.

Cobb set his drink down on a stylish end table and pulled out his notebook and pen. Trenton's eyes went to the notebook, then back to Cobb's face. He appeared relaxed.

"Do you mind telling us about your time working for Wendell Claiborne?"

"Not at all. I was in the landscaping business. Had a little company of my own, only one guy working for me. A lot of the work was lawn and yard maintenance, some smaller landscaping and planting jobs. Claiborne had hired me for lawn maintenance. We went there once a week for one season, and near the end of the season he asked me if I could build a retaining wall near the back of the property. I told him I could, gave him a quote, and got the job. I built the wall with old railway ties I was able to scavenge. I was there every day for a week, maybe a little longer."

"When was that?"

Trenton thought briefly before answering. "I would say maybe 1990 or '91." He thought some more. "It must have been '91. Anyway, the guy I had working for me was a young guy and he quit and went back to school. The next time I came to do the lawn care, Claiborne asked me if I'd like to work for him full-time. Of course, the yard and garden wasn't enough for full-time work, but he had other things he wanted me to do. A little chauffeur work, some minor home maintenance, and the odd time he'd ask me to help out serving the guests when he was entertaining. Eventually, the stuff in the house became the main part of the job, but I still looked after some of the other duties as needed."

"The stuff in the house," Cobb repeated.

Trenton nodded. "I was something of an in-the-house servant. Did all the cooking — something I'm quite good at — served the meals, continued to look after the guests when the Claibornes entertained ... sort of a combined butler, valet. It was a pretty good job and Claiborne paid me well."

I asked, "Did you live in the house?"

Trenton turned easily to me. "It was pretty much the same arrangement I have now with Ms. Hainsey ... Susannah." A small smile. "I had a bedroom upstairs that I used on evenings when I worked late or if there was any kind of function. The rest of the time I came here. I've lived here for thirty-one years."

"It's a very nice place," I told him.

Another smile. "I was fortunate to buy it when I did. I certainly couldn't afford it now. Anyway, I like it."

"The landscaping business — was that before or after you had a few ... brushes with the law?"

"Ah, you've done your homework. Good. It was after. And to head off your next question, I no longer have any ties or even contact with the people I associated with then. I've had a couple of parking tickets and one speeding violation in the last twelve, maybe fifteen years. As your research no doubt indicated."

I was trying to decide if I liked Trenton. There was a hint of something, almost a catch-me-if-you-can arrogance to the guy, but he wasn't unlikeable.

"Thank you," Cobb said. "We understand that you were somewhat enamoured of Susannah Hainsey when she lived with Claiborne."

His smile evaporated, but what replaced it wasn't nasty or unpleasant. "You *have* done your research." Trenton paused, then nodded slightly. "And, yes, I think that's a fair way of putting it. Susannah was a wonderful woman and always very kind to me. If she had not been with Claiborne, I would have loved to get to know her on another level. But she was, and I didn't."

"How did you feel about Claiborne being with someone you had feelings for?"

Another long pause. "It didn't bother me as much as you might think. They were a couple and I was their employee. I tried to perform my duties in as professional a manner as possible."

"Did she know how you felt about her?"

"If she did we never talked about it."

"Did he?"

"No, I'm quite certain of that."

"And how did you feel when he *broke things off with her* and she moved out?"

No pause or hesitation. "I was angry. I felt that he had treated her badly. She was a woman who deserved to be treated well by the man in her life. He was not good to her; he was disrespectful. I didn't like that."

"Disrespectful in what way?"

"It is one thing to be a philanderer. It is quite another to flaunt the other women in your very active life to the woman you're with. Even if she's not your wife."

"And when he ended it with her?"

"I wasn't working for him by that time. But when I learned he'd thrown her out, I didn't like it. I didn't like it at all."

"Thrown her out?"

"A figure of speech, Mr. Cobb. When he broke things off with her was I think how you put it; let's go with that. How are your drinks? Another?"

Cobb shook his head. "The drinks are fine. And no, just the one for me." They both looked in my direction. I shook my head.

"I want to go back to Claiborne's unfaithfulness."

"As I said, he didn't try very hard to hide it. I think his attitude was *this is who I am and what I'm about,*

*and if you don't like it, here's some money; I'll see you
around."*

"When Ms. Hainsey left … was asked to leave, did
you say anything to Claiborne?"

"No. Once he let me go I didn't see him but for one
or two times at functions. I never spoke to him about
Susannah or anything else."

"How long before the breakup with Ms. Hainsey
were you dismissed?"

"A few months."

"What did you do then?"

"Claiborne was generous, I'll say that. I had enough
money in my severance settlement that I could travel for
a time. I went to Europe, then Asia — saw some of the
world. When I got back here, I thought about getting back
into the landscaping thing, but I ran into Susannah —
Ms. Hainsey — and we had coffee a couple of times. She
offered me a job doing a lot of the same things I'd done
when she was with Claiborne."

"And you accepted?"

"To be totally honest, I was more interested in dating
her … maybe having a relationship. But she made it clear
that wasn't in the cards — she did it very nicely, but left
no doubt. Once I was okay with that, the job seemed like
a pretty good alternative."

"You weren't okay with it right away?"

Trenton looked away for a minute before answering.
"I cared very much for Susannah. So it took a while to get
to a different level with her."

"And that level's never changed?"

"You're wondering if the boss and the hired man get
it on from time to time?"

"Something like that."

He shook his head. "No. Never. And now that would feel pretty weird."

"Where were you the night Claiborne was killed?"

I recognized Cobb's strategy. Throw in the hard-hitting question when it's somewhat unexpected — see what reaction you get. We got almost none.

"I stayed over at my employer's home that night."

"Ms. Hainsey's?"

"Yes."

"Did you go out at all that night, before or after Ms. Hainsey went to bed?"

"No."

"Can she verify that?"

"I expect she can. Although I must say that after she's gone to bed, I should think I could leave without her knowing. I realize in telling you that, I may be hurting myself, but I'm sure you could figure that out anyway."

"What time does Ms. Hainsey generally retire for the night?"

"Not usually before midnight. I'd say most often between midnight and one."

"And the night Claiborne was killed?"

"As near as I can recall, she followed her established pattern. She likes to watch the news, generally runs a bath about midnight, and is in bed most nights around one or a little before."

Cobb leaned forward. "Do you have any idea who might have killed Wendell Claiborne?"

Trenton looked at Cobb for a while, chewing on his bottom lip. "I suppose one could look at exes — both those he married and those he didn't. And I understand there were husbands in some cases, so that might have created some motivation. But beyond that I really don't have any ideas that would be of much help."

"Business associates — you get to know any of them?"

"Not really. People came to the house, of course, for dinners and cocktail parties. But the hired help doesn't really mingle and chat with the A-listers at these things."

Cobb looked at me before saying, "We noted that Ms. Hainsey has a bit of a temper. Any chance, in your mind, that she might have lost it with Claiborne?"

"And shot him? Christ, no. Not a chance. Besides, as I've told you, I was there that night. I never went out and neither did she."

"Meaning that each of you can provide an alibi for the other."

"I suppose you could look at it that way."

"Just one last thing," I said. "In your time at odds with the legal authorities, did you ever have any dealings with the MFs?"

"The motorcycle gang?" He thought for a long moment. "No, not dealings. I might have met the leader, I can't think of his name right now, and, of course, he wasn't the leader back then, but I think I may have met him once or twice. Didn't like him."

"Rock Scubberd," I said.

"Yes, that's him." Trenton nodded. "You're not thinking there's an organized crime element to Claiborne's being shot?"

I shook my head. "No, just curious if you knew each other."

Trenton looked puzzled.

I glanced at Cobb, who looked equally puzzled. I shook my head to let him know I had nothing else. He stood up and I followed suit.

We shook hands at the door and Trenton looked as relaxed as he had when we'd arrived. He was either a guy with nothing to hide or a very good actor.

When we were on the road out of Bragg Creek, heading back toward Calgary, Cobb said, "You want to tell me what that was about?"

"The Scubberd thing? I'm not sure. It's like I told him, I was curious."

"You're getting better at the bad cop thing all the time."

"My true calling, I guess. To be honest, he doesn't look like the guy to me. You?"

"Hard to say. The alibi would be hard to break down in any case. I say we move him to the back burner for now. Maybe come back to him later if we need to."

"Why doesn't it feel like we're making progress?" I said.

"When have we ever worked a case together when it felt this early on like we were making progress?"

"Good point. So, what's next?"

"I'm going to see if I can get a look at the homicide report. Either the Lufts' lawyer or one of my few remaining contacts in the police service ought to be able to get me a look. How about I call you when I have it and we take a peek together. In the meantime —"

I held up a hand. "I know. The life and times of Wendell Claiborne."

"I think we might be narrowing our focus a little too much if we only look at wives and girlfriends. I wouldn't mind a list of the husbands of women Claiborne had relationships with."

"You might be right. I'm on it."

We were quiet the rest of the way back to his office, where I'd left my car. Cobb's hands-free announced an incoming call. It was his wife, Lindsay. I used sign language to let him know he could drop me in front of the building so he could get on his way home a little quicker.

I got out of the Cherokee and waved as he pulled away from the curb. I glanced at my watch, pulled out my phone, and called Jill.

She was out of breath when she came on the line. "Hi, babe. Love you."

"I love you, too. You been working out?"

"Uh-uh. Just ran up from downstairs. Laundry. Forgot the phone up here. How's your day so far?"

"Cobb and I are just back from Bragg Creek. We were talking to someone involved in the Danny Luft case."

"Okay; will you have to have it all solved by March fifteenth?"

"And that's because?"

"I won us a trip to Vegas."

"Are you kidding me?"

"Nope. Well, okay, I didn't win the whole trip. There was this promotion with one of the companies I do books for — you put your name in and there's a draw. The winner gets four days and three nights at New York–New York and a two-hundred-dollar voucher for meals and gambling and stuff. And guess who won it."

"Wow. I knew there was a reason I keep you around."

"And I just checked out flights and WestJet has a really good deal if we go around the fifteenth of March."

"I'm all in," I told her.

"Gotta run. I'm trying to get done before some cop show Kyla wants us to watch. Hope it's not too gory. That stuff bothers me."

"Me too. I'll call you tomorrow."

"Love you."

"Well, if I didn't love you before, I damn sure do now."

"There better be an LOL with that. Bye."

I hung up and headed for the car, a little more spring in my step and "Viva Las Vegas" playing in my head. With evening darkness settling around me, I beeped the doors unlocked and was reaching for the handle when I felt a weight hit me hard from behind and shove me up against the car. I tried to move but that wasn't happening. Whoever it was back there, he was strong.

"Wallet back left pants pocket," I rasped. "No need to get nasty here. I stay right where I am until you're gone."

"Shut up, Scribe. The package and instructions are on the front seat of the car. This is just a little reminder of what happens if you decide you're not a team player. You with me on this?"

He bent my arm in a direction arms don't normally go and I managed to say, "Yeah, I'm with you."

He gave a final shove and my face hit the top of the Accord. I stepped back and turned around. He was already walking away, gave a disdainful little wave without looking back at me.

Minnis.

EIGHT

I was sitting in the recliner in the living room of my apartment, looking out over the evening lights of Bridgeland and the rest of the city in the distance.

I was on my third Rolling Rock. My phone was sitting beside me but I hadn't called anyone. I wasn't about to. And I wouldn't be answering if someone called me.

I'd completed the assignment I'd been given by the MFs. I'd smuggled something into the U.S., met a guy at the Bin 119 restaurant in downtown Billings, Montana, a pretty cool restaurant if I'd been there with anybody but Truck McWhorters and if I'd been there for any other reason than to deliver a package that originated with the MFs.

When Minnis had finished roughing me up in the parking lot behind Cobb's office, I got into the Accord and sat for a long while before looking at the package and the note that sat on the passenger seat. I pulled out of the lot and drove to a well-lit area on 17th Avenue and parked again so I could read my instructions.

They were simple. Deliver the package to the Bin 119 within twenty-four hours. The note told me where to sit in the restaurant and to do that between 7:00 and 8:00

p.m. I would be contacted once I was in the restaurant. I would have to bring nothing back, which meant that the job was over once the package was in the hands of whoever I was meeting in Billings.

Of course, the tricky part would be getting through the border with the package — I suspected it was drugs, but I wasn't told and didn't care. I was damn sure it was something illegal or I wouldn't be the one making the delivery. The MFs must have assumed I had a valid passport and it crossed my mind to tell them I didn't, but I abandoned that idea. I wanted it over, still hopeful that this might be the one thing I'd have to do for them to even the score for the twenty-five-thousand-dollar gift to the Let the Sunshine Inn.

I didn't get much sleep that night. I worked out what time I'd have to leave to get to Billings in time to deliver whatever it was I was carrying, then sat up rehearsing what I'd say as I crossed the border. A guy crossing the border by himself — I didn't know if that raised alarm bells or not. If it did, and they searched the car, or worse, put the sniffer dogs to work, I was in big-time trouble. The MFs knew that and so did I.

Where you headed?
Billings.
Reason for going there?
Visiting a couple of friends down there.
How long you going down for?
Couple of days is all. Have to get back to work.
Carrying any firearms?
No, sir.
More than ten thousand dollars cash?
No, sir.

Taking anything with you that will remain in the United States?

No, sir.

I knew it was absolutely possible that the package contained money or a firearm or both, although I was still leaning toward drugs. Not that it mattered. If I was caught crossing the border with any of them in my possession, it would be a long time before I'd be sitting in my condo looking out over the lights of Calgary.

Whatever god smiles down on naive, stupid do-gooders was smiling down on me. The border crossing went without incident — there was a fairly long lineup, which I thought might be in my favour. I'd brought along a few props. A Tim Hortons coffee and sandwich, a couple of country CDs — George Strait and Alan Jackson. Michael Connelly's latest Bosch novel sat on the passenger side of the front seat. Just an ordinary guy heading down to the States for a couple of days of R and R.

I hoped the guard would just want to get through the line and would move me through without a whole lot of care and attention. And that's about what happened; in fact, it wasn't very different from my rehearsed version. When I got to Shelby, the first town of consequence on the I-15 heading south, I stopped at the Oasis Bar for a rye and diet. I was the only customer and I was pretty sure I was the first that day, as the place had only been open about twenty minutes when I dropped in. I ordered a second drink but changed my mind and didn't drink it, reasoning that a casual stop by a cop could become a big deal if I showed even minimal signs of having been drinking.

I travelled the speed limit all the way to Billings, not a hardship on the I-15 where the limit is eighty miles per hour. It got slower once I was off the interstate, but I complied there, too. I stopped only once more after the border — for fuel and a to-go sandwich in Great Falls — and nine and a half hours after I left my apartment, I was parked on 28th Street North in Billings, across from the Bin 119. It was just after seven.

I sat in the Accord for a while watching the place, but didn't see anyone go in or out that I figured might be the person I was meeting. The Bin 119 wasn't some seedy dump — in fact, it looked pretty upscale and hip, a place I'd have liked to take Jill sometime, under different circumstances.

At seven thirty I climbed out of the car, my package carefully in hand, and crossed the street. The restaurant was fairly busy, but there was no one in the corner of the place I'd been told to sit. I slid into a booth and set the package on the seat next to me.

I ordered a beer and had been studying the menu for maybe ten minutes when I felt the presence of someone at the front of the booth. I looked up at the gap-toothed grin of a short, wide expanse of a man wearing a slightly rumpled brown suit. He stuck out a beefy hand.

"Truck. Truck McWhorters. Great to see you again. It's been way too long."

I guessed the spiel was part of the subterfuge and thought I might as well play along.

"Sure, Truck. You're lookin' good as ever."

He slid into the seat next to me and glanced down, saw the package, looked back up at me, smiling.

"Trip down went well then?"

"Yeah, fine." I was already tired of the guy and hoped he wasn't planning to order food. Any friend or associate of the MFs was someone I didn't want in my life for any longer than necessary.

He looked around the place. "Nice spot. Never been in here before."

"You from around here?"

"Yeah. More or less."

I drank some beer as the server came over.

"Something for you, sir?"

Truck, if that was his real name, shook his head. "Thanks, but I have an appointment. Just wanted to say hello to an old friend. Spotted him through the window."

The server looked at me. "You, sir? Have you had a chance to look at the menu?"

"Maybe in a few minutes," I told her. "I think I'll just work on my beer for now."

She nodded and moved off and McWhorters stood up. The package was in his hand. I glanced around the restaurant to see if anyone appeared to be paying attention to us. It didn't look like it.

We shook hands again.

"Great to see you again, buddy."

"Likewise, Truck. Take care of yourself." What I wanted to say was *I hope you get run over by a truck, Truck, and the sooner the better*, but I didn't want to start a scene in the restaurant so I kept it courteous. Besides, it was possible that McWhorters was in the same spot I was — doing the MFs' bidding because he had no choice. Possible, but not likely. He looked like he was having too good a time for that to be the case.

"See you again … soon." He grinned at me.

I lowered my voice. "Don't bet on it."

"I think I will bet on that." The grin got bigger and he winked.

Then he was gone. I thought about following him, finding out a little more about him. For future reference. Decided against it. Drained the last of the beer instead.

I threw an American twenty-dollar bill on the table and left, relieved that I didn't see the server on the way out. As good as the Bin 119 looked, I suddenly wanted to be somewhere else. Somewhere that wasn't associated with my courier work for the MFs.

I stood on the sidewalk, watched twenty-somethings streaming into a nearby place that looked popular with that set. I crossed the street, climbed back into the Accord, and drove for a while. I was hungry and finally settled on Famous Dave's — another place that would have been great under different circumstances. I opted for ribs and a couple of rye and diets. I spent most of my time there thinking about how I'd deal with the MFs the next time they came calling. If Truck McWhorters's insinuation had any truth to it, I might be making the trip to the U.S. again, and soon. It was all unfolding exactly as Cobb had said it would, and that depressed me.

I didn't finish the ribs and passed on dessert. I nursed the second rye and diet for a while and listened to the music — it was country but it was okay. Mostly I stared at the wall decor and at a couple of families that looked pretty damn normal. Probably not one of them had cut any recent deals with motorcycle thugs.

I checked into a place called the Dude Rancher Inn. I thought about calling Jill and Cobb but called neither. I'd told them I had to run down to the States to meet with a distributor about my kids' books.

Jill had thought it odd that there had been so little lead time before the meeting, and I said the book people had given me a few options and this one seemed the best. More damn lies. Which was why I didn't call her. I was sick of listening to me.

The trip home was uneventful. I stopped at a mall in Great Falls and bought Kyla a Steph Curry jersey. I wasn't sure how many ten-year-old Canadian girls counted NBAers among their sports heroes, but I knew one who did.

I finished the third Rolling Rock and thought about a fourth — decided against it, twirled the empty third bottle in my hands while I thought. I tried to focus on the Danny Luft case and where we were in the investigation, which wasn't, if I were honest, all that far. In my mind I checked off everyone we'd talked to, replayed their interviews, and concluded there wasn't even a front-runner on the list.

The person I liked the least was Susannah Hainsey, but I realized that my personal likes and dislikes when it came to witnesses and even suspects were pretty much meaningless. I'd been putting together a list of potentially upset husbands, but of course, that list, in order to be comprehensive, would need to include husbands and boyfriends of women Claiborne didn't marry. And identifying the members of that potentially rather large group would be difficult, if not impossible, with the demise of the Philanderer-in-Residence.

I turned on the TV, turned it off before the end of the first commercial break, took a long, hot shower and tried to read, thinking it would likely be a long time before I fell asleep. I was wrong.

I was still asleep in the recliner when the banging on the door reminded me that way too many people seemed to be able to get by the intercom and security and into the building. I sat up and faced the door — not happy. "The guy who used to live here has moved. I'm a homeless person and I'm squatting here so bugger off."

"I've got coffee and I've got news, so get your ass out of bed."

Cobb. It was often Cobb who cut short my sleeping in. "*Good* news?"

"Feet on the floor, soldier, or I take my coffee out on the street and distribute it to *real* homeless people."

I stood up and started for the door, realized I was wearing shorts and a T-shirt, and detoured to the closet. I pulled on sweats and a Stampeders hoodie before padding across the hardwood to the door. Cobb was leaning against the door jamb looking dapper. I hated him.

I turned away and headed for the bathroom. After I'd washed my face and brushed my teeth, I decided to risk a return to the living room, the only room that constituted my bachelor *pad*. Cobb had set my coffee on the kitchen table. He had taken over my recliner and was sipping from his own cup as he stared out the same window I'd been staring out the night before. I moved to the hide-a-bed, pushed the covers out of the way, and sat. I took two sips of the coffee before I looked at him.

"Good morning," I said.

"You've looked better."

"Than what? You said you had news."

"Our client is out of jail."

"Bail?"

Cobb shook his head. "Uh-uh. Charges have been dropped. Or if they haven't been, they will be later today."

That jolted me awake. "I know you're not kidding so I won't say, *Are you kidding?* What the hell happened?"

"Someone confessed."

"Damn. Who?"

"Rachel Claiborne."

"Damn," I said again. "I didn't have her picked at all." I remembered that both Jill and Kyla had pegged her for the killer right off.

"Well, you might be right."

"What? You just said —"

"I just said she confessed."

I sat back, took a couple of sips of coffee. "You might have to help me with this."

"People confess to things they didn't do. Not often, but it happens. Usually it's because they're shielding the person who is guilty or, in this case, has been charged with the crime."

"You think she's taking the rap for Danny."

"I'm saying that's a possibility."

I thought about that. "So she's prepared to see her daughter deprived of both parents in order to save Danny's neck?"

Cobb looked at me. "I've been struggling with that, too. Maybe her moral compass is such that she couldn't stand to see the kid go down. Maybe she even blames herself for letting things get to this point."

"Or maybe she shot her husband."

Cobb nodded. "Or maybe that."

"So, what's next for us?"

"I submit a bill, Danny's father pays us, and we move on to our next case."

"Wow, not how I expected it to end."

"Or we could talk about your trip to Montana."

I tried to keep my face from showing alarm or surprise, but I wasn't sure I succeeded.

"Not much excitement there," I said. "Met with the book distributor, looks like we'll get more books into the U.S. … never a bad thing."

Cobb leaned back, sipped his coffee, and looked out the window again. "Sorry, but I think I'll have to call bullshit on that one, partner."

I knew that he had figured it out, or at least some of it. I decided not to make it worse by sticking to the lie. "What do you think you know?"

"I don't know a hell of a lot about publishing and selling books but I can't see some bookseller in Montana saying drop everything and get down here for a meeting so we can sell your books on this side of 49. On the other hand, I can see a criminal element saying we need you to get your ass to Montana for some activity that is written up in boldface print in the legal code."

"I didn't think I had a choice."

"I told you when they contacted you I wanted to know about it before you did anything."

"I know that, but to repeat —"

"Don't repeat it. I get that you felt trapped. How did it go down?"

I told him about Minnis knocking me around in the parking area behind his building and my trip to Billings and the delivery to Truck McWhorters.

He pulled out his notebook, jotted a couple of things down, then looked at me. "You okay?"

"Physically? Fit as a fiddle. Mentally, emotionally, not so hot. I hate lying to Jill and I'm not real proud of having to lie to you either."

"I know that. Did you get a look at what was in the package?"

I shook my head. "Didn't unwrap it. Didn't want to know."

"This won't be the last time. Hard to say how long it will be until you hear from them again. But you *will* hear from them again."

"Yeah, that's pretty much what McWhorters said."

"Okay, it looks like we've got some time off. Why don't you kick back with Jill and Kyla and forget about crime-fighting for a while."

"I can handle the kicking back part but it's a little tougher knowing that Scubberd and Minnis are out there and they aren't going away."

Cobb didn't answer. I could see he was deep in thought.

"I told you before, I don't want your help with this."

"Yeah." He nodded but was still absent. "Yeah, you did tell me that." At that he turned and looked at me for a long time. "Same rule though. I want you to tell me when you hear from them again."

When, not *if*.

"I don't know."

"I do. It's not optional, Adam. You call me."

"All right."

"Good. Time to change the subject," he said. "I talked to Yvette Landry. She's the lead investigator on the Kennedy killing. I met with her a while back and told

145

her everything we had learned and I threw in some of Kennedy's thoughts."

I knew Landry from a previous case Cobb and I had worked. She was a smart, relentless cop with a solid track record.

"Like how he thought there might be a dirty cop involved?" I said.

"I didn't use that term, but I did say that Kennedy had pointed out a few irregularities in the original investigation."

"And?"

"And she said she'd do some checking. She called me yesterday. She'd like to meet with us."

"Interesting."

"So, it's Friday. Take the weekend to be with your ladies. Maybe watch *Frozen*. I'll set up something with Landry for next week."

"Chisholm still her partner?"

"Uh-huh."

Andrew Chisholm wasn't as good as Landry, although he was still a pretty good investigator. He didn't like Cobb or me and didn't try very hard to mask his feelings.

I stood up. "Okay, *Frozen* it is. Which, by the way, I've seen at least four times and would happily watch again rather than the chick flick fare I'm often subjected to."

"Yeah, I'm feeling really bad for you."

I laughed at that and it felt good to laugh, for probably the first time since my encounters with Minnis.

It was neither *Frozen* nor a chick flick. Instead we watched *South Pacific* and ate popcorn. I'm a sucker for musicals, so it was a good night — and it actually got my mind off the MFs. I'd forgotten that "Some Enchanted Evening" was one of the hit songs. As it was being performed, I thought back to Cynthia telling us about Claiborne singing it to her. I was having trouble seeing Claiborne as Emile de Becque.

After the movie, Kyla kissed her mom, hugged me, and headed off to bed with a book, leaving Jill and me to finish off the bottle of Ripasso we'd opened with dinner. I leaned back on the couch and she curled into my chest and shoulder.

"So, tell me about Billings, Montana," she said.

I was glad we weren't looking at each other. "It was okay," I said. "I didn't get to see much of it, but what I saw I thought was pretty cool. I kept seeing places I thought would be fun to go to with you." That part was true.

"And your meeting? That go okay?"

I couldn't tell from her inflection if there was any doubt on her part. I hoped not.

"It was short but I think it went well. I guess I'll have to wait to see if anything comes out of it." *Stay as close to the truth as you can — makes lying easier.* I'd read that somewhere and hated that I was following that advice.

We sipped wine, cuddled, occasionally kissed, but neither of us said much. We didn't have to. The absolute joy of being close to each other didn't require conversation or even sound beyond the music Jill had chosen — k.d. lang's *Hymns of the 49th Parallel*, an album that had long been one of my favourites.

It was close to perfect. Close enough to make me almost forget the events of the last couple of days.

Almost.

Kyla came back out of her bedroom to give us a second set of hugs and whispered to me that she was reading a book about police work. We fist-bumped and she grinned and headed off to bed.

Jill smiled at me. "You two are crazy about each other. That's so cool."

"I hope she *is* crazy about me because I'm nuts about that kid."

"I can guarantee it." Jill was still smiling. "I think maybe we should follow her example, don't you?" Her head was tilted toward the bedroom.

"Seems like quite a good plan."

"I'm going to need more than a fist bump though." She took my hand and led me down the hall as k.d. performed Jane Siberry's "Love Is Everything."

NINE

Detective Yvette Landry was sipping green tea and nib-bling at some wafer thing. Chisholm, her sidekick, was concentrating on looking tough. We were sitting in the Higher Ground in Kensington, and Cobb and I were on the opposite side of the table working on coffee, no wafers.

There hadn't been much small talk — none from Chisholm. Apparently, discussing the weather doesn't fit the tough-guy mould Chisholm dedicated every waking moment to.

Landry was an attractive woman. She was wearing a tailored dark-blue suit; her hair was cut short, and she had just enough makeup to give a little colour to an already pleasant face. Chisholm was wearing a black leather jacket and a close-fitting toque. Looked like a bass player in a grunge band, but less friendly.

"We've looked into the points Marlon Kennedy, a.k.a. Kendall Mark, raised in relation to the murder of Faith Unruh," Landry said. "I'm not sure we've got much to offer you, but I wanted to follow up, let you know we hadn't blown you off."

"I didn't think you'd blown us off, Detective," Cobb said. "But we appreciate the update."

Landry opened a folder, took out a single piece of paper and retrieved a set of reading glasses from her purse. "As you know, Kennedy raised four points."

Cobb nodded. I drank some coffee.

"The first had to do with the lack of forensic evidence. No prints. No DNA match. He's right about that, and while it might be considered somewhat unusual or even bad luck, it's hardly evidence of any funny business at the police level. In fact, it doesn't really point to shoddy investigation." She looked at Cobb. "You were a cop, and you know as well as I do that the worst thing that's happened to murder investigations is CSI television. Every week a crime, no matter how complex, is solved in an hour. And almost always there's wonderful forensic evidence that just needs to be uncovered and correctly interpreted and bingo, the good guys are making an arrest."

Cobb nodded again. "And I know the real world isn't like that."

"Exactly. So while Kennedy was right on that point, it doesn't really smell bad."

"Did your research indicate whether there was no DNA evidence or that what there was had been contaminated by someone at the scene?"

"The report I read didn't point to one or the other. Which takes us to Kennedy's second point."

Cobb held up a hand. "Excuse me, Detective, but that's a rather quick move off of point number one. If there was DNA evidence and it was contaminated before or during the investigation, it seems to me that would require some scrutiny itself."

Landry nodded but it looked like an impatient gesture to me. "That's true but there is no indication that contamination of evidence took place. As I said, there was no discussion of DNA evidence beyond a mention that investigators were unable to rely on that data during their investigation. And now, back to point number two, if I may."

Definite impatience. I glanced at Cobb. He clearly wanted to pursue the DNA question further but realized it was pointless.

Landry went on. "One piece of Faith's clothing was recovered at the scene but later disappeared from the evidence room. Again Kennedy's right. As you know, Faith's body was naked but there was a pair of blue panties found nearby. They were suspected to be hers but sometime between the initial crime scene investigation when the panties were bagged and tagged and the sending of the evidence to the lab for testing, they disappeared."

She stopped and looked at Chisholm, who leaned forward, his voice flat and hard as he spoke. "I went back and talked to everyone who's still around who had anything to do with the case. I went through the homicide file. I talked to the lab people who were working for us back then — the senior person, a guy named Trudell, who's retired now, remembers the case, never saw the panties. I talked to a tech who worked in the lab at the time." He pulled out a notebook, flipped it open, found the page he wanted. "Cory Payne, she was Cory Selmar back then. She remembered that the missing panties came up after the fact — some of the senior officers were extremely pissed off — but nobody ever found them or found out what happened to them. My guess is it was carelessness, not malfeasance. Conspiracy theories are fun but they don't usually amount to much."

"I don't think Kennedy was interested in having fun," Cobb said. "And I'm not interested in your guesses. Truth is you don't know."

Chisholm's face reddened, bringing it much closer to the colour of his hair. I could see that he wanted to come back at Cobb but Landry cut that off. "Kennedy's third point had to do with there being no tip line. That's an administrative decision, and while it might be argued that the decision was short-sighted, again it hardly smacks of the corruption or dirty cop activity that Kennedy suggested might be the case."

"Hard to rule out completely though," Cobb said.

"Not for me," Landry answered, her eyes narrowing.

"Administrative decision," Cobb repeated. "Again, it would be interesting to know if Hansel and Gretel wanted one and it was overruled, or if it just didn't come up."

"Perhaps," Landry conceded without enthusiasm. "And that brings us to Hansel and his partner being removed from the case after seventeen days, then put back on it three weeks later."

"Let me guess," Cobb interrupted. "Unusual, but not criminal in any way."

A small smile appeared at the corners of Landry's mouth. It had nothing to do with humour. "Took the words right out of my mouth."

"Who were the other detectives who replaced Hansel and Gaspari?" I asked. I knew Gretel's real name and decided to veer away from the oft-repeated joke.

Landry glanced at the sheet of paper. "Senior guys. Joe Kinley and Jarvis Maughan."

"You follow up with them?"

"Not doable. Both deceased. And before you start wondering, both natural causes. Maughan, heart attack,

2008, just a few months after his wife died; cancer took out Kinley in 2011."

"Anybody ever ask them why they didn't have a report in the homicide file? They were on the case for three weeks and generated no paper. Or if they did, it, like the panties and possibly the DNA evidence, went missing. That make sense to you?" Cobb directed his question to Landry. I don't think he liked Chisholm any more than I did.

"No."

Chisholm drummed his fingers on the table. A little louder than necessary. "Stuff happens. You know that, Cobb. A sheet of paper gets misfiled. A piece of evidence goes missing. People make mistakes. They're human. It doesn't mean there's a dirty cop out there trying to undermine an investigation."

"No, but it doesn't mean there isn't."

Landry put her paper back in the folder and stood up. "We did what we came here to do, which was to share with you what we learned. We've got to get back to work on our own investigation. You're welcome."

Cobb showed them the palms of his hands.

"Just a second. You're right. I've been unappreciative —"

"You've been *rude*," Landry interrupted.

"Guilty as charged. And I shouldn't have been. I apologize if I've offended you. I do appreciate your keeping us in the loop. A little girl's murder has gone unsolved for a very long time. I guess I'm frustrated about that."

Landry's face relaxed. "No harm, no foul. And we're all frustrated, believe me."

Cobb stood up and shook hands with her, then with Chisholm. "Thanks. And good luck."

I shook hands with Landry but Chisholm was already on his way to the door. I guessed the snub was deliberate, and I was okay with it. When they'd gone, Cobb and I sat down again.

"What do you think?" I asked him.

"Kennedy was a loose wheel, there's no doubt about that. But he cared about this case as much as I've ever seen a cop care about any case. And he identified a couple of things that need to be looked at. A critical piece of evidence disappeared. And Kinley and Maughan wrote reports. Those aren't optional. Those reports have disappeared. Not one word of what they found, who they talked to — none of it is in the homicide file. That's two glaring mistakes. The DNA may or may not be another. Either this was an incredibly sloppy investigation or there was something else going on."

"If those things were deliberate, it would have to be someone close to the investigation, am I right about that?"

"Absolutely."

"Then the question becomes why. You think it's possible a cop murdered Faith Unruh?"

Cobb shrugged. "Or is protecting the person who did. Or had a grudge against the investigators and wanted them to look bad."

"Does that happen?"

"The police service is no different from any other business or organization. There's politics, inter-office jealousy, rivalries, even hatred."

We sat in silence for a while. "I just thought of something. We think Faith was lured by someone into that backyard. A kid could maybe be persuaded by a police officer — the uniform and everything?"

Cobb was shaking his head. "Non-starter. Detectives wouldn't have been in uniform."

"Yeah, you're right."

Neither of us spoke much after that. I got us refills, and when I came back, said, "What's next?"

"I'm not sure. I —" His phone rang. He answered, listened for a while, then spoke. "Sure, Danny, we can meet you. What's it about? … Okay, how about after school tomorrow? You want to get together somewhere near the school so you don't have to … You sure? Okay, my office, four thirty. Yeah, see you then."

He rang off.

"Danny Luft?"

"Yeah. Wants to meet. Wouldn't say why."

"If the kid has decided to confess, I'm getting into another line of work."

Cobb shook his head. "I'm not sure what's on his mind, but he sounded serious. You okay with tomorrow?"

"Yeah, no problem."

"And I need to think about where we go with Kennedy."

"There's part of me that says his death can't be related to Faith Unruh, and there's another part of me that says it's ridiculous to think otherwise."

"Yeah, I've got some of that going on, too. Look, I've got to run. Tomorrow, my office, four thirty."

"Got it."

He stood up. "It's your turn to buy."

Trying to lighten the mood.

"Got that, too."

I stayed a while and decided to step back in time — read the newspaper, in this case the *Globe and Mail*. One of the things that I'd found saddest about the continuing demise of newspapers was that one of my most pleasurable pastimes — drinking coffee and reading actual newsprint pages spread out over a table — might disappear altogether. Reading the *Globe* or the *New York Times* or the *Washington Post* on an iPhone or computer just wasn't the same.

I enjoyed a quiet hour catching up on the fortunes of the Flames, perusing the much-depleted entertainment section, and shaking my head at the most recent synapse failures of Donald Trump.

Finally, I set the paper to one side, took out my notebook, and for ninety minutes filled its pages with notes on three topics, hoping that forcing myself to analyze the three might lead to some useful ideas on at least one of the topics.

It did not.

I came no closer to some magical breakthrough on the Danny Luft case, the Unruh-Kennedy murders, or the MFs matter. That's how I titled that section — "The MFs Matter." Of course, it felt like a lot more than a *matter*.

The one conclusion I came to, and I had to admit it was based almost solely on gut feeling, was that there *was* a connection between the Faith Unruh and Marlon Kennedy murders. This wasn't new. I had come to that conclusion and then abandoned it several times already. Two events, twenty-six years apart, and yet it seemed inconceivable to me that Kennedy's brutal killing had nothing at all to do with the case that had been his obsession for a quarter century.

And that was my afternoon. Not a lot to show for the three hours or so that I'd been in the Higher Ground. In a way, working with Cobb when he felt he needed me was not unlike my years as a journalist, especially the time I'd spent and continued to spend as a freelancer. People struggle with the freelance concept just as they do with the idea of people working remotely from their homes, often thinking that the contract person working at home or out of a remote office is not actually working, or at least not working *much*. My own feeling is that the person working at home often works longer hours. It's just too easy to stay at the computer long after the normal working day is over, to take that late-night phone call, to tackle one more piece of paperwork.

I chuckled as I thought back to the time when there had been a knock on my apartment door, and when I opened it an elderly neighbour was standing there holding a copy of that day's *Calgary Herald*.

"Hi, Adam," he'd said, greeting me with a pleasant smile. "The kid who delivers the paper accidentally left two at my place today. And I said to myself, now who would have time to read the paper? And right away I thought of you." The implication being, of course, that I had nothing else to do.

I'd accepted the paper, thanked him, and closed the door — a bit quickly perhaps, but I remember being a little afraid he might suggest we sit around and read it together.

Once outside, I walked around Kensington for a while, enjoying the arrival of evening in one of my favourite neighbourhoods. Remembering the times Donna and I had taken walks very much like this one. I finally decided to drive by the house where Faith Unruh's body had been found. I hadn't done that since Kennedy's murder. Prior to that I had been something of a regular visitor to the back alley that ran past the garage beside which her body had been found, covered by a sheet of plywood. It had been those drive-bys and walk-pasts that had put Kennedy, courtesy of his surveillance system, on my tail.

Fifteen minutes later I was driving slowly down the alley. I had been there enough times that the landmarks were familiar to me — the huge pine tree in the corner of one backyard, the '53 Ford on blocks in another. I parked behind the house where the Faith Unruh murder had taken place, just yards from where Kennedy had met his violent end. I dug out the flashlight that I now kept close by at all times, and eased myself out of the car.

I directed the light to the door of the garage and stepped to the back fence to look over it at the place Faith's body was discovered. The feeling of intense sadness that swept over me every time I came to this place was there again. Not anger, not really — just immense, terrible regret that a little girl never got the chance to live out the rest of her childhood, to grow into adulthood, maybe have children of her own. All that had ended in this place, and as had happened more than once when I came here, I wasn't able to fight back the tears.

I stepped back from the fence and cast the light around the alley, remembering when I'd sat in for Kennedy while he'd been with his dying wife. I'd run the surveillance equipment for him for ten days and nights.

And once, only once, had I seen anything even remotely suspicious. A movement, a shadow really, fleeting … there and then gone. I had left his house and come to the alley to see if there was anything here. I'd found nothing.

It was later that Kennedy found the marks:

$$\cancel{||||} \ \cancel{||||} \ |$$

All had been carved into the bottom board of the wood frame that housed two garbage bins. Eleven marks in all. Then, in an email I didn't see until after he was dead, Kennedy had let me know that a twelfth mark had appeared.

I walked to the garbage bins, crouched down to look. I'd never seen the twelfth scratch-mark and wanted to see it now. I let the light find the marks, reached out to run my hand over the roughly carved lines. I jerked my hand back and for a few seconds found it hard to breathe. I bent closer to make sure I wasn't wrong.

I wasn't. There were now thirteen marks. Five, then another five, and three single marks. Thirteen.

Since I'd worked with Cobb, I had been in a few dangerous, pretty damn scary situations. But I don't think I'd ever felt my blood run as cold, my heart beat harder, or my hands actually shake the way they were now as I tried to steady the flashlight.

I stood up and backed away from the bins.

Suddenly, I whirled around. I hadn't heard anything or even felt anything. And nothing and no one was there. But I was spooked and I knew it. I climbed back into the Accord and locked the doors, the memory of Kennedy's encounter with someone right here sending fresh shivers up and down my back. I drove out of the alley, fighting back the temptation to floor it and get out of there as fast as I could.

I'm not sure why, but I employed some of the evasive tactics Cobb had taught me for when I suspected I was being followed. After my heart rate and breathing returned to near normal and nothing even remotely suspicious happened to rekindle my fear, I drove home. Once inside, I took a long shower, slid Lindi Oretga's *Faded Gloryville* into the CD player and sat with a rye and diet, and Guy Vanderhaeghe's *The Englishman's Boy.* But I didn't do much reading.

Cobb was at his desk. He hadn't spoken since I'd told him about the thirteenth mark. His hands were locked behind his head and he was staring at the ceiling. Finally, he lowered his gaze and met my eyes. "What do *you* think it means?"

I shook my head. "Kennedy had a theory that it was the guy who murdered Faith Unruh — that he was playing us, that he'd made a game of coming in and out of the alley, making a new mark every time. When there were eleven marks, Kennedy went back through the tapes and his notes and said he'd seen something, a shadow or something, nine times, and I'd seen it once, that made ten. He figured the other mark was for the time when Faith Unruh's killer had committed the murder."

"You never told me about seeing anything while you were filling in for him on the surveillance."

"I didn't think it was any big deal."

"Kennedy did."

"Yeah."

"There have been a few things you haven't told me about."

"Yeah, I know. I'm sorry." I meant it.

Cobb sat forward and rubbed his chin. Picked up a pen and jotted a couple of notes on his notepad, then leaned back and looked at me again.

"I asked you before what you think the marks mean. You told me about Kennedy's theory. I want to know what you think."

I took a breath and let it out before speaking. "I probably agree with him," I said. "It's hard to believe that there's no connection. A little girl dies in that yard next to the garage. Then weird stuff happens — shadows, marks. And then the guy who has been obsessed with finding her killer is also killed just yards from where the first murder took place. I have trouble seeing them as totally independent of one another."

Cobb nodded slowly. "I get that. The problem I have is the same one I've had all along — the time lapse. Faith Unruh was murdered in 1991. For twenty-four years there isn't a whisper. Then suddenly shit starts to happen. You and Kennedy see shadows in the alley behind the garage. Marks that seem to be keeping track of something, some number, appear. And then Kennedy is killed. But it's the twenty-four years of nothing I'm struggling with."

I stood up and crossed to the coffee maker, tossed in a pod, and started it pouring into the mug Kyla had bought for me — *Careful or you'll end up in my novel.* I hadn't written a novel; the kids' first chapbooks didn't qualify, but Kyla believed that one day there'd be a Cullen bestseller out there. Thus the mug. "I can't argue that. It's just bloody weird and I'm not saying I believe all of what I just said. It's a theory, that's all. You want one?" I tilted my head in the direction of the machine.

"No, thanks. Okay, here's what I think we should do. We make a list of everyone we can think of who has any connection to the case, however remote. And that includes the people who live there now. We start checking them out — you take care of that part. I'll tackle the homicide file again."

"By the way, how is it you're able to see homicide files? It's not like they're available to just anyone who'd like to peruse them." It was a question I had long wondered about. The homicide files, known as *murder books* in other jurisdictions, were for police eyes only. Yet Cobb had, from time to time, been able to access different files on cases we'd worked.

"Again, the advantage of having once been a cop and having friends in the service who are willing to risk their asses and let me take a peek."

"Handy."

He smiled. "Handy indeed. And speaking of former friends and colleagues, I'm thinking there has to be someone, either working or retired, who I can talk to, someone who remembers the case and can maybe tell us something about the investigation — maybe shed some light on the stuff Kennedy told us about."

"So you're not buying Landry and Chisholm's explanation?"

Cobb shrugged. "Maybe. Maybe not. Maybe it really was just shoddy work by either or both pairs of investigators. Which keeps bringing us back to the question I'd really like an answer to. Why were Hansel and Gretel pulled off the investigation and then put back on it?"

"That would be interesting to know. Who makes a decision like that?"

"I'm not sure. I don't remember it ever happening during my time there. I guess the captain or maybe somebody higher up, maybe even the chief. Hard to say. I'll do some sniffing around."

"I'll get to work on making the list and doing some checking. See if I turn up anything."

"While I'm at police headquarters, I'm going to see about getting the tapes. I know it will be dreary, but it might be a good idea to take a look. See if Kennedy missed something."

"How far back do we go?"

"About the time of the first shadow thing he saw."

"Yeah, I think that was about a year or more. Even with the most recent one missing, that's a lot of tape watching."

"I guess we have to decide if we're all in on this thing."

It didn't take long for me to make that decision. "I'm all in."

He got up. "Maybe I'll have that coffee after all."

I started a coffee for him. It always felt better when we had a plan, however nebulous. The action of investigating, of actually doing something and being fully committed to the investigation, gave me a feeling of purpose and even hope.

"What time are we meeting Danny?" I asked.

"About four thirty."

I handed him his coffee and looked at my watch. It was just after three. "I've got my gym stuff in the car and I haven't done much running lately. How about I go for a jog and I'll be back here in time to sit in?"

"Are you going to smell up the office?"

"More than likely," I said.

"Perfect."

Danny Luft's hair was a little longer and he seemed to have lost some weight, but he offered a smile as I greeted him at the door to Cobb's office. I steered him toward the same chair he had sat in the first time we'd met.

Cobb leaned across the desk and shook his hand. "Good to meet you at last, Danny."

"You too, sir, and thanks for all you and Mr. Cullen have done for me."

Cobb waved that off.

"Soft drink?" I asked him. "All we've got is Coke. Same as last time. Guess we need to expand our soft drink selection."

"A Coke would be great. Thanks."

I looked at Cobb and he nodded yes to another cup, so I made my way to the coffee machine and little fridge that stood in one corner of the office.

Behind me I heard Cobb say, "School going okay, Danny?"

"Yeah, I think so. I did pretty good on a math test yesterday, so that's all right."

"And how about at home? You and your dad getting along since all the … excitement?"

"Actually, things are quite a bit better. We even sat down and talked about drugs, and he never yelled once. I told him I wasn't interested in drugs beyond weed and he wasn't happy about the weed part but he was trying really hard not to get mad, I could see that."

I distributed the drinks.

"Thanks." Danny smiled at me.

"You're welcome."

Cobb waited until Danny had taken a long pull of the Coke and set the can on the edge of the desk. "So, what is it you wanted to see us about, Danny?"

"I wanted to talk to you about Mrs. Claiborne."

"Sure, what's on your mind?"

"She didn't shoot Mr. Claiborne."

Cobb glanced at me but kept his face expressionless as he looked back at Danny. "How do you know that, son?"

"She just said that — confessed, I mean — because she was worried that I'd go to jail for a long time. But Mrs. Claiborne couldn't kill anybody. She's a tough lady in some ways, but that's just not something she'd do."

Cobb took his time responding. "Okay, Danny, let's say you're right and it wasn't Mrs. Claiborne. You have any idea who *did* shoot Wendell Claiborne?"

Danny shook his head. "No, I don't, but I know it wasn't her."

He reached for the Coke but pulled his hand back. *Was it shaking?*

"Why did you lie to us earlier, Danny?" Cobb's voice wasn't mean or even argumentative, but it was firm. "Actually, a few times."

Danny moved around in the chair for a few seconds before answering. "I promised Adam — Mr. Cullen — that I wouldn't see Mr. Claiborne. And I figured you'd be mad when I broke that promise." He looked at me.

"Tell us what happened, Danny. How did your fingerprints get on the gun?"

Danny squirmed a little, but then settled and looked straight at Cobb. "I don't see why we have to talk about that now."

"We need the whole story if you want us to try to help Mrs. Claiborne."

Danny hesitated.

"How'd your prints get on the gun, Danny?" Cobb said again.

"I rode over to the house that night to see if I could see Glenna."

"What night was that?"

"The night Mr. Claiborne was killed." He looked over at me. "I know you told me not to, but I wanted to see her. Or at least try. I figured I could do it without seeing or talking to her dad, so I wasn't really going back on what I told you. But then as I was riding home I took sort of a shortcut and this car pulled up beside me and it was him. I didn't think I could just ride off. So I stopped … and he stopped."

Danny took a drink of the pop. I noticed his hand wasn't shaking anymore. Confession is good for the soul. "He got out of his car and he said something like 'We're still on for Saturday, right, Danny?' And then he pulled out this gun. I thought for a minute he was going to shoot me so I said, 'Oh yeah, we're still on,' and he said, 'Good, here, see what this feels like, make sure it feels okay.' And he held it out to me and I guess I was stupid, but I was also kind of scared, so I took it and held it for a couple of seconds."

"The shortcut you took, was that before or after you stopped at the 7-Eleven?"

"How did you know about that?"

"How about I ask the questions and you answer them. It works better that way."

I was a little surprised at Cobb's tone, but Danny just shrugged.

"After." He smiled then. "It's sort of funny. I was eating a bag of Cheezies when Mr. Claiborne stopped me, and when he handed me the revolver, I was worried I'd get Cheezie bits on it."

"Then what?"

"I gave it back to him and said it felt okay to me and he said that was good and that he'd be in touch on Saturday morning so we could plan things out. I might not have all of his words exactly right, but I think I'm pretty close."

Cobb leaned back and I saw his body relax a little. "You're doing fine, Danny. What happened then?"

"He drove off and I rode the rest of the way home."

"And that was it until the cops came to your house?"

Hesitation, then a slow shake of the head. "Not … exactly."

"What does that mean, Danny?"

"He phoned me."

I said, "Yeah, you told me about that. He phoned you and then texted. Then you tried to get back to him but weren't able to connect. That's what you told me. But is that exactly how it happened?"

"Yeah, but that was the first time."

"Whoa," I said. "You told me he phoned you and texted you around nine. Then you tried to call him back, but you didn't get him. That's how you told me it happened. Have I got that right, Danny?"

"Yeah, but that was before I went to the house. Then after I saw him when I was coming back home on my bike, he phoned me again."

Now I was angry. There was so much Danny had either lied about or left out, and I was getting really tired of it. I was about to say something, I'm not sure exactly what, but Cobb jumped in.

"What time was that?"

"I don't know. Maybe a half-hour after I got home."

"Okay, what time was *that*?"

"I think I got home around ten thirty, maybe a little later."

Cobb studied the kid for what felt like a long time. Danny had begun to move around in the chair, taking a drink of the Coke, then another.

"All right, Danny. Give it to me again," Cobb said.

"Give what to you again?"

"That night."

"Seriously?"

"Yeah, Danny. Real seriously. From when you got the first call. You see, Danny, you've changed your story a few times and you've left things out. One of the biggest problems lawyers and private detectives have is being able to do a good job when the client isn't truthful. So we need to hear it again, all of it, from the first phone call."

Danny looked contrite. I didn't think he was a flat-out liar. I thought he'd made some bad decisions about what to tell us and what not to tell us, and it was frustrating, but I still liked the kid. And I was pretty sure Cobb did, too, but both of us knew if we didn't start getting the truth, and all of it, pretty soon, we were going to have a hell of a time if the cops renewed their interest in him. And despite Mrs. Claiborne's confession, I thought that might still be a possibility.

"Okay, so Mr. Claiborne called me and texted me around nine o'clock."

"When he called, did he leave a message?"

"Yeah, just to call him back."

"What about the text, what did it say?"

"Same thing. He needed to talk to me, and I should get back to him right away. That he'd hate to have to talk to my dad about my little problem."

"Okay, go on."

Danny looked from Cobb to me, then back to Cobb.

"I knew I wasn't supposed to contact him, so I didn't. Not right away."

"But after a while …"

"I was afraid that he'd call my dad and tell him about the weed, so that's when I called him back, maybe around ten o'clock."

"Right, then what happened?"

"I didn't get him. That's when I decided to ride over there and maybe see Glenna if she was around. But I didn't see her, so I texted her and waited a few minutes, but she didn't answer, so I started for home. That's when he came along in the car and handed me the gun. All of that is exactly like I told you the first time."

Cobb said, "How long's the bike ride from your house to Glenna's?"

Danny raised his eyebrows like the question was foolish.

"Come on, I'll bet you've ridden over there a few times at least."

Slow nod. "Yeah."

"So, how long does it take?"

"You're starting to sound like those cops that came to the house to arrest me."

"How long?"

"Fifteen, twenty minutes. Not longer than that."

"Does it take longer at night? You go slower?"

"Not really, no. It's about the same."

"Did you leave your house right after you tried calling him back?"

"Yeah, pretty much. I just wanted to see Glenna. I guess I wanted to feel better, because I was feeling pretty crappy with all the stuff that was happening."

"Okay, so you left your house at about ten o'clock, maybe a little later. That puts you at Glenna's house a little before ten thirty."

"Yeah, I think so. That sounds about right."

"I don't want to *sound* right, Danny; I want it to *be* right."

"Yeah, well, that would *be* right." He spent a long time on the word *be*. I could tell he was getting pissed off.

"And then what, Danny?" I said gently. Good cop — a reversal of roles.

"I sat on my bike watching the house in case Glenna looked out a window or came outside for anything. But she didn't."

Cobb jumped back in. "And you didn't go up to the house."

"I didn't even go in the yard … I just stayed on my bike outside the fence."

"How long did you sit there?"

"I don't know, not that long. I thought it was kind of stupid, me sitting there looking at her house. Then, after a few minutes when she didn't text me back, I didn't want her to see me. I was afraid she'd think I was a total loser."

"So you left."

"Yeah, like I said, I stopped at the store to get the Cheezies, then a couple of blocks later Claiborne came along and showed me the gun and handed it to me and I took it. I gave it back to him, and he left, and I went straight home. That's the truth."

"I know it is, Danny," Cobb said.

"What do you mean?"

"And then Claiborne phoned you a little while after you got home."

"Yes, that's right." *Yes*, not *yeah*. I wasn't sure if that meant anything. Maybe the kid was just glad to be getting near the end of the story.

"Now, Danny, I want you to give me what he said, as close as you can remember it. Don't leave anything out."

Danny drank some Coke. "Okay, well, he started out all friendly. *Hey, Danny, really great to run into you, you get home all right? Didn't spill your Cheezies, did you?* Like he was trying to joke around."

"Right. Go on."

"Then he went totally serious. Like freaky serious. And he went through it all again. How he'd tell my old man about my *drug habit* — that's what he said, drug habit. Which is bullshit; it was just a little weed."

"Did you tell him it was bullshit?"

"No, I just listened. Then he said, 'Don't forget our deal, the bitch goes away and you get ten thousand dollars. You shoot one bitch and you wake up Sunday morning ten grand richer.' I think that's pretty close. I know he said bitch twice. I thought that was kind of ... I don't know ... *harsh*."

"Are you sure he said the word *shoot*?"

"Yeah, I remember that part really clearly. *You shoot one bitch.*"

Cobb thought for a minute, then said, "Okay, what else?"

"That was it. He said we'd talk about this on Saturday, plan the details, same thing as he'd said to me on the street. Then he hung up. Except for hello, I never said one goddamn ... uh ... one word."

Cobb leaned forward, elbows on the desk. "I need to ask you again. Why do you think Mrs. Claiborne didn't kill her husband?"

Danny thought before answering. "I don't know why. I just know she didn't. She couldn't."

"Not even to protect someone else?"

"You mean me?" He shook his head. "Not even for something like that. She'd say she did it — she'd do *that* for somebody else, but she did not shoot Mr. Claiborne."

"Okay, Danny, I'll tell you what, we'll talk to some people, ask a few questions, okay?"

"Okay, yeah, that'd be great. That's what I was hoping you'd say."

"You want a ride home, Danny?" I asked him.

"No, I'm good with the LRT and the bus. I do it all the time."

"Okay." I fist-bumped him and he grinned. Ordeal over. "We'll be in touch," I told him.

Cobb shook his hand and Danny left the office, I think a little happier than when he'd arrived.

Cobb jotted some things on a notepad. When he looked up, I said, "Well?"

"Yeah."

"That change your thinking at all?"

"Yeah, I'd say it does. Until now I wasn't sure that Danny wasn't the shooter. Even with Mrs. C's confession. Now I'm a little more confident that the kid didn't shoot him."

"Great, and part B of this two-part question — who did shoot Wendell Claiborne?"

"Yeah, part B is a little tougher. I'm going to have to think about that."

"Anything you want me doing while you think?"

"I think we stick to our game plan. We get back

to the Kennedy case. Get me a list of everybody you can think of, no matter how big or small, who's a part of this thing, and I'll do some checking with some cops I know on the points Kennedy raised about the investigation."

"Okay." I stood up and started for the door, then turned back. "One thing that puzzles me about Danny's story. It seems a bit of a long shot that Claiborne just happened along as Danny was riding back from the house."

"I doubt if it 'just happened.' I'm guessing Claiborne saw Danny out there on his bike and decided to apply a little more pressure, let him see the gun, handle it. Then he followed up with the phone call to reinforce the message."

"Claiborne was a piece of work."

"Amen to that."

"Hey, something I've been meaning to ask you. Actually, I'm asking for Kyla."

"Shoot."

"Any chance that someone with Crohn's disease would be ruled out as a candidate for the police service?"

He thought for a minute. "I would say it depends on the severity of the illness. You've told me hers is fairly manageable. I'm guessing that if that was still the case when she applied, it wouldn't be a deciding factor, especially if she's fit. Fitness is something they really look for."

"Thanks."

"She thinking about a career as a cop?"

"Uh-huh."

"Cool. You tell her she might have to deal with you and me?"

"Hell, no. I thought it best to look at the positives."

"Probably a good idea. Tell her anytime she wants to talk about it, I'd be happy to chat."

"Thanks, Mike. I will."

The list wasn't long. The four cops who actually investigated Faith Unruh's murder made the list: Detectives Hansel, Gaspari, Kinley, and Maughan. I included the two people who were involved in the autopsy, Dr. Abraham Trudell and assistant Cory Payne.

The people who now lived in the house where Faith's body had been found were Dennis and Charley Bevans and their daughter, Maizie, six years old; Charley was expecting another child sometime next year. Dennis owned a small business — sports apparel and accessories — while Charley worked in retail, managing a purse and handbag store in Market Mall.

And the people who lived in the former Unruh house were a little older — Dr. Jagdeep Sindhu, his wife, Maya, who was a pharmacist, and their son and only child, Ardesh, who was fourteen and a grade nine student at Central Memorial High School.

Faith's father, Del Unruh, had passed away in the years since the murder of his daughter. Her mother, Rhoda, had remarried about a year after her husband's death. I remembered Cobb telling me that there were unconfirmed rumours of an affair Rhoda Unruh was having before her husband's death. Cobb had indicated that all of the various strands, including Rhoda's new husband, Scott Curly, had checked out and that Rhoda and Curly had solid alibis for the time of the murder.

That didn't mean we wouldn't want to talk to them, but for now I saw them as back burner.

The friend Faith had walked home with before going the last fateful block by herself was Jasmine Kohl. Jasmine, now Hemmerling, was married with a family and lived in Salmon Arm, British Columbia, where she and her husband, Alan, owned and operated a couple of supermarkets.

And that was the list. In desperation I added Faith's teacher, Noelle Sensibaugh, and the school principal at the time, Everett Parr. Both had long since moved on to other schools and, in fact, Parr had retired in 2009. I was hoping that Cobb might have picked up a name or two during his conversations at police headquarters that would flesh out my rather pathetic list, at least a little.

I set the list on his desk and got ready to leave. It was my night to cook for the Sawley women and I wanted to walk down to Sunterra Market to get professional help for my vague menu plan.

The air offered hints of approaching spring and the walk felt good.

I picked up tourtière with mesclun and sun-dried tomato vinaigrette — the combination was one of Sunterra's specials. I realized I was kind of turning my night to cook into my night to warm stuff up, but I bought strawberries and hoped that strawberry shortcake and the strategic purchase of a nice Italian red might fend off criticism.

I'd been wary when heading to the parking lot behind Cobb's building ever since my unpleasant encounter with Minnis, and today was no exception. But despite my caution, I missed him. I'd opened the passenger door and set my purchases inside, and when I straightened up, there he was, a sickly-sweet smile on one of the biggest faces I'd ever seen. I quickly looked back inside the car to see if I'd missed something.

That made him laugh. "Just a social call, Scribe. Making sure everything's going well in your world."

"Until now everything was fucking great," I said.

"Now, that's not very friendly, Scribe. Especially to those who provided your lady's organization with twenty-five thousand dollars. That's just not friendly at all."

"What do you want, Minnis?"

"Today? Nothing. Nothing at all. Like I said, just dropped by to say hello to an old ... I guess maybe *friend*'s the wrong word."

There wasn't a face on the planet that I wanted to punch more than the one that was three feet away from me. Maybe that was the idea. Get me to snap, lash out. And I knew that if I did, as good as it would feel for maybe three seconds, Minnis would take me apart. I kept my mouth shut and my hands at my sides, willing the bastard to leave.

And he did. The job done, the intimidation once again applied, he turned and walked out of the parking area back toward 1st Street.

I stood for a long time, body rigid, hands shaking, stomach churning. What scared me most was the knowledge that this visit was a precursor to the next "assignment." I knew that the faint hope I had been clinging to was now dashed, and there would be a next assignment.

I decided to shake off the Minnis encounter and throw myself into the evening with Jill and Kyla. A gentle chinook had brought the temperature up to near-June warmth, and the three of us sat on the back deck, Jill and I drinking wine while Kyla worked on a Coke float. Then, in what seemed no more than seconds, the wind dropped away to not much more than a soft breeze, which was followed almost as suddenly by a very un-February-like rain shower.

But instead of running for cover, Kyla suggested we go for a walk in the rain. It turned out to be a brilliant idea, and we cruised the neighbourhood, the three of us holding hands, and telling a story — another of Kyla's ideas that involved rotating the telling between the three of us. First one would recite a line, then the next person would add a line, and so on. This story featured monsters (Kyla's creation) and talking vegetables (Jill); gorillas, a lot of gorillas (Minnis inspired?), were my contribution.

Back at the house, there was, as I thought there might be, a fair amount of criticism — some of it, I think, good-natured, directed at my "cooking." However, the strawberry shortcake, as I had hoped it would, saved my culinary butt. When the dinner cleanup was done, Jill and I sat on the sofa with a second glass of wine while Kyla headed for her room, book in hand.

After we'd sat for a while, her head on my shoulder, Jill sat up and set her wine glass down. She looked serious but not stern or worried. "I want to talk to you about the Let the Sunshine Inn."

I swallowed hard and directed my face to display anything but panic. I'm not sure it followed my directions, as one thought pounded out a nasty beat in my head. *She knows about the MFs. She knows about the MFs.*

"Celia announced today that she's leaving at the end of the year, and she plans to recommend to the board that I replace her. If I want to."

I quickly switched gears. This was important to Jill and that made it important to me. I had met Celia a few times. She had been the director of the place as long as I had known Jill and was a dedicated, tireless champion of the homeless, as well as those who used only the food bank part of the facility. "Do you want to do it?" I asked.

"I don't know. There's a big difference between being a volunteer for a few hours a week and being the person in charge. It's a pretty big deal."

"It's a *really* big deal. And just so you know, I think you'd be amazing at it. I'll do whatever needs to be done to support you if that's what you decide to do."

She leaned in and kissed me. "You are something special, you know that?"

"No, I'm not, but I know what the Inn means to you and I'll absolutely be in your corner whatever you decide."

"I'm going to think about for a couple of days."

"Good idea."

The next morning Jill and I were on our second cup of coffee and Kyla had just bolted out the door to catch a ride to school with her friend Josie when the phone rang. It was Cobb.

"What's happenin', bro?" I said when Jill handed me the phone.

"You are as un-hip as I am, so don't give me that shit."

"Nobody is as un-hip as you, my brother. Whassup?" It probably would have been more effective if I hadn't started laughing. Jill was shaking her head. "Anyway, I'm listening."

"I had an interesting chat with a guy named Herb Chaytors. You don't know him, but I do. Herb's been around the police service for a long time, was a detective in robbery for twenty years or so. Now he's kind of an administration guy — only a couple of years away from retirement. I've known him forever. He remembered a few things about the Unruh murder."

"Yeah?"

"You got time to get together later?"

"Sure. When and where?"

"How about the Rose and Crown? Beer and a sandwich, eleven thirty. Beat the lunch rush."

"See you then."

Cobb was there when I arrived, two beers already on the table. He looked up as I pulled out a chair and sat down.

"Thanks," I said and picked up my beer. We clinked glasses. "Here's to tracking a killer."

Cobb ordered a Reuben and I went with the shepherd's pie, my favourite at that place.

"Before we get into the latest on Kennedy and Faith Unruh, I want you to be the first to know — I had a visitor last night," I said.

His eyebrows shot up. "Oh?"

"Minnis."

"Another assignment?"

I shook my head. "Uh-uh. Just straight intimidation. Letting me know he and his pals are out there."

"And a reminder that there *will be* another assignment."

"Not that there was ever any doubt." I thought back to McWhorters's prediction that we'd meet again.

"Yeah, well, maybe we see if we can come up with a plan of our own."

"You have an idea?"

Much as I didn't want Mike to have to bail my butt out of a problem I'd made for myself, I was also hoping he might have some magic solution tucked away somewhere.

"Not really. Not yet. Just thinking about a couple of things."

We sat silent for a few minutes. I drank some beer, set my glass down. "Jill's been approached to take over as director of the Let the Sunshine Inn. You think there's any potential problem with that idea?"

"What kind of problem?"

"I don't know. The money I got from the MFs went to the Inn. You think if they decide to lean on me they might do it through Jill?"

He thought about that.

"I can't see how that would make a difference. They know where she and Kyla live — they can use them as leverage without involving the Inn. I can't see that they'd give a damn that she's working there."

"That's what I'm hoping. Other than the leverage part. I wish I could come up with a way to get that out of my life."

"Like I said, we'll work on that."

"I hope you realize how much I appreciate your help with this ... even though I told you I didn't need it."

"I know. But right now I haven't done anything to appreciate. I'll let you know when you can start bowing and scraping."

"Fair enough."

"Now, about Herb Chaytors …"

"Yes."

"I mentioned that I worked with Herb. Not closely; he was in robbery and I was in homicide, but I knew him and liked him. Kennedy knew and worked with him, too. A lot of people liked Herb. He had a reputation as a good cop. Some cops are liked by other cops but not so much by the public. Herb is a guy who has always been trusted by both the people he works with and the citizens."

"And you said he remembers the Faith Unruh investigation."

Cobb nodded. "I asked specifically about the missing evidence — Faith's panties going missing. He didn't know what happened, only that there was quite a kerfuffle in the department over that."

"No surprise."

Cobb nodded. "You're right. There was almost no physical evidence related to Faith's murder: here was the one thing they had, and the evidence disappeared before the analysts had a chance to examine it."

"Anybody get blamed?"

"Nothing official. Of course, Hansel and Gretel came under scrutiny but Chaytors says that was tossed on the scrap heap pretty quickly."

"Yet they were removed as lead detectives for a while."

"Yeah. Chaytors told me Jarvis Maughan was a favourite of the chief back then. Gerrard. J.G. Gerrard. Retired 2009."

"Let me guess. Deceased."

Cobb glanced at his notebook. "December 3, 2013. Fell through the ice on an ice-fishing trip. Drowned."

"Not a nice way to go."

"Someday I'll get you to write out a list of the ways that *are* nice."

"Point taken. Chaytors have any thoughts on Kinley and Maughan? Besides being in the boss's good book?"

"A few, yeah. Mostly on Maughan. Seems he got into trouble a couple of times. Was disciplined for inappropriate behaviour with a hooker. Had her in the car for questioning. But the story was there was more than questioning going on. And no charges were laid."

"Charges being the only thing that wasn't laid?"

"Something like that, yeah."

"You said 'a couple of times.'"

"Yeah, the second time he was actually disciplined for another sex-related offence. This time with a minor. Couldn't get details, only that the teen was involved with drugs, was picked up in a raid on a house party that apparently was completely out of control. Again, he had the girl in his car. Later he would only admit to making some suggestions, a little indecent exposure. The kid and her mother made a complaint, alleged it was a lot more than that, said he raped her. Maughan was suspended with pay, then a couple of weeks later the complaint went away and so did the suspension."

"Why did the complaint go away?"

Cobb shrugged. "Hard to say. The girl and her mom gave up, maybe they were intimidated, who knows?"

"When did these incidents happen?"

"Chaytors wasn't sure. Sometime in the early to mid-eighties was the best he could do."

"Interesting, though, that his transgressions were of the sexual kind."

"Yeah, that is interesting. But here's something else that's interesting. Maughan lived about four blocks from Faith Unruh's house."

That one rattled me. So much so that I said nothing, just stared at Cobb. Finally, I shook my head. "Maughan died in 2008. It would be a horrible irony if Kennedy spent most of his life sitting at those cameras waiting for Faith's killer to walk into the frame when the guy had actually been dead for almost half of that time."

"Yeah. But that's a possibility even if the killer isn't Maughan. And I don't think we want to jump to the conclusion that Maughan murdered Faith Unruh. Chaytors told me that Maughan was actually looked at — much later, when the trail had gotten pretty cold — because he lived that close to the victim. But he had an alibi. Herb couldn't remember what it was, but he did remember that Maughan was dropped as a suspect fairly quickly."

"Was that before or after he was actually one of the lead investigators on the case for a time?"

"Herb was pretty sure it was after. Hansel and Gretel were back as the lead team on the investigation." Cobb nodded. "Which, by the way, I asked Herb about — the thing with Hansel and Gretel being in, then out, then back in again. He couldn't tell me anything about that."

Neither of us spoke for a while. I busied myself twirling my glass in my hands while Cobb studied his fingernails.

"None of that gets us any closer to what's going on now, a quarter of a century later — the marks on the board in the alley, the shadows on the videos, and then the killing of Kennedy. If that's connected at all to the

Faith Unruh murder, then it makes no sense to think that the killer has been dead for a long time."

"Agreed," Cobb said.

"Any chance there were two people involved in Faith's murder?"

Cobb looked at me a long time before answering. "Anything's possible," he said. "I'm not sure that was ever considered. I reread the entire homicide file and everything in there seemed to point to one perpetrator. What are you thinking?"

"Just that maybe if it was Maughan and he had an accomplice, the accomplice is still alive and has resurfaced."

"Maughan and an accomplice," Cobb repeated.

I shrugged.

"Remember what I said about Maughan having an alibi?"

"Killers have had so-called ironclad alibis before," I pointed out.

"True. And maybe that's the case here. Or maybe Maughan had nothing to do with any of it and just happened to live nearby."

"Also a possibility." I nodded.

"I can tell you this. If Maughan was still alive today and was arrested for this, he'd be released almost immediately. Consider what we've got — two previous allegations of sexual misconduct, neither of which would be admissible in court, and the fact that he lived near where the victim lived and the murder took place … not exactly what might be called damning evidence."

"So we haven't got a lot more than we had previously."

"Hard to say. We're not a court of law, so we can pursue any avenues we want. Maybe we don't rule Maughan out just yet. How about I see if I can get the names of his assault victims, and maybe we can talk to them."

"So many questions and so few answers. Look, I know Landry's a damn good investigator, but I'm having trouble buying her responses on the stuff Kennedy brought up. I know I sound like a broken record, but wouldn't there have to be a reason Hansel and Gretel were dropped from the investigation and then reinstated later? And I'm just not convinced that the panties going missing was some innocent mistake, some administrative mix-up. Come on, that's a hugely important piece of evidence."

"On that one, I'd have to give her the benefit of the doubt. It's terrible that something like that could happen but the simple truth is it can. And does."

I wasn't ready to let it go. "And why no tip line? I know Landry said it's an administrative call, but you'd think in a case like that it'd be automatic?"

"It is now. In fact, there are two ways to call in tips. One is Crime Stoppers, which is always anonymous, and there's a direct line to the police, as well. Don't know if that was the case back then. To be honest, I think it's the least important of Kennedy's allegations. Interesting, though, that it didn't happen, no matter how big a waste of time a lot of those lines are."

"Yeah, I damn sure know about that."

I had set up a private tip line on a previous investigation and was deluged with calls from quacks and wackos, much to the delight of Cobb and both our families.

Cobb grinned now at the memory of it. The food arrived, and we suspended conversation while we salted, peppered, and ketchuped. A couple of bites and a long pull of beer later, Cobb looked at me. "Let's see if I can get those names of Maughan's victims. I wouldn't mind chatting with them if we can find them and they're not living in Poland or Beirut or something."

"Maybe I can help with that."

"Let me see how I make out and I'll call on you if I'm not doing well."

"Fair enough."

"Now let's take a look at your list of names."

I pulled the sheet of paper out of the ragged briefcase I always carried, a long-ago gift from Donna, and passed it across the table.

He looked over the list. "Okay," he said, "how about we divide this up? I know it'll probably be deadly dull, but why don't you dig into the backgrounds of the two families — the one in the former Unruh house and the other in the murder house."

"On it," I said.

"Meantime I'll take Trudell and Payne, who performed the autopsy on Faith, and I'll see if I can find Rhoda Unruh, Faith's mom — see if time has suggested anything to her she might have forgotten to mention in all the earlier questioning she must have gone through. Maybe the new husband, too — it'd be interesting to know when exactly he came on the scene."

"Something I wondered about ... the marks themselves, is it too much of a reach to think it might be useful to know what they were made with?"

"Nothing's too big a reach when we've got next to nothing to work with. I know a guy who works in a private forensics clinic. Maybe I'll offer to buy him dinner if he'd swing by there one evening after work and take a look at the marks."

"And the little girl who walked home from school with Faith that day …"

Cobb looked at the list. "Jasmine, formerly Kohl, now Hemmerling."

"I'm wondering if we should try her; maybe she's thought of something in the intervening years. I could call her."

"Can't hurt."

"Actually, it probably can. I'm betting it hurts every time she thinks of that day, and I'm going to ask her to remember it again."

"You're right. Collateral damage from the work we do."

"I know. But I do think I should call her."

"I think so, too. All right, we work this stuff for a couple of days and then reconvene."

We once again turned our attention to the food, content at having some direction, something to do, however small.

After lunch, as we got ready to go, Cobb reached across and took my arm. "One other thing, Adam … Minnis shows up, or any of his MFs pals, who you gonna call?"

I pointed to him and said, "MFs-busters."

Neither of us thought I was all that damn funny.

TEN

I spent the next morning at home online and on the phone. It didn't take long to remove the families who lived in the two houses associated with the Unruh murder from our list of people of interest.

Dr. Sindhu and his family had immigrated to Canada from Mumbai in 2008 and moved into the former Unruh home in 2009. They'd purchased the house from a woman and her teenage daughter after the woman and her husband had divorced. Dr. Sindhu didn't know if the woman had bought the house from the Unruhs, but he seemed to recall that the woman, her husband, and the teenage daughter had been living there a long time, fifteen or twenty years, he thought. I decided to add a note to my list that it might be worth checking with the woman, if we could find her, see if she and her husband were the first owners after the Unruhs, and if so, if she'd ever come across anything suspicious or at least interesting in the house.

And a year after the Sindhu family had moved into the neighbourhood, across the street and down a few houses, the Bevanses had moved into the house where Faith's body had been discovered. Dennis Bevans had grown up in Ponteix and Charley in Beechy, two small communities near Swift Current, Saskatchewan. They'd met in high school in Swift Current and married in 2005. Maizie, their daughter, was Calgary's New Year's baby in 2011. They'd bought the house from a retired draftsman and his wife, who'd lived in the house for twenty-eight years. That meant they had to have been living there at the time of the murder. Same note — might need to follow up with the previous owners if they were still around.

And that was it. I decided to turn my attention to Jasmine Hemmerling, who had been with Faith Unruh in the moments before her death. I reached her on my second call to Salmon Arm, explained who I was, and gave her an abbreviated version of Kennedy's role in the investigation into Faith's murder and now his own death under strange and clearly suspicious circumstances.

At first she didn't seem willing to talk about what was surely one of the most painful times of her life. But as I explained that Cobb and I were convinced there was a real chance that Faith's killer could still be found, even after all this time, she finally agreed to tell me what she remembered of that day.

"It wasn't any different from other days except that Faith had just had her birthday and was still excited about that. We were both into Barbies back then and she'd got a new doll that she was totally pumped about. That was what we talked about — well, *she* talked about — most of the way home. Did you know they put that Barbie doll in the casket with her?"

"I didn't know that, no."

"Anyway, we got to my house and for some reason we hugged — maybe because of her birthday, I don't remember. Back then kids didn't hug each other all the time like they do now, so it was unusual, but after … what happened … I'm so glad we did that … you know?"

I could hear her voice break and knew she was struggling with the memories. I waited.

Finally, she said, "I'm so sorry. I do this about once a year when I think about that day … even now."

"Please don't apologize, Jasmine. Did you see anyone suspicious or out of place that day as you walked home?"

"No. The police asked me that same question. I was questioned three or four times. But there was nothing about that day that was any different from any other."

"How about at school? Did Faith have any people she didn't get along with? Teachers? Other students?"

"I don't think so. Not really. The police asked me about that, too, but I don't remember anybody she really didn't like or who didn't like her. Of course, there were boys who bugged us and some girls we liked less than others, but I don't think there was anyone that stands out as somebody she really disliked. Faith was pretty quiet and really nice — she got along with just about everyone."

The answers so far had been about what I'd expected. I decided to see if I could learn something about the investigation itself.

"Do you remember the police officers who questioned you?"

"Not really. There were different ones. The first guys had funny names. I remember that much."

"Hansel and Gretel?"

"Yes, that's it. I'm not sure those were their real names, but they told us that's what they were called at the police station."

"Us?"

"Yes, my parents were with me for all the interviews. Except for the time Terry's dad talked to me."

"Terry. Who's Terry?"

"Terry was an older kid in our school, maybe grade nine, something like that. His dad was a policeman and he talked to me at school. I got called into the office and he talked to me there."

"Do you remember the policeman's name? Or Terry's last name?"

She paused. "I don't. I think I knew it back then, but I'm not sure now. I just remember that there was this kid at school, and his dad was a policeman, and then one day that policeman came to the school and asked me questions about Faith and what I knew about that day."

"Was that the only time that policeman talked to you?"

"No, there was another time at the station. He was with another detective that time."

"Do you remember that policeman's name — the one who was with Terry's dad at the station?"

"No; I'm sure he probably said it, but I don't remember."

I thought for a minute before my next question. "If Terry was in grade nine, how did you know him? I mean, kids usually hang with the kids from their own grade or fairly close, at least that's how it was when I went to school."

"That's how it was for us, too, but Terry was one of the boys who liked to tease us and bug us; that's about the only time we ever saw him — after school, or sometimes on our way to school."

"Do you remember if you saw him on the day Faith was murdered?"

Another pause. "I don't think so. I'm pretty sure we didn't."

"Jasmine, if I was to say a couple of names to you — if one of them was Terry's last name, would you remember?"

"Maybe. If I ever knew it. I just can't remember for sure."

"Okay, well, let's try it. How about Kinley?"

After a few seconds, she said, "No, I don't think I know that name. I'm sorry, it was a long time ago and I was so upset and scared after what happened to Faith … I was afraid whoever did it would try to get me next. I guess it's natural to think that. Anyway, it was pretty awful. One of my parents had to take me to school for the rest of that year and even the first couple of months the next year."

"That's understandable, and I can only imagine how terrible that had to be for you. Just one other name. How about Maughan?"

Again she waited. "That might be it. Terry Maughan. That sounds familiar. I'm not positive, but maybe. Why are you asking about the policemen and Terry? Do you think …?"

"No, Jasmine, nothing like that. We're just trying to tie up some loose ends with the original investigation, that's all. And you've been really helpful in that regard."

"I don't think I've helped at all. I wish I could. I'd give anything to see the person who did that to Faith caught and put away forever. It makes me sick that he's still out there having a life and she … and I'm still scared even after all this time that he could — "

She stopped talking then.

"We're going to do everything possible, but I can't lie to you, Jasmine, it won't be easy. And if you think of anything at all — no matter how trivial you think it might be — please call me. Will you do that?"

"I will. I doubt if there will be anything I haven't said twenty times before, but if I think of something, I'll call. I really will."

"Thank you, Jasmine, I really appreciate this."

We rang off and I sat for a long time, staring at nothing, thinking about my conversation with Jasmine and how it had made still more personal the murder of a little girl I had never met. And I began to understand Kennedy's obsession with finding the killer. My own loathing for whoever had ended the life of an eleven-year-old who was excited about her new Barbie doll — that loathing, that overwhelming desire, the *need* to have the killer pay for what he'd done — was as great as it had been all the years that the arsonist who took Donna's life remained at large.

It *was* an obsession.

I checked my watch. One thirty. I decided to head over to the school Faith had attended — see if I could find out if Terry's last name *was* Maughan. I wasn't sure it mattered, but the fact that one of the cops who investigated the murder had a kid who attended the victim's school — there was a chance it might be significant, if for no other reason than he might have some interesting perspectives on his old man. If I could find him.

I arrived at Kilkenny School just before two and headed straight to the office.

There was only one person there, a grey-haired mid-fiftyish woman with laugh lines around her eyes and bright-red lipstick on a wide, pleasant mouth. She smiled a smile that made me think she was the kind of school secretary who would be well-liked by the kids. I'd had a couple of those during my time in school. "Can I help you?" she asked.

"I don't honestly know," I admitted. "My name is Adam Cullen. I'm a journalist and I'm involved in an investigation into the death of a little girl who attended this school. She was murdered in 1991."

"Faith Unruh."

I nodded. "You're familiar with the incident."

She pointed. "That wall over there. There's a tribute to her, some pictures, and even a couple of things she did while she was here."

I turned and looked to where she was pointing, then back to her. "Did you know Faith?"

She shook her head. "I started here a few years after Faith was killed. But of course, I knew about it."

"Do you mind if I take a few minutes to look at the tribute?"

"Of course not. Go ahead. Can you just sign in first? Right here." She pushed a clipboard with a sign-in sheet toward me.

As I signed my name, she said, "I'm Lois Meeker. The kids call me Miss Lois, even though I've been married for twenty-seven years."

"Great to meet you, Miss Lois." I grinned at her.

She smiled a wrinkly-eyed smile back at me. "Can I get you a cup of coffee?"

"No, thanks, but I appreciate the offer. Excuse me for a minute."

I walked to the wall she had indicated. The tribute to Faith Unruh was a large framed board, maybe four feet high by six feet wide, and consisted of several pictures of her, a couple of annual school photos and several of her in school activities — sports, a Christmas concert, and one with two other girls that the caption below indicated had been taken only a couple of weeks before her death. There were two pictures she had drawn herself and a faded two-page story she'd written called "Mrs. Frisby and the Rats of Kilkenny." I scanned it. It was a cute takeoff on a book I remembered liking a lot as a kid. There was also a half-page piece entitled "One More Angel in Heaven" that talked about Faith as a little girl who loved her family, her friends, and her school, and who "would be forever cherished and missed."

I walked back to where Lois Meeker was just ending a phone call. She hung up and looked at me. "Moving, isn't it?"

I nodded. "Very."

"I get up and go over there and look at that at least once a month. Kind of reminds me what's important in our lives."

"I can understand that," I said. "Lois, I'm not sure of the protocol here. Should I be speaking to the principal?"

"I'm afraid she's away at a meeting. I can make you an appointment if you like."

"How long has she been here?"

"Only a couple of years."

"Then I don't know that she would be of much help. But there's something maybe you could do, if you would."

"Sure, if I can help."

"Are there records of former students here at the school?"

"They've all been digitized now and are at the board offices, but the original stuff, attendance books, things like that, are still stashed away in our storage room. Probably they'll be chucked or hauled away someday, but it hasn't happened yet."

"Is there any way you could check and see if there was a student here at the same time as Faith? Would have been a couple of grades ahead of her. Kid named Terry Maughan."

She looked at me for a long time. "You know that's totally against school board regulations, right?"

"I figured it was," I said. "And I understand if you can't help. All I can tell you is that it's been twenty-six years since a little girl was murdered and we're looking at every possibility, however tenuous, to try to find her killer."

She continued to look at me, not friendly or unfriendly — she was just thinking. Finally, she spoke.

"What did you say the name was?"

"Terry Maughan."

"Boy or girl?"

"Good point," I said. "Boy."

"It'll take me a few minutes."

"No problem. And, uh … are there any teachers who were here when Faith was a student here?"

She thought about that, then nodded. "Just one. She's got grade four this year. Mrs. Dole. Holly Dole. I can see if she could spare you a couple of minutes."

"I'd really appreciate that."

"I think I'll just walk down to her room and chat with her rather than use the intercom."

"Sure," I said.

She stood up. "Which means you're in charge of the phone if it rings."

"Seriously?"

She nodded. "It's not complicated — the students do it during the noon hour. Just say, 'Kilkenny School,' and take any messages." She passed me a pen and message pad.

"Sure, how hard can it be, right?"

"Right." She smiled at me and headed off past the tribute wall and down the hall. When she was out of sight, I turned and glared at the phone, hoping that if I looked threatening enough it wouldn't dare to ring.

I was relieved when Lois Meeker reappeared without my having to press my receptionist skills into service.

"She's going to get the kids working on a spelling quiz, then she'll meet you in the staff room." She pointed in the direction of a different hallway. "About halfway down on the left. How about I walk you there? Don't want you getting lost."

I guessed that her offer to show me the way had as much to do with school security as it did with courtesy.

"Thanks, Lois, I appreciate it. And by the way, there were five calls, no messages. I took care of everything."

She laughed. "I've heard every kid-lie you can imagine and I've got a pretty good built-in BS detector."

"What kind of kid would lie to the school secretary?" I tried to sound shocked.

"The kid who thinks lying to the school secretary might keep him — or her — out of the principal's office."

"I think I remember that now," I said, as she pointed to the staff room door, smiled again, and turned back toward the office. I tapped on the door, and when no one answered I went inside to wait for Mrs. Dole. A long rectangular table was the feature piece of furniture. There were a couple of comfortable chairs and a leather couch around the perimeter of the room, with less comfy chairs at the table. Part of a cake had been left on a platter; I guessed it was to celebrate a staff member's birthday. Sink, stove, coffee machine — likely standard fare for school staff rooms.

I had just settled down onto one of the comfortable chairs when the door opened and a woman who looked maybe a little older than Lois Meeker entered the room. She lacked the smile wrinkles, was a bigger woman than the school secretary, and had grey, straight-cut hair that was just slightly out of place. Not a harried look, really, but not completely relaxed either. Grade four teacher.

She came toward me, smiled, and held out her hand. "Holly Dole," she said.

I shook the offered hand, found it firm but friendly. "Adam Cullen. I appreciate your taking the time to chat with me. I'll be quick. I know you're in the middle of a class right now."

She waved that off. "This is grade four. There's always a nine-year-old girl who will probably be a teacher herself one day, a little bossy, loves to have extra responsibilities, doesn't mind ratting out the misbehavers, even if they're her friends."

"And you have one of those?"

"I *was* one of those. And I *have* one of those. They won't mess with her." Both of us laughed and took seats, Holly Dole on the leather sofa, me back on my chair. "I also have the TA from the next classroom sitting in for me. She can only stay a few minutes."

"Miss Lois told you why I'm here … why I wanted to talk to you?"

"She did, yes."

"I appreciate your speaking with me. Did you teach Faith?"

"I'm happy to say I did — the year before ... before it happened. Grade five. She truly was a wonderful person. Not a wonderful *child*, a wonderful *person*. I'm sure you will understand, Mr. Cullen, that it is not possible after thirty years in the classroom to remember every student. But you do remember some. Forever. I would have remembered Faith even if she had not been ..." She stopped, unable to say the word.

I nodded. "Did everybody feel the same way about her?"

"What do you mean?"

"Someone did her harm, Mrs. Dole. It's possible that someone hated her. Jealousy, maybe?"

"Wasn't it a sex crime?"

"Faith was naked when she was found, but she'd not been violated. The police believe the killer was interrupted or panicked without completing what he had started."

"But wouldn't that be random, then?"

"Possibly." I nodded. "But not necessarily. Faith went into that backyard, almost certainly having been tricked or lured there by the killer. It seems possible that she may have known her attacker."

"Killer, attacker," Holly Dole repeated. She leaned forward. "I'm hating this conversation, Mr. Cullen. Anyway, to answer your question, we get to know very few of the students outside the school. I wouldn't be able to say if there was someone out there who didn't like her. But I can't imagine anyone hating Faith enough to want to take her life."

"I apologize for dredging up terrible memories. Just one more thing — do you remember a student named Terry Maughan?"

She thought a moment, then shook her head. "As I mentioned, Mr. Cullen, I wish I could remember them all, but I just can't. I'm sorry."

"His father was a policeman. And one of the investigators on the Faith Unruh case."

She sat back down. "Wait … oh, yes, I do remember. Terry's father, the policeman. He came here a few times to do presentations to the kids. You know the kind of thing — there's no reason to fear the police; they're our friends — that sort of message. Then I remember him coming to the school and questioning people, including me. We saw a different side of him then, I remember. Very businesslike. Very serious. As you would expect, of course."

I thought about that. "So, did he ever come to your classroom to do a presentation?"

"Oh, yes, absolutely. Two or three times at least."

"So he might have done a presentation when Faith was in your class."

"I can't say that for certain, but I would think that's possible. I suppose it must have been very difficult for him, you know, investigating the murder of a child he might have met."

"Maybe," I said.

"Wait a minute, that's not where you're going with this, is it? You can't think —"

I held my hand up. "I don't think anything, Mrs. Dole. We're just trying to connect some dots. So far, we haven't been able to connect very many. So we ask questions and hope that one of the answers points us in the right direction. Believe me, it's nothing more than that. Just one last question: Now that we've established that Terry Maughan was the son of the investigating officer, does that ring any bells as far as Terry is concerned?"

"Let me think about that." She paused a moment, then nodded. "I don't remember him well, it was a long time ago, but I do remember that a lot of the kids thought he was kind of a big deal because his dad was a policeman. And I think Terry was part of the presentations a couple of times. Yes, his dad used him as an example a few times, it was quite funny."

She paused before adding, "Another thing I recall, as I think back on it, was that it really seemed that Terry worshipped his dad, wanted to be a policeman himself when he grew up. I don't know if he ever made it. Sorry, that's about all I can tell you."

"Okay, there's just one last thing."

"You've said that three times."

I held up two fingers. "Scout's honour this time. Faith's teacher that last year, Noelle Sensibaugh, I was hoping to talk to her, as well."

Holly Cole's shoulders sagged. "Another tragedy, and I'm not sure that it's totally unrelated."

"What do you mean?"

"Noelle and I were friends. Not get-together-every-day-after-school friends, but I went to her house, knew her kids, she came to our place a couple of times. She was a single mom and so was I, so we had that in common. Anyway, she was off on stress leave for the last few weeks of that year after Faith's death. She came back in September, but she didn't stay, just couldn't get past what had happened. They moved to Manitoba — Russell, I think it was — and she taught there for a number of years. We kind of lost contact. Then about ten years ago I heard that she was in a care centre in Regina with dementia. I contacted the facility, thinking I'd try to get out there and see her, but I was told that she was too far gone … she wouldn't know me."

She paused and looked down. I thought there might be a tear or two. "I'm ashamed to say I don't know if she's still alive or … I just didn't keep up after that."

She stood up then. The interview was over. I stood and shook her hand. "Thank you so much. You've been great, and it *is* helpful, believe me."

She nodded. Murmured something I didn't catch, and left the staff room, walking quickly to get back to her students and the kid in charge of kids. I followed her out and turned the opposite way in the hall, headed back to the office.

Lois Meeker's smile greeted me and she held up a weathered-looking file folder. "Bingo," she said.

"Whatever they're paying you, it's not enough."

She laughed. I leaned on the counter as she opened the folder, extracted an eight and a half by eleven sheet of paper and read. "Terry Maughan attended Kilkenny for two and a half years. Came here partway through grade seven and finished his junior high here in 1992. The school is K to eight now, but back then it went up to grade nine. I'm not sure what high school he went to after that, but living in this part of the city, it was probably Central or maybe Ernest Manning. I've got his academic record here, but it won't tell you much."

"What about disciplinary stuff?" I asked. "He get into any trouble while he was here?"

She scanned the pages again. "You understand that I can't give you specifics ... but in general terms it doesn't look like anything major. Got sent to the office a few times for acting out in class and once, no, maybe twice for bullying, it says here. But there's no details other than that he got a couple of detentions. If it had been serious, there would have been parent conferences, maybe suspensions, but I don't see anything like that."

"Doesn't say who he was bullying, I don't suppose."

Another glance at the contents of the file folder and a shake of the head. "Sorry."

"Any siblings?"

Another look at the file, a head shake. "Looks like he was an only child."

"Does the folder contain the address for Terry Maughan?"

This time she tore a small piece of paper from a notepad and, with a final look at the contents of the file folder, jotted something on the paper, then handed it to me.

"Listen, I really appreciate your help with this," I told her. "Both you and Ms. Dole have been great. I'm going to get out of here and let you get back to work." I stepped forward and shook her hand.

"Mr. Cullen, I wish you luck with your investigation. The closure would mean so much to so many people."

"We're going to do our best, but a case this old, this cold, I can't guarantee we'll be successful."

"Well, don't hesitate to call or stop by if there's anything else we can do. Especially if it's something that's not against regulations."

I smiled, said goodbye, and walked out into the southern Alberta sunshine that made summer amazing and winter bearable. But instead of climbing back into my car, I decided to walk the route Faith Unruh had walked the day of her murder.

It was four blocks to her friend Jasmine's house, then another block to Faith's home. But, of course, she hadn't reached home that day, had been lured somehow into the backyard of the house three doors down and across the street ... and murdered.

I walked the speed I thought kids would walk as they made their way home from school. Ten minutes later I passed the house where Kennedy had lived and conducted his surveillance for so many years. It was on the same side of the street as the Unruh home. I walked farther down the street and stood in front of what I called the murder house; I'd given it that designation only to differentiate it in my mind from the Unruh family dwelling.

This was the first time I'd really thought about the fact that the house where Faith was murdered was actually *past* her own home if she walked the normal way from her friend Jasmine's house. That, it seemed to me, clinched the fact that her killer had lured her to the yard where she died. He would have had to speak to her before she went into her house, and convince her to walk past her home — three doors down, across the street — and into the backyard.

I stayed there for maybe fifteen minutes, then walked to the end of the block, turned right, walked another half block, and came back up the alley behind the murder house, the alley where Kennedy's life had come to a violent conclusion.

I looked at the wooden frame that housed the garbage cans behind the yard where Faith had died. No new marks. Either the killer — if that's who had made the marks — had not returned to the alley since Kennedy's death, or he didn't feel the need to record his visits after Kennedy and his surveillance were no longer factors. I walked the rest of the way down the alley and made my way slowly back to the school and my car, thinking as I walked about what I'd learned that day.

Maybe there was something there and maybe there wasn't. But it was interesting to me that one of the cops who investigated the murder of Faith Unruh may have met her in another context. Although meeting one student in a classroom full of students — even in days when class sizes were manageable — may be of no consequence. Unless, of course, he knew Faith outside the school, as happens in neighbourhoods — people often know, or at least know *of*, the kids who populate that area. And what about *Terry* Maughan? He did know Faith; Jasmine Hemmerling had told me about the kid named Terry whose dad was a cop and who liked to bug her and her friend Faith. Could there have been a connection between the cop who did presentations in the school, the son who worshipped his dad and didn't mind doing a little bullying, and the little girl who lost her life just after her eleventh birthday?

I pulled out the piece of paper and read the address of the house the Maughans had lived in when Terry had been a student at Kilkenny School. It couldn't have been more than three or four blocks from the school, albeit in the opposite direction from the Unruh house. Still … we weren't talking a lot of distance.

I wanted to talk to Terry Maughan, assuming, of course, that he was still alive and that he lived in close enough proximity that a face-to-face chat was actually feasible.

I decided to abandon technology for the moment and try the local phone directory. It took much longer to actually locate a phone book than it did to learn that Terry Maughan was not listed. If he lived in Calgary, he had an unlisted number, or, like more and more people were doing, he had gone away from a land line and used only a cellphone.

I called Cobb and started talking before he finished saying hi. "Maughan's son went to the same school as Faith Unruh. He was two or three years older but he knew her, teased her sometimes."

Cobb didn't say anything for a while. "You get a first name?"

"Yeah. Terry. Tried to get a phone number. No luck. I haven't been able to find out if he still lives in the city or not. And something else — Maughan, the cop, came to the school from time to time to do presentations to different classes. It's likely that he did at least one of those presentations for Faith's class. And some of the time Terry helped out with the presentations."

"You get all this from Faith's friend?"

"Jasmine Hemmerling? Some, not all of it. I talked to the school secretary and a teacher who's still at the school and was Faith's teacher the year before the murder."

There was silence at the other end of the line. I was used to that — it meant Cobb was thinking hard about something, and it was better if I didn't interrupt.

"Good work on this, Adam. I need to think about how we follow up on what you've got here. In the meantime, it wouldn't be a bad idea to keep working on locating Terry. You get anything on the families that live in the two houses?"

"Yeah. Nothing there. At least not the people who live there now. Both moved to Calgary well after the murder, one family from Saskatchewan, the other from India. There was at least one other family who lived in the Unruh house between when Faith's parents owned it and when the people who live there now bought it. Want me to pursue that?"

"Maybe, but not right now. I've got something else for us to check out first."

"Sure, what's up?"

"I located Faith's mom, Rhoda Curly. The former Rhoda Unruh has moved back to Calgary from Victoria. And she's no longer married to the guy she took up with after Faith's dad died. She works at a pet shop in Bowness. She said we could come by the place tomorrow afternoon. She'll take her break when we get there. You got anything on?"

"Nope, free and clear."

"Good. *And* I've got a trunk full of tapes. The homicide cops were only too happy to have you spend the rest of your life looking at footage so they wouldn't have to. But the deal is, we see anything, we let them know right away."

"I'm good with that."

"Right, I'll bring them along. Gotta go. See you tomorrow."

He was gone and I sat staring at the phone, a little impatient. I felt that maybe there was something to the Maughan father and son lead and I was anxious to get at it. But I also realized that we were investigating a cold case — a twenty-six-year-old cold case. Everything would be the same tomorrow as it was today. And I knew that Cobb was less impulsive than I was. He liked to think about things — "let it soak" was how he often put it.

Impatience aside, I was in a pretty upbeat mood and called Jill to see if she and Kyla could do dinner.

"Sorry, babe, Kyla's sleeping over at Josie's house. They've got an early rehearsal of a play they've written. They're presenting it at noon tomorrow, so this is the last one before the big show."

"I believe that's called a dress rehearsal in theatrical circles."

"About which you know …?"

"Next to nothing."

We both laughed.

"If it's not too much of a disappointment for you, I'm available for dinner," Jill said.

"Well, I guess if you're all there is, I'll have to settle."

"Listen, mister, you know that option you sometimes exercise — the one that has you sleep at my house, in my bed?"

"Yes, I'm familiar with that option."

"You're about two seconds from having that option revoked for a really long time."

"Ha, like you could resist me."

We laughed again and I told her I'd pick her up at six. I called Caesar's and made a reservation for six thirty, then drove home, went for a long, slow run, and followed that up with a longer, slower shower before heading out to spend the evening with the woman I loved.

ELEVEN

"I've decided to take the job," Jill said as we waited for our dessert.

"I'm happy for you," I said. And I was.

Jill cared as much about the Let the Sunshine Inn as I did about every story I wrote for publication. She was as passionate and caring about every person who set foot in the place as it was possible to be. She'd be an amazing director, and I told her so.

"It's not enough to care," she told me, smiling Jill now replaced by serious Jill. "I hope I know enough and can learn enough to actually be good at this."

"I know I'm biased, and because of that, my opinion might be less valid than some, but I think the very fact that you recognize you'll need to learn in order to be really good is a huge first step."

"Thanks, Coach."

"Do you remember how we met?"

"Yeah," she was smiling again. "You and Mike were looking for Jay Blevins and you came to the Inn. I put you to work helping me sort food bank items."

"And that's my point," I said. "You recognized my obvious sorting talents though you'd never met me before — that's a sign of real leadership."

"I think maybe you've had too much wine."

"Not yet, but I might before the night is over. We're celebrating."

The celebration continued long after we got back to Jill's house; in fact, it continued through much of the night. But all celebratory thoughts disappeared the next morning when I climbed into the Accord and saw the package sitting on the passenger seat, a handwritten note scrawled on half a sheet of paper tucked neatly under it.

It read, "Same place as last time. 6:00 p.m. Tuesday. Do NOT let us down, Scribe. Jill and cute little Kyla wouldn't want you to either. Have a nice drive."

I got out of the car and looked around. Stupid. Minnis would be long gone. I walked around to the passenger side, but there was no sign that someone had broken into my car. When I thought about it, I realized it was better that I hadn't come face to face with the evil that was Minnis. I looked back at the house and was glad that Jill wasn't looking out, wondering what I was doing. I got back into the Accord and drove off.

I decided to head for Cobb's office, pull down all the blinds, sit in the dark, and drink coffee. Just to be sure I wasn't being followed, I used some of the evasive tactics Cobb had taught me.

Cobb was already there, sleeves rolled up and talking on the phone. So much for my plan to be alone. "I appreciate your candour, Ms. Deines ..." he was saying. "Yes, I hope so, too.... Thank you again.... You too."

He hung up as I swung into the most comfortable seat in the room.

"That was April Deines," he said, "once known as Lady Godiva, exotic dancer and sex-trade worker. Was able to beat a big-time heroin addiction and now manages a couple of hair salons. Ms. Deines — she was especially anxious for me to know that it's pronounced 'Dine-us' — was nineteen when she was picked up by a Detective Maughan and driven to a secluded spot where she was given a couple of options. She chose option A, which meant that when they were done, Maughan drove her back to her apartment and dropped her off, wishing her a nice evening."

"Hmm," I said. "No surprise."

"She never saw him again and wasn't able to give me much that would help us, other than to confirm what Herb Chaytors thought had happened. I haven't had any luck with the other Maughan victim. Maybe you should take a shot at it."

"Sure." I pulled out my notebook. "Name?"

"Sylvia Jarman. Last known address, 34th Avenue Northeast. See what you can find out."

"Okay, but it would be a lot easier if she lived in Billings, Montana."

Cobb's head snapped up.

"Seems I have another delivery to make to my pal Truck McWhorters."

"How was it communicated?"

"Same as last time … package and instructions left on the front seat of my car." I held up the package and the note.

"Let's have a look."

I dropped both on his desk and headed for the coffee maker. "You want one?"

He pointed to his cup. "On my second already." He bent to look closely at the note. "The first one handwritten like this?"

"Uh-huh. Just like that."

He studied it for a while, shook his head, set it down and pulled the package in front of him.

"You said you didn't open the first one?"

I shook my head. "Afraid to. I wasn't sure what was inside. I know that even coming in contact with the wrong shit can be deadly. And I'll be honest: the threat to Jill and Kyla had me spooked."

Cobb nodded. "They know that. That's why they make those threats. I think we'll have a look in this one."

The package was about the size of three bigger paperback novels stacked one on top of the other. But somehow I didn't think we'd find the three latest Louise Pennys in there.

Cobb pulled on a set of latex gloves, the kind you see doctors and nurses using. He took out his pocket knife and carefully removed the outer brown paper wrapping. As with the first package, there was no writing on the outside. Someone had used Scotch tape to seal it up. Cobb set the paper aside. The wrapping had been covering a cardboard box. He examined the box for a minute or so and appeared to find nothing of interest. He cut another piece of tape, then eased the top back. He reached in and removed something that looked almost as if it could have been a half pound of butter, maybe a little longer than that.

He set it carefully on top of his desk, extracted a second package, pretty much identical in size and shape, then a third. The weird part was the wrapping around the packages — it was colourful, to say the least. It looked like tie-dye art or a kid's colouring project. Disguising the contents, maybe? I'd seen lots of drugs of every kind during my time covering that side of the crime beat for the *Herald*. I hadn't seen the colourful artwork on the wrapping before. I didn't ask Cobb about it — again, not wanting to disturb his concentration.

As he peeled back the wrapping from the first of the packages, I noticed he moved even more slowly now, methodically. It looked as if he were being careful not to come in contact with what was inside. And he didn't. Didn't touch it, sniff it, nothing. Rewrapped it and set it back in the box.

"There are six packages in total. I'm betting heroin. Street value, tens of thousands, maybe more. You get caught crossing the border with this, they put you away for a *long* time." He drew out *long* to emphasize the point.

"You have a better idea?"

He shook his head slowly. "The note says the delivery has to be made by Tuesday. Today's Friday. We've got a little time. Nice of them to give you the weekend off."

"Yeah, they're all about considerate."

"We're going to put this away for now. Let me think about it. See if we can come up with an alternative plan."

"Mike, I can't put Jill and Kyla in danger."

"You've already done that."

That pissed me off. I stood up. "I know that, for Christ's sake. But I'm not going to make it worse. If you don't have an alternative plan, I'm taking that damn package and I'm going to Billings."

I thought he'd argue but he didn't. "I get that, Adam. I do. Let me see what I can come up with. In the meantime, have you had breakfast?"

I shook my head.

"Red's Diner sound like an option?"

"It damn sure does."

The heroin safely stowed in Cobb's office safe, we walked the four blocks to Red's. By the time the food came and we'd had a glass of juice and were working on coffee, I was feeling a little better, more relaxed. I was ready to think about Faith Unruh and Marlon Kennedy and the link, if there was one, between their murders.

We talked again about my conversation with Jasmine Hemmerling. Cobb thought for a long time before responding. "You're right; it would be nice to talk to Terry Maughan. It makes sense that when one of your classmates was murdered and your dad was one of the investigators, there might have been conversations around the dinner table about the case. Maybe he'd remember something — maybe he could even shed a little light on how it came about that his dad was the lead investigator for a while. He might be able to tell us what the homicide file hasn't: whether Maughan was at the crime scene right after the murder."

"The kid was fourteen years old," I said.

Cobb nodded. "Yeah, I know, and maybe all of what I just said is nothing more than wishful thinking. But we won't know if we don't ask, and in order for us to ask, we have to find him."

"I've got an even crazier thought," I said. "Let's say, for the sake of argument, that Maughan was the killer. Do you think it's remotely possible that Terry Maughan was in on it somehow, as a participant, or that he at least knew about it?"

"You asked if it's possible. The simple answer is yes. You and I both know there have been horrific crimes perpetrated by kids younger than Terry Maughan. And if we're right in thinking that Faith was lured into that backyard, then certainly it's reasonable to think that she might have gone there at the bidding of a classmate. So, yes, it's possible. It is also extremely unlikely. Those cases I mentioned where kids have done terrible things are, thankfully, rare. But that doesn't alter the fact that I'd like to talk to Terry Maughan. So let's work on that — see if we can find him. I'll check on whether he has a record; you keep working on getting a current address."

I nodded, though I had no clue where to start my search.

"By the way, did Jasmine mention whether Maughan had done presentations in her class?"

"She didn't, and I forgot to ask her. You think it's important?"

"Not really. Just corroboration, but I think with what you learned at the school, we've got what we need on that score."

We sat a while longer, Cobb drinking coffee, me looking at mine. My face must have given me away.

"Something's bothering you … what's up?"

"Oh, I don't know — there's just this little drug smuggling detail that's distracting me a little, that's all."

Cobb smiled grimly. "I get that. And I get that it's a lot easier for me to say relax than it is for you to actually do that. But like I said before, just leave it with me for now. Maybe I'll come up with something that might help."

As much as I wanted to follow his advice, my pessimism meter was still running pretty high, which is why I ate only about half of what was on my plate.

When we'd finished a second cup of coffee, Cobb said he had things to do, and I told him I'd use the office while I tried to track down Sylvia Jarman and Terry

Maughan. I started with Jarman and spent a fruitless hour in pursuit of a clue to her whereabouts. I was about to give up when I came across a note online that referred to a minor hockey coach named Les Jarman. I checked back in my notes. Sylvia Jarman's parents were Les and Ruth Jarman. Les Jarman had coached the West Mount Pleasant bantam team in 1986 and I knew West Mount Pleasant was a neighbourhood not all that far from the 34th Avenue Northeast address Cobb had given me.

I reasoned that if Sylvia Jarman's encounter with Jarvis Maughan had taken place in the late 1980s and she'd been a teen at the time, she'd be maybe forty-five or fifty today. There was at least a reasonable chance that one or both of her parents were alive and out there somewhere. I attacked that possibility for the next hour, made more calls, and finally found a Ruth Jarman, living at last report in Red Deer.

I got a number and called, but got her voicemail. I left a long and fairly detailed message about the reason I hoped to talk to her and ended the call thinking it was 50-50 at best whether I'd hear back from her.

I spent another half-hour online trying to get a line on Terry Maughan. Nothing.

I decided to turn my attention to other things. I hadn't done anything lately about my second career, that of budding children's book author. My first two books — *The Spoofaloof Rally* and *The Spoofaloof Goof* — much to my surprise, were selling well. I had started a third but was floundering, mostly because I simply hadn't got down to it. I knew that being a successful writer depended a lot more on diligence and discipline than it did on inspiration and brilliance. Lately I had been neither diligent nor disciplined.

I fired up the iPod and turned to Alessia Cara to provide the audio track while I cast about for some creative juice. I had wondered whether there was any particular reason for there to be a third Spoofaloof book and wasn't sure that Kyla's wanting one was sufficient. But now that I was committed — a signed contract with my Toronto publisher — it was time to actually write something. I spent an unproductive hour starting, deleting, then starting again, until I was convinced that the part of being a writer I really hated was the writing part.

My gnashing of teeth was short-lived, as April Wine's "Roller" announced an incoming call. The caller had a soft voice that I had to work to hear, but I made out the words *Ruth Jarman*.

"Ms. Jarman, thanks for calling back. Before I take up any of your time, can you confirm that you are the Ruth Jarman who once lived on 34th Avenue Northeast in Calgary?" The same soft, tired voice confirmed that she was that Ruth Jarman.

"As I mentioned in my message, my name is Adam Cullen. I'm part of an investigation that's looking at a former policeman named Maughan. We know about the incident involving that officer and your daughter, and I was hoping to be able to reach her in order to ask her about what happened when Maughan had her in his car for questioning."

"Well, first of all," the little voice responded, with just the slightest increase in volume and energy, "you won't be able to talk to Sylvia. She passed away in 2014 from a drug overdose."

"I'm so sorry to hear that."

"Yes." There was a long silence and I was just about to pick up the conversation again when she continued, though she spoke slowly. "She was a wonderful little girl, but things began to go all wrong as she got older." There was a catch in her voice and another silence followed, this one not as long. I heard her take a deep breath. "And after what happened to her that night with the policeman, the bad stuff seemed to speed up."

"Go wrong how, Ms. Jarman?"

"Sylvia struggled ... wait, what's this about?"

"I'm sorry, I should have been clearer," I said. "Ms. Jarman, I'm a journalist and I work with a private investigator named Mike Cobb. In connection with another case we're investigating, we spoke with someone who was familiar with the incident involving your daughter. I know it can't help Sylvia, Ms. Jarman, but it could be helpful with our investigation if you could tell us what happened that night."

There was silence for a while and I hoped she was digesting what I'd said.

"Sylvia suffered from depression and that led to her drinking more and more; then weed was next ... not really for, like, recreation; it was fulfilling a need for her. And then everything spiralled down from there. Do you know anything about addiction, Mr. Cullen?"

"I do, yes. I've written about Calgary's drug culture during my time at the *Herald*, and after I left the paper and became a freelancer. I've seen the pain it's caused a lot of people. I'm sorry you and Sylvia had to be among them."

"That's right, you said in your message that you're a journalist. I guess that's a problem for me, Mr. Cullen."

"What problem, Ms. Jarman?"

"I don't want another story about Sylvia, I'm sorry."

"I understand that, Ms. Jarman, but this is not for publication. As I said, Mr. Cobb and I have encountered Jarvis Maughan's name in connection with one of our investigations and we'd like to follow up — find out all we can about him."

"But he's been dead for some time."

"Yes, ma'am, he has. And I'm not able to tell you why it's important to us, but please believe me, it would be very helpful if you could see your way clear to telling the story one more time."

A pause, then she began slowly. "We were strict parents. Sylvia was only fifteen, and like most fifteen-year-olds, she was looking to exercise her independence. I couldn't really blame her. We knew she'd smoked up a few times and we were okay with it as long as it didn't get out of hand and her marks didn't go down — that kind of thing.

"That night at the party there were quite a few of them that had smoked some weed and I guess the problem was that there were several underage kids there. A neighbour complained and the cops showed up, three or four cars. Maughan took Sylvia to his car, told her he wanted to question her, then drove off with her."

She stopped then and I thought I could hear her crying softly. "My daughter had never been with a man, Mr. Cullen, and for it to be like that ... she told me she begged him to stop. But he didn't. We lost our daughter that night. Oh, she lived almost thirty more years, but she was never the same." Another pause, then she said again, "We lost our daughter that night. We never got her back. After that, it was like I said, drugs, booze, an endless succession of men, almost all of them jerks. She got pregnant, lost the baby ... it's awful to watch your child go through what Sylvia did, Mr. Cullen, especially when there is nothing you can do."

"Did Maughan ever come around again?"

"I don't think so. I think Sylvia would have told us; she hated him so much. But after that night I'm quite sure she didn't see him again."

"Did you try to have him charged?"

"Sylvia wouldn't allow it. She said she couldn't relive that night in a courtroom full of people."

"Ms. Jarman, I want to thank you. I know this was very painful for you, but I need you to know that you've been very helpful."

"I know that man's dead, and I know there's nothing that can be done to him now, but whatever it is you say I've helped you with, I'm glad, and if it causes Jarvis Maughan to be diminished even a little, that would be good."

We said goodbye and as I hung up I was consumed by a festering hate for a man I'd never met. And never would.

After talking to Ruth Jarman, I felt that I needed to step back from the world of crime for a while. I drove slowly across town and parked in front of my apartment building. There had been times when I was ready to walk away from writing about crime. And now here I was, not only writing about that world but becoming more and more a part of it by working with Cobb on investigations. It was often a sordid place, and I felt it was taking a toll on me. And maybe in turn on Jill and Kyla.

I sat for a long time wondering what I'd be doing if it wasn't this. I didn't come up with an answer. And I realized, at least for now, that it didn't matter — I had no choice but to keep doing what I was doing. I couldn't turn my back on Faith Unruh or Marlon Kennedy. And I wanted to see through to its end the Claiborne case, though I wasn't sure what we could do, or more precisely what we'd be *allowed* to do to help Rachel Claiborne. And whether I liked it or not, I was ensnared in the heinous crimes of the MFs.

I called Jill and got her voicemail. Without telling her I was down, but knowing I'd be lousy company, I let her know that I needed time at my place that night. Hinted that it was work-related. I wanted to soak in the tub for a long time, spend some time with a good book, and maybe hit the sack early.

That's not how my evening went.

I got through the bath part and had been reading for maybe ten minutes when the phone rang. It was Cobb. "I need you in a meeting right now."

"Shit," I said.

"Yeah, life's like that sometimes. But I need you to get in your car and drive to an address I'm about to give you."

"Just a minute." I fumbled for a pen and paper and was finally ready. "Okay, give me the address. I'll get there as soon as I can."

He gave me the address of a less than stellar motel in the northeast part of the city, the Big West Inn, Room 204. Then he hung up. No details. No reason for the "meeting" given.

I thought about shaving and finding a fresh shirt but decided the kind of meeting that would take place in the Big West Inn required neither. I figured whoever was there would have to settle for clean.

The drive took twenty-six minutes. By the time I got there, I was even less enthusiastic about the place than I had been just thinking about it. It was dumpier than I remembered. The exterior was a tapestry of chipped paint and cracked plaster, the parking lot littered with pages of ancient flyers, fast-food wrappers, and plastic containers of every shape and size.

I ran up a set of outside stairs to the second floor and found room 204. Part of the *4* was missing but there was enough of it there to tell me it was the right room.

I tapped on the door. No answer. I knocked again, louder.

Cobb's voice called out, "Yeah."

"It's me," I said. "I'm coming in."

"Yeah, come on."

I turned the handle on the door and pushed.

The place was hazy — not cigarette smoke but something, I wasn't sure what. It smelled of musty carpet, overripe bananas, and old sweat. Not a welcoming combination. I took two steps into the room. There were five people sitting around a table in the centre of the room. The table looked as if it might have been nice once — maybe when it had been part of the furnishings at one of Calgary's first speakeasies.

There were several beer bottles on the table. Poker night, it seemed. Cobb was at the far end; the chair at the end closest to me was vacant, presumably awaiting my arrival. I recognized a couple of the people at the table — I'd seen them in action before. They were former cops, one retired and one on disability. They were also fearless, as ruthless as the worst of the bad guys, and often well-armed. I nodded in their direction, received a nod from one, a near-smile from the other.

I knew one more member of the gathering. Ike Groves, who preferred to be called "The Grover," was an informant Cobb had used when he was still on the force and had kept in touch with. He now and again showed up on the payroll of Cobb's private enterprise. The Grover was a slimy little worm with a permanent whine in his voice, but his intimate knowledge of life on the streets of the city made him occasionally pretty valuable. I wondered what the occasion was.

There was a fifth guy at the table whom I didn't know. He looked totally out of place — not geeky exactly, but a long way from macho. Three more guys, all *really* macho, were leaning against the wall to one side of the table. And there was someone else — someone I'd missed at first glance. A girl. She was sitting in a shadowy corner of the room drinking a Tim Hortons coffee.

Cobb gestured at the vacant chair. "Introductions are in order. Let me do the honours," he said. "Gentlemen, lady — this is Adam Cullen." Cobb started with the geeky guy I didn't know. "That's Chip." He pointed to the two ex-cops next. "You've met Frenchie and McNasty. And, of course, you know The Grover. Those three are Malibu, Taurus, and Patriot." He paused, waiting for me to say something. I knew better. The introductions, of course, were useless. Clearly, Cobb either didn't want the people in the room to know each other's real names or he didn't want me to know them. This was already feeling like one of those *the less you know the better it is* arrangements.

When I didn't respond, he continued. "As the conversation unfolds you'll begin to understand what this is about. At the end, if you have questions, you can ask." He looked from one to the other around the room, then said, "Grover, you're up."

Ike Groves leaned forward, fidgeted for what seemed like a long time, pulled out a package of cigarettes, looked at Cobb and put them away. I was feeling nervous already, and nothing had been said so far. "What do you want me to say, man?"

"What I want you to say, Grover, is exactly what we have been saying in this room for the last hour. I need my man here to get a feel for what we're doing, and it will do the rest of us good to review it one more time."

More fidgeting. "I wasn't planning on telling this to a whole shitload of people."

"Grover, there is exactly one person in the room that wasn't here when we went through this earlier. Somehow that doesn't feel like a shitload to me."

"Still, bro, I wasn't planning —"

"Plans change."

"Yeah, I guess … but —"

"Look, Grover, I'm getting tired over here," Cobb said in a low, cold voice. "Now we can cancel our arrangement and you can walk out of here, or you can start telling this whole shitload of people what we have been talking about."

The Grover nodded. I'd caught his act before, and I knew that Cobb would get what he wanted. The Grover knew it, too. He nodded a second time.

"Okay," he said. "Like I told you before, Rock Scubberd has a son from a previous lady. The kid's name is Brock and he's nineteen years old."

The bigger of Cobb's associates — the one he'd introduced as McNasty — chuckled at that. "Rock's kid's name is Brock. Rock and Brock. That's just fucking groovy."

The Grover didn't react — stared straight ahead. I

was never sure if Grover was as fucked up as he made out or if that was part of the act.

"Turns out Brock likes 'em young. Like I said before, the younger the better. Been in a couple of scrapes because of it, but so far Dad and his boys have been able to convince people that pursuing things might not be a good idea. Up to now the kid's managed to stay out of big trouble."

Grover hesitated and looked at Cobb like he hoped he was finished.

"Tell us again about his MO for his … activities," Cobb prompted.

"Mondays and Thursdays every week, like clock-work. He's got a couple of connections, punks who wanna be tough guys. They find the girls for him. Usually kids that're messed up on something and will do pretty much anything to get either a couple of hits or some money to make a buy. Pretty simple stuff. The guy that brings the girls most often is a guy named Ernie. Don't know the last name. Don't even know if he's got one. There's another guy, but most of the time it's Ernie."

"And Brock has a place where all this goes down."

"Yeah, he's got this little house in Ramsay."

Cobb held up a piece of paper. "Address and map. Everyone here has one." He tossed the page across the table to me. "Now you do, too. Sorry to interrupt, Grover. Please continue."

"A girl, sometimes more than one, is brought there and they party a while with Brock; then the tough dudes take the girls back to wherever they want to go, and the kid goes off home like he's been at the movies or something."

"The old man know about his party pad?"

The Grover shook his head. "I don't think so."

"And when the party's over, he always goes home."

"I can't say that for sure. I'm not there watching what's going down. But from what I've been able to learn, it seems like that's the way it happens, yeah."

"And does he ever go there at any other time? Just to hang out ... anything like that?"

"Again I'm told no. The living room is set up for his ... romantic inclinations. The bedroom is storage so there's no real reason for him to be there when he doesn't have a girl there."

I glanced over at the girl drinking coffee. She looked like she was paying attention but like what she was hearing was no big deal.

Cobb looked at me. "My friend Grover here is far too modest. The truth is he's been watching the place — with a little help from his friends — and everything he's said here is good information. I know because I've checked it out myself. With a little help from *my* friends."

I thought I saw Frenchie and McNasty move their heads up and down a little, but I couldn't be certain.

Now Cobb looked around the table. "I've told all of you that there's a time crunch, so this has to happen Monday night." He turned his gaze back to me. "I wasn't intending to involve you, but we lost one member of the cast, so the understudy has to step in. On Monday night you will arrive at Brock's party pad with Pink here." He indicated the girl.

"Pink?"

"Is an entertainer. Dances to Pink's songs. Thus the name. Pink does other things to entertain her clients, and for the record is twenty-one years old —"

"Twenty-two," Pink interrupted. "It was my birthday Monday."

"Happy birthday," Cobb said. "Of course, what is of particular interest to us is that, as you can see, Pink looks *fourteen*. Right up Brock's alley. Turns out The Grover is a man of many interests. Among other things, he does a little pimping — Pink is one of his ladies."

"I dislike that term," Grover's whiny voice intervened. "I see myself as a business manager. And I want you to take good care of my baby when she's in there."

"I think it's fair to say she'll be a lot safer with us looking after her than in some of the situations you put her in."

Grover opened his mouth to answer but changed his mind and closed it again. I studied the girl named Pink. She didn't seem to mind or even notice that she was being referred to in the third person. In fact, she'd stopped paying attention and had pulled out her phone.

Cobb spotted her out of the corner of his eye. "Sorry, you can't use that in here. No calls, no texts."

She looked at him, shrugged, and put the phone away. She picked up a travel magazine that lay on the table beside her. I didn't see Pink planning a European vacation anytime soon. Vegas maybe? But I knew I was being unfair in thinking that way. She looked up at me at just that moment and I smiled at her. The smile wasn't returned. I didn't blame her.

Cobb turned his attention back to the table. "Everything will be as usual as far as Brock knows. He's a creature of habit, so it's best if everything happens the way it always does."

He nodded in my direction. "Except that in place of Ernie, who's under the weather at present, it'll be you making the delivery."

McNasty chuckled again at that. I had an idea that it would be a while before Ernie was out from whatever weather he was under.

"You will drive Pink to the house and walk her up the sidewalk to the door," Cobb continued. "Brock will hand you some money; you turn and leave. And you're done. The house will be wired and there will be a couple of cameras. By the way, I've been in the house and his computer is loaded with kiddie porn. Bad stuff, the kind that could get him behind bars for a long time. With that and Pink's performance, we'll have all we need and more."

It was starting to come together in my mind. It was a con. And once we had all the damning evidence on Brock, I was sure there'd be a meeting with his father and maybe Mrs. Scubberd, too.

Cobb turned to Pink. "You know at what point you call out?"

She nodded.

"And what exactly will you say?"

"We've been through this," she complained. "I'm not stupid, you know."

"And I'm not suggesting that you are," Cobb said gently. "What would be stupid is if we did this without sufficient preparation. What exactly will you say?"

"I'm supposed to say, 'I'm only fourteen. You can't do that to me.' Then I scream, 'Please don't.'"

Cobb nodded and said, "Good. That's perfect." He turned then to the two ex-cops I'd met before. They didn't need prompting.

Frenchie, the smaller of what Cobb liked to call his "operatives" — I knew from previous encounters that he was French Canadian — spoke next. "We'll be in the car across the street and down a few houses. We move on the word fourteen. We hit the door when she screams. Once in the house, he takes Scubberd," he nodded to his partner, "and I get the computer and Pink and we're out the door."

The bigger operative, McNasty for this operation, added, "I get Scubberd dressed and out to the car."

Cobb looked at the three guys leaning against the wall. "That's you, Taurus."

The middle guy, who didn't look much older than Pink, nodded. "Got it. The minute they're out of their car, I do a U-turn and pull up in front of the house. I'll be there."

Grover leaned forward. "The kid ain't no pussy. He's not going to be easy to get to that car."

McNasty spoke again. "I'll get him to the car. The boss said he has to be alive. He didn't say anything about being gentle. If he gets ugly with me, I won't be gentle." A pause. "When we get to the car, I put him into the back seat and I get in beside him. We drive away."

Frenchie picked it up at that point. "Pink and I get into the second car, the Malibu." Another nod from another of the guys leaning against the wall. "I deliver Pink to Grover, who will be waiting for us about a mile from Scubberd's house. In front of the Old Shamrock Hotel." He patted a pocket. "Once Pink is back with Grover, my chauffeur and I bring the computer back here."

Chip spoke up then. "As soon as everybody's out of the house, that's when I go in. I figure I need ten minutes, fifteen at the most to pull down the technology. As soon as I'm loaded, I'm out of there. I join you in the van."

"Where I'll be in the back calling the show," Cobb said.

Calling the show. Very theatrical. Which was in keeping with how carefully scripted all this sounded.

Cobb continued, looking at Chip. "We take you around the corner to where the last car — Patriot — is waiting. Your driver will bring you straight back here."

McNasty spoke again, looking at Cobb. "I get a call from you on my cellphone. I sound very concerned. When the call is over, I tell the kid there's been a fuckup, apologize all over the place and we take him back to the house. Once he's out of the car, I leave and we all meet back here and drink some beer."

"You drink beer," Chip said. "I process the video and the audio and pull what we need off the computer. Once you have that in hand, I'm out."

"Good," Cobb said. "Any questions?"

Frenchie said, "Any way of knowing if the kid will be packing? And what do we do if he is?"

"The scenario as it unfolds will have Brock naked, so even if he's carrying, the weapon won't be *on* his person, so to speak. And if when you guys hit the door, he dives for his gun, you do what you need to do. But he comes out of there alive. Is that clear?"

"I can probably help with that part," Pink said. "I'll make sure he's ... busy at the moment you guys come into the house."

"Good." Cobb nodded. "More questions?"

"I have a few," I said. "But I guess they can wait."

"Anybody else?"

There was general shaking of heads. "Okay. We meet here at eight p.m. Monday. I want everyone ready to roll so we're at Brock's house at nine. That's when Ernie normally brings the girls. Eight o'clock," he repeated. "Clothing, cars, weapons, everything ready. We good?"

This time there was nodding in unison. Slowly they made their way out of the place. Grover and Pink were the last ones to leave. Grover turned back to look at Cobb, like he wanted to say something. He must have thought better of it. He turned, took Pink by the arm, and they were gone, leaving Cobb and me alone in the room. I went to the fridge, pulled two beers out of the box that was the only thing in there. I sat back down, pushed one of the bottles across the table to Cobb. I opened mine and took a long pull.

I didn't know whether to be pissed off or run over and give him a hug. I settled for somewhere in the middle. "How much is this little production costing you?"

He shrugged, drank some beer. "Actually, not that much. I called in some favours, reached out to some people I know, and bingo, we're ready to perform. I think I'll call it *All's Well That Ends Well.*"

"I believe that name's taken."

He laughed. "Damn."

I set my beer down. "I don't like it."

"Why not?"

"Too many moving parts. Too many people involved. If there's even one fuckup, the thing becomes *Macbeth* in a hurry."

Cobb raised his eyebrows.

"Cursed," I said.

"Anything else?" Cobb's face had turned dark, rigid.

"Don't get me wrong, Mike. I appreciate what you're trying to do for me. And if it works it'll get the MFs off my back forever. Nothing would make me happier, believe me. But I don't want a whole lot of people put in harm's way to get me out of a mess I created for myself."

Cobb looked at me for several seconds before answering. "I get that, Adam. And that is exactly what is uppermost in my mind. Nobody in this wants to get hurt. And everybody knows exactly what they have to do to make it work."

"Not everybody."

Cobb smiled at that.

"Your role will be minimal."

"It doesn't feel minimal."

He went through it again. "You and Pink pull up in front of the house. You walk her up to the door. When Brock answers the door, you say Ernie couldn't come and he sent you. You wait for him to give you the money for Ernie and you ask him what time he wants you to come back for her. He'll tell you that and you turn and leave. You get back in the car and you drive away."

"Uh-uh. Once I leave the house, I want to be in the van with you and Chip … the command centre. I want to see how this goes down."

Cobb started to shake his head. I held up my hand. "That's not negotiable. I want to be there."

Cobb closed his eyes, then opened them, nodding slowly. "Okay, we can do that." He pointed to the map. "When you get in your car after you leave the house, you continue straight down the street and turn right at the first intersection, then take the next right and then right again. In other words, you drive around the block. Park on the side street immediately west of the house." He pointed again. "The van will be a couple of houses east of Brock's pad in front of the corner vacant lot. We'll be able to listen to what's going on in the house. If it seems that Scubberd might be coming out of the house or looking out the window for some reason, I'll put my foot on the brake pedal. If, when you come around the corner, you see brake lights, you don't approach the van; turn around and retrace your steps back to your car."

"Got it."

"Everybody's going to be mic'ed up so you can talk to us. We'll hear your conversation with the kid when you go to the door."

"Can I hear you?"

A pause. "I don't think so. Too risky. The only people who can't hear us are you and Pink. Everybody else will have two-way communication with me in the van. Because you two are the ones who will actually be face to face with Brock, we can't take the chance of somebody talking when they're not supposed to and Brock hearing it."

"Yeah, I get that."

"Good."

"What happens after you have the video, the audio, and the porn stuff from the computer?"

"Then we set up a time to sit down with Scubberd senior and we chat."

"And what's going to stop him from shooting our asses and taking the stuff."

"Come on, Adam. I bet you know the answer to that one."

I thought. "Copies."

"Bingo. I make it clear that if you or I disappear, there are several people with instructions to release all of it to the police and the media immediately. I think that will keep the MFs in check."

"And get me out of their clutches."

"That's the plan."

"You trust all the people you have in on this thing?"

"Trust? I wouldn't trust The Grover as far as I can throw him."

"Which is the reason for the goofy nicknames."

Cobb nodded. "Exactly. I want Grover to know only what he needs to. Pink is a wild card. I don't know her. But Grover owes me and I think they'll deliver. The rest of them are good, even the drivers. I know them all, and I know they'll do what's needed. I'm hoping you'll do the same."

"I'm pretty sure I can handle it. But I still don't like —"

He cut me off. "Adam, the alternative is you keep making runs to the States until you get caught, and Jill and Kyla can visit you in prison. Let me know if that's your preference, and I'll give everybody Monday night off." He didn't sound angry so much as tired of having to convince me that this had to be done.

I knew he was right and I nodded slowly.

He smiled. "We can end this, Adam."

"If everything goes according to plan."

"Yeah."

We both drank the beers, thinking hard about what lay ahead.

"Oh, and by the way, we've got things to do in the meantime. I've got us a Monday morning audience with Rachel Claiborne. Well, Kemper made the arrangements."

"Busy start to the week."

"Monday, Monday," Cobb said. "I'll pick you up at your place at nine."

I picked up rye bread, herb pâté, an onion, an English cucumber, a small jar of apricot and chili cheese spread, and a bottle of Cabernet Sauvignon from Southwood Vineyards in Ontario, and headed across town to Jill's.

All of my purchases were designed to curry favour with a couple of people who may have lost faith in my culinary talents after the Sunterra Market extravaganza — all of the food wonderful but none of it actually prepared by me. And while there wouldn't be a lot of cooking involved on this night either, I was confident I'd win them over.

I cheated a little and picked up a book for Kyla, a public relations move that had never failed me. I opted for Linda Bailey's *Seven Dead Pirates*, reasoning that pirates, alive or dead, were a surefire way to win over a ten-year-old's heart.

And I actually felt upbeat, maybe even optimistic. There was at least a reasonable chance that Cobb's plan would work. And if it did, the MFs and the endless threat of them owning me would go away.

After a pre-dinner game of Scrabble — Jill prevailed over the well-read kid and the journalist — I cut up onions and cucumber, set out the rye bread, pâté, and the jar of spread. It was perfect. The great thing was that, with each bite requiring a little more work than simply loading a fork, there was ample time for conversation and laughter, and there was plenty of both.

Dinner over and the cleanup done, Kyla scuttled off to her room, new book in hand. Jill and I, as we often did, topped up our wine glasses and took to the sofa, where we sat as close to each other as possible without actually sharing clothes.

After a few moments of silence, Jill took my hand. "You seem funny tonight, as happy as I've seen you in a while. If I was looking for a word to describe you, I'd say you were carefree … or maybe relieved."

I thought about the best way to answer without lying any more than I already had.

"You're probably right," I said. "It feels like maybe Cobb and I are making a little progress with a couple of things we're working on."

"Wanna share?"

"Maybe not yet. Not tonight. Give us a few days to see if we really are going in the right direction. Then we'll talk, okay?"

"Of course."

"Thanks, babe."

"So, can I ask you a question?"

I held my hands in a gesture of surrender. "Okay, it's Jennifer Aniston. I admit it. She's the one I think of when we're making love."

Jill punched me on the arm. "Idiot, that wasn't the question."

"Oops."

She punched me again.

"Okay, I'm serious," she said. "Let's say we couldn't live here and we couldn't live in your apartment … where would you want to live?"

I sipped my wine. "Wow, that's a tough one. Well, I always thought I'd want to live in one of those family-type neighbourhoods, like maybe Lake Bonavista, but I'm not totally sure. I love a lot of the older parts of the city, too."

"Like Bridgeland?"

I nodded. "I do like where I live. I like it a lot. I'd want wherever we lived to be really great for Kyla, that's important to me."

She kissed me then.

"I have to say, I like that a lot better than the punching."

She laughed. "If you'd behave, you'd get more kisses and less punching."

"I'll keep that in mind. What about you? Where would you want to live?"

"I guess I'm kind of like you. There are quite a few places I could be happy in."

"What about the country? With your love of horses, I'd have thought you'd like a home out of the city."

She nodded and smiled. "Yes, that too. Decisions, decisions." She smiled and moved in close to me, the smell of her hair and the nearness of her warmth pushing aside, at least for now, the thoughts of what was to come on Monday.

TWELVE

"Thank you for seeing us, Mrs. Claiborne," Cobb said as we slid into chairs on the opposite side of a cold grey metal table. I had anticipated we'd be separated by glass with a speaker on each side, so this was better.

Rachel Claiborne smiled. It wasn't a big smile and didn't involve her eyes. She looked smaller than I'd expected. I guessed that jail, even a remand centre cell, could do that to you.

"Mike Cobb, Mrs. Claiborne; this is my partner, Adam Cullen. I believe your attorney told you that we have been representing Danny Luft."

"She did, yes."

"They don't give us a lot of time here." Cobb leaned forward, his elbows on the table. "So, I'll get right to it. Danny told us that you didn't shoot your husband, Mrs. Claiborne."

A pause. "And he would know that how?"

"He said he just knows. He told us he's sure you're covering for someone."

"I shot my husband. He deserved to be shot, and I'd do it again if I was faced with the same opportunity. Danny Luft is a nice boy … but he's wrong."

"What opportunity was that, Mrs. Claiborne?"

"What do you mean?"

"I mean when did you shoot your husband and how did it take place?"

"What difference does any of that make now?"

"Did you have the gun with you when you entered his office?"

"What?"

"The gun, did you bring it with you? We know that he kept it upstairs in a bedside table. Had you planned to kill him? If so, I expect you brought the gun with you from upstairs."

Cobb was firing the questions at her, I assumed to try to catch her off guard.

"I ... I told you I don't see the purpose in any of this. I don't need to answer any of your questions. And I'm not sure why you are asking them. Your client is in the clear. He's no longer a suspect. Which he shouldn't be, because I'm the one who shot Wendell."

I spoke for the first time. "Danny was very firm in his belief that you didn't shoot your husband, Mrs. Claiborne. He doesn't think you are capable of killing someone."

She looked at me. "Do you know anything at all about me ... about my life before I married Wendell? Because I promise you, Danny Luft, as fine a young man as he is, knows nothing about me and what I'm capable of."

Cobb said, "As a matter of fact, we do know about your former life, Mrs. Claiborne."

"Then you know that the world I inhabited was dark. Dark and dirty and dangerous. Human life was not as valuable as the next sale of crack or the next john's blow-job. Money ruled everything. And it ruled my life. So forget about what Danny thinks of me or even what you think of me. I know what I've done in my life and I know what I did that night. I think this interview is over." She stood up.

"Mrs. Claiborne," Cobb said, his voice low and flat. "I know who killed your husband."

She started to turn away, then turned back, the mask that had been her face until that moment now gone, replaced by anger. Anger and maybe fear. "What is it you think you know?"

"First of all, Mrs. Claiborne, I promise you that we will not reveal what we know without your permission, and I know you can't give that permission. We both know that, don't we, Mrs. Claiborne?"

She didn't answer. Her features were tight, as if they were glued in place. "I'm going to give you and this fantasy of yours thirty seconds more, Mr. Cobb. Then I will walk out that door and in a few weeks I will be sentenced to a number of years in prison for shooting my husband. And that's exactly as it's supposed to be. *Crime and Punishment.*"

The room was quiet for a moment, and in that time I knew, or at least I thought I knew, what Cobb was saying to her, without actually saying it.

"Did you ever read that novel, Mrs. Claiborne, *Crime and Punishment*?"

She looked at me and shook her head.

"In it, the main character is a man — Raskolnikov, who murders two women. His punishment is internal — the guilt he feels at what he has done. This is different — this is a case of someone willing to bear the punishment for something she *hasn't* done."

"Actually, I wasn't talking about the book, Mr. Cullen. But thank you for the literature lesson."

Chastened, I didn't have a response. Cobb stepped in. "I'd like to ask you a few specific questions, Mrs. Claiborne."

"You can ask any questions you like."

"And I'd appreciate it if you'd answer those questions."

"I will if I can."

"Did you bring the gun with you from the bedroom upstairs?"

She looked at him a long time before she nodded.

"Did anyone else see you shoot Wendell Claiborne?"

"No."

"Where was your daughter when the shooting took place?"

"She was outside taking our dog, Tater, for his evening walk."

"Did she hear the shot?"

Hesitation. "Yes … no. Wendell was already … I'd already shot him. Glenna had come back into the house and still had her coat and mitts on; it was a cool night. She came into the office to say good night to her father and saw him lying there."

"What did you do with the gun after you shot your husband?"

"I … I dropped it."

"Then what?"

"What do you mean?"

"What happened after you shot your husband and dropped the gun on the floor?"

"I called 911."

"Right away?"

"Well, there might have been a few minutes — I was upset, as you can imagine."

"And what did Glenna do after she came into Claiborne's office?"

"What did she do?" she repeated the question.

"You said she came into the office and saw him on the floor. I'm wondering what she did. Did she scream, did she run over to her father's body, did she run back out of the room?"

"I … there was some confusion, as you can understand. I'm not sure exactly what. It took me some time … I mean, to recover myself … a few minutes."

"Recover yourself," Cobb said.

"Yes, I … Glenna ran into the room and she screamed, and she, I believe, went to her father. She was … in shock … as you might expect. Then she came to me and we held each other."

"Did you come into the office before or after your daughter shot her father?"

I glanced over at Cobb. This was the homicide detective on full display. Aggressive, relentless, determined and pulling no punches. Rachel Claiborne looked like she was thinking about leaving again but this time changed her mind before she got to her feet.

"That is absurd."

"Please tell us what happened in that room that night, Mrs. Claiborne," Cobb said. "Sometimes there are extenuating circumstances. We may be able to help. And I reiterate my promise that we reveal nothing of what you tell us without your permission."

"You seem quite confident that you are right."

"Mrs. Claiborne, I think Danny Luft was right when he said you would take the hit for someone else. But not just *anyone* else. You'd do it for Danny Luft because you knew he was innocent. And you'd do it for your daughter because you are her mother."

The room was quiet for a time. Rachel Claiborne was looking down at her hands. Finally, she looked up.

"You are right about that, Mr. Cobb. I would do anything for my daughter. But it was Danny who had been arrested and charged. And all of us in this room know he didn't kill my husband. I'm told that the police had sufficient evidence — phone messages, texts, his fingerprints on the gun — that he may well have been found guilty. I couldn't let that happen."

Cobb was gentler now. "Mrs. Claiborne, your first statement to the police was very different. It talked of your coming into your husband's office some minutes after he was shot and discovering him lying on the floor."

"Of course. That was when I believed we could perhaps convince the police that someone else had killed Wendell, some stranger breaking into the house. But, as I said, once I learned about Danny and the evidence the police indicated they had, well, I had to … I had to do what I did."

"I understand," Cobb said. "Mrs. Claiborne, I'm going to present a slightly different scenario. I'd appreciate your hearing me out and I'd like to hear your reaction. I'm thinking that you and your husband were discussing something, perhaps arguing. Maybe it was about money. Maybe it was about women. Or maybe it was about the fact that he wanted you gone from his house and his life. The argument became heated, nasty. Your husband picked

243

up the gun that was on his desk and was threatening you. Glenna came in from outside, having taken the dog for a walk. As you said, she still had her coat and gloves on. She looked in to say good night and saw Mr. Claiborne waving the gun around and pointing it at you. The gun, by the way, was not upstairs in the night table, because he had it with him to show Danny earlier that evening.

"Now I doubt that he was going to shoot you because, of course, he already had a plan in place for that. But Glenna couldn't know that he was only threatening. She saw him out of control and threatening her mother with a firearm. She did the only thing she could think of. She ran at him to keep him from shooting you. There was a struggle, the gun went off and your husband fell to the floor.

"Perhaps you, too, became involved in the struggle … it doesn't matter. What does matter is that you are protecting your daughter and have been all along. And while that is understandable and even admirable, it may not be necessary."

"Mrs. Claiborne," I said. "I covered the crime beat for the *Calgary Herald* for several years, sat in on a lot of trials, wrote about dozens of cases from fraud to robbery to murder. If this came to court, a jury would almost surely be very sympathetic to your daughter and to you. This was someone trying to disarm someone with a gun. You both should be — and, I think, would be — looked at as heroes."

Rachel Claiborne looked first at me, then at Cobb, her mouth, her posture, and her voice combined in one thin, unyielding line. "I will not allow some lawyer to pick apart my daughter in a courtroom and I will not have her sit there while that same lawyer dredges up every sordid detail from my past. Neither of those things is going to happen, gentlemen, and that is my last word on the matter."

"Glenna doesn't know about your former life," I said.

"She does not and she will not find out about it in a courtroom surrounded by people she doesn't know and, you'll forgive me Mr. Cullen, by reporters who couldn't care less about breaking a young girl's heart as long as the whole vulgar story is told."

Sadly, she was speaking the truth. I nodded my head.

"And I remind you that you began this conversation, Mr. Cobb, by giving your word that you would say nothing of this insane little potboiler of yours. And I most assuredly do not give you my permission."

Cobb looked worn but he nodded. "You don't need to remind us, Mrs. Claiborne. We will keep our word." He took out a business card and handed it to her. "If you change your mind or if you ever want to talk some more, you can call me anytime. Thank you for taking the time to speak to us. We wish you well."

Rachel Claiborne stood up. "Thank you, Mr. Cobb … Mr. Cullen." She shook our hands. "I appreciate what you are trying to do. But I'm going to hold you to your promise. You will say nothing; you will do nothing, as we agreed."

She rapped on the door to let the guard know the interview was over. As he opened the door, she smiled at us a last time. I nodded to her and she was gone.

Cobb's business card still lay on the table.

"This doesn't feel like a win," I said.

Cobb and I were sitting in Ric's Lounge and Grill in the Sheraton Four Points Hotel in northeast Calgary.

We were working our way through a plate of nachos and listening to Justin Bieber's "Purpose" on the house sound system.

Cobb took a sip of his Caesar and shook his head. "No, it doesn't."

"So, what now?"

"You heard the lady. We're out. Our client has been cleared."

"So we just let a woman we know is innocent go to jail."

"If you can think of a way we can keep that from happening without breaking our word to Rachel Claiborne, I'm all ears."

I shook my head. "I wish I had even the makings of an idea."

"Me too." He looked at me over his glass, a nacho in hand. "You okay for tonight?"

I shrugged. "You want the truth? I'm scared to death. I'm scared something will go wrong and somebody, maybe several somebodys, could get hurt. Maybe hurt bad. But it's a little like the situation with Mrs. Claiborne; I don't have a better idea. And I'm willing to try almost anything to get the MFs out of my life."

Cobb nodded. We ate some more nachos and I drank some of the Rickard's Red I had barely touched.

"You really believe this can work?"

There was no hesitation. "Obviously, I think it will work. But if you're wanting a guarantee, I can't give you that. All I can tell you is that I've been through the thing a hundred times in my mind, including all the things I think can go wrong, and I believe this will happen as I've laid it out."

I held up my glass and he tapped it with his. "Mike, I haven't been nearly grateful enough. And that's bullshit. What you and everyone else are doing tonight is because of my screw-up. Don't think I don't know that and don't appreciate it."

Cobb nodded and glanced at his watch. "Monday, Monday."

"I'm not sure that's the song you want to be our theme music for this operation. There's a line in there about not trusting that day."

"I guess I was thinking of another line. Besides, what do you know? You're the Canadian music guru. You're not supposed to know anything about the Mamas and the Papas."

"Ah, but that's where you're wrong. Denny Doherty was Canadian. Maritimes, maybe, I'm not sure."

"And Denny Doherty, I take it, was one of the Papas?"

"Check."

Cobb drained his Caesar. "I should have known better than to doubt you."

"Canadian music guru," I said. "Not a particularly marketable skill." I pushed my beer away, thinking too much to enjoy it.

Cobb saw the gesture and nodded. "I say we get out of here and grab a nap before the big show. It might be a long night."

We both threw money on the table and headed out to Cobb's Cherokee. On the way back to the office and my car, neither of us talked and he kept the radio off. Alone with our thoughts, and in my case a prayer or two.

THIRTEEN

I got to the motel a little early, but I wasn't the first one there. A voice answered my knock with, "Yeah, who is it?" I said my name (Cobb hadn't given me a nickname) and the door opened. I walked in and nodded to McNasty, who had opened the door. He returned the nod and his mouth made some of the motions associated with smiling. He stepped back and I followed him into the room.

Cobb was at the same place he'd been when I was there previously. He had a school-type notebook on the table in front of him and was making notes. Frenchie was also there, leaning forward and studying whatever Cobb had written or drawn on the page.

There was tension in the room. I wouldn't say they were nervous, but it was far from a relaxed atmosphere. Cobb looked up at me. "Adam, how are you?" His face tried a little harder on the smile and was more successful. "Have a seat, there's coffee and doughnuts if you feel like either."

"I think I'm good," I said and took the same seat I'd had the last time.

"There's one change to the plan. I'll fill you in before the rest of them get here."

"Okay," I said and looked at each of Cobb's men, neither of whom gave any indication that anything was amiss.

"When you leave the house after you drop off Pink, you don't get in the van that's in front of the party house." He held up a crude, hand-drawn map. "That van will be there, but I want you to drive one block farther east and turn left. You'll see another van parked on the side street almost at the corner. You park your car, get out, and walk down the street away from the van; then cross the street and walk back to the van. You climb in the side door of that van."

"I said I wanted to be in the command centre."

Cobb nodded. "And you will be. Chip and I will both be in there along with Jean-Luc … uh, Frenchie, once he drops off Pink with Grover and joins us with the computer in hand."

The little French Canadian laughed and wagged his finger at Cobb's gaffe.

"I don't get it," I said. "Who's in the other van?"

"Nobody."

I didn't say anything but my face must have given away my confusion.

"It's a decoy," Cobb said.

I shook my head. "I don't get it. Decoy to do what?"

"It's just precautionary. I told you the other day I believed everybody would do what they're supposed to. But just in case they don't, we have a little backup plan."

It wasn't hard to guess who the weak links in this chain were. "You think Grover and Pink might pull something?"

"I can't say," Cobb admitted. "I think Pink is okay, but Grover …? If he tries anything I want to be ready."

I had a few more questions, but they remained unanswered as the other players in Cobb's production began to arrive. Once everyone was there, Cobb went around the room again, asking everyone if they were clear what they had to do and if they had any questions. I spent some time looking at Grover, but there was nothing that indicated he was anything but a team guy. No one had questions. I noticed that Pink had chosen clothes and a small amount of makeup that, if anything, made her look even younger. My disgust for Brock Scubberd rose another notch.

They stood around in groups of two or three, some drinking coffee and talking in low voices. The doughnuts went untouched. Nervous stomachs, maybe. I knew mine was. Chip went from person to person, attaching tiny microphones and earpieces. Pink and I didn't get the earpieces. Grover didn't either.

"What the fuck?" he whined. "I need to know what's goin' down, for Chrissake. My baby's gonna be in there and I need …"

He stopped talking then because Cobb had risen out of his chair and walked to where Grover was sitting, Pink to his left.

"You need nothing," Cobb's voice was low and slow and it was the only sound in that room. "You don't need to hear anything, and you sure as hell don't need to talk to anybody. Including right now, Grover. You understand what I'm saying to you? All you have to do is be sitting in your car in front of the Shamrock when Frenchie arrives with Pink."

Grover's eyes narrowed and for a brief moment it looked like he might challenge Cobb. He wisely decided against it. He gave a brief nod and leaned back in his chair to create a little more distance between himself and Cobb.

It wasn't long before Cobb looked at his watch and said, "Okay, cellphone ringers off." He waited until everyone had complied. "All right, let's go."

He didn't want everyone to leave at once, so again we filtered out in ones and twos. Pink and I were the last ones to leave. By the time we got to my car, everyone else had left the motel's parking lot. Except Cobb and Chip. Cobb stepped to the driver's side window. I opened it.

He looked at his watch. "What time have you got?" I looked at the car's clock. "Eight thirty-seven," I said.

"Okay, at a quarter to, you head out. You don't have to rush but don't dawdle either."

I nodded, preferring not to ask my voice to do anything just then. "Good luck," Cobb said. He crossed the parking lot to his Jeep. Seconds later he and Chip were gone.

Pink opened her window and lit a smoke. Normally I'd have asked her not to light up in the car, but I decided to let it go. As the clock hit a quarter to, she tossed the cigarette out into the parking lot and I started the car.

Once we were on the street, she said, "Full tank. Good idea." It was the first time she'd spoken directly to me.

"Yeah, I figured it wouldn't be good to run out of gas tonight."

Neither of us said anything more after that and we kept the radio off, the car's engine the only noise around us.

As we drove by the last cross street before Brock Scubberd's house, I saw the decoy van sitting in front of the empty lot on the corner.

Scubberd's party pad was the third house in.

The house between Scubberd's and the corner lot was boarded up. On the other side of the Scubberd house, another older bungalow, not very different from the party house, was dark. I hoped the residents, if there were residents, weren't home. The fewer people around to see what would be happening over the next hour or so, the better. Farther down the block, there were lights on in some of the houses, but no one outside that I could see. There were a few cars parked on the street and in a couple of driveways. In one of them, I knew McNasty and Frenchie were waiting and watching.

I eased to the curb in front of Scubberd's. I decided to shut the car off, not wanting to appear to Scubberd too eager to get out of there. I looked over at Pink. "You ready?"

She nodded.

"Okay, let's do this."

We climbed out and she waited for me until I came around the car; then we walked the rest of the way to the house together, up two steps to a concrete landing with an iron railing on the sides. Scubberd opened the door before we could knock or ring the bell. That threw me a little. That wasn't how I'd rehearsed it in my mind. He stood at the door, dressed in jeans and a Mötley Crüe T-shirt. He was scowling at me.

"Who the fuck are you?"

"Ernie couldn't make it tonight. He asked me to bring her."

"What do you mean he couldn't make it? He didn't say anything to me."

I shrugged. "Shit, I don't know. He just called and told me he had something he needed me to do. I didn't ask no questions." I grinned stupidly in the direction of Pink and he looked at me for a couple of seconds longer, then switched his attention to her.

"Well, well, aren't you just the sweetest little piece ever. What's your name, baby?"

"My friends call me Pink," she said.

"Pink." Scubberd chuckled at that. "Well, I certainly plan to be your friend … Pink. You better come inside. It's chilly out here." He looked up and down the street, checking maybe to see if anyone was watching.

He held out his hand, stuffed a couple of bills into mine. "You tell Ernie that I'm going to kick his sorry ass next time I see him. And" — he glanced again at Pink, but he was talking to me — "you can come back at midnight. I might just want to take a little extra time tonight."

I nodded, and as Scubberd stepped back to let Pink inside, I turned and walked back to the car, willing myself not to look around, especially not back at the house. I got in the Accord, started it, and drove off, following Cobb's instructions, rolling one more block east before making the left. As I did, I saw the second van in place. I drove halfway down the street and parked on the opposite side. I got out, locked the car, and walked up the street away from the van. Then I crossed over and strolled back, trying hard for the look of someone taking his evening constitutional and enjoying the walk.

When I got to the side door of the van, I tapped. Chip slid it open and I climbed inside, pulling the door shut behind me. Chip turned away and began fidgeting with a couple of dials on a receiver. There was a small screen set up so that both he and Cobb could watch it.

Both were wearing sophisticated-looking headsets with attached microphones.

Cobb was sitting in the driver's seat, but had it swung around so he was facing the back of the van. He was looking at the monitor. "He's just poured her a drink," he said. "I don't think his MO has included date-rape drugs, but be ready. If it sounds like she's starting to lose consciousness, we may have to move — no, there she is, I've got her now. She's telling him that she wants to be a Hollywood actress. I can't see her, but she sounds pretty convincing. Okay, everybody listen now. Everybody focus."

He looked at me then and gave a thumbs up. Chip handed me a headset.

The first voice I heard was that of Brock Scubberd. "Okay, baby, I think it's time you and me got a little better acquainted." There was the sound of people moving, I couldn't see the monitor but guessed he was kissing her and clothing was coming off. "Oh, baby, you look good, you look real good. This is gonna be a night both of us are gonna remember for a long time." More rustling noises. Lasted a little longer this time. "Oh, yeah, that's good, this is gonna be so good. Okay, baby, my turn now. Oh, you wanna do that. Aren't you a bad girl. Hey now, easy with that shirt … that's first-class material right there, just like what's inside the shirt … and especially what's inside the pants. Oh yeah, you come here."

Then Pink spoke, the first time I heard her. "Hey, handsome man, what's that?"

Scubberd answered. "Just one of the tools of the trade, baby, nothing for you to worry about."

"It scares me. Not too close, okay. Can you put it over there?"

I'd moved to where I could see the screen. The camera was behind Scubberd, so we were seeing only his bare back. He was blocking Pink from view. Scubberd moved out of view for a few seconds, then returned.

"Thanks, honey," Pink said. "That's better."

"Good girl," Cobb said. "She's letting us know that the gun is a little ways away from them. Shouldn't be long now."

"For you, baby, anything." Scubberd's words were slightly slurred, perhaps an indication he was on something, or a combination of things. "Now let's get those little guys off and you and me gonna have some fun the Brock way." More rustling, accompanied by some moaning this time.

Cobb said, "What about the other camera? Can we bring it up on the monitor?"

Chip shook his head. "It's recording, so we'll have the pictures, but I couldn't set it up to go back and forth between cameras. I had to pick one. Looks like I picked the wrong one."

"This is fine."

We could see that they were both naked now and Scubberd was on her, moaning and grunting. Not a gentle lover. Then the monitor went black.

"What's wrong?" Cobb said.

"Not sure," Chip answered. "I'm hoping it's the monitor and not the camera."

"See if you can get it back."

"On it," Chip said, working furiously at a keyboard and what looked like a small mixer board.

"Okay, everybody, we've only got sound for the moment," Cobb said.

A couple of minutes passed before either of them spoke again. It was Pink. "Hey, baby, that hurts, don't be too rough, okay?"

"Rough is how this game is played, sugar." There was an unidentifiable noise, then what sounded like a slap or a punch. Then I heard a groan — someone in pain. I looked at Cobb.

He had both hands on the headset and he was staring at the floor, every part of him concentrating ... straining to hear more.

"Come on, Pink ... come on," he hissed into the mic that he knew she couldn't hear.

"Hey, I'm —" Pink's voice cut off by the ugly sound of someone hitting again, of someone else being hit. And the groan was lower, weaker.

"She's hurt. She can't do it. She can't say it. Go. Now! Go, go, go!"

I looked through the windshield and could see the house on the next block. From one of the cars across the street and down a few houses, two figures hit the pavement running. I picked up a pair of binoculars from the front seat and was able to train them on McNasty and Frenchie as they sprinted for the house. And even from here I could see they both had their guns drawn. McNasty took the stairs first and without breaking stride aimed a kick at the lock side of the door. It crashed open and they disappeared inside, the little French Canadian closing the door behind them.

From that point on it was back to the audio feed.

"What the fuck do you think you—?" That's as far as Scubberd got. I guessed that McNasty had either hit him or kicked him and Scubberd had gone down or at least been silenced.

The silence was momentary. "You stupid fucks. Do you know who I am? Do you know who my old man is? You assholes are the other side of dead and —"

Again the sound of fist contact. Hard contact, followed by a loud groan. "Now you listen, you piece of shit." It was McNasty, and he was almost growling. "You see what I'm holding? You feel that against your head? Now, my orders are to get you out of here and into that car that's outside. But the orders don't say if I have to deliver you dead or alive. I'd prefer dead, so if you open your mouth one more goddamn time, I'll blow your fuckin' head off."

"What about Pink?" Cobb said into the mouthpiece.

"She's okay," I heard Frenchie say, his voice barely more than a whisper. "We're just getting her covered up, and we'll be ready to go in a couple of minutes."

McNasty spoke again, barking out an order. "Okay, motherfucker, get your pants on, and if you even think about reaching for that piece, it'll be the last thing you ever do."

The only talking after that was Cobb's man directing Scubberd. "Now the shirt ... your shoes, asshole, get your shoes and put them on. Now."

I lifted the binoculars again and saw the two cars, the Taurus and the Malibu, pull up in front of the house, on schedule.

Seconds later, the four of them came out of the house, Frenchie supporting Pink and helping her down the sidewalk, McNasty with his gun against the back of Scubberd's neck.

Cobb was looking through another set of binoculars. "You sure she's okay? Does she need medical attention?"

257

The answer came back in French.

"English," Cobb ordered. "I want everyone to know what's going on."

Frenchie switched to English. "She says she's okay. She'll have a black eye and she's got some blood in her mouth. She says her teeth are sore but none of them are loose or gone."

"Stay with her," Cobb told him. "I don't want her by herself. When you get to Grover, give him your headset and microphone, I'll want to talk to him."

I could see Frenchie gently helping Pink into the back seat of the second car. What was happening at the front car was anything but gentle, and I wondered what might have happened if Cobb hadn't given the order that he wanted Brock Scubberd alive. I watched McNasty open the back door and shove the kid inside. I wasn't sure, but it looked like Scubberd hit his head on the roof of the car on the way in. McNasty piled in beside him and both cars sped away.

Chip was already out of the van and jogging toward the house.

"Does he need help?" I asked Cobb.

He shook his head. "I don't want anything left behind and he's the only one who knows the exact set-up." He glanced at his watch. "He said ten to fifteen minutes at the most. I hope he's right."

I followed his lead, stole a look at my watch. I was as impatient as Cobb. I wanted to be the hell out of there, and the sooner the better.

Eight minutes in, a voice crackled over the headset. It was Frenchie. "Cobb, you there?"

"Yeah ... go."

"Grover's not here."

"What?"

"He's not here."

"You sure you're at the right place? North side of the old Shamrock Hotel.

"I'm there … and he ain't."

"What about his car? Old red Caddy, you see it anywhere?"

"*Rien* … nothin'."

"How long have you been there?"

"Couple of minutes."

"All right, give it three more minutes, then get away from there. Get back here but stay away from the house. Park behind my van … not right behind. A few car lengths back."

"Got it."

"Goddamn it," Cobb whispered, then hissed into the microphone, "Chip, you nearly done?"

"I'm out that door in thirty seconds," came the answer.

"Right." Cobb looked at me. "Grover's pulling something, that son of a bitch. Reach down behind your seat there. There's a rifle — get it."

This whole thing was starting to worry the hell out of me. For all Cobb's careful planning, we both knew Grover was the loose wheel, and now it looked like … I didn't know *what* it looked like.

"Christ," I said, "I didn't expect there to be shooting."

"Get the rifle."

I reached back, lifted it off the floor. Looked at it. Bolt action — looked like a deer rifle, maybe.

"You know how to shoot, right?"

"I know how to shoot."

"And you can use one of those?"

"Yeah, but —"

"Good, it's loaded. You don't shoot unless I tell you to, but if I tell you to, you shoot, okay?" He pulled a handgun out of a shoulder holster I hadn't noticed and set it on the seat beside him.

"Okay." I set the rifle on the floor at my feet, picked up the binoculars again. Chip was out of the house and running for the van. He dropped something on the lawn, bent down to pick it up, was running again.

Cobb started the van. "Open that door for him."

I pulled off my headset and slid the door open.

Chip started handing me cameras and microphones and some stuff I didn't recognize. I piled it into the back of the van. When all the equipment, most of it smaller than I expected, was inside, Chip climbed in. As he did, I looked back and saw Frenchie and Pink and their driver pulling to the curb a few car lengths back of us. I pulled the door shut.

I heard Cobb in the front seat on his cellphone. "Everything good?" I couldn't hear the answer. "Okay, we take a little time now. Start to sound concerned."

I put the headset back on and could hear McNasty as he talked to Cobb on his cell.

"Aw fuck, you're kidding," he said.

"That's good," Cobb said. "Keep going. Give me more of that."

"You gotta be shitting me. What the fuck am I supposed to do now?"

"Okay," Cobb said. "Is he paying attention?"

"Yeah, yeah. I don't fucking believe this."

"Okay, get ready to hang up, think about it for a few seconds, then tell your driver to take you and Scubberd back to the house. Is he okay to make it from the car to the house on his own?"

"Yeah. I do not believe this. Jesus Christ."

Cobb ended the call and pulled his headset back on. We heard McNasty swear some more, then say, "Okay, drive us back to the house."

The driver said, "What?"

"You heard me. Just do it. What a bunch of shit."

Scubberd must have said something because McNasty said, "You shut the fuck up or I'll plant this thing so far into your skull they'll have to dig it out with a shovel."

There was silence in the car then. And I guessed it was moving and would be back at the house in a few minutes.

Cobb looked at me. "I want you to go back to Frenchie's car and get the computer. Bring it here."

I nodded and was out the door. I walked quickly back to the car. Frenchie had the passenger side window down and passed me the computer. I looked into the back seat to where Pink was. I could see bruising and swelling on both sides of her face.

"You okay?" I asked her.

"I've been better … but yeah, I'm okay."

"You did good in there," I told her and tapped Frenchie on the arm. "You both did."

I hurried back to the van and let myself in. I set the computer next to Chip and got myself back to where I'd been before. The seconds ticked by, it seemed to me, in slow motion. I could feel the rifle at my feet and hoped that's where it would stay.

We heard McNasty say, "Looks like this is your lucky day."

"What the hell does that mean?" Scubberd demanded.

"This is what it means, you little turd. It means we're taking you back to your house, where I'm going to drop you off and you get to go inside and make yourself a cup of tea. Trust me. I'd love to shoot your ass right now. But somebody fucked up and I don't get to do that until next time."

The kid said, "Fuckin' losers."

"Don't push your luck, piece of shit. I haven't knee-capped anybody in way too long."

That ended the conversation for the moment.

Cobb put the van in gear, moved to the intersection, and rolled through it. At the next corner he turned left, drove for two more blocks, then about halfway down the third block pulled in behind a dark-brown SUV with Patriot at the wheel.

Chip, who had been sorting the stuff in the back of the van, including the computer, into a small duffle bag, said, "I've got everything I need. I'll see you at the motel."

Cobb nodded and Chip rolled the side door open, climbed out of the van and into the passenger seat of the SUV.

"Turn your cellphone on," Cobb told him. "In case I need to talk to you."

Chip nodded. We waited a few seconds until the driver pulled away from the curb. When it was out of sight, Cobb made a U-turn and we retraced our route back to where we'd been previously. Another U-turn and we were in almost exactly the same place we'd been.

We were only there a minute or so when the Taurus pulled up in front of the party house and Brock Scubberd pulled himself out of the car. He took a couple of steps, turned, and unleashed a barrage of curses at the car that was already pulling away. Then he continued unsteadily on his way up to the house and disappeared inside.

"Your guy McNasty's a pretty good actor," I told Cobb.

He shrugged and came close to a smile. "I'm not sure he was acting."

"Yeah, I sensed that he didn't like Brock Scubberd."

"I got that same sense."

"Kneecapping what I think it is?"

"You shoot the victim in both knees."

"Yeah," I said. "That was my guess. What do you think the kid's going to do?"

"Well, I don't think he's going to phone up his old man and ask for help. So that limits his options. I expect he'll think about it as much as his IQ will allow him to, and then he'll shrug his shoulders and get on with his life. Maybe call Ernie and tell him to get him a girl. But I doubt if that will happen tonight."

"Okay, so what's next for us?"

"We're wrapped here. Time to reconvene back at the motel." He pulled his headset onto his head again and spoke into the microphone. "Okay, everyone, one last thing … anybody see Grover?"

There was a chorus of *nos* and *uh-uhs*. Cobb nodded and started to speak, then stopped, slid the headset down over his neck.

"Frenchie, you read me?"

"Yeah."

"Ask Pink if she wants us to take her to the hospital."

We could hear Frenchie relaying the message. "She says no, she just wants to go home."

"You got her envelope?"

"Yeah."

"You have any money?"

"Yeah."

"Put an extra two hundred in her envelope. I'll settle with you when we get to the motel. You have that much on you?"

"Yeah, I got that much."

"Okay, then I want you to take Pink downtown and put her in a cab. If this is a set-up, I don't want you driving into an ambush. Then you head for the motel. You got it?"

"Yeah."

"Good, I'll see —" Cobb stopped in midsentence. "Oh-oh," he said softly.

I looked at him and saw that his attention was drawn in the direction of the house. I picked up the binoculars and looked down the street. A block past the house, a car, its headlights out, was moving slowly up the street. It was too far away to know for sure, but it looked like there were two people in the front seat. I couldn't tell if there were more in the back.

Cobb spoke into his microphone. "Everyone stand by. There's a car approaching the house. Lights off. Not one of ours. Nobody moves except on my command, but be ready."

The car slowed even more and came to a stop alongside the decoy van. From that distance I was certain there were at least two people in the car. The person in the passenger seat opened his door and, though I couldn't say for sure, it appeared that he — I was fairly certain it was a man — threw something under the van. He slammed the door shut and the car roared toward us, lights still off.

"Get down!" Cobb barked.

As it roared by us, I managed to glance up over the dash and was sure it was Minnis I'd seen in the passenger seat. I wasn't positive, but I thought I saw Grover in the back seat. And I knew the driver, too — Rock Scubberd, the kid's dad.

All three of the car's occupants were staring straight ahead, grimly concentrating on the road in front of them, not looking right or left. Not seeing us.

I turned to Cobb, who, like me, had stolen a peek over the dash.

He said only one word. "Grover."

We sat back up and Cobb started to speak into the microphone once again. He didn't get the chance.

The explosion, though it was more than a block away, was powerful enough that the van we were in rocked from side to side and I felt myself actually shifted to my left. A huge fireball raced up into the night sky while metal debris from the other van flew like shrapnel in every direction. What looked like part of the hood or a door landed on the pavement just a few feet in front of us.

As the initial noise died down, there were a few smaller bursts and concussions. Cobb spoke into the microphone. "Code Orange," he said. "Code Orange. Does everybody read me?"

One by one everyone identified himself and acknowledged the Code Orange, whatever the hell that was. A part of me almost wanted to laugh at the action movie scene unfolding in front of me. But I remembered that Cobb had made the call on the decoy van, a call that I realized now had saved lives, one of them quite possibly mine. So, whatever his Code Orange was, I was okay with it. When he was satisfied that he'd heard from everyone, Cobb threw the van in gear and wheeled left around the corner, heading in the same direction as the MFs car.

I knew we weren't chasing them; that would have been stupid. What was important now was for us to be out of there fast, before curious eyes noticed us leaving the area. Cobb was careful not to speed. As we headed east, I looked back at the scene behind us. People were already starting to appear at front doors and windows of houses on both sides of the street. The gawkers would be fascinated, at least for a while, by the flames that were soaring skyward and consuming what was left of the other van. And as I continued to stare back at the chaos on the street, I realized there wasn't a hell of a lot of it left.

Cobb's voice was calm as he spoke into the headset. "Okay, everybody. I imagine most of you heard that. The MFs and The Grover blew up the other van. We're okay. I want everybody moving now. Nobody gets followed, nobody gets stopped by the cops — I want everyone back at the motel as soon as you can get there. I repeat — make sure you aren't tailed, and don't speed or do anything else to get yourself pulled over. Remember, it's Code Orange. If you've got questions, ask them. Otherwise get moving."

There were no questions and Cobb pulled the headset off and tossed it behind him.

"They could've killed Scubberd's own kid if some of that flaming debris hit the house," I said.

"Yeah," Cobb said.

"Could have been bad for us, too."

"Yeah," Cobb said again.

"Okay, I've got a question."

"Shoot."

"If we'd been in that van, we'd be dead now."

"That's not a question," Cobb said.

"The question is this — how did you know that was a possibility?"

"I didn't."

"Then why the second van that everybody on the team knows about except Grover? You had to have some idea."

Cobb glanced over at me then back at the road. "Look, Adam, I've known Grover a long time. Long enough to know that he'd sell his mother for the right price. He's one of the sleaziest bags of shit on the street. Up to now, he's played by my rules. But I always knew that anytime Grover was part of something, I had to keep looking over my shoulder. That's what I was doing. I honestly believed this would go off just the way I'd planned it. But because Grover was in the mix, I needed a little insurance. That old van I bought off a guy for three hundred dollars? That was the insurance."

"Actually, except for that little episode back there, it did go off pretty much the way you planned it."

"We're not done yet. We haven't got you off the hook."

"When does that happen?"

"Right away. Once we get back to the meeting place and Chip is sure we have what we need, I make a call."

"I asked you once before, how much is our night's charade costing you?"

"If things work out, I'm hoping nothing. We'll know soon enough."

It wasn't long before I learned what Code Orange was. The rendezvous had been moved to a second motel, at least as unpleasant as the first. That eventuality had to have been set up in advance, another example of Cobb's attention to detail. And maybe his concern about The Grover.

When we got back to the new motel, Cobb circled the block twice, staring at every parked car and eyeing the three people we saw on the street — a woman walking with an elderly man and, on another street, a kid in a hoodie. I wondered about him but Cobb seemed satisfied that he wasn't a threat. This place, which from the outside looked marginally less grungy than the first, sported a sign that announced it was The Hillside. Terrific name. Not a hill within ten kilometres.

The third time we went by the driveway leading into the motel's parking lot, Cobb turned in. It was pretty straightforward after that. Everyone was there. Cobb dismissed the three young drivers, handing each an envelope and shaking hands with them. They then left at five-minute intervals.

After they were gone, the rest of us — Cobb, me, and Cobb's guys — drank coffee while Chip checked video and audio and downloaded it onto a second computer.

"Good news," Chip finally said. "The cameras worked perfectly, both of them. It was only the monitor that crapped out. I've downloaded all the video and audio onto your laptop. I think you'll be happy with it. Should be just what you need to spoil someone's day."

"You have the email addresses where I want the copies sent to?"

"I do," Chip responded. "They'll be delivered within minutes."

"I've spoken to all of them. They — and you — know what to do if something happens to me or" — he angled his head in my direction — "him."

"Absolutely." Chip nodded. "I hope I don't ever have to do it, though."

"Well, that makes me feel better," I said, trying for a laugh, not managing one myself.

We gathered around the computer to watch. We'd heard the audio so had a pretty good idea what we'd be seeing. No real surprises. Once some of Pink's clothing came off, Brock was in a hurry. I flinched the first time he hit her and again when he did it a second time. She appeared to be at least stunned by the blows and it looked to me like Cobb was right to send the guys in when he did. It didn't look like Pink was in any shape to remember, let alone say, the cue lines she and Cobb had agreed on.

And as I had expected, McNasty was far from gentle with Brock Scubberd once he and Frenchie were in the house. I wanted to cheer when I saw him hit the kid with an elbow that snapped his head back and sent him sprawling to the floor.

We watched the whole thing twice and Cobb nodded approvingly and fist-bumped Chip.

"You're right. We've got exactly what we need. As long as Grover doesn't spill to Rock Scubberd that Pink was his girl and she's not a minor. And I don't think he'll do that. Scubberd might not approve of Grover's offering to be part of this even if he claims he only did it so he could out us. I don't think Grover will want to have to deal with Scubberd's temper. And when Scubberd learns there was nobody in that van, Grover's credibility will be in the tank."

"Along with his body?"

"It's possible. Apparently, that was a risk The Grover was willing to take."

"When do we make the contact with the MFs?"

"Now seems like a good time. Why don't you help Chip pack up while I make the call?"

Chip was already packing up his equipment, and I crossed the smallish room to give him a hand. "You did a damn good job," I told him. "Seeing as this thing's a wrap, at least this phase, how about you tell me your real name."

He looked at me and grinned. "Albert Playfair." We shook hands. "But the funny part? I've been called Chip since junior high school ... about the time I started fixing friends' computers. My buddy's dad called me that after I put a hard drive into his machine, and the name stuck."

We weren't long getting his stuff packed away in two good-sized cardboard boxes and ready to go. Frenchie drained the last of his coffee and stood up. "I'm giving you a ride back to your car," he told Chip. "Here, let me carry one of those."

They started for the door, with McNasty close behind. He threw a perfunctory wave in Cobb's direction and turned to me. "Luck," he said, and followed Frenchie and Chip out the door.

Cobb was standing at the window, looking out at the parking lot. His cellphone was at his ear. I wondered how he knew Scubberd's cellphone number.

"Scubberd. It's Mike Cobb. You sound surprised to hear from me. Yeah, I'm tickled to be chatting with you, too. I've got some bad news. First of all your little IED missed its target. Sorry to have to ruin your evening. Yeah, cut the bullshit and listen up because I've got some more bad news. I seem to have acquired some rather damning material that will reflect badly on your son. The young lady he was with tonight was a little too young to be totally legal.

"There's all this video and audio that's just crying for an audience. Oh, and there's his enthusiasm for kiddie porn. You might want to call him and ask him if he's seen his computer lately. It might be missing. But see, Rock, that's where the good news kicks in. I happened to have found the young man's computer and I'd really like to return it. The cops look unfavourably on that whole kiddie porn thing — about the same way they seem to regard guys like Brock taking advantage of underage girls. And slapping them around. The cops are real funny about that kind of stuff. So it seems like it might be a good idea for us to meet.… Well, I was thinking tonight would be a good time. I think you'll want to get on this sooner rather than later … otherwise one of the various copies I've made might just find its way to the cops or the media or maybe both."

There was a pause as he listened to Rock Scubberd. I assumed Scubberd was less than cordial.

"No problem, Rock. I'm happy to fuck off. And right after I do that I'll make a couple of calls and maybe we can all get together tomorrow and watch Brock on the news. That would be fun."

He ended the call and turned to me, smiling. "Well, I learned a few new words. I'm guessing he's talking to the kid right now and will call me back." He crossed the room to the well-worn sofa and sat down.

"What if 'fuck off' is his final answer?"

"For that to happen, he'd have to be willing to throw his son to the dogs. And don't forget the son's last name. All of this would reflect rather badly on a guy who portrays himself as a respectable businessman biker. I think he'll call. He may want to talk to his wife about it, too. But he'll call. Or she will."

We sat and waited. For the first time in a very long while, I wished I was still a smoker. I was worried that the evening's charade might have made things even worse, although I wasn't sure what could be much worse than having to smuggle drugs across the Canada-U.S. border and having people trying to blow us up. Cobb was much calmer about things. The cards had been played and he seemed pretty happy with his hand. I just wanted all of it to go away. It was twenty minutes before the call came.

Cobb took his time answering. "Scubberd," he said by way of greeting. Then he listened. "We'll be there. Forty-five minutes."

He ended the call and stood up. "Time to go. We have a stop to make on the way."

"Where's the meeting?"

"Hose and Hound. He's booked the whole upstairs. Probably a pretty good choice from our perspective. Lots of people downstairs. I doubt if he'll want to shoot the place up."

"You doubt?"

Cobb smiled. "I told you before — no guarantees, my friend. But I think we'll be okay."

Cobb gathered up his laptop and we left just as the hands on the clock radio indicated eleven. The stop we had to make was at the office. He pulled into the parking lot behind the building and parked next to his Cherokee. "Time to switch vehicles." He beeped the doors open on the Jeep, stepped out of the van, and loped toward the back door of the building. I swung out of the van and climbed into the Jeep, glad to be out of the command centre.

Cobb reappeared a couple of minutes later with the package I'd been scheduled to deliver the next day.

"That going to factor in?" I asked as he settled in behind the steering wheel.

"It might."

We didn't talk any more after that. It was a short drive to Inglewood and the Hose and Hound Pub. I'd been there a few times and had always liked the place. I hoped I would still like it an hour or so from now.

We parked across the street, and Cobb placed the drugs in a small carrying case and handed it to me. He carried the laptop as we made our way to the pub.

The downstairs area was fairly full for a Monday night and as loud as one might expect from the post–11:00 p.m. revellers.

Cobb led the way to the staircase and I followed him up. Scubberd, Minnis, and a couple more MFs thugs were seated at a large table in the middle of the room. There was another guy who looked like an accountant who sat at a table by himself. I wasn't surprised that the lovely Mrs. Scubberd was also there. She was at an adjoining table by herself, sipping a glass of white wine.

No one spoke. No greetings, not even nods were exchanged. Cobb set the laptop on Mrs. Scubberd's table, turned it on, and tapped keys for a few seconds. Then he turned the computer so that she could see the screen. Scubberd stood up and moved to a spot behind his wife. When the show was over, Mrs. Scubberd closed the cover on the computer and sat back. Scubberd went back to his seat. Both of their faces were inscrutable.

Scubberd broke the silence. "I'm guessing I know what you want. Scribe, you have anything to say?"

I shook my head. This was Cobb's deal and I didn't want to mess it up.

Mrs. Scubberd looked at me. "We had a deal. You're reneging."

"I don't see it that way," I said.

"I want the product," Scubberd said.

Cobb pointed at the bag I was holding and said, "It's for sale."

"Bullshit," Scubberd roared. "You push me too far and I don't give a shit what's on that computer — I'll blow your asses straight to hell."

Cobb reached into his jacket pocket and pulled out a sheet of paper, which he handed to Scubberd's wife. I wondered if Cobb deliberately demonstrating that he was dealing with her and not Scubberd was a good idea. "That's a list of expenses — what it cost me to put together tonight's event. It comes to eight thousand six hundred and fifty-*three* dollars and forty-seven cents. I'm prepared to waive the forty-seven cents."

He turned to Scubberd. "You get the product, and we both know how much it's worth, so you're getting a bargain. Eight thousand six hundred and fifty-three dollars. Cash. Then we walk away from each other and we're done."

"And if I decide to take that package and turn my fellas loose for a few minutes, there's exactly zero you can do about it."

Cobb turned his body and his eyes to Mrs. Scubberd. "I think that would be a mistake. The simple truth is we don't like each other. And your husband is right — you can cause my friend and me a lot of grief. And clearly we're able to be a bit of a pain in your asses, as well. So I'm proposing that we declare a moratorium. We agree that each of us leaves the other alone. You get the product and we get the money. Nobody gets killed, nobody gets beat up, and no one outside this room ever sees that" — he pointed at the computer — "ever again. Everybody lives happily ever after."

Scubberd was on his feet. Droplets of spittle flew from his mouth as he leaned on the table and held up one fist. "You chickenshit fucks. You put that bag on the table and get the fuck out of here and you've got ten seconds to do it."

Cobb didn't move. I had a bit of a job convincing my legs not to do what they desperately wanted to do, which involved turning and bolting back down the stairs.

The seconds ticked off. No one moved. Finally, Scubberd straightened up and nodded to Minnis, who reached for the shoulder holster that had been very much in evidence since we'd walked into the room.

"Deal," Mrs. Scubberd said, and suddenly the room was a tableau. Minnis froze and looked at his boss, who was looking in turn at his wife. She ignored them both and stared hard at Cobb. "You're proposing a truce."

"No." Cobb shook his head. "I said moratorium. Truce sounds to me more like peace. And I don't think there will ever be peace between us. Moratorium means we agree to stop fighting each other. It can be permanent or it can be temporary. If one side screws up, the moratorium ends. If, for example, anyone associated with the MFs does anything to either of us or any member of our families, the deal's off and the copies are distributed to the media and will appear on social media. And if either of us does anything that harms any of you or your … business interests, same thing, the deal's off."

"We're out twenty-five large," Scubberd said.

"No, you're not," Cobb argued. "Mr. Cullen here made a trip to Montana that helped make you a lot of money. I'm guessing the profit was a hell of a lot more than twenty-five thousand dollars. The only thing you lose is a delivery person. And I'm sure you can find a few more of those."

"A delivery person and eighty-six hundred and fifty dollars," Mrs. Scubberd said with the small smile I'd seen a couple of times before. That smile made her one of the most beautiful women in the world, and I was pretty sure she knew it.

"Eighty-six hundred and fifty-three," Cobb said, returning the smile.

"Of course." Her smile was accompanied by a little laugh. She turned and passed Cobb's list of expenses to the little guy sitting by himself. He had a pencil-thin moustache that didn't look good on him and I put him at around fifty. He was carrying a briefcase and I was fairly sure he packed that briefcase pretty well everywhere.

"Pay the man," Mrs. Scubberd said.

He nodded, turned away from us and dug around in the briefcase. I thought it interesting that he didn't look to Scubberd for confirmation. A moment later he passed a pile of bills to Mrs. Scubberd, who, without looking at the money, passed it along to Cobb.

Cobb set the package on the table in front of her. Then he stepped back and touched his hat as if he was ready to leave.

Finally.

Mrs. Scubberd spoke in a soft, firm voice. "There's something I want to say to you before you go, Mr. Cobb. And to you, too, Mr. Cullen."

Cobb nodded and waited, his face impassive. I tried for the same look. The tricky part was figuring out *where* to look. I didn't want to make eye contact with either Scubberd or Minnis. And I wasn't sure if looking at Mrs. Scubberd was a good idea. I finally settled on a spot on the wall just over the head of the guy with the briefcase.

"You may see this as some kind of victory, and because of that you might also see us as weak. That would be a mistake. We're agreeing to this because I believe, and I think my husband will agree over time, that it is counterproductive for us to be at war. People will get hurt, some may die — and it will cost all of us time and money that could be used much more effectively in other avenues of our businesses and our lives.

"And please don't think that because it appears that I make some of the decisions for our organization, that my husband and his colleagues are somehow lesser men. Again, that would be a serious error in judgment on your part.

"This moratorium" — she drew out the word — "that you have proposed works for us at this time. It makes sense to put what has happened in the past and what happened today behind us. We are prepared to do that. But I warn you both. Don't ever be so foolish as to underestimate us."

It was weird, but the whole thing felt to me like being called to the principal's office and hearing a lecture about acting out in class. Except that this lecture was about living and dying, and everyone in the room understood that. I wondered how Cobb would respond.

He waited a moment before answering. "Message received. And you can believe me when I say that I have never in the past underestimated you, nor will I ever in the future." Cobb looked at them in turn. "Any of you."

He looked at me. "We're done here. Let's go."

I glanced around the room before following Cobb back down the stairs. He didn't slow down; he didn't speed up. I moved up alongside him at the bottom of the stairs as we made our way toward the door.

"I'm assuming you'd prefer to go somewhere else for a drink," Cobb said.

"Yeah, that would be good."

Outside on the street we stopped and took a few deep breaths before climbing into Cobb's Cherokee. I couldn't resist a quick look over my shoulder and was happy to see that no one was running toward us, guns drawn and bullets flying. Nevertheless, I was relieved once we'd pulled out onto 9th Avenue and put a few blocks between us and the Hose and Hound.

"I have to say this. Holding out for the money was insane."

Cobb shook his head. "What I said to them was true. They still came out thousands, tens of thousands ahead. It wasn't worth killing us for less than ten thousand dollars."

"Would you have tried that if it was Scubberd you were talking to instead of his wife?"

"Scubberd would kill someone for ten dollars. He's also not rational. So the answer to your question is no. And I was only fifty-fifty on going after the money even with her until I saw the guy with the briefcase. I thought he might be their accountant type. Meaning that at least some thought had been given to the possibility they'd have to spend some money. And we weren't holding them up for ransom on the stuff we had on the kid. They might have thought what we were asking for was a bargain. Maybe we should go back and ask for more."

"How about I buy you a drink instead?"

He grinned. "I'm okay with that. You have a preference?"

"How about the Whiskey Down at the MGM Grand?"

"Good spot all right, and Vegas is nice this time of year, but do you have a second choice?"

"Okay, how about the Nash? It's close and it's pretty cool."

Cobb nodded. "Good choice."

"Yeah, and we can celebrate the fact that we're still alive … stuff like that."

The Nash was once the National Hotel. The place opened in the early 1900s as a hotel and bar, mainly serving a working-class clientele; decades later it was one of Calgary's seedier spots. It then stood empty for over a decade before reopening as a hip new restaurant and bar. Jill and I had met up at the restaurant a couple of times after her shift at Let the Sunshine Inn ended, as it was just a few blocks away. Tonight, it was the Off Cut Bar that beckoned.

Cobb parked in front of the equally historic livery stable that stood next to the Nash. As we walked to the entrance, I glanced over at Cobb, who looked like he might have just left his kids' Christmas concert. "How do you live the life you do and not spend all your time looking in your rear-view mirror?" I asked.

He smiled. "Adam, I try to weigh all my options and come up with the one that will be most effective. I don't want to get killed any more than you do. But once I've made a decision, like I did tonight, I have to trust my instincts and my judgment. If I'm wrong, then that's going to be bad, but when I'm sure I'm right — and I was pretty sure tonight — then I do what I have to do and trust that I don't have to look in my rear-view. When I can no longer do that, it's time to get into another line of work."

"*Pretty* sure, eh?" I said. "As opposed to *totally* sure?"

"I'm seldom totally sure."

Inside, Cobb ordered a red wine. I went with tried and true — a rye and Diet Coke — which I drank way too fast. I ordered another.

"So, what would it be?" I asked.

"What would what be?"

"The other line of work. If you weren't a private investigator."

Cobb sipped some wine, set his glass down, and grinned at me. "My old man was a baker. When I was a kid I spent a lot of time in that place. I loved the smell, never got tired of that, and I thought it was neat that my dad knew just about everybody who came into the place by name. And a lot of times he knew what they wanted before they said a word. I always thought that was pretty cool, too."

"That *was* pretty cool."

"Good thing I decided to do something else though. The small neighbourhood bakery is a thing of the past. The chain doughnut shops have pretty well killed them off."

"Too bad."

"How about you? You ever think of being something other than a journalist?"

"For me there have only ever been two things … baseball and writing. When my baseball career ended, it seemed like the right time to pursue the journalism option."

"Ever regret it?"

"Until I hooked up with you, never."

He laughed at that, then turned serious. "I guess I *have* put you in what looked like harm's way a time or two. I apologize for that."

I shrugged. "I brought this on myself. And you saved my ass. I won't ever forget that. Besides, I'm a big boy. If I felt I couldn't do this, I could always walk away."

"I hope you don't. We're not a bad team."

"Just remember — you get me killed and you'll have to deal with a pissed-off Jill."

"I've thought about that. Scary."

We both laughed. Relieved laughter.

"So, what's next?"

"Well, we've got a couple of items on our plate. I'd like to get back on the Faith Unruh–Marlon Kennedy thing."

"I'll start looking at tapes tomorrow. That should get my mind off Scubberd and company."

Cobb started to respond but didn't get the chance as his phone rang. He looked at the number and answered. "Yeah?"

That was the last word he said. He listened for a while, then ended the call and put his phone away.

He took a drink of wine, more than a sip this time. "Grover's disappeared," he said.

That jolted me back to the reality of what had gone on earlier that night. "Disappeared as in dead?"

Cobb shook his head. "That was Rock Scubberd. He told me Grover had screwed him around. He didn't elaborate, just said nobody does that and when he finds Grover he's dead. Told me he wanted me to be the first to know."

"Meaning what?"

Cobb pursed his lips and thought for a minute before he answered. "Knowing Grover, it's entirely possible that he did try to pull something on those guys. That's how he rolls, on everything. I imagine he's now concentrating on keeping his ass on the top side of the grass. So maybe the call was a warning to us, a message — if I know where Grover is, Scubberd will expect me to give him up."

"And?"

"And happily for all of us, I don't know where Grover is."

"Think he'll try to get out of Calgary?"

"Hard to say. This city is what he knows. He might stay and see if he can come up with a way of getting back in Scubberd's good graces." A pause. "Or, hell, he might be on his way to Vancouver."

"So, if you did happen to come across Grover, would you make the call?"

"I'm kind of hoping I never have to answer that question."

Cobb finished his wine. "I don't know about you but I'm ready to call it a day. It's been a long one."

I no longer wanted the rest of my drink. Like Cobb, I needed this day to be over. And I hoped the next one and the ones after that might be a little quieter, a little easier. I paid for the drinks and we walked out into the night.

A north wind had come up, and the temperature was falling fast. A fitting end to Monday, Monday.

FOURTEEN

The weather had definitely turned. We were in the throes of a protracted pre-spring cold snap — the forecast being several days of temperatures in the minus teens, with windchills considerably lower.

The Accord and I felt pretty much the same way about prairie winter. Neither of us was keen to get started, especially in the frigid early morning hours. It was the fourth day of well below normal temperatures with lots more to come. I was already gritting my teeth.

I had finally finished the third book in my kids' Spoofaloof series, gone through dozens of surveillance tapes, cursed Kennedy for not moving to newer technology that would have been easier to work with, and drunk several gallons of coffee.

Ninety-six hours of self-imposed solitary confinement: me, the computer, the tapes, the coffee, and, later in the day, quite a number of cans of Rolling Rock. And now even the beer was gone. The only thing the tapes had given me was a persistent headache, which I admit may have been, at least in part, facilitated by the beer.

I'd found all of the points when there seemed to be some unexplained movement on the tapes going back a little over a year. And though I was certain there was human activity in that alley — the marks on the wood were proof of that — the tapes revealed nothing I didn't already know. I remained convinced, however, that there was a connection between the marks on the garbage bin stand and Kennedy's murder. I was a great deal less certain about the puzzle that troubled me every day and about which I changed my mind every other day — the connection between Kennedy's death and the horror that ended Faith Unruh's life so many years before.

The tape-fest concluded, I was sitting on the sofa at Jill's place, both of us enjoying a near-ritual post-dinner glass of wine. I decided the time had come to do something that was long overdue. I was scared to death that what I was about to do would jeopardize what we had together, but I couldn't continue to deceive someone I wanted never to deceive.

I set my glass down and looked at her.

"Serious time," she said.

"Yes," I said. "Very. There's something you need to know about the twenty-five thousand dollars the Inn received from that anonymous donor."

"You know who the donor was?"

"I do, yeah."

And I told her. I told her all of it, left out nothing right up to and including the confrontation with the MFs at the Hose and Hound Pub a few days before.

When I finished I picked up my wine glass as she set hers down.

"There's one more thing I want to say," I told her. "I am so sorry that I kept this from you. I thought I had good reasons, but there aren't any reasons good enough for me to lie to the person I care about most in this world. I … I'm sorry."

She didn't say anything for a long time. The longer she stayed silent, the more worried I became.

Finally, she spoke. "I'm not sure if I should yell at you or hug you."

"Yeah." I thought it would be funny to say *I know which one I'd choose* but I didn't. This wasn't the time for funny.

"I love you for caring enough about the Inn and what it means to me that you'd do anything to help save it. But Mike was right. It was incredibly dumb to think you could deal with people like that. You could have been arrested or killed. Do you know what that would have done to Kyla and me?"

She stopped and I saw a solitary tear on her cheek. I didn't move to brush it away. I didn't speak.

She took a couple of breaths. "As for lying to me, well, I guess you didn't really. You just didn't tell me the truth. Splitting hairs, maybe, but I'm trying to give you the benefit of the doubt here."

"Yeah," I said again.

She picked up her glass, took a drink. A long moment passed before she spoke again.

"This is over now. I don't want to talk about it now or ever again."

"So you're not going to throw my ass out in the street?"

"You big dumb twit. There are men who abuse their wives or girlfriends; some are addicts, some gamble, and some fool around. And I'm going to throw you out for trying to do the right thing and being willing to risk your life for something I care about? That would make me as dumb as you."

It had taken no more than ten minutes. Ten minutes for me to confess and apologize and to be forgiven. Turned out to be some of the best minutes of my life. Then Jill leaned in to me and gave me a long, slow kiss that reminded me again that an amazing woman loved me and that I was one lucky big dumb twit.

Cobb and I sat across from Detective Yvette Landry in her cubicle. She'd asked us to come in for a chat. There were a couple of cops at other cubicles in the room, but her partner Chisholm wasn't one of them. I thought that was interesting; maybe Landry was trying for a slightly more cordial ambience this time.

"How's it going with Unruh-Kennedy?"

I looked at Cobb. We'd already agreed on the way into the building that he would do the talking. "I'm not sure we've made much progress," he told her. "Still chasing down a few things."

"Like?"

"Oh, you know … this and that … here and there."

"That's it?"

"Guess so."

It looked to me like Landry saw Cobb's answer for what it was: evasion.

She sat back. "Have you thought any more about Kennedy's contention that there might have been irregularities with the investigation?"

I thought that was an interesting question and wondered about her motivation in asking it. Had she or the department uncovered something?

Cobb seemed to be on the same page. "That's something I was planning to ask you."

Landry smiled. "I asked you first."

Cobb shrugged. "The irregularities, the mistakes, whether they were deliberate or not, are undeniable. But did they impede the investigation? Hard to imagine how they couldn't."

"As I told you earlier, we looked at it and there was an internal inquiry a long time ago. Neither came up with anything substantive."

Cobb waved that off. "Lots of internal inquiries tend to find nothing substantive. Did this one look at Maughan?"

"As a saboteur or as a suspect in the murder?"

"How about both?"

"I can't answer that off the top of my head. I can tell you that I read the report and checked his alibi and it holds up as well now as it did then."

"And what was his alibi?"

"He was working that day. The case was the unexplained death of an elderly widower in northwest Calgary, circumstances suspicious. It was determined fairly quickly that he had been murdered. Maughan and his partner caught the case and were interviewing potential witnesses that afternoon."

"Together?"

"I read the homicide file. The notes said they spoke to three people that afternoon."

"Anybody follow up with those three people?"

A pause. "I don't know."

"They clear the case?"

She shook her head. "An arrest, but no conviction."

"Any chance we can get a look at the file?"

"To what end?"

Cobb shrugged. "Because we just like chasing our tails. Or maybe we think Maughan deserves a closer look. Either way, I'd like to have a peek at the file."

"You know that's not allowed."

"Yeah."

"And I know you've seen homicide files before."

A pause. "Yeah."

A half-smile played at Landry's attractive mouth. "A little quid pro quo?" she said.

"What can we do for you, Detective?"

"Word is that you've used the services of an inform-ant named Ike Groves before."

"The Grover? I may have chatted with him from time to time, back in the day."

"How far back?"

Another shrug. "It might help if you were to tell us what you're looking for."

"One of Groves's girls is dead. It was a nasty one. Your name came up as someone who knows the guy."

"I know the guy. Pretty street-savvy player. Knows where the bodies are buried, so to speak."

"Yeah, well, now he'll have one of his own to bury."

"I heard something about it."

Landry leaned forward, tapped a pencil against a cheekbone. "Where'd you hear it?"

"Out there," Cobb waved an arm. "The mean streets of our city, Detective. Word gets around."

"You remember who passed it along to you?"

"Anonymous. Someone called me, didn't identify

himself, said he'd heard I knew The Grover and wanted me to know."

"You hear anything else? Like maybe who took her out?"

Cobb shook his head. "A guy like The Grover had enemies. Probably lots of them. In fact, someone like him, even his friends might deserve your attention."

"So, why wouldn't those enemies take out Groves himself?"

"Like I said, he's a slimy operator. Might be hard to find. I don't know. Guess if they couldn't find him, they went after her."

"This girl have a name, Detective?" I asked, thinking and hoping that The Grover had lots of girls and that I didn't know this one.

She checked her notes. "Leah. Leah McDaniel. Dancer and prossie. Her stage name was Pink."

I forced my face to remain still. I met Landry's stare, but didn't blink. She turned her gaze on Cobb. "You mentioned Groves's friends. Any in particular I should be paying attention to?"

"Can't help you there," Cobb said. "I didn't hang with the guy. Either he or I would arrange a meeting; he would pass along some information if he had what I needed. He'd get paid and we'd part company. I can't say I know much about him beyond his criminal activity, which I'm sure you are as aware of as I am."

Landry looked unhappy. "Care to hazard at least a guess as to where I might start my investigation?"

"Grover was a street guy. I'd probably start by talking to some of the people who knew him, people who lived their lives the same way he did."

"Street people. Crack addicts, dealers, pimps. That's who you'd recommend?"

"Be a place to start. When can I come by and pick up the homicide file for the old guy?"

"You don't. Come by tomorrow. I'll photocopy the *relevant pages* and leave them at the desk. Sealed envelope, your name on it. Nobody sees those pages but you two."

Relevant pages meant we weren't getting everything in the file. Cobb didn't argue. He knew, as I did, that Landry could get in trouble for giving us anything. "Thanks, I appreciate it. Anything else you'd like to chat about?"

"The higher-ups don't believe there's a connection between Faith Unruh's murder and Kennedy's. There was a meeting and that was the only item on the agenda."

"You at the meeting?"

"I was, yes."

"And is that your thinking, as well?"

She shook her head slowly. "I don't know. How do you explain it? Twenty-five years after a little girl is murdered, a guy who spent all that time trying to find the killer gets himself killed just a few feet from where she died. On the one hand it's hard to believe they're *not* connected. But it's twenty-five years, for God's sake."

"We've had that same conversation ourselves," Cobb said. "More than once."

"Do you really like Maughan for Faith Unruh?"

Cobb shrugged. "Did you know he gave *The Policeman Is Your Friend* presentations at the school Faith attended?"

Landry sat up. "You sure about that?"

"One hundred percent. And there's a chance he gave at least one of those presentations to Faith's class."

"Where'd you …? Doesn't matter." She shook her head. "That's not much."

Cobb nodded. "By itself, no it's not. But *if* he was part of the group that was first at a crime scene that had some evidence go missing and *if* there's a chance that he knew or at least had met the victim … well, it makes you think, doesn't it? Then you factor in his being given the lead in the investigation for a time, then having it taken away. There's starting to be some building blocks there."

She shook her head. "Cards maybe, not blocks. It's still pretty flimsy. And if it was Maughan, does that mean you agree with the brass that the Kennedy killing is unrelated?"

"They're either unrelated or there were two people in on the Unruh killing."

"So you think that somehow Maughan ditches Kinley, hooks up with his accomplice — they murder an eleven-year-old girl — and Maughan is back on the job an hour or so later?"

"Whoa!" Cobb held up his hands. "So far, all we have to say that Maughan and Kinley were working that day is the report in a homicide file, a report that one of *them* would have written. And if there was an accomplice, who's to say it wasn't Kinley?"

"Kinley's dead, too. So that blows any theory that the Kennedy and Unruh murders are related pretty much to hell."

Cobb shrugged. "Whoa again. That's never been my theory. It's been a question I've asked, just as you have."

She nodded. "But damn near impossible to prove there's a connection."

"And damn near impossible to prove there isn't."

"I don't know if you know this, but the way the law works, you have to prove guilt, not innocence."

"I've heard that."

"I know it's a pain in the ass sometimes, but that's the way the system operates. So you're going to need a whole lot more than a cop giving presentations at a victim's school and a weird chain of events in the investigation to even get out of the batter's box with this."

"I know we haven't got much. And believe me, that frustrates me as much as it frustrates you."

"Good luck finding more."

"Thanks," Cobb said. "That starts tomorrow with the homicide file on the old man's death. What time do you get in?"

"Nine o'clock."

"I'll be there just after nine. I'll bring coffee."

It looked like we were wrapping up. Turns out we weren't.

Landry turned back to me. "Why don't you tell me about the time you spent in Kennedy's home?"

I'd been waiting for this moment, but when it happened I was taken by surprise, which was likely how Landry wanted it to happen. I thought about trying to buy time by asking how they'd found out, decided that would be a bad idea.

I wanted to glance at Cobb to see if he was in favour of my answering her or if he wanted me to keep my mouth shut. But I knew Landry would see my look at Cobb and probably regard it as suspicious.

I opted instead for the truth, knowing that talking to the cops without a lawyer present was seldom a good idea. I decided I'd start and if things looked like they were getting greasy, I'd clam up and wait for counsel.

"He asked me to man the surveillance system for him while he was away with his wife, who was in the last stages of her life. I did that. He came home after his wife's funeral and I left. End of story."

"You would have had to be quite expert with the various elements of the cameras and recording equipment."

"I'm not sure I would call me an expert. He gave me a bit of a crash course on the workings of the equipment, told me to note everything I saw that looked like it might deserve his attention. But you likely already know that from the notations I made in his notebooks."

She glanced at her notes. "You showed up in the alley a few times prior to your filling in for him, and you went into the alley again on one occasion during your time in Kennedy's house. So tell me about those visits to what was once a murder scene. And was about to become one again."

Things were moving into dicey territory and I wasn't sure how much more I should say. But again I opted for candour, this time a little less confident that honesty was the best policy.

"I'd first heard about the murder of Faith Unruh from my girlfriend's daughter and her friend. Cobb filled me in on what details he knew about the case, and to be honest I became somewhat obsessed by it. I drove down that alley and walked there a few times, as well. Of course, Kennedy saw me; he tracked me down and eventually confronted me in the area behind my apartment, where I park my car. I was able to convince him that I was not the person he was looking for. As for the time I went there while I was looking after the surveillance, that was because I thought I saw movement, something in the alley. I went over to check it out but I didn't see anything suspicious or otherwise."

"This confrontation with Kennedy, tell me more about that."

I decided it was time to deviate slightly from my being honest and forthright with her.

"He was waiting for me in the lane behind my apartment. He asked me what I'd been doing in the vicinity of where Faith's body had been found. I told him. He seemed a little doubtful, but when I told him about my connection with Cobb, he seemed more inclined to believe me."

"That doesn't sound like a confrontation." She was looking hard at me. "It sounds more like a conversation."

I nodded agreement. "Confrontation might have been the wrong word."

"Where were you the night Kennedy was killed, Mr. Cullen?"

Trick question and I knew it. If I fired out the answer right off the top of my head, it would look like I knew I'd need an alibi at some point. And if I floundered around too much, I knew that, too, would make me look bad ... or worse, suspicious.

"Sorry, I can't remember. But I'll look back at the date and let you know."

"Do you drive an SUV?"

"No." I shook my head. "Honda Accord."

"But you do." She turned again to Cobb.

"Yes, I do. In fact, it's in the parking lot right now, if you'd like to check the tire impressions from the homicide vehicle against mine."

"I might want to do that at some point." She stood up. "I think we're done here. Thanks for coming by. I do appreciate it. You think of something useful on Ike Groves or this girl who worked for him, I'd be grateful for a call."

Cobb and I stood up. I wanted to yell, "She's not this girl! She has a name!" but I remained silent.

Cobb spoke instead. "See you in the morning."

Landry nodded and Cobb and I turned in unison. No goodbyes. I didn't get a sense that we parted on bad terms, but it wasn't cordial either.

When Cobb and I were out of the building and standing on the sidewalk, I took a long, deep breath, let it out slowly. "Shit," I said.

"Yeah."

"Shit, shit, shit."

Cobb pointed down the street with his chin, indicating maybe we should walk. It felt like a good idea. I'd barely known the girl named Pink but I was sickened that her life was over. Another horribly premature death.

And most sickening of all was the thought that her death might have been connected to the Scubberd set-up. And the fact that operation only happened because of my getting tied up with the MFs in the first place.

We walked a few blocks in silence. Finally, I said, "How'd I do under cross-examination?"

"Not bad," Cobb replied. "You didn't over-talk it and that was good. She could have gone after you a lot harder and she didn't, so maybe she doesn't see you as worth pursuing. Or she's planning to take another run at you when I'm not there and Chisholm is. I'd get your alibi sorted out right away. Call her tomorrow. I'm hoping that wasn't a night you spent at home by yourself."

"Yeah, I'm hoping that, too."

We'd circled around and were back at the parking lot. Cobb took hold of my arm. "This isn't on you."

"Isn't it?"

"No, it's not. The world that people like Grover and Pink live in is dangerous. People die in that world. Drugs kill them, they kill each other. Every day — lots of them die very young. They choose the life they live. And in a way they choose the way they die."

"She didn't choose this … I did."

"We don't know that."

"I know that." I fumbled for my keys.

"You up for a late breakfast?"

"I had breakfast."

"How about an early lunch?"

"Inventive," I said. "Yeah, okay … lunch."

Forty-five minutes later I was staring down at a good-looking bowl of chili at Bumpy's Café while Cobb was enjoying the first bite of the mac and cheese.

I needed to talk and I needed the topic to be something other than Pink's death. "I've been having this weird thought," I said.

Cobb gestured with his fork that I should continue.

"I keep coming back to the idea that Maughan's kid was an accomplice in the Faith Unruh thing … or at least involved. Is there someone deranged enough to take his kid along to be part of a rape and murder?"

Cobb chewed, swallowed, and set his fork down. "One of the things I learned as a cop is that you cannot overestimate the extremes of human degeneracy. So, in answer to your question, yes, it's possible. But it seems to me there are other possibilities. There's the possibility that Terry Maughan could be the perpetrator. So, let's think about that. It's likely that Faith was lured into that backyard. She was eleven years old and not likely to go there with a stranger. Could she have been drawn there by a schoolmate? Maybe. And there's the fact that the murder was, in many ways, botched. A lot of it points to an amateur as the attacker. Maybe it wasn't even supposed to *be* a murder. Maybe the perp intended only to rape her, but things went wrong — maybe she fought harder than he expected, and he panicked and killed her. And in one of those remarkably lucky situations for the killer, things got messed up in the investigation either deliberately or otherwise and he got away with it."

"She was strangled. You think a thirteen- or fourteen-year-old kid would be strong enough?"

"Don't know. I'd have to see the kid."

I nodded and worked away at the chili for a while. It was very good but I wasn't giving it my best effort. "Why didn't you tell Landry about Maughan's kid going to the same school and knowing Faith?"

"I don't like to give away all of our bargaining chips at once."

I had another thought. "That could explain the irregularities in the investigation. Maybe it was Maughan, but he wasn't messing with the investigation into his own crime. He was covering for his kid."

Cobb shrugged. "It's a possibility. It would be good if we could talk to Terry Maughan."

"I haven't been able to find him yet."

"Maybe we need to concentrate on that for the moment."

I nodded. "Makes sense."

"I'll make a couple of calls in the morning. You okay?"

"Yeah, why?"

"You look a little shaky is all."

"Guess I'm not used to being a suspect in a murder."

"If you were a serious suspect, that would have been a very different conversation. The bad cop wasn't even there. She was doing her due diligence in case it gets asked about at a meeting. So don't flatter yourself — you're not that big a deal. At least not yet."

"Gee thanks, I feel a lot better now."

Cobb grinned. "Anytime."

Drake and Rihanna's "Take Care" announced that I had a call.

"Whoa." Cobb stared at my phone in something close to disbelief. "I'll say one thing, you are full of surprises."

I smiled and took the call. It was Lorne Cooney.

"Hey, what's up, Lorne?"

"Hey, Cullen, I'm on my way out the door, but I just got a little insight into your friend Claiborne."

"The *late* Claiborne?" I said. "He was never my friend."

"Yeah, well, friend or not, it seems that the gentleman liked to patronize ladies of the evening."

"Hookers?"

"So the story goes."

"That surprises me. This is a guy who had gorgeous, interesting women at his side almost all the time."

"Key word in that sentence is *almost*, mon. Apparently, that wasn't quite enough for him. Anyway, like I said, I gotta split. Thought you'd like to know."

"How solid is this, Lorne?"

"I wouldn't call if it wasn't solid."

"Much appreciated. Have a nice evening."

"That's the plan, my friend. Later."

He ended the call and I looked at Cobb. "You get all that?"

He nodded. "I think so. Claiborne apparently enjoyed the company of prostitutes."

"Yeah," I said. "I guess I didn't see that one coming. Question is, how relevant is it to finding the killer?"

"Good question. Maybe gives us a few more people with reason to take Claiborne out."

"Maybe," I said, "but it also provides another motive for Rachel Claiborne."

"Yes, it does. The cops will like that."

We sat for a couple of minutes in silence. I wasn't sure what Cobb was thinking about, but my own thoughts weren't pleasant ones.

"Damn it, Mike … Pink."

He nodded slowly. "That's a tough one. I'm not sure how they found her or even found out *about* her."

"You think it was the MFs?"

"That's where I'd put my money."

I had to agree. It was where I'd put my money, too — about twenty-five thousand dollars.

"I know what you're thinking," Mike said. "And if you're all about self-recrimination then you better take a look at the other half of this partnership. I was the one who came up with the idea for the con, put the plan together, decided that one of Grover's girls would be perfect — if he had one who looked young enough. He did and I ran with that. Now Pink's dead. So if blame's the game you need to play, then pencil me in for a big share. And just so you know, it's not my first time in the Fuck-Up Hotel."

There wasn't much I could say to that, at least nothing that came to me right then.

Our server came by, topped up our coffees, asked about dessert — we both declined — and he moved on to another table.

Cobb added milk to his coffee, took a long, slow sip and set the cup down. He stared out the window blankly. Then he began to talk. "I'd been in homicide for just under two years. My partner was a veteran who'd been on the force for twenty-six years, about half of that in homicide. Glenn Sheffield. It's a quiet afternoon and we're interviewing a witness in a homicide we're investigating — a fairly famous sportscaster — Gilbert Arnold — was messing with a guy's wife and the husband didn't take kindly to it."

"I remember Arnold," I said. "The guy was a legend. Hockey, football, he did it all. And I remember reading about his murder. But I don't know if I paid attention to the details."

"Yeah, well, the details were pretty straightforward — jealous husband plunks wife's boyfriend. Slam dunk. Except that the guy has an alibi — provided by the wife.

"So, Glenn and I are interviewing another of Gilbert's former flames, a singer in a blues band that was kind of a big deal at the time — they were called The Blue Blues Confederation."

"Heard of them, too," I said. "In fact, I'm pretty sure I have one or two of their albums in the collection."

"I'd be surprised if you didn't."

"Yeah."

"The singer's name is Iris Speck — and we're just trying to get a little background on Arnold and his meanderings."

"Looking for dirt."

Cobb shrugged. "Essentially, yeah. Though we prefer the term *evidence*. So, we get to her house and she's got a guy there, a guy named Louis D'urrville; I'm pretty sure it's a fake name — the guy's as French as a Ford Fairlane. We can see right away that he's on something and pretty mouthy. Glenn was pretty cool in those situations, but I was a bit of a hothead and wanted to do a little damage to this guy. Glenn kept me from doing that. Anyway, while we're trying to interview her and keep D'urrville quiet so we can actually talk to her, there's pounding on the front door. It's the next-door neighbour.

"This guy is fruitcake nuts right from the get-go, but he's figured out that we're cops and he wants to lay a charge against D'urrville about some damage he did to the neighbour's house when he was cutting down a tree in the backyard. Tree fell the wrong way and totalled the guy's deck and pretty much destroyed his barbecue.

"So now we've got the blues singer, who, by the way, was a right bitch. She had a tough time getting through maybe six words, seven tops, without the use of some derivative of *fuck*. And we've got the methed-out boyfriend and the nutso neighbour. Sounds like a scene from a bad sitcom, except these people were real. So, while I'm trying to usher the neighbour back out the front door, Iris freaks out and is trying to get at the guy. Glenn's holding her off. I finally get the neighbour out and the door closed and I turn around and D'urrville's standing there holding a rifle. There's a shitload of noise — both Iris and D'urrville are yelling, the guy outside is pounding on the door again, and Glenn's trying to get people settled down.

"But all I see is that gun in the hands of a space cadet. I give him the spiel, the one they teach you in cop school — *I need you to put the rifle down, Louis.* About then in all this chaos, Iris loses what little sanity there is left in the whole goddamn mess, and she's trying to hit Glenn with a poker from the fireplace. So now we've got two people and both of them have weapons. She misses with her first try, but I'm thinking if she hits him with that thing she's liable to kill him. And Glenn, as he's trying to dodge her attack and keep his head from being caved in, trips over something, a piece of furniture or something, and falls.

"And that's when the comedy show ended and the shitshow began. Looking back on it now, I honestly believe Iris had realized this whole thing wasn't good and was about to pull back. But then D'urrville comes racing across the room with the rifle and he's screaming."

Cobb's voice got quieter. "I'm sure he's going to shoot Glenn. I assume the position and yell for him to freeze. He slows down but he keeps moving toward Glenn. I yell again but he still doesn't freeze and now he's six feet from Glenn, who's still on the floor, and he has the rifle pointed at my partner for Christ's sake, and I've got to do something. I fire my weapon. First time I'd ever had to do that, and maybe that's why I missed him. Point-blank and I miss." Cobb stopped then, swallowed, looked at me for a second then back outside.

"At least I miss D'urrville. I hit Iris Speck. She goes down and D'urrville drops the rifle and throws himself across her on the floor and now the screaming's started again.

"And then suddenly it's over. It's all over. She's lying there on the floor and D'urrville's on top of her crying. Glenn gets up off the floor and we call for backup and an ambulance."

Cobb stopped talking, almost as if he were resting from the exertion of telling the story.

"She ... Iris ... did she live?"

Cobb nodded. "Yeah, she lived. She's a paraplegic. I've gone to visit her once a month ever since. She's never said an unkind word to me, never failed to smile at me when I walk in the door."

"Nobody could ever blame you," I said.

"No?" Cobb looked hard at me. "The rifle D'urrville was carrying was a pellet gun. Might have posed a big-time danger to a squirrel."

I thought about that. "Doesn't matter. There's no way you could have known — it was an insane scene and you did your best."

"That's right," Cobb said, his voice January-cold. "I did my best and I messed up. So don't talk to me about making a mistake. I put that woman in a wheelchair for the rest of her life. And I'd give anything to live those two minutes of my life over again. But that's not how it works. You get on with doing what you're doing because it's important. There's no guarantee that I won't make another mistake or that you won't. But think about the good things we've done. Think about those things when you're not too busy feeling sorry for yourself."

Cobb stood up. "I'm picking up that homicide report from Landry in the morning. I should be in the office by ten. It'd be good if you were there to look at it with me."

He turned and walked away.

FIFTEEN

I arrived at Cobb's office just after ten with a coffee in each hand. The light in his office was on. He was already at his desk, head down, concentrating on what I guessed was the report on the homicide that had been investigated by Maughan and Kinley, as I struggled with the door, cursing the coffees that were depositing hot liquid on my hands. He looked up and smiled. "How's that goin' for ya?"

"I say we switch to orange juice."

"We could do that, but we'd both be either in therapy or dead within a month."

"Both of which might be preferable to scalded hands." I set his coffee on the desk in front of him. "Learning anything?"

"Maybe." He picked up a page he had set to one side. "Take a look at that."

I shrugged off my jacket, wiped my wet hand on the inside of the sleeve, and took the page. It appeared to be notes written by one of the investigating detectives, followed by a more formal typed report incorporating those notes. The notes covered the top third of the page and were almost illegible — a doctor's prescription on steroids — so I skipped down to the report itself ...

I took a call at 4:28 p.m. from a female caller, it was a 911 call rerouted through our dispatcher. The call was from a Rosalyn Meers — she was somewhat hysterical but I was able to ascertain that she had discovered her next-door neighbour, Lionel Hilmer, lying in the living room of his home just inside the front door and that Mr. Hilmer was unresponsive and there was a lot of blood. I asked Ms. Meers if she had touched anything, she indicated she hadn't, I had her give me the address — the 2200 block of Capri Avenue NW. I told her to go back to Mr. Hilmer's house but not to enter and not to let anyone else enter. I was on my way to the scene within a couple of minutes of her call. Kinley was in with the Chief Inspector and I didn't feel it was appropriate to wait for him so I left a note on his desk and left the building en route to the crime scene.

I was at the Hilmer home approximately 26 minutes after the call came in. An ambulance was on scene — one paramedic had gone inside only to check the vital signs and was able to ascertain that the victim was deceased. The paramedic was back on the front porch waiting alongside his female partner. I gloved up and opened the front door; my initial observation confirmed that

Mr. Hilmer was deceased. I called the Medical Examiner's office, then questioned Mrs. Meers, who informed me that the victim lived alone, that she had gone to his home to invite him to have dinner with her and her husband, that the front door was unlocked and when he didn't answer the bell she got worried, tried the door, looked inside and discovered the body.

Once the Medical Examiner personnel and Detective Kinley were on scene, Kinley and I split up and did a rough search of the grounds around the house. Found nothing but, of course, the search was cursory and a more detailed search was undertaken later by two more detectives, Linder and Snead, and three uniformed officers. Detective Kinley and myself went to the house on the other side —

"How far are you?" Cobb interrupted my reading.

"They're just going to one of the neighbouring houses."

"Spoiler alert. They learned nothing, so you might as well quit reading. Instead, tell me what you make of what you're seeing on the page so far."

"What do you mean?"

"I mean look at what he wrote and tell me if you see anything interesting."

I stared hard at the page, read each word again. "It's a murder; I guess that makes all of it unusual."

"Okay." Cobb shook his head. "I apologize. I'm not trying to play Sherlock Holmes and I'm damn sure not trying to make you look silly in any way. It's not the content I'm interested in. Look at the time Maughan says the call came in."

I looked again, then up at Cobb. "Four twenty-eight. How is that unusual?"

"Now look at his notes up above, he notes the time of the call there, too."

I looked again. "Four twenty-eight. Exactly the same time." I was beginning to wonder if Cobb was behind on his sleep.

"Now look at the numbers themselves. Anything?"

I stared at the numbers, first in the handwritten notes, then in the typed report. "You mean that they're smudged?"

"Yes, but is the whole number smudged?"

One more look. Then closer. "No, it's just the middle digit in both numbers. It's like maybe ... maybe someone erased that digit once."

"Right, so let's think about this. Faith's school dismissed every day at three thirty. That's noted in the first homicide file. Let's say it took even ten minutes, which is pretty fast, for the girls to get out of school and walk to her friend Jasmine's house. Even if everything after that happened very quickly in terms of her being lured into the backyard, murdered, and covered with the plywood and the perpetrator making his escape, it is virtually impossible for all of that to take place and for the killer to get to the police station by four twenty-eight to take that call."

"Meaning Jarvis Maughan couldn't have been the guy."

And then suddenly I saw where he was going. "But if that smudged number was changed —"

"Right," Cobb said. "Let's say, just for argument's sake, that the original middle digit was a four or maybe a five, making the time of the call four forty-eight or four fifty-eight — now it becomes much more feasible for the time frame to work. And don't you think it's odd that only one of the three digits looks smudged and it's the middle digit in both cases — one handwritten and one typed?"

"That seems like an unlikely coincidence for sure. But let's think about it. Is there another reason the digit could be smudged in both instances that *doesn't* point to deliberately altering the report to reflect something quite different from what actually happened?"

"Well, if Maughan was sitting here I'm sure he'd say he just made a mistake, realized it after the fact and changed the number to reflect the actual time the call came in."

"But you're not buying that."

He shrugged. "All I'm saying is that if that time was altered to show an earlier time than was actually the case, it's more of the same kind of evidence we already have, all of it circumstantial and all of it pretty damn flimsy."

"I agree that it's circumstantial, but I'm not sure I'd agree that it's flimsy. Maughan could have known Faith, either through his visits to the school or through his son, who we *do* know was acquainted with Faith. We've got a cop with a past record of using his power and position to sexually assault women and who lived within a short walk of Faith's house. And through all of this, there's been his alibi, which has always been in his favour. If there's a possible hole in that alibi, it feels to me like that could be a game-changer."

Cobb smiled. "Now that's the optimism I like in my partner. Okay, there are a couple of things we need to do. I've written down the names, addresses, and phone numbers of the three witnesses Maughan, and maybe Kinley, spoke to that day. It's a long shot, but maybe, if we can find them, one might recall the actual time that the call was made to the police or maybe the time when Maughan arrived on scene, which he indicates would have been between approximately four forty-five to four fifty-five p.m. And I've got the last known address of Terry Maughan. Four years ago he was living on McKenzie Towne Gate. So we've got a couple of things we need to pursue. Let's divide them up. You want the ladies or Maughan?"

"You have a preference?"

He shook his head.

"Okay, I'll take McKenzie Towne. There's a good pub out there somewhere, I think."

He closed up the folder, slid it into the top drawer of his desk. "You okay?"

I nodded. "Yeah, I'm glad we have some lines to follow up on. I need to get my mind off things."

He stood up. "Good. Let's roll."

SIXTEEN

I was right. The house Terry Maughan had lived in was within a block of the Kilt & Caber Ale House. I passed it on my way to the address on McKenzie Towne Gate.

I went first to the house. There was a Honda Odyssey, the ultimate kid packer, in the driveway, and with deductive powers that would have made Holmes (and Cobb) proud, I guessed there might be children in evidence. I rang the bell and a midtwenties redhead with a baby on her hip opened the door a crack and looked out at me, the door bound by the chain I could see dangling between it and the frame.

"Ma'am, my name is Adam Cullen. I'm working with a private investigator on a matter, and we're hoping to determine the whereabouts of a former resident of this house, Terry Maughan. I was hoping you might be able to help me."

I passed a business card through the opening and she stared at it for a few seconds. "I can't let you in the house," she said, not in an unfriendly way.

"I absolutely understand and I'm happy to stay here on the front step. Did you and your husband buy the house from Terry Maughan?"

She paused and looked off, thinking. "I think that was the name. We never met the people. The house was vacant when we bought it and we went through a realtor."

"Do you know if Mr. Maughan, if that's who it was, had a family?"

"I think so. Again, we never met them, but Jay Keeling across the street, I think he was kind of a friend of his, he said there had been three people living here — the couple and one child."

"Which house does Mr. Keeling live in?"

She pointed with her free hand. "That storey-and-a-half over there, the brown one."

The baby apparently saw that as his cue and began crying. A small child, maybe three years old, arrived at that moment and peered around her mother's legs at me. I smiled at the woman and said, "Looks to me like I should get out of here and leave you to take care of these guys. Thanks for your help. Do you know if Mr. Keeling is around?"

"He might be. He travels sometimes — he's got a sales job, I think — but I don't know if he's in town right now or not."

I thanked her again and headed across the street to the Keeling house. A newer Chevy Equinox was in the driveway, but that didn't mean he was home. My repeated knocking and doorbell ringing confirmed that no one was at the Keeling residence. Just to be certain, I looked the number up on my phone, called, and reached a voicemail. I left a message explaining that I was trying to locate Terry Maughan about a matter dating back several years and I'd appreciate it if Mr. Keeling could call me when it was convenient.

Things went downhill from there. I canvassed the houses on both sides of the street. A number of people weren't home, and the lone resident I did speak to had lived in the area for only two years and hadn't known the Maughans. I hoped Cobb was having more luck with the witnesses.

I decided I deserved at least one beer and stopped off at the Kilt & Caber for a Stella.

The place was almost empty, so I sat at the bar. The bartender looked to be around thirty and was tattooed to within an inch of his life. He handed me the Stella and a glass, took the money I'd set on the bar, and smiled when I waved off the change.

"How long has this place been here?" I asked.

"Opened in '99."

I looked around, let him know I liked the layout of the place, which I did. "How long have you been working here?"

"I started in '05, left in 2008. Came back for a second tour of duty in 2012. Been here ever since."

Two twenty-something women came in and took a table on the other side of the bar. He moved off to serve them. He returned to the bar, got their drinks, a glass of red wine and a Scotch and something, then visited with them for a couple of minutes after delivering the drinks. He got back to me maybe five minutes later.

"Ready for another?"

I shook my head. "A friend of mine used to live around here. Terry Maughan. He might have come in here. You know him? He moved away about four years ago."

The bartender moved a cloth around the bar in front of my drink.

"You say you were a friend of Terry's?"

"Yeah. I'd like to catch up with him again. Haven't seen him in a while."

"I didn't know Terry had any friends."

I immediately regretted my lie, realizing it would restrict what I could ask. A friend would know, for example, where Maughan worked.

"When was the last time you saw him?"

The bartender shrugged. "He still came around once in a while even after him and Carly split up and they sold the house. Haven't seen him for at least a year, though, maybe more."

"Yeah, that's about when I lost track of him, too. You hear anything after that?"

"Hear anything? Like what?"

I shrugged. Keeping it casual. "I don't know … where he got to, what he's doing now, that kind of stuff."

"Well, you know Terry, doing as little as he could, always a new scam — he'd call it a business opportunity. I think the latest one was furnace cleaning — not door to door exactly, he had some woman in an office call ahead, or maybe he'd call himself, then he'd come by, driving a van that looked kind of official. I figured the thing was borderline illegal, but like I said, that was Terry."

"He actually clean the furnaces at the places he made appointments with?"

"Sort of, I guess. Change the filter, fuck around a little, stuff you and I could do."

"Yeah." I shook my head like someone wishing good ol' Terry would get his shit together. "Weird though, the guy just up and disappears, that's pretty nuts even for him."

The bartender gave the bar one more wipe, was now looking at the two women, who clearly were more appealing conversation partners than I was. "I guess," he said.

"Who knows, maybe he's in jail. Wouldn't surprise me. Sure you don't want another?"

"No, just the one for now. Got to get back to work. Not like Terry, you know?" I chuckled.

"Yeah. What do you do?"

"I'm a writer."

"Writer," he repeated, clearly puzzled. Probably didn't talk to a lot of writers. "You mean like insurance?"

I didn't even know what the hell that meant. *Under*writer maybe? "Yeah, something like that."

Outside I called Cobb.

He came on right away. "How's it going?"

"Not bad. You?"

"Not good. One of the women they talked to that day passed away four years ago. One moved away — the Maritimes, nobody's exactly sure where. And Mrs. Meers, the one who called it in, was very pleasant and wanted to help but couldn't remember anything related to the exact time she made the call or when Maughan arrived on scene. So I hope you did better than me."

"Maybe," I said. "A couple of things. Terry Maughan's wife's name was Carly. They split about four years ago. That's why the house was sold. But maybe she's still in Calgary, and if she is, maybe we can find her. Terry was still around, part of the local scene up until about a year ago, then pretty much disappeared. But before that he was doing some kind of quasi door-to-door furnace-servicing thing. Sounds a little scammy, but the thing I wondered about, could it have put him at or maybe even *in* Kennedy's house?"

Cobb was quiet for a long minute. "That's certainly a possibility. Hard one to check though, with Kennedy gone."

"Any chance we could get back in the house, go through Kennedy's back bills and receipts? I mean, I know it's a long shot, but might be worth a look."

"Leave it with me," Cobb said. "I'll talk to Landry. Don't know if the place is still vacant or if it's been sold."

"It looked dark and pretty vacant last time I was there."

"Could be the cops haven't released the place yet. I'll do some checking. Why don't you see if you can find Carly Maughan."

"Okay. One more thing. The bartender threw out that Terry was a bit of an outlaw. Maybe we should make sure he's not in jail."

"Bartender?"

"Yeah, this research gig is a hard, hard life."

"I see that. I'll find out if Terry's languishing in prison somewhere. Let you know."

"Okay. I'll get going on Carly."

"You might have to drag yourself out of the bar to do that."

"Damn, you sure can spoil a guy's fun."

Cobb laughed. "Later."

It felt good to be back doing something, though I wasn't at all sure how effective what I was doing actually was. Still, it was a lot better than sitting around moping.

To further solidify the good feeling I was enjoying right then, I found Carly Maughan in less than five minutes. Courtesy of Facebook, the world's biggest time-waster but, every once in a while, the source of quite useful information. I searched her name, found it, went to her timeline, and, because she was selling some kind of beauty products in what sounded to me like a pyramid scheme, I came to a couple of posts that gave me an address — a high-rise apartment not far from Mount Royal University in southwest Calgary — and a phone number.

I thought about phoning but changed my mind and decided to try for a face to face with the former Mrs. Terry Maughan. As I drove across town, I thought about what I'd say to her. I knew I couldn't suggest that her former husband may have been an accomplice in a murder twenty-five years ago and that her former father- in-law may have been the murderer. I finally decided to fall back on my favourite introduction — that I was working on a story — this time the story was looking at the children of cops: how difficult was growing up when the kids knew what their mom or dad did; how many became cops themselves; and how many went in the opposite direction altogether and stumbled into a life of crime. As her ex had been a policeman's son, I'd like to get her perspective on how she thought he turned out. Not altogether bullshit; in fact, I *was* very interested in her thoughts on Terry Maughan.

I refined my cover a little during the drive, and by the time I was parking on the street in front of her solid sixties apartment — not upscale but far from a dump — I was feeling good about my chances if I could actually get an audience with the former Mrs. Maughan.

Once in the ground-floor entrance, I buzzed apartment 816, waited thirty or forty seconds, then buzzed a second time, getting an almost instant response. A younger voice than I expected, pleasant, maybe even friendly. I laid out my spiel, ending with a plea that she give me just a couple of minutes of her time. I heard her speak to someone else, and finally came a cautious though not altogether reluctant agreement.

I rode up the elevator to the eighth floor. When I got to apartment 816, the door was ajar, as if Carly Maughan were inviting me in, but I knocked anyway. I'd pictured in my mind the woman who went with the voice, and those things are almost always terribly wrong. But not this time.

She'd had a cheery, agreeable voice on the intercom, and a cheery, agreeable woman in her mid- to late thirties came to the door, pulled it the rest of the way open, and smiled at me. She was wearing jeans and an *I ♥ Hawaii* T-shirt. She had short brown hair and large, expressive eyes. Attractive. Behind her a boy I would have put at about twelve or thirteen was watching me. Protective. The look on his face much less friendly.

"Hi, I'm Carly, come in."

"Adam Cullen." I stepped into the apartment, offered a hand; she shook it and I followed her to the living room.

"I've got some coffee on. Would you like a cup?"

"Thanks, I'd appreciate that."

"Chance, why don't you talk to Mr. Cullen while I get the coffee. You want a juice?"

Chance shook his head and sat in a recliner near the window, leaving a patterned chesterfield for me. I sat and looked at the kid for a moment, wondering if Terry Maughan was his dad and if he looked like him. I wasn't sure I saw any resemblance between Chance and Carly Maughan, but that may have had something to do with the smile that seemed a permanent feature with her, a distant memory for him.

He was, however, wearing a faded Blue Jays shirt, providing me with an opening.

"You like baseball, Chance?"

"Not really." He saw me looking at his shirt. "I took it out of the lost and found at school."

"Good work," I said. "It's a great look."

He apparently missed my sarcasm or didn't feel the need to respond, opting instead to stare at my shoes. I was pretty sure it wasn't that my footwear fascinated him so much as that I didn't.

"Actually, your name is a famous one in baseball," I told him. "A big part of history. Tinker to Evers to Chance. Double play combination for the Chicago Cubs in the early 1900s. Chance was the first baseman. There was a very cool poem about them. I wrote a paper about it when I was in university."

I reached for my phone to look it up. Chance nodded but he was clearly underwhelmed by my dullness. I had lost him at *actually*. I left the phone where it was.

Carly Maughan mercifully re-entered the living room, two coffee mugs in hand. I stood, took one, and sat back down. She surveyed the seating arrangements, started to sit on the couch with me, then changed her mind.

"Chance, maybe you should leave Mr. Cullen and me to talk. Maybe you can find something to do in your room."

I'm pretty sure Nero Wolfe could have gotten to his feet in less time than it took Chance. He slumped off down the hallway and a few seconds later we heard the door close.

"He's fourteen," Carly said as she settled in the chair Chance had vacated. I wasn't sure if she offered her son's age as general information or as an excuse. I decided that if this was a preview of what we could expect from Kyla when she hit fourteen, I'd hurl myself from a tall building the night before her birthday.

I pulled out a notebook and pen, partly to add credence to my cover and partly to jot down anything she gave me that might be useful in finding her former husband.

"Thanks for taking the time to see me, Carly."

"You said you were writing a story about Terry."

"Yes, I understand you two haven't been together for a while."

"A little over four years. Four wonderful years."

"Terry was … difficult, was he?"

"No, he was not difficult. He was impossible, at least to live with."

"Abusive?"

She shook her head. "I wouldn't say abusive. It was … it was as if everything I ever said or did just bored him to death. Other than when we had sex. And I'm not sure that after a while, even that …" She shrugged.

"What did Terry do for a living?"

"It would be faster to tell you what he didn't do. Let's see, he was a Transit System bus driver — that was a good job, benefits and everything. He lasted maybe two years. He was a plumber's helper, worked for a short time in the oil patch, sold shoes in a store in Southcentre Mall, and he got into every get-rich-quick online scheme, make that *scam*, there was. We were always broke. My parents bailed us out on mortgage payments and other bills until I just couldn't ask them anymore, and that really pissed Terry off. That's when we split. In fairness, I will say the thing Terry wanted most was to be a cop like his dad. And he tried, twice. Failed the written test both times."

I nodded sympathetically. "Someone I spoke to said Terry did some sort of door-to-door sales."

"That's true. I mean, it wasn't like encyclopedias or vacuum cleaners or anything like that. It was a little more twenty-first century — there'd often be some technology element to it; he liked that, but it was always the same: it didn't quite work out and it was always someone else's fault. Sad, really."

"Have you seen Terry recently?"

"I haven't, and that's kind of different. He hasn't seen Chance or even called him in a really long time. We used to see him every now and then, at least for birthdays and stuff, but not at all for quite a while now."

"How long is a while, Carly?"

She thought for a moment. "I'd say a year, maybe year and a half. Oh," she jumped up, "let me top up your coffee."

"Just half a cup," I said.

She picked up my mug and disappeared into the kitchen. Without Chance to talk baseball with, I decided to look around the living room. There were pictures, lots with Chance as the subject, some with him actually smiling. There were a few of Carly, some with her and her son together, but none with a man in them.

Carly came back about then and handed me my coffee. I thanked her and sat back down. "So, what do you do, Carly?"

"Receptionist in an accounting office. Four days a week. Today's my day off and it's cool because this is a half day at school for Chance. We get some time together."

I nodded, sipped the coffee. I noticed she hadn't mentioned the beauty products. "I don't want to keep you too long, but I wondered if you knew where I might find Terry. I'd really like to talk to him, interview him for the story."

She shook her head slowly. "I'm sorry, but I really don't. I know he was living in a furnished suite for a while but then I heard he came into some money. After his dad died, Terry's mom remarried and I think the new guy had quite a lot of money. So maybe Terry got a nice inheritance or something."

"Which I take it he didn't offer to share."

She shook her head again. "I didn't care about it for me," she said, and I believed her. "But it would have been nice for Chance if we had a little extra every once in a while."

"Terry ever talk about his school days?"

"School days?"

"Yeah, you know, people he chummed around with, teachers he liked, teachers he didn't like, just the stuff people talk about when they think back to school."

"Well, I guess he might have said something from time to time, but I can't honestly remember any of it, so I don't know if it was all that interesting. I guess I didn't really pay attention."

"I heard he sometimes helped his dad with presentations in schools — you know, the kind where they talk about the police with the kids. Terry ever mention that?"

"Yeah, I think so. I remember him saying something about 'all that time I spent with my dad talking about how great cops are should get me into the force.' But it never did."

"So you can't give me any idea where I might look for him."

"I can give you the address of the place he was renting, but I phoned a couple of months ago and he's been gone from there for quite a while."

I nodded and stood up. "Thanks, I'll take that address anyway, and the last phone number you have for him, if you don't mind."

"Sure, I'll get those for you."

"Oh, one last thing. Do you happen to have a picture of Terry I could borrow?"

Her face came as close to a frown as it looked like it was possible for it to get. It took a few seconds for her to make up her mind.

"I guess so. I'll be right back."

She disappeared into the kitchen and I moved to the door to wait for her. Chance came out of his room and over to where I was standing.

"It was good to meet you, Chance," I said.

He looked at me. "Words that are heavy with nothing but trouble: Tinker to Evers to Chance," he said, then grinned at me.

The last two lines of the poem. Good ol' Google. Someday I'm going to learn not to judge people on first meeting them. Chance Maughan had just taught me that lesson, again.

We were in the middle of a high-five when his mom emerged from the kitchen with a piece of paper and a small photo. "Did I miss something?"

"I was just saying so long to a pretty cool kid."

The smile returned to her face in a big way and she handed me the paper and the photograph. "I don't need the photo back."

"How about I just take a picture of it — that way you

don't need to part with it." I pulled out my phone. "I keep forgetting about the technology."

Chance gave me a little wave and I grinned at him as he headed back to his room. When the door had closed, Carly said, "That doesn't happen very often."

"I'm glad it happened today," I said.

"I guess he thinks you're a nice guy. I do, too."

"Thanks, and right back at both of you."

I took a couple of pictures of the photo, put my phone away, and turned for the door.

"If you ever wanted to have another cup of coffee sometime … I'd … uh … be up for that."

I turned back to her. There was some pink in her cheeks as she made the offer.

"Thanks … I …" I hoped the smile on my face told her that couldn't happen. The smile on hers told me she understood.

"I really appreciate your help," I told her.

She smiled again. "You're welcome, Adam."

When the door closed behind me, I sent a wish to wherever wishes are supposed to go that she'd meet a great guy one day and the three of them would have a nice life together.

On the street in front of the building, I looked at my picture of the photo. I probably wouldn't have need- ed it. Chance was his dad minus twenty-five or thirty years. I climbed into the Accord and GPS'd the address she'd given me. The place where Maughan had rented a suite was only a couple of blocks from the house he and his family had lived in when Terry was in junior high at Kilkenny School, and only a couple more from the school itself.

I decided to drive by the place, see if anyone there might offer up something on where the elusive Terry Maughan could be found. I made a drive-through pick-up at a Starbucks on the way and relied on Stan Rogers's *Northwest Passage* — the album, not the single — to provide the accompaniment for the drive.

More and more I felt that Terry Maughan might be connected somehow to what happened in 1991, but how direct or tenuous that connection was, I had no idea. Was he a teenage murderer? Was he an accomplice? Was he the guilt-ridden family member who'd found out what his father had done and had had to live with that knowledge ever since? All of those and probably a couple more scenarios I hadn't thought of seemed possible.

And could that mean he was also connected to Kennedy's murder? And where the hell was he? Why the disappearance that roughly coincided with the time the first shadows began to appear on Kennedy's surveillance tapes of the alley behind where Faith's body had been found? Or was the whole thing wishful thinking — a couple of coincidences and some circumstantial evidence that added up to nothing?

The GPS directions took me right by the school, and a couple of turns led me to the address Carly Maughan had provided. Big house, I would have guessed seventies vintage. I tried to visualize where the suite Maughan had rented was situated in the house, and realized I had no idea. I got out of the car and headed for the front door, rang the bell, waited, rang it again.

After a lengthy wait, I finally heard movement on the other side of the door. It was opened by an unshaven guy in jeans and an undershirt, his body language and facial expression screaming pissed off.

"You have trouble with readin', Mac?"

I looked where a fat, flabby finger was pointing. A faded sign read "No soliciting." "Actually, I didn't see the sign, Mac, but we're okay, I'm not soliciting, not selling anything."

"I work nights and you interrupted my sleep, so if you ain't selling, what the fuck you want?"

What the fuck I wanted was to kick this man in the chimichangas, but I opted for restraint and a smile. "I'm looking for a former tenant of yours, Terry Maughan."

"Well, if he's a former tenant, then that pretty well means he ain't here, wouldn't you think that's what it would mean?"

The chimichangas, through no fault of their own, inched closer to a date with destiny.

"He leave a forwarding address?"

"No, what he left was a month and a half of unpaid rent. Who the fuck are you, anyway?"

I decided to change my approach. "*Calgary Herald*," I said. "Just working up a feature on illegal suites. If you wouldn't mind staying right about where you are, I'm just going to step back a little and get a shot of you at the front door. Yeah, that'll be perfect."

I started to back up, moving my hands like I was lining up a photo. "This will look great," I said.

"Whoa, whoa, whoa, just a minute," the guy said. "We don't need any pictures here or any stories. You know what — there's a nice lady rents that suite now, single mom, has a daughter at university; she comes home on weekends sometimes. You don't wanna see somebody like that out on the street, do ya?"

"Hell, no," I said. "That's why this is a totally sympathetic story. No fake news here, brother. I see you as a hard-working guy, works nights, has a little thing on the side that he rents out to people who are just as nice as he is. See how great that will be on page eight?"

I continued to set up my photo, checking the light, the angle. Apparently it hadn't occurred to the gentleman that the taking of a picture required a camera, which I was lacking. I stepped back up on the landing, pulled out my notebook and pen.

"Can I get the correct spelling of your name?"

"No names, no photos, okay? Come on, all right?"

"Okay," I said. "The last thing the *Herald* would want is to cause anybody any stress. So tell me about Terry Maughan."

"What do you wanna know?"

"I'm assuming that when you rent a suite to someone, you ask a few questions. What did he do for a living?"

"He ran some kind of home-based business, some on-line thing. That's what he said. I try not to interfere with other people's business."

I'm pretty sure there was a message for me in there somewhere. I ignored it.

"Maughan have many visitors?"

"No, hardly any. A couple of women, so at least he wasn't a fag. I'd have thrown his ass outta here if that was the deal."

"Yeah, good for you. Did he go out much?"

He nodded his head. "A lot at night. Not every night but I'd say quite a lot. The suite is set up so people can come and go without my knowing — you know, give 'em their privacy — but he had a fairly loud vehicle. So I knew when he was leaving."

"How about when he came home? Did he stay out all night?"

"I told you, I work nights, so I wasn't here most of the time when he got home. A couple of times on my days off, I noticed that he got back maybe two or three in the morning."

"The loud vehicle — what did he drive?"

"SUV."

"Remember the make?"

"Nope."

"Big, little, midsize?"

He shrugged. "I'd say maybe somewhere in the middle."

"Older, newer?"

"Somewhere in the middle."

"What about during the day?"

"I told you, I was usually sleeping. Like I oughta be doing right now. But sometimes he was gone during the day, too. I know that from my days off. I figured he was doing whatever his business was all about." A big yawn, exaggerated for effect.

The longer I stood on that porch, the more I felt that my body was being infested by poisonous insects. I'd had enough.

"Well, thanks, Mr. ...?"

"Uh ... Smith." He winked at me.

"Right." I winked back and turned to walk up the sidewalk toward the street. Just before I got to the Accord, I wheeled around, pulled out my phone, and held it up as if I was taking a picture.

He opened the door and yelled, "Hey, we agreed no pictures. What the fuck ya doin'?"

I pretended to click, then waved as I dropped into the driver's seat. "So long, Smitty."

I resisted the desire to race home for a shower, opting instead for soup and a sandwich at the Avenue Deli in Marda Loop. The sandwich was Montreal smoked meat, and it provided the needed antidote to the noxious aura of the man I had just talked to.

As I ate I flipped through my notebook, pages of jottings and recapped conversations, focusing on the notes I had made following my visit to Kilkenny School. I recalled walking the route Faith and her friend Jasmine had probably walked on their way home that terrible day in 1991. I thought about the Maughans — the cop and the son.

Terry Maughan had returned to the old neighbourhood, at least for a while, when he was renting from Mr. Personality. It was within blocks of Kilkenny School and the former Maughan home, and not far from the site of the Faith Unruh murder. Significant? Maybe. Except he wasn't there now.

I finished my food and called Jill. I figured she might be on a break at the Inn. She was, and picked up, her voice radiating the joy the job gave her every day.

"Hey, girl I love. How's your day?"

"Busy but good. Lots of drop offs at the food bank and a couple of new people wanting to stay at the Inn. Just processing them right now."

"Okay, won't keep you. Just needed to hear your voice."

"I love that you called. Don't forget Kyla and I have a baseball meeting tonight."

"Right," I said. "I *had* forgotten. Maybe because it's the dead of winter. You guys planning spring training in Phoenix?"

She laughed. "I wish. Gotta run, babe. See you later tonight."

We ended the call. I checked my wallet for Detective Landry's business card. I called her number, got voicemail, and left a message detailing my alibi for the night Kennedy was murdered. "I was at my girlfriend's home for dinner; then we went to the launch of a book I'd written at Owl's Nest Books. Forty or fifty people saw me there; I'd be happy to provide names. In fact, Mike Cobb came in partway through the event and told me about Kennedy. I'm not sure why I didn't remember that earlier — probably just flustered at being a person of interest. Let me know if there's anything else I can do for you."

While I was talking to Landry's voicemail, I received a text. It was from Cobb.

> Heard back from lab guy. He checked lines on trash can platform. Made with a common pocket knife. Same knife for all? Can't tell, but similar. T Maughan not in jail — here or anywhere else in Can. BTW we get an hour in Kennedy's house tomorrow 9:30 AM. The cops haven't released it to the executor yet; I'm not sure why. But the good news is we can still get in there. The bad news is Chisholm will be our watchdog. C U there.

SEVENTEEN

I arrived at Kennedy's old place at 9:25. Both Cobb and Chisholm were already there, standing outside on what was less than an ideal morning for being anywhere but next to a roaring fire. I parked behind Cobb's Cherokee and joined them on the sidewalk. It was hard to tell if either of them had actually spoken before I got there.

"Mike," I said and nodded. He returned the nod. "Detective Chisholm." He ignored my greeting.

"Okay, let's get this over with," the detective barked. "Here's the rules. Nobody goes anywhere without me. None of this splitting up, one upstairs, one down. I'm in the room you're searching at all times."

"Going to take longer that way," Cobb said.

"Might take longer, but it won't take *long*. You get forty-five minutes. Your time may not be valuable, but mine is. And rule number two is whatever you come up with, I see it. Rule number three — nothing leaves the house."

"How about we give our word that we share anything we find that might be at all relevant?"

"The word of a cop who couldn't cut it and a fake media guy. I don't think so. Let's go."

Until that moment I had Chisholm pegged as someone who was naturally surly but who could be effective as a homicide detective. This morning changed all that. He was just a jerk.

I noted that the police tape that had been in evidence for quite a while was now gone. We moved through the snow on the unshovelled walk and Chisholm unlocked the door. We stomped around getting snow off boots and shoes. The furnace had been turned way down in the house, and the forty-five minutes that had seemed way too short a time now looked like a frigid eternity.

"What are you actually looking for?"

"Not sure." Cobb shrugged. "Evidence that someone might have been in the house at some point and found out about the surveillance equipment — knew enough to find and take the tape of himself killing Kennedy."

"Look no farther than your partner there. Ran this shit for a while. Knew all about it."

"Yeah. How about we get started."

"Be my guests." Chisholm stepped back, arms folded.

"Let's start upstairs," Cobb suggested and we headed up to the room where the surveillance cameras were trained on the alley behind the murder house. I had spent a lot of hours in this room while I pinch-hit for Kennedy when he'd been with his dying wife. It looked different without the stacks of tapes everywhere — the tapes that were now in my apartment.

There weren't many places in this room that could possibly yield anything that might help us. Cobb checked the table while I concentrated on the shelves. We moved fast, and once we determined there was nothing there of interest, we moved on to the two upstairs bedrooms.

We found nothing useful in either, made a quick pass through the upstairs bathroom and a hall closet. We were twenty minutes into our forty-five minutes allotted time. We moved downstairs as Chisholm, following us, chortled and said, "Well, I'm sure glad this isn't a waste of time."

The second of the two surveillance areas would have been a living room in a normal home configuration. As was the case the first time I had come to the house, I was startled by a large blow-up photograph of a young girl on one wall. I knew the girl in the photo was Faith Unruh. My guess was that the photo had to have been taken in the year prior to her death. Again, there weren't many places to check out in that room, and I was glad that we were in and out quickly. The hall, downstairs bathroom, and dining room got cursory looks at best, but that was probably sufficient in that there were few places that might house the kind of thing we were looking for.

That left the kitchen. I figured if we had any chance at all, that's where it would be — the elusive clue that might tell us if someone had been in the house for some commercial venture, a renovation, a carpet cleaning ... furnace maintenance. I was wrong. Though there was a drawer that was clearly where Kennedy had kept receipts, bills, bank statements, and miscellaneous papers, nothing in that drawer or anywhere else yielded anything interesting.

Shivering and disappointed, I turned for the front door, where Chisholm was already looking at his watch. Cobb and I exchanged looks. He shrugged. We'd tried; there was no use dragging our heels. The only good thing about leaving that house was the Accord's reliable heater, which beckoned and promised to thaw frozen body parts.

Chisholm, unable to keep the gloating off his face, opened the door and stepped back to let us exit. Cobb led the way.

"Wait," I said. "There's one place we didn't look."

Cobb and Chisholm both looked at me, Cobb's face questioning, Chisholm's a mask of scorn.

"What the fuck are you trying to pull? I told you —"

"The basement. I know it's unfinished from my time here before, but I just need a quick look. Just give me a couple of minutes."

"Your time's up. Let's go."

Cobb said. "Hey, it's a basement. Just let him have a fast look. How long can it take?"

"I'll tell you how long it will take. Two minutes. If your ass isn't back up here in one hundred and twenty seconds, I'm coming to get you. And you don't want that."

I turned and raced down the stairs. There was no furniture, drawers, shelves, or even cardboard boxes down there. But none of that would have interested me if there had been any. I was looking for only one thing — the furnace. I remembered that my dad used to keep the user manual for our furnace resting on the main duct leading away from it. If someone had done maintenance on the furnace, real or bogus, could Kennedy have done the same thing with the paperwork? *Maybe maybe maybe.*

I got to the framed-in room where the furnace, hot water heater, and a smaller soft water tank were located and wasted thirty seconds trying to find the light switch.

When I did, I started my search, the seconds ticking off in my head. I didn't know if Chisholm would actually come down here after me, or if Cobb would let him, but I didn't really want the answer to either of those questions.

Come on. Come on. Come on.

Chisholm's baritone boomed from upstairs. "Thirty seconds, bud. Don't make the mistake of thinking I'm kidding."

And suddenly there it was — a nondescript piece of paper the size of a restaurant bill. Four lines — handwritten.

Record of Service.
Foothills Furnace Maintenance.
May 18, 2016.
$157.50 including GST.

It was held in place by a single tired piece of Scotch tape. I tore it off the outer wall of the furnace and stuffed it in my pants pocket.

Now the tough part. I had to reign in the elation, walk up those stairs and onto that main floor looking like my dog had died. I turned off the light and started up the stairs just as Chisholm appeared at the top. I trudged up and past him and headed for the front door. Cobb was leaning against the doorframe watching me. "Sorry, Mike," I said. "If there was anything down there, I didn't have time to find it."

Behind me Chisholm snorted. "You wouldn't have found shit if I'd left you down there all day. Let's go."

Cobb and I moved out of the house, off the step and onto the sidewalk, the snow again surrounding our boots. As we got to the front sidewalk, Cobb turned to

Chisholm. "Thanks, Detective," he said. "You're a pleasure to work with."

"Fuck you, Cobb." Chisholm climbed into his car and raced away from the curb, eager to report back on our lack of success.

"Maybe we should get us a coffee," I said to Cobb. "I'm pretty close to hypothermia."

"What did you find?" Cobb asked.

"What are you talking about? I told you I struck out. Besides, don't you remember Chisholm's rules two and three?"

"Yeah." Cobb grinned. "That hangdog act might work on Chisholm, but you're not good enough to fool me. What did you find?"

"Maybe we should have coffee," I said again.

We were sitting in the Phil and Sebastian's in Marda Loop, one of my favourite people-watching places in the city. But on this day I wasn't interested in watching people, other than maybe Cobb, to gauge his reaction to my find in Kennedy's house.

"I feel bad about not inviting Chisholm to join us. He makes every day brighter," I said as Cobb looked over the furnace maintenance receipt.

"There are a hell of a lot of good cops. Chisholm isn't one of them," Cobb said, without looking up from the faded writing on the paper in front of him.

"Foothills Furnace Maintenance," he mused.

"It fits the time frame," I said. "It wasn't long after that that the first shadows began to appear on the surveillance tapes."

Cobb nodded. "Checking the furnace might have taken whoever wrote this to other parts of the house and a view of the surveillance set-up."

"It's possible," I agreed. "I know this isn't the smoking gun, but it just might have put Terry Maughan in Kennedy's house at least once."

"I'd really like to find this guy," Cobb said. "We need to talk to him."

"Any idea how we do that?"

"I'll check with Motor Vehicles, see if they've got a vehicle registered to him."

"I missed the neighbour across the street when I went by his place in McKenzie Towne. He hasn't called me back, so I'll give him a call, see if he can give us anything."

"How about where he grew up? We know it wasn't far from the school or from Faith Unruh's house. I wonder if he ever pops around to the old stomping grounds at all."

"More than that. He rented a suite in a house in the old neighbourhood. He's not there now but he was in the last year. If he is the moving shadow in the videos and the guy scratching the marks on the platform, then obviously he's been in the area. Maybe I should ask around. I've got the picture of him. Maybe somebody's seen him."

"Worth a try."

"I haven't got a lot going on this afternoon. I'll get started after lunch."

"Okay. See how you make out. And if you're at it again tomorrow, you'll have to start a little later in the day, because you do have something in the morning."

I looked at him. "What's up?"

"Come by the office about ten. I've got something I want you to see."

"Sure," I said. "Care to give me a hint?"

Cobb shook his head. "I don't think so. Don't want to spoil the surprise."

Lunch was a fast-food burger that reminded me why I seldom do that. I started with a call to Jay Keeling, Terry Maughan's friend from across the street when he'd lived in McKenzie Towne. This time I got Keeling. He was fine with talking to me, apologized for not getting back to me, but added next to nothing about Terry that I hadn't already learned from his ex-wife and the bartender at the Kilt & Caber. That is, until near the end of our conversation.

"It's funny he doesn't come around anymore; we were pretty good friends," Keeling told me. "I figured he must have left town. That was Terry, too, always talking about greener pastures — maybe he'd have better luck in Vancouver or Montreal, places like that. But then I actually thought I saw him not that long ago, so I guess he didn't go anywhere … or if he did, he's back."

I perked up at that. "You saw him? Where?"

"On the Deerfoot. I was stuck in traffic. And so was he, going the other way. I'm not one hundred percent sure it was him. He was talking on his cellphone, which is another thing Terry was doing all the time. Chasing a buck however he could get it."

"When was this, Mr. Keeling?"

"I don't know, a few weeks, maybe a month ago."

"What was he driving?"

"Well, if it was him, it was a white van, kind of dirty."

"Any writing on the van?"

"Yeah, there was, but there were other vehicles between him and me, I couldn't make it out. I thought it might have been something Furniture. Sorry, I wasn't sure."

"Did you actually see the word *furniture*?"

"Hell, I can't remember. Maybe, or maybe part of it, I'm not sure."

"Any chance the word might have been *furnace*?"

He thought about that. "Could have been, I guess. Which would make sense, because he was hustling some furnace cleaning and maintenance deal last time I saw him. Tried to sell me a package."

"He have the white van back then?"

"No, he had an old beater SUV — Chevy Blazer. That thing had been through the wars. Anyway, he was pissed at me because I didn't buy the furnace package, and that was the last time I saw him."

"And he didn't say where he was living that last time you guys talked?"

"Just somewhere downtown," he said. "Didn't say exactly."

After I ended the call with Jay Keeling, I drove around the neighbourhood, stopping at convenience stores and gas bars, showing Terry Maughan's photo to clerks and cashiers, getting the occasional *might have seen a guy that looks like that but I'm not sure*. Finally, just after four, I lost heart and gave up for the day.

Three texts and a couple of phone calls later, dinner with Jill and Kyla at Redheads Japa Café in the Beltline was on. Donna had spent time in Japan before we were married and had introduced me to Japanese cuisine and Redheads. This would be the first time Jill, Kyla, and I had been to the place, and it was also my first time there without Donna. The plan was for me to pick up Kyla and meet Jill at the restaurant after she got off work at the Inn. The arrangement left me time to run, shower, and change clothes.

Kyla was outside waiting for me when I got to the house. We talked baseball all the way downtown, but I didn't like her colour. I asked her if she was feeling okay, the dreaded spectre of her Crohn's disease always embedded in my consciousness. She swore she was fine and deflected my concern with a question: Who's going to bat cleanup for the Yankees?

And while the evening was pleasant, it was less so because Kyla didn't eat much, excused herself to go the bathroom twice, and just wasn't her perky self. During her second washroom absence, Jill said what was on both our minds.

"I don't like it, Adam, she's not quite right."

We both knew that there would be down times in a disease that was as cyclical as Crohn's. I hoped that that's all this was — a temporary bout with an illness that would always be there but, with care, could be managed. I suggested we pack up the remaining food and take it with us.

When Kyla returned from the washroom, she didn't fight that suggestion, further evidence that she was a long way from a 100 percent. There was a tacit agreement among the three of us that on those days that Kyla wasn't feeling well — thankfully there had been relatively few of those — I would stay at my apartment. One of the effects of Crohn's was difficult diarrhea, and when that was the case, Kyla preferred privacy and the company of her mother only. And though I would rather have been there for her, to do whatever I could, I respected her wishes and understood the embarrassment she would feel if I were there. I hoped that if Jill and I were to become a permanent partnership, Kyla would be okay with my being present during the unpleasant moments we all knew would recur from time to time.

Once the two of them were in the house with Kyla in her pyjamas, the leftovers in the fridge, and chicken noodle soup warming on the stove, I gave them both hugs and got ready to leave.

"Chin up, sweetheart, and bounce back soon, okay?" I said as I gently hugged the girl who'd become like a daughter to me.

"Sorry I ruined the evening," she whispered.

"None of that," I said. "The only thing you did wrong all night was to pick Judge to hit fourth for the Yanks when any sensible baseball person knows it's going to be Stanton."

She stuck her tongue out at me and headed off down the hall.

"Keep me posted," I instructed Jill, as I gave her a quick embrace and turned for the door. "I want to know how she's doing. I *need* to know how she's doing."

"I will, babe. I love you."

I had made a habit of looking around the yard and street whenever I came out of Jill's house. I did that now and saw nothing out of place — no suspicious characters leaning against light standards, no dubious vehicles idling in the street, no unsavoury men with turned-up collars and pulled-down hat brims sneaking peeks at the house.

I eased myself into the Accord and pulled away from the curb. I was restless, partly because of the lack of progress in finding Terry Maughan and partly because I always felt that way when Kyla was feeling the effects of her illness.

For a few minutes I drove aimlessly, before finally heading toward the house once occupied by the Maughan family. I'd wanted to drive by the place and maybe even see if there might be a neighbour or two around I could ask about the family, a bit of a long shot, as Terry Maughan had probably moved out of the house in the mid- to late '90s, his father then succumbing to a heart attack in 2008. So it had been a while. Still, it was only a few minutes away.

I checked the address that the school secretary, Lois Meeker, had given me and circled the block a couple of times, stopping directly across from a medium-sized 1960s bungalow with a single attached garage. Blue siding, living room to the right, bedrooms to the left. The place looked decent, yet there was no sign of life, as if it were uninhabited. Blinds were pulled down over all the windows except in the living room, where floor-length drapes were drawn. The sidewalk hadn't been shovelled, though there were some footprints and tire tracks in the driveway. Not uninhabited after all. I checked my watch. It was just after 8:00 p.m.

I slowly climbed out of the Accord and looked up and down the street. No one was in the neighbouring yards or strolling along nearby. I hurriedly manufactured a story in my head about looking for an old pal who had once lived here and crunched my way through the snow to the front door, mounted three steps to a small landing, and rang the bell.

I waited a minute or so, then rang it again. No answer, no sound or light inside the house. I flipped up the lid on the mailbox. Empty. I turned away from the door, stepped back to the path that ran both to the front walk and the garage. I walked to the garage, noting that the snow had been stomped down to a thin layer, an indication that whoever lived in the house went to the garage for the car more often than they walked out to the main sidewalk. And apparently didn't believe in the snow shovel.

If those were my takeaways, I hadn't learned much. At the garage I took in that there were no windows, and, just for the hell of it, tried the garage door. Locked shut from the inside. I decided against bothering neighbours at that hour. I'd come back the next day, after whatever "surprise" Cobb had in store for me.

For now it felt like a great night to retire early with a glass of wine and a good book. As I climbed back into the car, I pulled my cellphone out and called Jill. "Hey," I said, "how's the patient?"

"A little better, I think. She's sleeping. I'll see how she fares through the night and into tomorrow morning, then I'll decide if we need to get in and see the doctor."

"Okay, let me know if I can do anything."

"I will. And I'll call you in the morning in any event. I think I'm about to call it a day."

"Funny, I was just thinking the same thing."

"I love you."

"I love you, Jill."

EIGHTEEN

When I opened the door to the office, I saw right away that Cobb wasn't alone. Someone was sitting in the chair opposite his desk, his back to me.

"Sorry," I said. "I'll come back a little later."

Cobb gestured. "No, no, come on in, Adam. You know our visitor, I think."

As I crossed the office, I glanced at the person in the guest chair and stopped dead.

Ike Groves. The Grover.

His look told me he wasn't any happier to see me than I was to see him.

I decided to play it cool, so instead of taking a seat, I headed for the Keurig machine like this was the most normal morning ever and spending time with someone who had recently tried to blow us up was the sort of thing that happened every day around here.

"Coffee, guys?" I offered.

"Love one," Cobb replied. "Grover?"

"Uh, yeah, I could use a coffee. Thanks."

I made up three mugs. "Milk or sugar, Grover?"

"A little milk would be good."

I passed the mugs around. "You picking up a suit downstairs, Grover?"

"No," he held his hands out to display his ensemble — a burnt-orange blazer over a pink shirt and a tie that was wide, colourful, and hideous. "Do I look like a dude who needs a suit from down there?"

"No, you're da bomb, Grover."

I heard Cobb sputtering at that as I took a seat. I'm not sure Grover got it.

Cobb leaned back, coffee in hand. "It seems that The Grover has a problem."

I had a dozen snappy comebacks at the ready but thought it best to keep them to myself. "Something we can help with?" I said.

Cobb shrugged. "Maybe." He turned his gaze to Grover. "You want to tell him about it or would you like me to?"

"You go ahead, man. I trust you to tell it right."

Cobb sipped his coffee, then began. "It seems that our friend Grover has had a falling out with the MFs. Grover has explained that he has worked with Mr. Scubberd and company a few times over the years, including a recent *situation*. Apparently, in the execution of a course of action related to that situation, Scubberd concluded that Grover may have provided faulty information that resulted in a serious problem for the MFs. Grover is convinced that his life is in danger and would like our help in keeping the MFs from finding him."

"Did Grover happen to mention what the particular situation was that has led to his being in danger?"

"He prefers not to give details that he feels are irrelevant."

Grover had been nodding as Cobb laid out the problem he was facing. I realized then that Grover was not aware that we knew he had tipped off the MFs to the van in front of Brock Scubberd's home — the one that was blown to bits the night of the con involving Pink and the younger Scubberd … the one Grover thought we were in at the time of the explosion.

"Irrelevant," I repeated. It was a struggle to keep myself from grabbing Grover by his long, skinny neck, but I had a hunch that Cobb had another idea.

He continued. "Grover and I have been discussing an exchange of services. I believe I can provide a place where he can live out the rest of his life in relative safety. And he, in return, is willing to do something for us."

More nodding from The Grover, this time even a bit of a grin. Mr. Co-Operative.

"Are we going to get to any specifics of what it is we are all doing for one another?"

Cobb shook his head. "You and I will get into that after Grover leaves us. I'm sure you can understand that he's a little anxious about being discovered by members of the MFs and would like to be on his way as soon as possible. To wit …" Cobb waved an arm, "our friend's chariot and charioteers are here." I turned to see Jean-Luc, a.k.a. Frenchie, and McNasty — I still didn't know his real name — entering the office.

Cobb stood up. "Everything clear outside?"

Frenchie nodded. "The car's in back. Nobody followed us and nobody's watching the building."

Grover stood up and slowly turned to them. "You get my stuff?"

"We got it," Jean-Luc said. "One suitcase. One computer case, computer inside. Paperwork right here." He patted his pocket.

Cobb looked at his watch. "Okay. You've got time. No need to speed or do anything that will draw attention from the cops or anyone else."

Grover turned back to Cobb and offered a hand. "Thanks," was all he said.

Cobb shook his hand. "Remember, Grover, if you screw this up even a little bit, I let Scubberd and company know where you are and you're a dead man. And that's a promise."

Grover nodded. "Got it."

McNasty, who hadn't spoken a word, turned and led the way out of the office, Grover behind him and Jean-Luc the last one out. He closed the door without looking back at us.

Cobb sat back down.

"Why is it I get the feeling we're back in the Old West again, riding on the wrong side of the law?"

Cobb didn't answer. Instead he passed me a single eight and a half by eleven sheet of paper, typed text covering most of the page. I read it slowly, then read it again.

> The following is my complete and truthful statement as to what happened on the night of February 2, 2017. That evening at just after 10:00 p.m., I was admitted to the residence of Mr. Wendell Claiborne on Willow Park Green Southeast in Calgary, Alberta, Canada. I was there to confirm details of a plan Mr. Claiborne had to contract his daughter's boyfriend, named Danny

Luft, to shoot his wife, then make it look like there had been a break-in and that Mrs. Claiborne had been shot by the intruder. Mr. Claiborne and I had known each other a long time. He enjoyed the services of some of the ladies in my employ on a number of occasions. My job in this instance was to be the break-in artist. Two nights later, on Saturday night, I was to break his office window, enter the office, leave a fairly obvious trail in and out and then leave. Mr. Claiborne didn't give me the details of how Danny Luft would carry out the shooting of Mrs. Claiborne. But while we were discussing the final plan for Saturday and what I was to be paid, he refused to pay the 50 percent up front that had already been agreed upon. We argued about that, and I told him if he didn't pay what he owed me, I'd go to the cops and tell them what he had in mind for Mrs. Claiborne. The argument got louder and nastier. Claiborne lunged for a revolver that was sitting on his desk at the time and had been there from the start of our conversation. I got to it first and when it looked like Mr. Claiborne was reaching for the drawer in his desk, where I was concerned there might be another gun, I shot him once in the chest. Clearly this was self-defence, as there was no doubt in my mind that Claiborne was reaching for a second weapon. I was going to take his wallet and search the office for other money or goods to make it look like a robbery, but I didn't get that chance, as I heard a scream upstairs and figured someone in the house had heard the shot and would be coming downstairs and into the office. I exited through the front door and left the area. Unfortunately, a couple of nights ago I let slip that I had shot Claiborne to a couple of guys who know Mike Cobb, who is an ex-cop and someone I have provided information to on a number of occasions. Cobb had a couple of his associates bring me to his office, where I admitted that I had shot Mr. Claiborne. Cobb told me he would have to turn me over to the police homicide unit but I insisted that I give him my full and truthful confession because I do not trust the cops. I am making this confession freely and of my own will. And now that I have done so, Cobb is having the same two associates who brought me here take me to the police station, where I will be handed over to homicide detectives.

Signed on this 22nd day of February, 2017.

Grover's signature was at the bottom of the page and I had no doubt in my mind that it was, in fact, Ike Groves's signature. It was probably the only thing on that piece of paper that *was* legitimate. I leaned forward and set it on Cobb's desk.

"You're kidding, right?"

"About what?"

"About giving that to the cops. That is so junior high it's embarrassing. And you'll probably end up in jail. And you thought my deal with the MFs showed poor judgment. They'll peel Grover like a stale grape and that whole bogus thing is going to blow up bigger than that van in front of Brock Scubberd's house."

Cobb was smiling. "Of course it's bullshit and of course the cops are going to suspect it's bullshit. But a few things you need to consider. The first one is I don't have a better idea, do you?"

"I can hardly think of a worse one."

"That's not what I asked you. We don't have a lot of options. Mrs. Claiborne has forbidden us to do anything that might point the finger at her daughter, and we gave our word on that. The only way we get her out of there is to find another person the cops can hang this on. So what we've got is a lowlife with a lengthy criminal record who has confessed to shooting Claiborne. Yes, the document itself and even the idea is junior high, as you call it, but what's more important than that is that it could work. Grover has included just enough truth in his confession that it just might fly."

"Jesus Christ, Mike."

Cobb held up both hands. "Consider this. The police and the Crown prosecutor have a very sympathetic figure in Mrs. Claiborne, whom nobody wants to see behind bars except maybe a dickhead like Chisholm. I spoke to Kemper and he told me he's seen cases with less reasonable doubt than this result in acquittals. By the way, he's talked to Rachel Claiborne and she has given a tentative go-ahead for our little plan."

"Tentative," I said.

"Yeah, she wants to know it will work. Kemper relayed my *there ain't no guarantees* speech but he also told her it has a decent chance. And as for the cops ripping Grover to shreds, well, that isn't going to happen." He glanced at his watch. "Because by now, The Grover, that crafty son of a gun, has somehow managed to escape his escort and is on his way to a place that will provide him with safety and anonymity for the rest of his life. The police, and more importantly, the MFs, will not find him because there are only three people in the world who know where Grover will be by this time tomorrow. Those three people are Grover, me, and a man a very long way from here who will be Grover's guardian angel and watchdog all at the same time."

"Your own private witness protection program."

"Something like that, yeah."

"I still can't believe it'll work."

"You might be right," Cobb admitted. "But it's what we've got. And it gives Rachel Claiborne a chance. Which is more than she'll have if we do nothing. And, by the way, since you aren't part of this, all you have to do is tell the truth. You saw Grover leave in the company of two of my associates and after he had been escorted from the office, you read the confession that he wrote. By the way, that confession was taped and videoed as he made it and I have to say The Grover was pretty convincing. He won't win the Academy Award, but then neither did *La La Land*."

"Landry's going to hate this," I said.

I was right.

Detective Yvette Landry was sitting in Cobb's office across the desk from him and I could see it was a monumental effort for her to keep from screaming. So far she'd been able somehow to maintain control. I was on my observation perch over near the Keurig machine, Chisholm was standing, his back to the windows that looked down on 1st Avenue. Both of them had declined coffee.

She had spoken for several minutes, had not raised her voice, had not sworn, yet had managed to convey in absolute terms what she thought of Cobb and me and what she thought of the fact that Rachel Claiborne was going to be released later that afternoon.

Cobb sat back in his chair. He didn't look smug or smartass. He had listened to what Landry had said, had not interrupted, and had nodded a couple of times. Now he was ready to respond.

"Detective Landry, I understand your frustration, I really do," he said. "I've done the job you're doing and I watched people walk who in my mind were absolutely guilty. It was the most frustrating part of the job and was probably the biggest reason I finally left the police service. But all of us in this room know that Rachel Claiborne confessed in order to prevent Danny Luft from having a murder conviction over his head for the rest of his life.

"She did that because she knew that Danny did not shoot Wendell Claiborne. She was prepared to go to jail for a very long time to protect that young man. And if one of Calgary's seedier citizens, who had a long association with Claiborne, seeing to his penchant for hookers, had not been overheard bragging about killing Claiborne, which led to his confessing to the shooting, Mrs. Claiborne would have been one of this city's most tragic wrongful convictions in our history."

"That, if you'll forgive the vulgarity, is bullshit," Landry answered. "The woman shot her husband, perhaps with good reason, I concede that, lied to us at first with some cock-and-bull story about finding him after some unidentified prowler had shot him. Then, to her credit, she didn't want a young man to be convicted and jailed for something he didn't do. She confessed, finally telling the truth, but only because she had to. Then along come Cullen and Cobb with a load of crap, cooked up with a piece of street shit, and because Mrs. Claiborne has been painted by the media as the female counterpart of a knight on a white charger, she will go free today."

Cobb looked like he was ready to argue again but changed his mind.

"But I didn't come here to debate her guilt or innocence," Landry continued. "I know you'll ride your nonsense story as long as that horse will carry you. I came here to make two promises. The first is that I ... we" — she included Chisholm for the first time — "are not about to let this go. There has been no trial; there is no double jeopardy here. We will keep looking for your lowlife friend, and if we find him, we will get the truth from him. And when that happens we will see your asses behind bars for a very long time. And we will see Rachel Claiborne charged with and tried for murder, as she should be.

"My second promise refers to the time from now until that day comes. I will be watching you. Oh, I know Cullen and Cobb are little cult heroes in this city but you are not heroes to us. If you so much as fail to dot an i or cross a t; if you step offside in one of your investigations by so much as a half-stride, my partner and I, and a hell of a lot of people in the Calgary Police Service, will be there, and you will pay the price. Believe me, you will pay the price."

She stood up. Cobb and I joined her. There would be no handshakes, no *see ya later* smiles. This was a declaration of war, and while it might be a long time before the battles of this war would be fought, if they ever were, the line had been drawn and the arbiter of that line would be Detective Yvette Landry. Of that there was no doubt.

NINETEEN

The confrontation bothered Cobb, I could tell. I made us a couple of coffees after Landry and Chisholm had left, but we didn't talk much and he declined my suggestion that we grab some breakfast at Red's Diner, a sure sign that he wasn't himself.

Cobb liked Landry, and more than that, he respected her. She was a straight shooter and a good detective, and for him to know that she didn't see him the same way was tough to take. I'd come around a little more on what Cobb was trying to do. He didn't want Glenna Claiborne charged and tried in the death of her father, and it wasn't right that her mother should possibly spend several years incarcerated to keep her daughter out of jail.

I got that. And I was starting to get that Cobb realized that the only way to keep those things from happening was for there to be another suspect. And with Wendell Claiborne's consorting with prostitutes and Ike Groves's long history as a pimp, the connection, however dubious, was there. And, of course, all of it was complicated by the fact that Cobb could not tell Landry who the real killer of Wendell Claiborne was. He'd done what he felt he had to do, using the resources he had.

Cobb was as tough a person as I'd ever known, but he was also a decent, at times gentle man who loved his family and was passionate about his work both as a former homicide detective and now as a PI. And I could see it would be a while before he'd be able to put the loss of respect that Landry had professed behind him.

I got the sense that he wanted to be alone, and I headed off to see if I could get a line on where Terry Maughan was living. I returned to the neighbourhood where he'd lived as a teen and where he'd lived again recently. I hit pizza places, a couple of Tim Hortons, more convenience stores, and gas bars — all to no avail. And I tried the former Maughan neighbours — only three nearby houses had people at home and all of them were too recently arrived in the area to have known the Maughans. As dark was beginning to settle in, I stopped to fill up at a Fas Gas on 37th Street. Because it was a little farther away from the neighbourhood I was focused on, I wasn't going to bother showing the attendant the photo of Maughan.

But when I got inside, the guy manning the till — his name tag told me he was Vihaan — was pretty chatty. After we had both lamented the bitter cold and shared where we'd rather be when the thermometer flirted with minus twenty-five — his chosen destination was Vancouver; mine was Hawaii — I decided to show him the photo.

He looked at it and nodded right away. "Oh, yes. I know him, he stops here often, fills up, always buys one of those." He pointed at the large Kit Kat chocolate bars that were on a small rack right below me.

"You know his name?"

A shrug. "No, he never has said it and he pays at the pump with a debit card."

"What's he drive, did you notice?"

"Not always the same vehicle — sometimes a van, I think a company truck, writing on the side, and he also has a quite old, very rusted SUV, blue and white, I don't know what kind."

"The van, you remember what the business name was?"

Another shrug. "I did not pay attention."

"When was the last time he came by, do you remember?"

"A few weeks, maybe." Vihaan hesitated. "Why do you want to know all this?"

I had something ready should that question be asked. "I'm on the committee for our school reunion — we're supposed to spread the word to people we went to school with. If this is the same guy, his name is Terry Maughan, but nobody seems to know his address and I'd really like to make sure he's on the invitation list, you know?"

"Yes." Vihaan nodded and smiled. "Well, it shouldn't be so hard. He told me a few months ago that he had bought his old house — not so very far from here. I remember that because I never heard of that before, someone buying for a second time a house they lived in before."

"You mean ... wait, did he say if it was the house he'd grown up in?"

"Yes, I think so. He said it was his parents' house a long time ago and it was for sale and he bought it. You're his friend, so you must know the house."

I nodded slowly. "Yeah, I know the house. Thanks, Vihaan." I grabbed a package of gum and threw a twenty on the counter to pay for it. When he'd run it through the till, I declined the change.

"That's for you, my friend. You've made my day."

"Thank you," Vihaan said.

As I started for the door, he called out, "Wait. Money!"

I turned back to him. "What? Oh, I paid at the pump."

"No, his name ... I think maybe his name is Money. I just remembered that. One time only he said to me, we were out of the Kit Kat bars and he said, that's no good, you better have them next time I come in here. You look after Money and Money will look after you. I told him I didn't understand look after money, but he said, 'No, not money — *I'm* Money.' He pointed at himself then."

I didn't understand it either, not at first, then I said. "Are you sure he didn't say Monny? You look after Monny and Monny will look after you?"

"Monny ... Money." Another shrug. "There is no difference."

"You might be right. Except that Monny just might be a nickname for someone with the last name Maughan. Anyway, thanks a lot, Vihaan, you've been a huge help."

I stepped outside and for a while was barely aware of the cold. Were we finally getting close to answers that had eluded Cobb and me and everyone else for so long? Answers about the Kennedy killing? And maybe even the murder of Faith Unruh?

I shivered. Maybe it was the cold, or maybe it was realization that the night before I had been skulking around the house that Terry Maughan might once again be living in.

Terry Maughan.

Monny.

I got back in the Accord, started it, and cranked the heat. I called Cobb and got his voicemail. "Hey, I might have found Terry Maughan. Call me when you get this. And if I'm right, every time you pass a Fas Gas from now on, give 'em a tip of the hat."

I was hoping an upbeat message and maybe even a breakthrough might raise his spirits.

I pulled out of the gas bar lot and headed back in the direction of what was once the Maughan residence. And might be again. I circled the block a couple of times, drove down the street the blue-sided bungalow sat on, once in either direction, slowing both times as I passed in front of the house, peering at what looked like as lifeless a place as it had been the previous night.

I parked down the street for a while, waiting for Cobb to call back. Still no sign of life around the house, nobody coming or going on foot or in a vehicle. I decided to check it out once more, see if maybe I could find something that would confirm that it was Terry Maughan's house and that he was still living there, even if he wasn't around right now.

I walked quickly; it was too damn cold to dawdle. Except I wasn't sure what I'd do when I got there. If it was Terry Maughan and he answered the door, what then? I looked again, no lights on, decided to check the mailbox again. There was a flyer this time, no name on it. I looked around and decided to try the yard — maybe one of the windows back there wasn't covered and I could get a look inside.

I had to pass the garage on my way, and just for the hell of it, I tried lifting the overhead door, expecting it to be locked, as it was the night before. But this time it yielded easily. I pulled it only far enough to get a look inside. And there on the near side, right in front of me, was a dirty white van. I straightened, looked around and lifted the door a little more, just enough to let me inside to have a look at the side of the van. There was enough light from the nearest streetlamp to give me a bit of a look around. The far side space was empty, so I guessed that Maughan was out in the Blazer.

I eased my way along the van and peered through the semi-light at the writing on the side — I could just make out the words — Foothills Furnace Maintenance. I stepped back and looked around the garage, but couldn't make out much more than shadowy shapes. But one set of shapes interested me. What looked like a pile of tires up toward the far corner of the garage. I moved in that direction, pausing with each step to make sure I didn't bang a shin on some piece of wayward machinery. Or kick something over and make a bunch of noise.

I got to the tires — there were four of them — and I tried to get a look, at the same time running my hands over them to determine if I could tell what vehicle they might have been from. I guessed they didn't belong to the van. Too big and awfully wide. Meaning that if they belonged to the Blazer, they might be the ones that had driven repeatedly over the helpless body of Marlon Kennedy until the last vestige of life had been crushed out of him. I bent over them, hoping to get a better idea of what brand they were, but it was too dark.

Suddenly, I heard a noise behind me and froze, hoping it was the wind from outside moving something around. I heard it again, closer now, and started to straighten and turn. I wasn't fast enough. Pain detonated in my head — pain I'd known only once before, when an opposing pitcher had run a ninety-eight-mile-an-hour fastball off my right cheek and temple. But this wasn't a fastball. The result, however, was much the same: a heavy, black curtain of swirling darkness settled over me, and I slid to the floor.

TWENTY

I woke up with a headache that registered 8.5 on the Richter scale, a horrific ringing in my ears, and the taste of blood in my mouth. Even in my less than solid mental state, I knew I was in serious trouble.

"Well, well … I was beginning to wonder if I'd hit you too hard. Welcome back."

I looked up and saw a face I knew, the face from the photo — Terry Maughan. I tried without success to make my mouth work. The blood in my throat choked out the sound. I was lying on my side in the back seat of a vehicle, I guessed the Chevy Blazer. I looked around and saw that I was sharing the space with various fast-food remnants, a small gas can, and at least a couple of old furnace filters.

Maughan's leering face was looking at me over the back of the front seat. I tried to sit up, but quickly realized that wouldn't be possible, since my hands were tied behind my back.

"I figured we'd meet up sometime, but I didn't think it would be this easy," he said. "You are one dumb son of a bitch, you know that?"

I still couldn't get my voice to quite work so I nodded. He was right. And leaving my cellphone in the car while I'd prowled around Maughan's garage put the exclamation mark on the point. There would be no clever manoeuvring of bound hands to somehow turn on the phone and have Cobb or someone listen in.

I croaked out a word, coughed, swallowed, and tried again. "I know you killed Kennedy … did you also murder Faith Unruh?"

Maughan chuckled. "Cut right to the chase, eh? Probably a good idea, as you haven't got much time. Actually, I didn't, but I know who did."

He laughed like that was the funniest thing he'd heard in a while.

"As soon as I heard about it, I knew he'd killed her. He'd done a couple of presentations at the school the week before — had Faith up there at the front of the class helping every time I turned around. I could tell he was thinking about doin' the dirty, and like I said, when I heard she'd been killed, I knew exactly what had happened. But for a pretty good cop, the old man was kind of a fuckup as a criminal. Got into trouble a few times for boinking the suspects. Hell, this time he didn't even get the ol' peter out of his pants. Turned out little Faith was a scrapper, popped him one in the nose, he bled like a stuck pig and I'm guessing that's what caused him to lose it. Then panic set in and he got the fuck out of there. I guess you can understand he didn't share all the details with me, even when I told him I knew he'd killed her. But I'll give him credit — he didn't try to lie about it — just told me he'd made a mistake and was going to get help and begged me not to tell anyone."

"Admirable," I said.

He laughed hard at that.

"Admirable? Not so much. But do you know how fucking awesome it is being a kid who knows the old man's worst secret? There wasn't a whole lot of *No, Terry, you can't do that, No, Terry you can't have that* after we had our little talk. I kept thinking they'd figure it out, and maybe they did, but they didn't have enough to put him away. As bad as he fucked up, he was awful lucky. He covered her up with a four by eight piece of plywood and then hauled ass out of there. He got back to the station, no sooner walked in than he caught a suspicious-death call — headed out, did the homicide investigator bit on that one, but made sure he'd be around to be part of the Unruh investigation. Got to the crime scene that he was pretty damn familiar with, conveniently cut himself, contaminated the shit out of the DNA that would have had his signature all over it."

"And it was him who made the panties go away."

"Yeah, there was blood on them and he was afraid it might be his — made sure they never got to the lab. So there it is — our dirty little family secret that's going to stay a secret because that famous back alley is about to add another page to its … um … interesting history."

"Why have you kept the secret all this time? Why would you give a shit if people knew what he did?"

"Kind of gets in the way of my career path when the old man's a known killer, you know what I mean?"

"You still think you're going to be a cop?"

He turned serious at that. "You better fucking believe it."

My mind was a lot clearer now. I tried moving around, seeing if whatever he'd used to bind my hands was at all loose. It wasn't and he laughed again. "Yeah, that won't work. Cullen. That's your name, isn't it? I saw you on the tapes sneaking around back there. I must have been driving you assholes crazy with all the stuff I did to make it look like something was going on in the alley. I laughed my ass off over that. Then I did a little checking — your vehicle when you stayed at Kennedy's place was a giveaway. I've been a couple of jumps ahead of you all the way."

"Yeah, you're a smart guy, Monny. Too bad you're not smart enough to pass the written cop test. But hey, I hear they're looking for forty-year-old illiterate guys. So hang in there."

He reached over and punched me hard on the side of the face. I decided it might be best to keep my mouth shut.

"Let's go, asshole. It's time I tested this new set of tires."

He turned back to the front and we drove off, moving fast. He turned the stereo up loud, maybe so he wouldn't have to listen to me. I worked hard at the bonds that held me and had the same lack of success I'd had earlier. I reasoned that if we were starting out from near his house, we were only a couple of minutes from the alley where Kennedy had died and where I was scheduled to be the next victim.

Then Maughan turned the stereo down and slowed the vehicle to a crawl. I could see he was looking around, his head on a swivel, making sure there weren't people hanging out to witness what was about to happen. The ride got bumpier; I guessed we were in the alley. A few more seconds ticked off and we rolled to a stop. One last look around, then Maughan leaned over the back seat, grabbed my hair with one hand, and with the other forced some kind of dirty cloth into my mouth. Having reduced to next to useless my last line of defence, he threw the driver's side door open, climbed out, jerked the back door open and grabbed me by the shirt. He was bigger and stronger than I'd thought he would be, and he hauled me out of the back seat with ease, dragged me around the other side of the vehicle to where the trash can platform stood and forced me to the ground. He had a rope and he pulled it noose-like around my neck and wrapped the free end around the platform's two-by-six posts.

"Good night, piece of shit," he growled. "Oh wait, I almost forgot." He reached in his pocket, pulled out a pocket knife and bent to make one more mark on the platform. He straightened and grinned at me. But he'd made a mistake. He was close enough that I could get in one kick. I did, behind the knee, and it took him down.

Problem was, that's all I had. My hands bound, and now with my neck in the noose, I couldn't follow up the kick with anything useful. All it got me was one more punch in the face, this one stunning me a little.

I sensed him leaving and closing the back door of the Blazer; he got into the driver's seat and backed the car up, maybe twenty feet or so. Ready.

I heard the roar of the accelerator and saw the lights of Blazer coming at me. He was behind me: it was my head he'd crush first, and I knew that I was seconds from my last moments on this earth, visions of Jill, Kyla, and Donna the last pictures my mind's eye would see.

Maybe it was reflex, but I squeezed as far to my right, as close to the platform as I could get, and realized there was a tiny space under the platform. I wiggled and squirmed as hard as I could and got at least some of me underneath it.

Some but not all. My left leg was still sticking out and the pain was beyond terrible as first one tire, then the other rolled over it. Even with the noise of the engine,

I heard the snap of breaking bones. I wanted to scream, tried to scream, but couldn't.

The Blazer came to a stop just past me and Maughan jumped out again, ran to where I was still partly under the platform, reached down and dragged me clear of it.

"Nice try, I'll give you that. But I'll bet you can't do that again."

I knew he was right. I needed both legs to squirm my way back under and I no longer had that capability. It was over, and we both knew it.

He didn't try for a cool exit line, just walked quickly back to the Blazer and climbed back in. Wanting it over with.

I tried; I actually tried to make my body repeat what it had done before, this time with one leg useless and crushed. It was no good. I closed my eyes and tensed, heard the roar of the engine again, waited for the inevitable.

Maybe it was because my eyes were squeezed shut that I didn't see the headlights. But I suddenly realized the Blazer was moving away from me. Toward the other end of the alley, where a second set of headlights had now appeared.

I was dimly aware of brakes squealing, gravel being thrown from beneath spinning tires, vehicle doors being opened and slammed shut, and finally what sounded like gunshots. Then voices, familiar ones.

"Christ, I almost ran over him myself," one of the voices said. "Just saw him at the last second."

The owner of that voice leaned over me. It was McNasty. Beside him Cobb's concerned face peered at me as he reached down to pull the cloth from my mouth and gently remove the noose.

"Hang in there, buddy, you're okay, an ambulance is on its way. We got him."

"Is he still alive?"

Cobb looked over his shoulder, then back at me. "I don't know. Jean-Luc's with him."

"His father murdered Faith. And Terry killed Kennedy. He told me." I had to say that much in case I didn't live to tell it later. They had to know.

Cobb nodded. "Good job, partner. You did damn good. Oh, and, by the way, you were right about the Fas Gas guy except you might owe him more than a tip of the hat. You might want to buy the guy a coffee. Now just take it easy, I hear the siren — the ambulance will be here in a few seconds."

He was right. I could hear it now, too. It was the last thing I heard before that curtain — the same one as before — like the ones at the front of theatres, thick and dark, slowly descended — taking me into the world of unconsciousness one more time.

Terry Maughan didn't survive the night. When he'd realized he was trapped, he'd stopped the Blazer, leaped out, and run at the vehicle that was blocking the far end of the alley, a gun in hand and firing. Likely blinded by the headlights, he fortunately didn't hit anyone. From both sides of the Cherokee, Cobb and Jean-Luc returned the fire, and Maughan was hit three times.

The Medical Examiner's office said later that two of the three wounds Maughan had suffered could have proved fatal.

It was two days before I was able to give a statement to Detectives Landry and Chisholm. I told them exactly what Maughan had told me. There were, of course, some unanswered questions, but there were also answers, and most importantly, the resolution of two investigations.

Cobb, who had been at the hospital most of the time since I'd been hurt, came into my room as I was completing my statement to the police. When I was finished and had answered all of the questions the detectives had as best I could, Cobb filled in the blanks about what had happened two nights earlier. It was the first time I'd heard it, as doctors hadn't allowed much in the way of conversation up until then.

When he'd been unable to reach me on my cell, he got worried, so with Frenchie and McNasty assisting, he phoned every Fas Gas on the south side of the city. It was Cobb who connected with Vihaan, who at first thought it odd that there was so much concern over a school reunion contact, but finally told Cobb what he'd told me — that Terry Maughan had purchased the house he'd lived in as a boy.

When Cobb got to the house and saw the Accord parked down the street, cellphone still sitting on the front seat and no one at the house, he guessed the worst. After a fast search of the house, garage, and yard, Cobb figured that maybe Maughan wanted to complete the cycle with one final killing in the alley.

It was that correct assertion that saved my life. My leg had required a lengthy surgery to repair, but I was assured it would be "reasonably close to as good as new" in ten or twelve weeks.

When Cobb and I had finished giving our statements, Landry put away her notebook and looked first at me. "I'm glad you're going to be okay. I wouldn't have wanted this to end with you dying in that alley. You did good work and I realize there's no point in my saying you might have wanted to bring us into this sooner. The outcome might have been different on several fronts."

She then turned to Cobb. "The police service is grateful that you and your partner have brought about the completion of two long-standing crime investigations. But this doesn't change what I said before, doesn't change it at all."

With that, Landry turned and left the hospital room, Chisholm following.

Cobb patted me on the arm. "I'll let you get some rest. I'm around, so anytime you need something, just let me know."

"You don't have to hang around here, Mike. I'm doing fine and I know you've got better things to do."

"You're wrong. Number One son's running things at home, and so far Lindsay tells me it's not going all that badly. The house is still standing, no one's left home, and the neighbours haven't noticed I'm gone. In fact, rumour has it there's a movement afoot to keep me away for another month or two."

It hurt to laugh so I kept it to a smile. We shook hands and he headed out, but I knew he wouldn't be far away. Jill and Kyla were next in, Kyla sending Mike her brightest smile as they passed in the doorway. I knew Mike had been talking with her about the police service and I also knew Kyla was loving their chats.

She and her mom had also been there virtually the whole time I'd been in hospital. Jill bent over, kissed me lightly. "Time to get some sleep, mister. We'll be right over there."

She pointed at the two chairs she and Kyla had been sitting in for most of the forty-eight hours since I got out of surgery. I tried to argue but didn't have a whole lot of fight in me right then. I was asleep before they had sat down.

It was four days later that I received a couple of surprise visitors. I was sitting up and had just finished the final installment of Lorne Cooney's three-part piece on the Faith Unruh murder. It had been titled "Faith Unruh — The Last Chapter in One of Calgary's Saddest Stories Is Finally Written." Lorne had done a good job, as I had expected he would. He'd avoided the maudlin and the sentimental and had told it all with straightforward honesty, some of it hard to read, even now.

"Hey, Danny, come on in." He stepped in and reached behind him to pull a slender, pretty girl along with him.

"Hey, Mr. Cullen. This is Glenna."

"Hi, Glenna, great to meet you. Danny's told me all about you."

Blushes from both of them. Glenna, freckled, reddish-brown hair, athletic-looking, soccer maybe or volleyball, the shy smile still in place.

"Why don't you guys pull up those chairs?"

"No, that's okay," Danny said. "We can stand. We just wanted to say hello. We heard you were hurt pretty bad, and we wanted to come and see you. I hope that's okay."

"Of course it's okay. In fact, it's better than okay. Thank you."

"We brought you these." He handed me a box of chocolates.

"Hey, that's great. Chocolate is a food group around my house."

That brought a laugh.

"You two doing okay? I mean, after everything that happened?"

Danny nodded. "I guess so."

"How about you, Glenna?"

"Pretty good, I guess." Her voice didn't sound convincing.

"Things will get better with time," I told her, not sure how true that really was.

She nodded but didn't answer right away, her eyes downcast. When she raised them to look at me, there were tears there.

"I know my dad did some bad things, Mr. Cullen, but seeing him lying there like that — I … that's hard to get, like … to take, you know?"

"I understand, Glenna."

"It's kind of weird. Seeing him upstairs and he's just my dad and then a few minutes later he's not anymore … it's …" She stopped and there were more tears. Danny put an arm around her shoulders.

There was something that sounded off in what she was saying. I let her recover and wipe her eyes and nose with a tissue.

"You saw your dad upstairs? When was that, Glenna?"

"He'd just come in from being out. I guess that's when he had gone to talk to Danny and showed him the gun. Of course, I didn't know that then. But he had gone up to the bedroom and I was just coming out of mine and I saw him in there putting something in the drawer by the bed. I was going to take Tater outside and I didn't even stop and talk to him right then. I wish I had said something. I could have told him …"

"I'm betting your dad knew you cared about him a lot." I waited again as she dabbed at her eyes. "Glenna, can I ask you a question?"

She sniffed and nodded, trying to be strong.

"What happened after you took Tater for a walk?"

"I don't know. I came back in the house and Tater ran off to the back door where his food dish is. I saw lights on in Dad's office, so I thought I'd just tell him good night. I went in and that's when I saw …" She stopped again, took a breath. "He was lying there and Mom was there, too. I didn't see the guy who shot him. He must have run away before I got back to the house."

It was either an Academy Award–winning performance or I had just heard something I never wanted to hear. If Wendell Claiborne had actually gone upstairs after he'd returned from his meeting with Danny, had he put the gun back in the drawer?

And had Glenna actually entered the office after her father was shot?

If the answer to both of those questions was yes, then Cobb and I had it wrong. Cobb's premise was based on the gun being in Claiborne's office. But if he had returned it to the upstairs bedroom, then someone had to get it from there to the office. If that person was neither Danny nor Glenna, then there was only one person who could have taken it there. A person with a motive. And the charade with Ike Groves and his bogus confession was everything Landry had said it was.

No matter how valid the reasons were for Rachel Claiborne to shoot her husband, if she did, she had committed murder. Maybe a jury would have been lenient, but we would never know that. There would be no trial and no jury.

We had made it possible for a killer to go free.

I looked at Danny and Glenna for a long time. Searching for a trace of guilt or guile that might indicate that Glenna was lying. I saw none.

"Glenna, I'm sorry you're having to go through this. I could throw out a lot of useless clichés and sayings, but none of them will be much help. You're a terrific kid and I really believe it will get better with time. And if there's anything Cobb and I can do for you — either of you — just ask, okay?"

"You already did, Mr. Cullen. You gave me my mother back. And I know one thing; I couldn't do this without her. If she'd gone to prison to protect Danny ... I want you to know that ... well, I just thank you so, so much."

"You're welcome, Glenna. Thanks for coming to see me. And thanks for the chocolates."

They smiled, bobbed heads, and slipped out into the hallway. I didn't know if what Glenna had said at the end of the visit made it any better. But it did remind me of what Cobb had said a while back. *Think about the good things we've done.*

I decided to give it a try.

TWENTY-ONE

Corny, hokey, sentimental — it would be all of those things. But since those three words describe me rather well, it was also somewhat apt.

After a couple of months of mostly frigid temperatures and grey skies, the last few days, the first days of April, had brought a welcome respite from winter's ferocity. Temperatures were in the mid- to upper teens on the plus side of Anders Celsius's temperature scale, and blue skies felt, as the song's lyrics proclaimed, as if they were smilin' at me.

I was hoping that the sky wouldn't be the only smile I would see on this day. I'd had my full leg cast replaced by a smaller version, and I was at least a little more mobile than I had been for the past five weeks.

It was time.

Time for an outing. The day had started with Kyla and me delivering coffee, biscuits, and strawberry jam to Jill in bed. Timing is everything and ours had been near perfect, as our arrival coincided with the first flutter of eyelids.

Our carefully rehearsed plan had Kyla announce that we would be heading off for the first picnic of the year — to Reader Rock Garden, a one-hundred-plus-year-old park located just south of the Stampede grounds. One of

Calgary's best-kept secrets, it had long been a place I had gone to, most often alone, to relax, to read, and to think pleasant thoughts.

And while the flowers would not yet have appeared and the plants and shrubs were mostly dormant, the promise of beauty and joy not far off was, I thought, symbolic and in keeping with the day's plan.

The drive to the park was quieter than usual, what with Kyla more nervous than I was, and Jill enjoying the sun on her face as she drove — that being a task I was not yet up to handling. Once parked, we didn't have to hike far to find the right spot — a park bench near the rock walls William Reader himself, then Calgary's Parks Superintendent, had erected a century before to keep the hillsides around his cottage from eroding.

We ate and talked and laughed. It was a perfect day.

"I have a request," I told them both. "The new cast requires new signatures. I was hoping you would both sign my plaster. Kyla, would you do the honours first, please?"

She agreed and I pulled a Sharpie from my pocket and handed it to her. I turned and raised my leg as best I could to accommodate her. She fussed and wrote for what seemed rather a long time, finally prompting her mother to comment, "He said an autograph, not a novella."

Kyla handed Jill the Sharpie. "Oh, rats, I forgot my phone in the car. I want to get some pictures of this place. Can I have the car keys, Mom?"

Keys in hand, she bolted down the hill to the parking area.

I swung around to face Jill. "Okay, your turn. But do me a favour — can you sign right on the knee? I want your name in a prominent place."

She started to bend down to get in position to sign the cast.

"That's okay," I said. "Stay right there." I stood and, awkwardly I'll admit, was able to get my leg up on the park bench next to her. And as she leaned forward she saw the ring that Kyla had so carefully two-sided-taped to my cast — right on the knee.

She dropped the Sharpie and the tears came.

"Jill," I said, "I'm sorry I can't do this on bended knee like I said I would, but I did want the knee to play a role nevertheless." I bent and removed the ring from my cast and pulled the tape off.

"I want you to know that you make me unbelievably happy every single day and I'd like to try to do the same for you ... today and every day after this one. Will you marry me?"

I lowered my leg back to the ground and Jill stood up and pressed in against me.

"I love you so much, Adam Cullen." She kissed me, long and warm and soft. And then whispered, "But can I give you my answer after your accomplice gets back?"

"Deal," I said.

And within a minute, Kyla was racing back up the hill, cellphone in hand, and out of breath. Neither Jill nor I spoke.

Kyla looked from one of us to the other and back, concern starting to show her face.

"Did I miss anything?" she asked.

"No, you didn't," Jill said. "I wanted you to be here for this." And she turned to me and said, "Yes, I will marry you, Adam Cullen. Yes, yes, yes, yes, yes."

A group hug followed. Tears, laughter, and a hug that I hoped and believed would be the first of many ... many.

TWENTY-TWO

I was sitting on the back deck having coffee with Jill. The *Calgary Herald* was resting on the table in front of us but I hadn't looked at it. Time for that later. Lorne Cooney had called to say there was a positive review of the soon-to-be-released third Spoofaloof book on page 27, but that, too, could wait. These moments on the deck with Jill were precious to both of us and I had no desire to cut this one short.

It had rained during the night. Jill and I were watching a couple of robins industriously enjoying a hearty breakfast of fresh worms, which convinced me I should put off making our own breakfast, at least for a while.

Kyla was at a weekend baseball camp with two of her girlfriends and would be home later that day.

I'd started running again — slowly; Jill was positively radiant as she basked in the fulfillment of her work at the Inn. We'd been in the house two months. Our search had ended when we had walked through this place in the Roxboro neighbourhood a second time. When we got back outside we looked at each other, both of us with the expression that said *please tell me you love this place as much as I do.* We closed the deal that afternoon.

Character home, it's called. A two-storey old-timer with original hardwood floors, a beautiful backyard, and a fair number of items that needed attention, which is probably why we could afford it.

There had been several long discussions among the three of us about whether to buy in the country, but we finally agreed that there was much about this city that we loved and wanted to be a part of every day. And we were getting our country fix two or three times a week when we headed to the stable where our three horses were boarded. Jill had been saving for a couple of years and my latest Spoofaloof advance topped up the horse fund. Talented quarter horse geldings for Jill and Kyla, a quiet old mare for me.

There had been no honeymoon, nor had there been a trip to Vegas. The tour company had been great and agreed to let us reschedule for the fall, when my leg would be completely healed.

Jill's job at Let the Sunshine Inn was demanding, but she was loving it. She'd taken the morning off after spending much of the weekend alternating between the food bank and the homeless shelter. Kyla had had a couple of minor bouts with the Crohn's lately, but for the most part was managing it well and treated it with the same disdain with which most people regard the common cold.

The phone rang. I looked at the number. It was Cobb.

Mike and I had met for a couple of lunches and the occasional beer since that February night in the alley, but the talk was always casual. No business, no talk of cases or crimes, no planned pursuits of evildoers. And I'd been fine with that. More than fine.

And, of course, he'd been at the wedding. Church wedding. May 9th at Scarboro United Church, Reverend

Lee Spice presiding. I glanced at Jill and she nodded. *Take the call*. I hoped Cobb was calling to tell me he had tickets to the Stampeders game or the Stampede rodeo and could we join Lindsay and him.

I picked up the phone.

"Hey, Mike, how are things?"

"Things are good, amigo. How about you?"

"Right at this moment, awfully close to perfect."

"Liking the new place?"

"No, *loving* the new place."

"Getting tired of the life of leisure yet?"

"Not yet. Maybe ask me in about ten years."

"Have you seen the *Herald* this morning?"

"It's right here, but I haven't cracked it yet."

"When you do, take a look at a little story at the bottom of page two. There's a note about a disturbance in the Stampede infield last night. No details, because Stampede security closed off the area to everybody, but there were cops and an ambulance."

"And you're telling me this because?"

"I got a call late last night from a rodeo cowboy — guy named Johnny Stringer. I think you know the name."

"Johnny Stringer," I repeated slowly. "The String Man?"

"That's the guy. He said he knew you."

"Johnny rode broncs," I said. "He was pretty good in his day. I haven't seen him in a few years."

I'd done a feature on Stringer ten years earlier, maybe more. Years before that, he'd been part of a search that went on for weeks after a plane went down in northern California. The plane had four Canadian cowboys aboard, and dozens of people, including cowboys from both sides of the border, flew into the rugged mountain ranges between Cloverdale, British Columbia, and San Francisco in search of the downed plane. Johnny was one of those guys — he had his own plane and put his own rodeo career on hold to help in the search. The search went on most of the summer but was finally called off.

The wreckage was found months later by a hunter. It was a tough moment for a sport that defines itself by its fearlessness and independent spirit. Johnny Stringer talked quietly and reluctantly about his part in the search. His story was a compelling one and I won a couple of awards for the piece when it was published. Those plaques were among the things that were destroyed in the fire that claimed Donna's life in 2006.

"Been a while since I've talked to Johnny."

"He remembered you."

"He asked about me, did he?"

"No, he asked *for* you."

I didn't get that. "*For* me. I don't understand."

"He called me because he couldn't find your number, but it was you he wanted to talk to."

"About what?"

"Well, that takes us back to that incident at the Stampede grounds last night. Seems a rodeo contestant ended up spread-eagled in the middle of the infield. Large Bowie knife buried up to the hilt in the guy's chest. The body was found late last night. Word spread among the cowboy community. Turns out the guy was a friend of Stringer's, and The String Man, as you refer to him, called me about midnight."

"Uh-huh." Suddenly I wasn't sure I liked the direction of the conversation.

"Naturally there was widespread concern among competitors and Stampede officials. Johnny told some people that he knew a guy named Cullen who's been involved in some high-profile investigations with some other guy whose name he couldn't remember at first." Cobb chuckled at that.

"It finally came to him. Johnny said he'd make a call. I was the call he made. Looking for you."

"So you said. Johnny ever hear of the police?"

"Apparently the rodeo folks aren't confident that the local constabulary are up to the task."

"They made that assessment after a couple of hours?"

"I think it's more ingrained attitude than assessment."

"What did you tell him?"

"I said you were on hiatus but that I'd talk to you."

"Did you tell him that you're the actual investigator?"

"I mentioned that, yes."

"So, why this call?"

"Like I said, I told him I'd talk to you. He wants both of us. *Cullen and Cobb.* And actually, so do I. I could use your help on this."

Cullen and Cobb. Funny how that phrase had worked its way into the lexicon of the city. I'd even heard that Mayor Nenshi had mentioned Cullen and Cobb during a speech he gave to a group of urban planners in Toronto. And I had to admit I liked the phrase — the sound of it, what it meant … what it had meant to me.

"I don't need an answer right now," Cobb said. "Just think about it, okay?"

"Yeah."

"Seriously, I need you to think about it."

"I will. I'll think about it."

"Give Jill and Kyla hugs for me."

"I will. My best to your clan, as well."

We ended the call. Jill took our mugs, went into the house and came back a few minutes later with refills. She set mine down and touched my arm before settling back into the lawn chair, her feet tucked up under her. She didn't say anything. Didn't have to.

I thought back on what had happened in the time I'd worked with Cobb — we'd done some good, that was true, but I had to weigh that against the horrors I'd seen, the face of evil I'd looked into and that had looked back at me. I'd sworn after that night in the alley that I was done. And I saw no reason now to change my mind.

I looked at Jill. She was watching me. Looking for a sign? She smiled a little smile at me. I smiled back.

Cullen and Cobb. It did sound good.

I reached for the *Herald*.

ACKNOWLEDGEMENTS

The Cullen and Cobb series has been one of the great joys of my literary life. I look forward to spending time with Adam, Mike, and their families, and I love the time writing this series has afforded me to spend prowling the streets and hideaways of my beloved Calgary. The series could not happen — and that is certainly the case with this book — without the amazing contributions of so many. That group includes everyone at Dundurn, from Kirk Howard and (the now departed — I miss her) Beth Bruder; the editing team for *None So Deadly* — Allison Hirst (developmental editor), Jenny McWha (project editor), and Claire Wilkshire (freelance copy editor); art director Laura Boyle (cover) and freelance designer Lorena Gonzalez Guillen (interior); and publicists Michelle Melski and Tabassum Siddiqui. Thanks as always to my tireless agent, Arnold Gosewich. And special gratitude to the people I consulted with and who were so generous with their time and expertise: Dr. Adam Vyse, retired policeman Mike O'Connor, and particular thanks to Detective Michael Cavilla, CPS Homicide Unit, who went way above and beyond in his help with this book.

On a grander scale, I thank, most of all, my family— my late dad who instilled in me early on a love of reading and, in particular, of reading crime fiction; my mom, who fostered in me my love for all things Calgary, my sons, Murray and Brad, and their families, and my daughter, Amy, and her family — their love and encouragement has meant so much. And, again, Barb, ever supportive, a wonderful first reader and the one I lean on … a lot.

Thank you all.

Book Credits

Developmental Editor: Allison Hirst
Project Editor: Jenny McWha
Copy Editor: Claire Wilkshire
Proofreader: Shari Rutherford

Cover Designer: Laura Boyle
Interior Designer: Lorena Gonzalez Guillen